The Lost Diary

OF MEHMET THE CONQUEROR

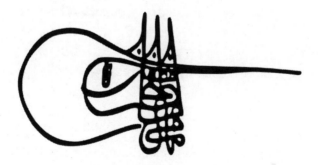

HASAN ZIA

BISAC Categories:
FIC014000   FICTION / Historical / General
FIC081000   FICTION / Muslim

Summary:
Mehmet Ahmet Osman is an 18-year-old Muslim-Turkish-Canadian. He is a typical teenager, but he learns from his grandmother that he is descended from the Ottoman imperial family. In fact, he is even named after the great sultan, Mehmet the Conqueror.

Mehmet is obsessed with history, which he is studying extensively, assisted by his professor, Dr. Abbas Rizvi. At university, Mehmet is making new friends and studying hard. But there is something eerie about the diary, and Mehmet soon finds himself at the center of the emerging Ottoman Empire—in the 15th century!

EMERALD
BOOKS

DEDICATION

To my Dadiama, who like Mehmet's Babaanne,
never fails to inspire.

TUGHRA (SEAL OR SIGNATURE) OF
MEHMET THE CONQUEROR

PORTRAIT OF
MEHMET THE CONQUEROR
IN HIS YOUTH

سلطان غازی بایزید خان وقتداشی شهزاده جم ایله یکشنبر اوکن عظیم جنك ایدوب شهزاده جم منتوب مصر
سلطان غورله واروب انده جم كنه عاتشه سی مجددن كلد كده بنه عسكر جمع ایدوب جنك ایلدی بنه صكل
دربادن فرنكستانه فرار ایله یافی عمرینی الله مكودری   وسلطان بایزید خان اوتوز یا مشنده هفنه جلوس
ایدوب بادشاه اولدی سازلودردوه نفرریض نجمشنده وفات ایلدی رحمة الله علیه رحمة واسعه

فتوحات غازی سلطان بایزید خان

كلی	آقكرمان	اطنه	قلعه انا وردن	قلعه حتون	فرون	خروج شیطاقولی
سنه ۸۸۷	سنه ۸۸۷	سنه ۸۹۵	سنه ۸۹۲	سنه ۸۹۲	سنه ۸۹۲	سنه ۸۹۷

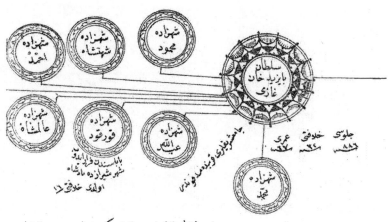

استنبوشهزاده لراجل موعود لربله یكتجیزاده واصل رحمت حق اولدیلر

LINE OF MEHMET THE CONQUEROR AND HIS ISSUE

A PAGE OF DRAWINGS FROM MEHMET THE CONQUEROR'S JOURNAL

Public Domain Licensed by Creative Commons

"Verily you shall conquer Constantinople. What a wonderful leader will he be, and what a wonderful army will that army be!"

—Prophet Muhammad (SAW)

1. Mehmet

"I copied your cadence, I mirrored your style
I studied the greats, I'm the greatest right now."

My favourite lyrics to "Middle Child" by J. Cole come blaring through my phone alarm, hollering at me to wake up, forcing me to look for the time.

5:15 a.m.

I grunt, tap dismiss, and get up.

Waking up is no issue for me today. I didn't get any sleep. This happens to me every year the night before school starts. This year is slightly different, though. The sleepless night has come early, on the last Sunday of August, exactly one week prior to the start of the school year.

This is a special year. Starting next week, I'll be studying history and political science at Queen's University in Kingston, Ontario, one of Canada's top universities.

I shake my head. I get up and walk over to the washroom, taking a look at my sleepless face in the mirror. "My name is Mehmet Ahmet Osman. Today I will do good, have fun, and not stress."

I say this to myself every morning, yet I rarely ever do the "have fun and not stress."

Okay... Maybe I sound like an ungrateful wannabe edgy bastard

1

right now, but you see, I feel as though I wear a mask every day. I show the world that I'm a nonchalant nerdy kid, who loves history, books, and sports. However, inside I lack confidence, and at times feel quite anxious and insecure.

The insecurity starts from the moment I look into the mirror. I don't like the way I look, and it's disgusting that I feel that way. My curly hair never sits right, even though I keep it longer; there are zits on my forehead that I try to cover with my hair, but it just...doesn't work. I have a short and thick beard, which I like, but people my age see it and assume I'm much older. My body used to be athletic, but I clearly gave up on being fit after I got benched during my final high school hockey game.

I suppress these thoughts, make *wudu,* and pray the Fajr prayer, the first of five daily prayers. It gives me a moment of peace.

I typically get annoyed that I never left a mark on anything in high school. I've felt my entire life that I've been sent to Earth to do great and wonderful things. I probably place high expectations on myself because my family is very accomplished. My father is a well-known Canadian Muslim leader, whose organization provides a platform for Muslim-Canadian youth to display their talents and grow as individuals and has helped educate thousands on the true beauty of Islam. My mother is a professor at an online Islamic college. She also instructs Muslim women and children in our neighbourhood about Islam, and they all just love her.

The feeling I've not yet done anything in my life severely agonizes me. I had opportunities in high school. I had tons of friends and played on the varsity soccer and hockey teams. I even won the provincial championship back in my freshmen year for hockey. However, I feel like I threw all that away, never taking advantage of the opportunities I had.

I sometimes replay the moment from this past February after I caught my "friend" Harris cheating on his girlfriend. The next day, he was determined to silence me. He and his friends cornered me, then declared to the entire school, "not a single person in this school gives a damn about you. The only reason why anyone even talks to you is because you were my friend."

Words that have pierced my brain every day since.

Not because Harris said them, but because nearly everyone, even people I assumed were my friends, people I assumed respected me, sat in silence as he mocked my existence. Those words stung me for the rest of the school year because I believed they were true. I never got people to care about me because I always had my guard up and portrayed myself as someone who did not care about anything, even though that isn't exactly true.

High school did not totally suck. I do have some great memories of playing soccer, hockey, and ping pong for the school team, playing cards in the back of the class, hating math class, loving English class, and hanging out with friends. I just hate how it all ended with an empty feeling in my stomach—an emptiness that still remains to this day. I hate how I never spoke my mind and let people dictate what I did.

But today is going to be different. Today will be the start of something new. I get a fresh start at a completely different place. I'm beyond excited and terrified. It's my chance to make new, better, and stronger friendships. I hope to meet people who respect me for the person that I am. I will take off my mask and be myself around people. I'm annoyed that I will have to live two hours and fifty-two min-

3

utes away from my bed in Mississauga, Ontario, but it'll be amazing to finally take classes that actually interest me, like the *rise of empires*. Most of all, I'm delighted for the opportunity to become a leader and generate a positive impact in my new community.

I know, I know... you guys are rightfully thinking, *What kind of 18-year-old dude is worried about whether he becomes a leader or makes a positive impact on his university community during his last week of summer vacation prior to his freshman year?*

But I've just got lofty aspirations. I want to be the first Muslim to become the Canadian Prime Minister. The plan is to get a dual degree in poli-sci and history at Queen's, go to law school at McGill University in Montreal, learn French, eventually become a politician, and work up to being a Prime Minister.

I know I'm reaching for the stars. Heck, anyone I've ever told my plan, has laughed straight in my face, which definitely hurts. However, I just believe that this is the best path towards fighting for marginalized communities in Canada. Throughout my years in school, I've witnessed the Islamophobia, racism, sexism, ableism, and other forms of discrimination. I know there are people living in my neighbourhood who struggle to pay for necessities such as rent, food, and medication. My hope is to lead Canada to a future without hate and with hope, and going to Queen's is only step one.

I glance at my phone.

6:02 a.m.

Okay, time to sleep for an hour before getting ready for my three-hour drive to Kingston.

I close my eyes for what feels like two seconds. I hear the door blasting open. My mother comes into my room, pulls off my blanket, and yells at me in Turkish. "Get up, get up, you need to leave for Queen's in 30 minutes."

I look for my phone.

7:31 a.m.

Crap.

My mother comes into the room again, holding a bucket, hollering, "If you don't get up, I will throw this bucket of ice on you!"

"I'm up, I'm up!" I slip outta bed.

I quickly shower, change into tan pants with a button-down navy top. It's a cloudy and cool summer day in August. At 7:50, I head to the kitchen, carrying my duffel bags, and find my mother, father, and grandmother.

"*Assalamu Alaikum!*" I cheerfully say as I warmly smile at my father. I wrap my mother and grandma in a bear hug.

"*Walaikum As-salaam,*" my mother Dalia, whom I call Anne (An-nay), replies. She passes over a plate of my favourite breakfast, chocolate chip pancakes.

"Mehmet!" my dad, named Ahmet, happily says. "Are you excited about moving into your dorm today?"

I shrug and reply, "Sure, Baba... I guess."

"Come on! You must be excited to get away from us, right?" he jokes.

"Of course I am," I smile. "Only thing I'm gonna be missing here is Anne's cooking and Babaanne's stories, but definitely not your long talks."

"Hey! I know you secretly love those," Baba retorts.

"Nobody does, Baba."

My grandma snorts and says, "I love you, Mehmet," in Turkish.

"I love you too, Babaanne," I warmly reply with a smile across my face. I take a few bites of breakfast.

"I can't believe you are about to move away for university," Anne cries out. "It feels as though it was just yesterday when I was holding you in my arms."

"I know, it's wild," I say unenthusiastically while peeking at my phone. "Hamdan should be here any second."

"So why on earth is he driving you all the way to Kingston, when he is going to school in Toronto?" she inquires. "Does he not have anything better to do?"

"Because Hamdan and I have been best friends literally since we were babies. He is basically my brother," I reply. "Besides, a road trip is always fun."

Truthfully, I also think Hamdan is dumb for driving me three hours north of Mississauga for school. When I told Hamdan that, he simply said, "We're brothers, we should always be there for each other no matter what."

"I just wish we could take you to school ourselves," Anne says. "We could have helped you settle into your dorm and met your roommate."

"Don't worry, Anne, I'll be fine."

At that very moment, my phone buzzes. Hamdan's waiting for me outside our building.

I turn to my family and awkwardly say, "Well, he's downstairs, so I guess that means goodbye..." I turn back towards the door.

"Don't be crazy! We will see you to the car," Anne states.

When we get downstairs, we see Hamdan leaning against his white Kia Sorento.

Hamdan is of Pakistani descent with his full name being Hamdan Naeem. He's lanky, has flowing wavy black hair swept to the side and he rocks a very thin beard. Today he's wearing a nice white Adidas shirt with blue working-man type jeans.

He waves at me and calls, "Hey Mehmet!" To my family, he says his *salaams* and shakes my father's hand.

After Hamdan and I load my belongings, Anne quickly squeezes me in a tight hug. Soft tears roll down her face.

"I'm going to miss you. Have a great year, Oğlum."

"I'm going to miss you too Anne," I restlessly say. "I'll be home by reading week, which is halfway through October."

I then hug Babaanne as she mutters in Turkish, "Mehmet, have fun at school, make sure you work hard, so that you may be successful. Remember, success is in our blood. You know how our family is directly descended from Osman, the founder of the Ottoman Empire. Since then, we have had many great people like your namesake, Fatih Sultan Mehmet and Kanunî Sultan Süleyman honour our name. Now, I know you do not necessarily care about your heritage, but you are studying history this year, I do hope you learn about the great legacy of our family, and take the good that they did as inspiration, so that you may carry the torch for the next generation."

"I will, Babaanne, I promise."

Next, Baba gives my hand a firm shake and says, "I know I've given you a hard time. I'm always trying to get you out of your comfort zone. I've done all that to prepare you for when you will have to live on your own. Make sure you enjoy your first year. Remember that Allah is always with you. Work hard, and you will be rewarded. Be sure to call us when you get there."

Hamdan honks three times and bellows out, "Hey, Mehmet! We're going to be late for the start-of-the-year party!"

Baba frowns, which gets me to laugh out loud. "Don't worry, Baba, I don't even like parties."

He relaxes and demands, "You boys be careful and drive safely."

"We will, Ahmet Uncle," Hamdan calls out.

"I'm controlling the music!" I exclaim.

I look back at my apartment building in Central Mississauga for one last time—the last time I'll ever see it.

2. MEHMET

We speed along towards Kingston with "Chosen 1" by Polo G blaring from the car speakers. While listening to Polo, I think back to what Babaanne said about my Ottoman heritage. She thinks I don't really care about it, and I can see why. At school, I've always felt that people see me differently due to my religion and heritage. At times it's unintentional, like teachers disliking that I'd have to miss half a period on Fridays for Jummah prayer, or when hockey coaches would feel burdened by having to get *halal* food following big wins. Students constantly made jokes about Islam and terrorism. Eventually this started getting to me, so I'd refrain from asking teachers for permission to leave class for prayer, instead asking to use the washroom. In public, I wouldn't speak Turkish, using English even to speak to my family. Now, I rarely use Turkish, even at home. In my opinion, that doesn't mean that I don't care about my Islamic and Turkish heritage.

Babaanne's always told me the stories of all the great Ottoman sultans. When I was younger, I'd constantly badger her for all the stories about Fatih Mehmet, aka Mehmet the Conqueror. The fact that he conquered Constantinople when he was only 21 is incredible. Hearing about his successes from my grandmother makes me proud to share his name. I mean, sharing the name of a man known as "The Conqueror" is pretty darn cool. Aside from Babaanne's stories, I've never really bothered to learn anything about Ottoman history. Okay, there was this one time in grade 11, for a debate, where I did research Ottoman history. I had to make the case that the Ottomans were the greatest empire in world history.

Their architecture is brilliant. The *masjids* they built are amongst the most beautiful in the world. I remember the remarkable feeling I had when I walked into Ottoman-era *masjids* like the Blue Mosque or the Süleymaniye Mosque while visiting Turkey a few years ago. The Ottomans were also incredibly organized. At the empire's peak, the army was swift and powerful. Most notably, they lasted for an incredible duration of over 600 years. It's all unbelievable that I descend from an empire that vast. It makes me proud, but also sorta embarrassed—there are aspects that fail to impress me. Rather, they shock me in the most upsetting way.

I discovered that they would force some young Christian boy slaves to accept Islam, which is completely forbidden in the religion. Next, I learnt about the Armenian Genocide, which is disturbing to say the least. It also doesn't help that my family's dynasty is constantly ripped on Twitter by Eastern Europeans. These actions are disgusting to me. Like...you want your family to be perfect. All of my family's faults are out there for the world to see. I don't know if Babaanne is correct in saying that we are descended from the Ottomans, but if we are, I feel ashamed of these acts and because I learnt of them, I didn't go any further into studying the Ottomans. I had enough already to win a high school level debate.

I've also never really bothered to learn about Islamic history, which is sorta embarrassing. I've always been a religious Muslim; I've even memorized the entire holy Quran. I've read about the Prophet Muhammad's life many times. I know about the lives of many of his companions. I just never bothered to learn about how Islam spread and why it caught on so quickly throughout the Middle East. I never bothered to learn about the Islamic dynasties.

I'm about to major in history. I think it may just be the time to learn more about Islamic and Ottoman history. I feel that learning more will help me feel more pride about my heritage. At least more pride than I presently have.

As I play "Thnks fr th Mmrs" by Fall Out Boy on the aux, I feel Hamdan punch me on the shoulder.

"Why are you so quiet?"

"I just can't believe I'm moving three hours away from home. It doesn't feel real quite yet," I reply. "Reality should set in soon enough, maybe when I get to my dorm."

"True," Hamdan mumbles, driving silently for a moment. "Remember how we used to beg our parents to let us sleep over at each other's houses?"

"Yeah, and I always ended up kicking your ass at wrestling during those sleepovers."

"Hey! That only used to happen because you were super fat," Hamdan jokes.

"I was never fat!" I exclaim. "You were just extremely skinny... I mean you still are."

We laugh, and I feel so happy to have him by my side.

"We used to be so obsessed with Spider-man as kids. We'd watch the Tobey Maguire movies all night," Hamdan recalls.

I nod. "I was always more of a DC guy, but those Spider-man movies were great."

"Ah, those were fun days," Hamdan reminisces. "Sometimes, I wish we could go back."

"Um, I would absolutely not like to go back to those days."

"Why not?"

"Because we can now do so much more," I explain. "We can drive to Kingston and back. We don't have to rely on our parents for everything, and we can actually pursue our interests."

"True," Hamdan slowly replies. "But we didn't have responsibilities back then."

"The fact that we have responsibilities and fears is what makes the fun times even better," I state. "Think about it, if we partied all the time, we would eventually get bored doing things we find fun. Balance is important. If I don't do something important, I feel useless and bored."

"Okay, but you still better go to parties at Queen's," Hamdan says. "Being in your dorm and reading or studying all the time is going to make people think that you're boring."

"I don't like parties. Way too much drinking, which is *haram*. The music is too damn loud, and you have to shout to talk to people. I would much rather hang out with friends and play cards or FIFA," I say. "Anyways, I like to read and study random topics. That's actually fun. Why else would I study history and political science at uni?"

Yes, I know I sound like the cheesiest guy in the whole world. I probably sound like a stupid character from a teen show like *One Tree Hill* or *Dawson's Creek*. However, the only person I feel I can share this stuff with is Hamdan, who prefers the truth about everything, even if I do sound a little weird.

"Whatever, man," Hamdan says. "It's okay to let loose sometimes."

"Don't worry, I will," I promise.

"So, what's your roommate's name?"

"Some guy named Jacob Brannan," I respond. "He's in math and stats."

"Seems boring," Hamdan says. "You've talked to him then?"

"Once."

"What did you talk about?"

"Just coordinating what to bring. I'm bringing the Xbox, while he's bringing a screen. We're going to get a printer and a mini-fridge in Kingston," I say.

"Couldn't you leave the console at home?" he asks. "You'll be playing games all day."

"There's nothing wrong with that!"

Hamdan shakes his head. "Anyways, we should be there in thirty minutes."

I nod my head, hoping that Jacob is going to be someone that I get along with.

We get to Queen's around 11 a.m. The place is absolutely humongous, and the campus is just so beautiful and picturesque. It's exactly how I dreamed of a university being. There are stone buildings with beautiful architecture, making me feel as though I'm walking through a smaller part of Hogwarts. There is ample space for hundreds of people, and it'd take a considerable amount of time to walk from one side of the campus to the other. As we pass the Joseph S. Stauffer Library, excitement fills my heart. My high school in Mississauga was small and only held around 700 students. Here, I'll be attending school with thousands of students. There are so many avenues to pursue, so many ways to get involved, so many people to meet. Hopefully at least one or two of them will be friends that I can hold onto for life. I feel as though I'm in a larger world, even though Mississauga is a much larger city, with a greater population.

"So... what building are you moving into?" Hamdan asks.

"Victoria Hall."

"Where is it?" he impatiently asks.

"How am I supposed to know that?"

After searching for about 10 minutes, an upper-year student helps us find the building.

Hamdan and I take my belongings into the double room and place them by the entrance. The room has two twin beds that are pushed against opposite walls. On each side of the room, there is one desk and one dresser. To say I'm disappointed would be an understatement.

"You should probably claim a bed before your roommate gets here," Hamdan asserts.

"Jacob and I can decide how we set it up when he gets here," I say with a hint of finality hidden in my tone.

"What should we do now?"

"Well... we could go look around the campus."

"Okay," he replies. "Can we just get some pizza first?"

"I will never say no to pizza."

We find a *Pizza Pizza* right by Victoria Hall. After Hamdan and I split a medium cheese pizza, we start going around the campus. This is my first time at Queen's University, so over the next couple of hours, we tour the whole damn place, starting from the football field, which is right in front of Victoria Hall. I look for the buildings in which I have to attend lectures throughout the term. Hamdan talks about how excited he is for his architecture program at Ryerson University in downtown Toronto. We talk about sports, particularly how exciting the hockey season is going to be this year, and as we walk into Stauffer Library, I just know that I'm totally going to love my year at Queen's. My only wish is that Hamdan remains here with me.

After checking out the Athletic Centre, which has an amazing basketball court, we walk back towards Victoria Hall.

On the way back, we hear from a few freshmen that there's going to be a concert tonight, which I am not particularly interested in, but as we enter the building, Hamdan says, "You have to go to that concert."

"You know I don't like concerts. I'm not going."

"You have to start making friends. It's 3 p.m. I'm going to leave, so you have to make friends and go to that concert."

"Whatever man, I'll just stay in my dorm and set up."

We continue arguing about the concert all the way to my room.

When we enter the dorm, we find a very tall and athletic white guy with flowing curly red hair and stormy grey eyes setting his belongings onto one of the desks.

"Hey," he says, "are you Mehmet Osman?"

I nod. "You must be Jacob Brannan."

"Yeah, I am," he replies. "But you can just call me Jake. Did you bring your Xbox?"

"Yes," I reply. "Did you bring your screen?"

"Yep," he answers. "I also bought a mini-fridge and a printer. We can split the cost."

"Sure."

Jake points to Hamdan and asks, "Who are you?"

"Hamdan Naeem." He shakes Jake's hand.

"Are you guys going to go to the concert later tonight?"

"I'm not," Hamdan abruptly says. "I've got to get back to Mississauga. I only came to drop Mehmet off. Mehmet loves concerts, he will definitely go."

With that, he quickly shakes my hand, tells me to text him later, awkwardly nods at Jake, and leaves the dorm room.

"You should probably know that I don't like concerts at all."

"It's okay," he says, "I'm not a huge fan either."

For the next hour or so, Jake and I work together to set up the dorm. We move the beds around, set the mini-fridge, printer and console. All while interrogating each other to get to know the other better. I find out that he's from some small ass town called Simcoe, has a girl at Western University named Priya, is an athlete, and a massive gamer. He learns that I'm a hockey obsessed history buff who also loves to game.

"FIFA?" I ask. "Let's see how good you are, lad."

"Oh, you'll see how I good I am, boy," Jake replies as he snatches the better controller from my hands.

As we pick teams, I ask why he chose Queen's over Western, or a school closer to home.

"I just wanted to leave that town, man. I know everyone that lives by me. I also didn't want to go to Western. I want to be on my own for a bit," he says. "I like my girlfriend, but both of us can live without each other for a couple weeks. We'll still see each other every month or so, and during school breaks."

I nod while choosing to play with Manchester United, my favourite soccer team. Jake selects Real Madrid. When we start, he asks why I chose Queen's.

"I only applied to two schools, Queen's and University of Toronto. I also really wanted to get outta my comfort zone." I answer. "If I went to UofT, I'd still live at home. I came to Queen's to get outta that comfort zone and to be more independent."

Jake nods as he scores the first goal of the game.

"Bro, you are so much better than I thought you would be."

"I told you I love video games," Jake restates while smiling.

"I can see that," I mutter as I bear down and focus on the game.

It's a hotly contested match. Both of us trade chances on net and talk our shit. A defender on Jake's team picks up a red card to start the second half. In the end, I score two unanswered goals to earn the victory.

"Holy! That was a great game," I say. "Run it back?"

"Bet."

We play a best of 7, trading wins. There isn't much that separates us, but I still eventually pull out to win the series four to three.

"Bruh, that was fun!"

"Whatever," Jake grumbles. "FIFA isn't really my game."

"Okay, let's run 2K," I suggest. "If you a man?"

"Bet," Jake accepts. "But after the game, we're going to that concert."

"Do you know who's performing?" I ask.

"Two guys I've never heard of."

"So, what's the point of going?"

"We could meet people, and it'll probably be fun," Jake says. "It marks the start of orientation week. I'm going, and you should too."

I reluctantly agree.

"Okay!" Jake excitedly says. "I pick the Raptors."

"And I'll go with the Lakers..."

We head down to the football field for the concert around 8 p.m., following the Asr prayer. In the lineup heading into the field, we meet two other first-year students, an African-Canadian student named Tre and an international student from Lebanon named Hussein. We decide to hang out together during the concert. By 8:36, we get let into the field and rush to stand as close to the stage as we possibly can. As people continue to file in, the DJ starts to play popular songs that everyone knows like "God's Plan" by Drake or "Sicko Mode" by Travis Scott. The DJ also plays classics like "Bye Bye Bye" from NSYNC or "Lose Yourself" by Eminem. We sing along to all of the songs and so far, I'm having a great time.

Next to come on is a random local rapper, whose name I don't catch. He's great, but I don't know a single song by the artist. The whole crowd is going crazy even though I keep hearing people say they have no idea who this guy is. The rapper plays to the crowd by asking us to wave our arms or turn on the lights from our phones and direct it towards the stage. He takes off his shirt to the delight of many, displaying his six-pack. He even attempts to crowd surf but fails miserably.

At this point, the field starts to get really congested and a bunch of people start getting crushed together. I feel like I've been stepped on and pushed by at least thirty people. All I can smell is sweat. One couple even attempts to make out with the girl pushed up against my back. A shouting match breaks out about 3 metres away from where I'm standing. I stand uneasily with my head throbbing. While the music is good, it's not nearly good enough to have a fun time while being uncomfortable.

This is precisely why I prefer smaller gatherings.

As the main artist comes on, I yell, "JAKE! I'm gonna head back to the dorm!"

Without waiting for a reply, I fall back and try to slip through the maze of people in my way.

When I finally get to the dorm, I realize that I smell like the sweat of other people, so I throw my clothes into the laundry basket, take a quick shower, and pray the Maghrib prayer. After that, I open my laptop to connect to the residence Wi-Fi.

I call home, and Baba picks up. I talk to him, Anne, and Babaanne. I show them my room, tell them about Jake, my impressions of the campus, and about my day. I tell them that I think I'm gonna have an amazing year. Anne tells me to take advantage of free food as much as I possibly can and promises to send food as soon as she can. Baba reminds me *again* that I need to work hard to do well.

We say our goodbyes, and at that moment, Jake walks back into the room.

He tells me about the main performer, some guy named Lil Dre.

We talk for a bit about what the rest of orientation week has in store. We also talk about movies and TV shows.

By 10:30, I've convinced Jake to watch the show *Friday Night Lights*.

I decide to start my research on the four major Muslim dynasties tonight by reading about the beginning of the Rashidun Caliphate, and the first caliph, Abu Bakr, the Prophet Muhammad's closest companion.

At this point, I should probably mention why I'm obsessed with history. So... I truly am a curious person. When I started reading and watching historical fiction books and shows, I began to research what actually happened in history, and I found the actual history just as fun, if not more so, than the shows and books. Eventually, I just started loving history, and I'm gonna force each and every single one of y'all to absolutely adore it as well.

Okay, anyways... so when the Prophet Muhammad, peace and blessings be upon him, died in 632 C.E., the majority of Muslims decided that Abu Bakr would succeed as the caliph. He was selected for his piety as well as his loyalty and close companionship to the Prophet of God. Abu Bakr also happens to be the first adult male to accept Islam.

At the start of his reign, certain tribal leaders saw the Prophet's death as a way to go back to their pagan ways. Others decided they could use the death of the Prophet to gain fame by claiming prophethood of their own. Islam had its centralized government in Medina, just like the Prophet had established. Pre-Islamic Arabs had a tribal system and did not adhere to a central government. Particular tribes, mainly Bedouin tribes, decided to stop paying their Zakat (alms) to the caliphate as an act of rebellion. They disliked centralized rule and did not want to join a unified Arabia.

Although not all the tribes who refused to swear allegiance to Abu Bakr left Islam; they were mixed into the group of those who left Islam and the people who claimed to be prophets, as apostates. This term was political more than a religious. Many of the rebels sought to attack Medina, particularly those who claimed prophethood.

All I gotta say is that rebelling against the smartest and most honourable person in Arabia was the greatest mistake the rebels could have possibly made.

These battles are known as the Ridda Wars, which means the Apostate Wars. Abu Bakr was forced to defend Medina from those who wished to harm it. The goal was for a unified Arabia. He divided his army into eleven and gave strict instructions not to use force unless it was absolutely necessary. The army was instructed to use the call for prayer, the *ezan*, as a signal for peace. If the rebels answered peacefully, diplomatic talks would take over. If not, the army prepared for battle. Abu Bakr used a mixture of diplomacy and active warfare to overwhelm the rebellion.

The brilliance of Abu Bakr and the Muslim leadership unified Arabia, a place that was never unified, under the banner of Islam. Many people who had memorized the Quran to protect its authenticity, died during the process of unifying Arabia, so Abu Bakr, who had memorized the Quran himself, began the compilation of the Quran into the physical book that we see today.

Abu Bakr, the first caliph of Islam, is just so brilliant, and learning about that brilliance is all honestly pretty wicked. That's why I gotta keep studying Islamic and then Ottoman history.

Hasan Zia

Okay, I should stop for tonight. It's only a few minutes till midnight.

Time to pray *Isha* and go to sleep because this day has just been tiring.

3. Mehmet

"Get up, Mehmet, get up!"

Tre, Hussein, and Jacob are standing right over me.

"What time is it?"

"3 a.m.!" Hussein answers. "More importantly, it's time for Capture-the-flag!"

I groan and slip outta bed. Jake yells that they'll be waiting right outside of Victoria Hall.

Orientation Week has flown by quickly, and I find myself settling into a different lifestyle.

Hmm... let's see... There was a headphone disco, which I found to be extremely weird. Oh, and one night, students got into a mystery bus, which took us to different places in Kingston. The bus Jake and I chose took us to a go-karting centre. Also, upper-year students have organized BBQs, water-gun battles, ping pong tournaments, and more.

There are SO many parties happening all around campus, it's actually wild. Throughout the week, I've been waking up to the sound of drunk and rowdy students returning to their dorms during the night. Jake and I have avoided most parties, aside from the one held in Victoria Hall.

The most important part of Orientation Week are the friendships I'm making. My friendship with Jake is quickly blossoming.

We can talk for hours about sports, TV shows, movies, school, and he even finds history interesting. We play video games day and night. Jake triumphs at *Call of Duty* or *Mario Kart*, and I win at sports games like *FIFA*, *NHL*, and *NBA2K*.

Oh, and the guys we met at the concert, Tre and Hussein; we've been hanging with them too. Tre is absolutely jokes and GREAT at soccer. Hussein is simply just a lovable lad.

I've also been making sure to continue studying Islamic history. Every night, before I go to sleep, I spend an hour reading. I am done reading about the first four caliphs. Lemme just quickly tell mention what I've been reading.

The first four caliphs, Abu Bakr, Umar, Uthman (Osman in Turkish), and Ali are known as the rightly guided caliphs. All four were close companions of the Prophet Muhammad, peace and blessings be upon him.

This early period was characterized by quick territorial expansion, as Islam spread West towards Tunisia in North Africa, north towards Eastern Europe, and east towards Iran and South Asia. The new Islamic empire toppled the Sassanian (Persian) Empire and conquered significant areas of the Byzantine Empire.

Now, just pause to think about it...

In one generation, Islam engulfed all of Arabia, toppled the whole of the Sassanian Empire and weakened the Byzantines. The spirit and courage of that generation is inspirational, and it should motivate everyone. We should display that sorta courage and spirit for Islam and for everything we stand for, like human rights.

The swift spread of Islam is profoundly impressive. It also shocks me that anyone who knows this history can claim that Islam was spread only by the sword. Yes, there were military expeditions, but all four caliphs preached peace. Abu Bakr gave strict orders to his armies not to harm any land or civilians, a sentiment followed by his successors. The leaders were also tolerant of other religions in their empire.

Umar, the second caliph, has become my favourite historical figure. He was the first to hold the title Commander of the Faithful. He was extremely humble and was known for his firm stance on justice. He is also known as Al-Farooq, which translates to *the one who distinguishes between right and wrong*. He established institutions that Arabs had never been exposed to, such as police, courts, and parliaments. He created a special department to investigate complaints against his appointed officers of state. He would punish those in power who did not treat civilians with dignity, compassion, and justice. Those in power had to take an oath promising they would not live luxurious lifestyles. He also kept a financial record of those who held positions of power to ensure they did not use their position to grow their wealth. Umar would frequently walk around the streets of Medina at night to see if he could help his citizens. His army peacefully conquered Jerusalem, without killing a single person and staying extremely tolerant of the Christians and Jews in the city, something the Crusaders could have learned from.

In my opinion, if he were alive today, he'd be considered a progressive politician. Umar Ibn Al-Khattab is very admirable, and I've absolutely got no clue why he isn't revered by historians, the way they celebrate Julius Caesar or Alexander the Great. Umar is exactly the type of person and leader I wish to be.

"MEHMET!" I hear Jake yell. "What's taking so long?"

Bloody hell.

I've been standing at the sink for well over ten minutes now, just thinking about history. I quickly splash my face, change into some dark clothes, and walk out.

Tre looks at me as I walk out the front doors of Victoria Hall and says, "We've already split into teams, the other team has already gone off."

"How do we ID them?" I ask. "We're not wearing any sort of uniform or anything."

"They sprayed some green stuff over their hair. That's how we'll recognize them," Jake replies. "What's our plan?" he asks everyone.

Well, this shouldn't be too difficult. Half our team is intoxicated. I can just smell the beer and weed. But a few on our team aren't, including my friends.

"Tre and Jacob," I say, "go with the drunk people and figure out where the other team's flag is. When you locate it, Tre and the drunk kids will run off to distract the other team's defensive unit. Jake, you'll grab the flag."

"What will you do?" Tre asks.

"Someone's gotta defend this flag," I say pointing to the orange flag on the ground.

"Where's our flag going?" someone asks.

"The roof," I answer as I grab the flag and drag three people up so that they can come with me.

"Mehmet, just remember that anything goes, so be ready to get tackled," Hussein says.

"Oh, don't worry, I'll be fine."

We enter the hall and I yell out, "Barricade the main entrance! The elevators too!"

I'm gonna try to funnel the opposition straight to the roof and trap them there. The flag will actually be in the common room by my dorm and shall be left undefended there while we set the trap on the roof. We reach my dorm room, and I grab a sheet and Jake's weighted blanket, then stroll over to the cozy common room and place the flag over the armchair like a regular cloth. Next, we head straight to the staircase, making sure that the stairs are the only way one can go up and down the building. When we get to the roof, I work with my teammates to place the sheet as a tripwire, so that when the other team does come up here, they will trip up straight away.

I've texted Jake about the ploy, and he's making sure word spreads that our flag is on the roof.

Now, all we gotta do is wait.

And wait we do. For the next thirty minutes, we sit in silence, deadass twiddling our thumbs. The door suddenly opens and a girl with a green streak in her hair trips over our trap. I throw the weighted blanket over her as I dodge a punch from some dude, who clearly seems like her boyfriend. Five people from the opposing team stream out from the door behind him.

"GET THEM!" I yell as I try to wrestle the boyfriend to the ground. He's bigger than me so I go low, grabbing him from below the waist, lifting him and throwing him down, and then I fall over his body. At that moment, I hear shouts from afar. Beautiful fireworks are set off, lighting up the night sky in a splendid display of colours. Everyone on the roof looks up at it, but I look down to see Jake, thrusting the opposing team's flag up in the air in pure jubilation.

What a fun night.

Today is the first official day of classes, and I'm starting with three lectures right off the bat.

First, I have Introduction to Microeconomics at 2 p.m. I don't really have any interest in econ, but I took it on the insistence of my father.

Next, I got the Historical Rise of Empires at 3:30. I've been *waiting* for this class to start since the beginning of summer.

Finally, I've got Government, Politics, and Power at 7 p.m. It's a political science course introducing students to the Canadian government, electoral system, and political theory, like conservatism and Marxism. It sounds pretty basic.

The other two courses I'm taking this semester are Canadian History from the 1800s and International Relations.

Honestly, these don't seem to be that hard. I'm sure if I stay on schedule and work hard, *inshallah*, I'll be okay.

Around 11 a.m., I stumble out of bed and start to get ready. I take out my favourite white button-down shirt, blue jeans, and white AF1s.

At 1:33 p.m., I head towards my first-ever university lecture, and I get there fifteen minutes early. Surprisingly, there's a huge crowd of freshmen waiting outside the lecture hall. When I finally get inside, I'm forced to sit near the back of the lecture hall, and the lecture has already started. Christopher Oraham, the professor, is a middle-aged man, wearing a full suit. In my mind, he looks like someone who has failed in the corporate world and instead decided to become an academic. He definitely has the world's most mundane voice. He goes on talking for forty minutes, introducing the concepts of the course and assignments. When he finally finishes speaking, it takes me a couple minutes to get my bearings. I fell asleep during his talk.

I seriously hope that college is not this boring all the time.

Remembering the fact that I had to sit in the last row of my Econ class, I run over to the next lecture hall to ensure I get a good seat for history.

I get there around 3:14 p.m., which is around the time my school day finished in high school. When I enter the lecture hall, it's mostly empty.

I go to the corner of an empty row adjacent to the left wall. I sit down, take my phone out, and start to scroll through Twitter.

A moment later, I feel a tap on my shoulder. I look up to see a kinda short but breathtaking girl standing over me. She has very light-brown skin, dark hair that beautifully curls at its ends, and lovely chocolate eyes that could mesmerize a man for hours.

"Hello!" she energetically says as a warm smile reveals her dimples. "Is it alright if I sit down here?"

My mind is trapped in awe, but somehow, I manage to nod.

She sits down but leaves a one seat gap between us. I take out my laptop and act like I'm just going about my business.

I feel another tap on my shoulder. It's the girl. "What's your name?"

"M-M-Mehmet O-Osman," I stammer. "What's yours?"

"Sally MacLeod, it's nice to meet ya!" she exclaims.

Her bright energy immediately puts me at ease. She seems very cordial and not-at-all intimidating.

"It's great to meet you too!" I say. "Are you planning to major in history?"

"Sadly, I'm not. I'm actually looking to major in anthropology," she replies.

"I honestly don't know much about anthropology, but that sounds fun," I say.

"I want to be a forensic anthropologist, and that's definitely cool," Sally states.

"I have no idea what a forensic anthropologist is."

"Basically, they apply skeletal analysis and techniques in archaeology to solve crimes," she explains.

"So, you'll be able to solve all of the *Unsolved Mysteries* on TV?"

"Exactly," she replies while smiling, "I could possibly minor in history or international relations, and this class sounds cool, so I'm taking it."

"Yeah, this class definitely seems like it's going to be nice."

"What are you planning to major in?" Sally asks.

"History and political science."

"So, you like history?"

"History is dope," I reply. "I know that a lot of people find it lame, but think of it as a TV show that's actually happened. More often than not, the history is a lot more entertaining,"

"If you say so..." she says with her eyebrow raised.

"I know most teachers don't teach it well, but it actually can be fun," I say.

"Okay," she says.

Yeah, I know. I probably just blew my only chance of sounding like an interesting or fun person. In my defence, history is most definitely cool. I just wish for once I met someone who agrees.

Sally nudges me. I look over. "Could I have your number?"

I'm actually shocked. I'm 1000% sure I sounded like a boring loser, but I guess she doesn't mind talking to boring losers.

"Sure," I say, convincing myself that I definitely sounded cool.

At that moment, our history professor trots into class leaning against a cane.

Great.

Another teacher who probably doesn't know how to make history seem fun.

As soon as he starts talking, I realize that I probably shouldn't have judged him by his appearance. The professor introduces himself as Dr. Abbas Rizvi. He starts the class by displaying quotes of many great historical figures, like Prophet Muhammed, Julius Caesar, and Alexander the Great, amongst others.

He explains that the class will focus on prominent empires, including the Roman, Persian, Byzantine, Islamic/Arab, Mongol, Mali, Ottoman, Mughal, Spanish, Portuguese, French, and British. He promises to also incorporate lesser-known empires like the Aztecs.

Overall, I love his energy and passion for history. Even though this lecture is only an introduction to the course concepts and major empires, I can see his passion for history and for teaching spilling through each word. He's a storyteller, and his whole face glistens anytime someone interrupts him to ask a question.

After he finishes class, I run up to introduce myself. I'm literally the only one to do so.

"Hello!" the old man cheerfully says as he scrambles to organize a few papers.

"Hello, Professor," I say with a quiver in my voice. I mean, I am scared to talk to him. "My name is Mehmet. Mehmet Osman."

Professor Rizvi leans on his cane as he looks up to me, then pushes up his glasses.

"And what is it that you'd like, Mehmet Osman?"

"Just to introduce myself, sir," I reply as calmly as possible. "And explain that I have an immense passion for history."

"Is that so?" he whispers. "And what in history do you find most interesting?"

"Ottoman history," I reply. "I am Turkish myself. But also, I am focusing on trying to read as much as I can on Islamic history in general."

"What is it that you know of Islamic history, Mehmet Osman?"

"Just that there is way too much that I do not know yet, Professor Rizvi," I reply. "There is so much I want to know."

"I shall assist you on this vast journey." Professor Rizvi sits back at the desk with a huge grin, then pulls three books from one of the cupboards. One focused on the Umayyads, another on the Islamic Golden Age, and the last on the Ottoman sultans. "This should help you, Mehmet Osman."

"Oh my gosh, sir," I mutter as I gaze over the books. "You do not have to."

"It makes me very happy to hear a young man interested in history," Professor Rizvi replies. "Let alone Islamic History. It would be my pleasure to assist you with your research, Mehmet Osman."

"Thank you, sir." I'm absolutely awestruck.

"And Mehmet..." Professor Rizvi says as he starts towards his office. "Perhaps you may prove to be helpful for my own research..."

I smile and turn to start walking outta class when I immediately notice Sally waiting for me by the exit. I walk over to her. "Do you wanna get some coffee with me? I have a few hours before my next class."

"Okay, sure," she replies with a bright smile that could light up the horizon.

We get some coffee and donuts from Tim Hortons and sit on a bench outside a nice-looking hall. We talk for about an hour, and I start to get to know her. Sally's room is also in Victoria Hall. She's from a small town in Ontario called North Dumfries, which is the hometown of my favourite country music duo, The Reklaws. She loves animals and even owns a horse. She plays soccer, was on an equestrian team, and is competent at archery. We love the same TV shows and like to read. Oh, also, her mother is Punjabi, so she's part-desi, which is pretty cool.

She gets up to go to her dorm around 6:48 p.m., and as I walk to the poli-sci lecture, I simply can't stop thinking about Sally. She just seems so genuine and pure.

I get to the lecture five minutes before its scheduled start. The professor, Dr. Liban Jama, starts the lecture at 7 p.m. sharp. He fills the room with his booming voice as he runs around the room, thundering about aspects of the Canadian government. He probably went through three cans of Canada Dry during the two-hour lecture.

When he finally dismisses us, it's after 9.

I walk to my dorm exhausted by the insane length of the school day.

In the room, Jake and Tre are playing *Call of Duty*. I nod to them and head towards the bathroom to wash and change into my sleeping shorts and a Pittsburgh Penguins sweatshirt.

We tell each other about our day and for some reason I don't mention Sally at all.

By 11 p.m., I'm in bed reading about the Umayyad Caliphate.

Tre leaves to go back to his dorm room, and Jake pulls out three massive textbooks and starts to work on math problems.

"Why on earth are you doing math this late at night?"

"I've already got 3 assignments due on Friday," he replies. "And I mostly forgot what I learned last year."

"Dang, I guess it sucks to be you," I say, giggling to myself.

"Yeah, it does," he says. "What are you doing? History?"

"Just some light reading."

After about a half hour of reading and listening to Jake moan about how difficult calculus is, I fall asleep.

4. Mehmet

University is so much tougher than I initially thought it might be. I got a ton of assigned readings that I skim through for my history and political science classes. Paying attention in my micro class is a struggle because of how boring my professor is. As the calendar turns to October, I've started to get busy with my midterm essays due prior to reading week, and my econ midterm is the following week.

Surprisingly, I don't find the actual content of my courses difficult. The problem I'm having is that the professors go through information so fast. What usually took a week to cover at the high school level, the professors will cover in a single lecture.

Outside of class, I'm having a great time. I've started volunteering for a mental health clinic in the Kingston area. I'm currently part of the events committee and help out a bit with marketing. At this time, we're planning a charity gala on New Year's Eve for Queen's students.

At school, Jake and I are always hanging out, at times joined by Tre and Hussein. On Tuesdays and Wednesdays, we play basketball at the athletic centre. We make sure to play video games every day, go out to different restaurants on the weekends, study in the library between classes, watch the Queen's football team play on Saturdays, and they've even (sadly) convinced me to go to a couple parties.

I'm getting used to the fact that I live with a roommate. I make sure to keep my side of the room clean, something I never did at home. I don't play music out loud at night. I also have to be very careful to not wake Jake up when it's time for me to pray the Fajr prayer and be sure to read the Qur'an at the *masjid* or when Jake has class to not disturb him.

I think it's wonderful that we are friends. Sometimes it feels I'm just sharing a dorm with a brother. I've learned that he's a fairly religious (Baptist) Christian. Honestly, I've never heard the dude swear. He doesn't get drunk like the other guys do. I've even seen him coming out of a few Bible study sessions. Jake and I often talk about the differences between Islam and Christianity.

I continue to study Islamic history on Fridays, which is the one day I have off during the week. I've quickly gotten through the Umayyad and Abbasid Caliphates.

I'm so completely mystified at how ignored these great dynasties are. I mean, the Islamic world was going through a whole Golden Age while the Europeans were stuck in their Dark Ages. Under Umayyad and Abbasid rule, the Islamic world grew exponentially. The Abbasids had the House of Wisdom, in which scholars congregated and revolutionized mathematics, science, and philosophy. The Europeans can thank these scholars for preserving the knowledge of the Ancients for them. I hate how ignored this is by the West, when they try to portray us Muslims as barbaric and uncivilized.

My research on the Islamic dynasties is helped immensely by Dr. Rizvi. As he promised, he passes me books and explains certain events to me over email and after class.

His history course is easily the best course I've ever taken.

After his lectures, I usually hang out with Sally. I may only see her for a couple hours a week, but I seriously enjoy talking to her.

She's funny, smart, and always so relaxed, which puts me at ease when I'm stressed. However, I do feel there is something slightly different about this friendship. We both act a bit awkward with each other. As if we're trying too hard to be perfect.

I'm probably just stupidly overthinking something when I shouldn't.

I texted Hamdan about what was going through my head, and all he did was respond, "Overthinking is your M.O. Stop doing that."

So now I just try to simply enjoy her presence.

Hamdan and I make sure to Facetime at least once a week. He loves going to school in downtown Toronto and enjoys that he still gets to live at home. He plans on coming to Queen's the day before reading week to spend time with Jake and me before we go down to Toronto to watch the Leafs play the Penguins. We also booked a hotel in the downtown area.

Honestly, I can't wait.

Tomorrow is October 9th, and I've been working on essays for my two history classes and the two political science classes. Luckily, I started on them the first week of school. So all I had to do was fix or proofread my second or third drafts.

While I work on my essays, Jake studies all night for his midterms, even though the guy is a full-on math genius. Unable to sleep while he's awake, I shifted my focus to the final great Muslim dynasty—the final caliphate, my family's dynasty, the Ottoman Empire.

Every night, I stay up until sunrise studying the Ottoman Empire. I want to go as in-depth as I possibly can. I want to learn all of the intricate details of their court and military. I'd like to learn about their trade relationships, and how they treated their citizens. I want to know about their accomplishments.

I've skimmed through readings covering the initial rulers of the empire, up until I got to Mehmet II, the sultan my parents named me after. He was known as Fatih (Conqueror). I read as much as I can about him. I've learned about his personality, leadership style, ambitions, and accomplishments, reading anything I could possibly find.

I guess you could probably say I'm a tad obsessed.

I binged a docuseries on the conquest of Constantinople in one night while taking notes. I checked out books from the library about it and read them one by one.

Tonight is the eve before I leave for reading week, so I get on my laptop to look through school stuff and find that Professor Rizvi has sent me an email.

Dear Mehmet,

I know that you are almost certainly about to start researching the Ottoman Empire. Since our first class following reading week will be on the fall of Constantinople, I would like to give you an interesting reading on the topic, which I have recently got my hands on. Please be at my office at 8 AM sharp so I may give it to you. You may hand in your essay at this time as well.

Dr. Rizvi

Crap... I completely forgot to proofread my essay.

Screw it. I'm gonna fall asleep and pray that the essay will be good enough for the A.

I wake up around 6 a.m. to "Royals" by Lorde playing from my phone alarm. I go over the final draft of my essay one last time, fixing a couple of grammar mistakes.

By 7:36, I've printed the essay, showered, and changed into a white T-shirt under a baggy grey sweater with black pants.

After grabbing coffee from the Tim Hortons right by my dorm, I walk towards my professor's office. I arrive about ten minutes early. I knock twice, hoping he is in the room.

"Come in," the energetic voice of my professor calls out from the room.

"Um, hello sir," I say. "How are you doing?"

"I feel incredible," he joyfully answers. "Now, I hope you finished your essay, Mehmet?

"Yes, sir," I reply. I hand him the printed copy.

"Ah, well this certainly looks good," Professor Rizvi says while skimming through the essay. "Although I'm disappointed with the generic title. I expected something creative."

"I'll keep that in mind for the final essay, sir," I affirm.

"Now you're probably wondering about the reading I called you here for," he starts.

I nod and wait for him to show me the book.

Instead, he continues on. "In 1451, Mehmet the Conqueror became the Ottoman sultan for the second time, with one goal—to conquer Constantinople, the Red Apple, a place now known as Istanbul. No one ever thought Constantinople would fall, yet he accomplished the amazing feat at the age of twenty-one, leading an army of around 80,000 against the most fortified city in the world. He was broad-minded, freethinking, cunning, passionate, courageous, and brutal to his enemies. He's praised by followers and feared by his enemies. Mehmet rode his white horse into the city on May 29, 1453, following a fifty-three-day siege, and he proclaimed himself to be the Caesar of the Romans. As he entered the Hagia Sophia cathedral, he picked up a handful of dirt and declared, 'There is no God but Allah, and Muhammad is his messenger.'"

I whisper, "My parents named me after him. My grandma claims he is my ancestor, that our family is descended from the House of Osman."

Professor Rizvi looks shocked. "Unbelievable! I should have seen it. Your first name is Mehmet, the name of six Ottoman leaders. Osman is the Ottoman family name. I've heard reports that some survivors of the Ottoman imperial family live in Canada. Your appearance is also eerily similar to reports of how Mehmet the Conqueror looked when he ascended the Ottoman throne."

"Well, my parents prayed I would be like him, perhaps the fact that I look like him is the answer to that prayer."

"No, I believe you are like him. I don't know you well, but I know you are intelligent. You are clearly passionate, or else you would not be here in my office at 8 in the morning to talk about Ottoman history. I suspect there is a great leader in there somewhere," Dr. Rizvi asserts as he points to my heart.

40

Yeah, I think to myself. *I would be a great leader if I had any degree of confidence, which I don't.*

Professor Rizvi continues, "Well, I think it's time to show you my collection of notes and books on the Ottoman Empire."

We walk towards a huge bookshelf that stretches all the way to the ceiling and is spread across four separate walls, filled with books, scrolls, and artifacts.

Professor Rizvi gestures towards six rows of books. "This is everything I have on the Ottomans," he says as he pulls out a box from the shelf. "And this is everything I have on the conquest of Constantinople."

Professor Rizvi and I go over details of the conquest. We discuss Fatih Mehmet's first reign, when he was only a 12-year-old boy. He faced continuous opposition from his grand vizier. The janissaries were also not pleased with the boy sultan. The European Christian world, knowing there was a boy on the throne, organized a Crusade against the Ottomans. Fatih Mehmet called upon his father, Murat II, to lead the Ottoman forces, and they prevailed against the Crusaders. At that point, Fatih Mehmet sought to capture Constantinople; he had been obsessed with the idea since he was a young child. However, Çandarlı Halil Pasha incited a revolt from the janissaries to urge Sultan Murat back onto the throne. Fatih Mehmet was partially banished to Manisa, a city in the Aegean Region of the Ottoman Empire, and he became the governor of a province called Saruhan.

Next, we moved onto Constantinople. It was re-founded in 324 C.E. by Constantine as the new capital of Rome. For over a thousand years it held strong as the capital of the Eastern Romans, known as The Byzantines. Constantinople is designed by geography

41

and history to be the capital of a great empire. It's surrounded by water on three sides. To the north lies a harbour called the Golden Horn, which is one kilometre wide and six kilometres long. To the east lies the Bosphorus, a narrow strait that separates Europe and Asia, and divides Turkey by separating Anatolia from Thrace. To the south lies the Sea of Marmara, which connects the Aegean Sea to the Black Sea. The city enjoys easy access by sea from the Mediterranean and the Black Sea.

After ascending the Ottoman throne for the second time, Fatih Mehmet quickly removed all threats against him. He made sure everyone fell in line and followed his orders. He did face opposition, but Fatih Mehmet prevailed. He expanded the Ottoman navy. He gained control of the Bosphorus with the construction of the Rumeli Hisari. He hired a master gunsmith to build cannons larger than anyone in Europe had seen, to tear down the strong walls of the city. He maneuvered his ships into the Golden Horn by moving them around the Genoese colony of Galata, and finally took the city with the final assault on its walls on May 29, 1453. After the conquest, Fatih Mehmet built up the city to be the worthy capital of a great empire.

Professor Rizvi and I discussed Fatih Mehmet's strategy, the pros and cons of each move, and the significance of the conquest.

At around 9 a.m., he says, "Okay, I have a class to teach in about an hour, and I would like to prepare. The reason I asked you here is to give you a very important diary."

He walks over to his desk. Slowly, he reaches down to a drawer and takes out an old and dusty diary.

Now you're probably thinking of a diary that's about ten to fifteen years old. This diary, however, looks as if it's hundreds of years old.

"I got this two days ago," Professor Rizvi explains. "It was recently discovered in Adrianople, which is now known as Edirne. I gave up a hefty fortune for this—it is the lost diary of Mehmet the Conqueror. Archeologists and bounty hunters have been searching for it for half a millennium. It's supposedly a first-person perspective on the Conquest of Constantinople filled with many secrets. It takes the perspective of Mehmet, one of his viziers, a janissary soldier, and a female servant."

"That's unbelievable," I mutter. "But why are you giving it to me? This is priceless."

He chuckles. "You should have let me finish. The account is written in Turkish; I can't read the language, but you can. So, I'm giving it to you in hopes that you may help me by taking detailed notes. Perhaps you can even translate important portions. Perchance we may discover something that no other historian has."

He hands me the diary. The design on the cover has faded. The pages are a yellowish brown. I look over a page and remark, "It's in Ottoman Turkish. Modern Turkish has changed a great deal. If I take it home during reading week, I can go through it with my grandmother, who can somewhat understand Ottoman Turkish."

Professor Rizvi looks at me for a moment, then sternly says, "I want to see the diary and your notes at our first lecture following reading week."

"Of course, sir."

"Okay," he relents, flashing a smile. "Enjoy your Friday and reading week."

"Have a good day, professor," I exclaim as I leave the office.

When I get to my dorm, Jake's eating breakfast.

"Where have you been?" he asks.

"Just went to hand in my essay," I answer. "Look, I'm tired, man. I'm going to sleep for a bit. Wake me when Hamdan gets here."

"Sure."

I jump onto my bed, pull on my covers, and fall asleep.

I'm sitting on a white Arabian horse entering a once-beautiful city that has clearly been devastated by war. I assume that I'm dreaming about the conquest of Constantinople from the perspective of Fatih Mehmet. I ride towards the Hagia Sophia, seeing it as a church. I marvel at its beauty, and I'm glad the Ottomans preserved it. From the corner of my eye, I see the Ottoman flag being raised with the crescent and star.

I reach the Hagia Sophia, pick up a handful of dirt, and cry out, "There is no God but Allah, and Muhammad is the messenger of Allah!"

Then, all of a sudden, I feel someone slap me. I look around and see no one. I turn to face the Hagia Sophia when I feel another slap.

I blink and see Hamdan and Jake standing over me.

"You're here?" I croak out.

"Yeah, I am," he answers. "Now get up. We need to go pray the Friday prayer before heading to Toronto.

"Aight," I say.

"You drooled all over your sweater," Hamdan says with a laugh.

44

I wipe off my sweater, still shaking at how real my dream felt.

"You were talking in your sleep," Jake adds.

"Yeah, I had a weird dream," I grumble while rubbing my eyes.

"Get ready, man," Hamdan exclaims. "We're gonna be late."

I get up, wash my face, and exchange my grey sweater for a black one.

"Let's go."

We pray the Friday prayer at a *masjid* about twelve minutes from the campus. The imam gives an excellent sermon about patience and leadership, mentioning how the best leaders are the patient ones. He states that patiently persisting is integral for people who wish to achieve their goals.

Following the prayer, we pick up Jake and go for burgers in the downtown area of Kingston (if you can call it that). We talk about the opening week of the NHL, the upcoming NBA season, and the recently concluded World Series, with the Nationals defeating the Astros. Jake turns the conversation to school, so we speak about what we like and dislike about university. Jake worries about failing his stats midterm. I tell him that he probably did an excellent job.

Around 2:30 p.m., we head back to Victoria Hall to pack our belongings.

"You should come up with us," I suggest to Hamdan. "We've

been so busy that neither of us really packed. It should only take about half an hour."

When we enter the dorm, Jake and I start to shove clothes into our bag.

I spread out the six outfits I wanna take home. I probably shouldn't need any more. If I do, I have clothes at home. I spread all my books across my bed to decide which to take home.

"Man, that is a LOT of books," Hamdan calls out.

"Yeah, I've been doing a ton of research," I say.

"Well, I hope you still made sure to have fun," he grumbles.

"Don't worry, we've had a lot of fun so far," Jake asserts.

"Glad to hear that," Hamdan mutters.

At that moment, someone knocks on the door three times.

"Didn't you tell Tre and Hussein we're busy today?" I ask Jake.

"I thought I did..."

I shrug and open the door. Sally's standing there in sweats, with her hair tied up in a messy bun, iced coffee in one hand, and her laptop in the other.

"Um, hello..." I cautiously say.

"May I come in?"

"Sure." I step back.

I look at Jake's puzzled face and say, "Um, Sally, this is my room-mate, Jacob, and that is Hamdan, a good friend of mine from Mississauga."

"Oh, so you're busy?" she asks.

"Kinda, but what do you need?"

"I was gonna ask you to proofread my essay, and then hoped that we could hand it in at the same time," Sally answers.

"Well, I've already handed mine in, but I can definitely proofread yours."

She smiles and says, "Great!"

We sit at my desk, and I start to read the essay. Out of the corner of my eye, I see Hamdan examining some of my books on Islam and the Ottoman Empire.

I read Sally's essay as fast as I can, pointing out the mistakes and confusing statements for her to fix, which she does right there with me.

"The essay is solid," I say.

"That's good to hear, I only completed my draft this morning."

"Well, it doesn't seem that way," I reassure her.

"Hey Mehmet!" Hamdan calls out. "This book is blank. Well... every page is blank, aside from the first."

I look over to find him holding the lost diary Professor Rizvi gave me this morning.

"That can't be right," I say as Sally and I walk over.

I grab the diary and flip through it. He's right. The book is blank, apart from the first page.

"This can't be," I mutter. "I skimmed through it this morning."

"Well, it is," Hamdan states.

I remain quiet and try to decipher the Turkish writing on the first page.

I read it aloud, "To fully understand history, you must experience reality from all perspectives."

As soon as I utter the words to Hamdan and Sally, the dorm starts to violently shake, with books falling off the tables, chairs tipping over, and Jake tripping as we struggle to keep our footing. Suddenly, we hear a loud whistling sound out of nowhere.

"What's happening?" Sally cries as she grabs my arm.

"I've got no idea," I say while frantically looking at Hamdan and Jake.

Hamdan grabs the wall as he cries out, "We're going to die!"

Jake shouts, "It's an earthquake! Take cover!"

We duck under the desks. I look at Sally and Hamdan, praying we don't die.

Just in case, I utter the Shahada, "There is no god but Allah, and Muhammad is the messenger of Allah."

I see a shining light coming from the diary. I feel Sally grabbing for my hand, and I release the tension from my fingers to accept hers. At the very moment our hands join together, the light from the diary gets brighter, and I black out.

After what feels like an eternity in an abyss, I feel someone shaking me. At first, I think it is Munkar and Nakir, the fearsome angels who question people about their faith in the grave. However, when I open my eyes, I see a very tall, wonderfully dressed man, with a thick black beard, wearing a black, turban-like headdress.

"Shehzade, you are awake," he says in Turkish.

I stare at him, and in English, I ask, "Who are you?"

He blankly stares at me as I look across the room. It is beyond marvelous. It looks like it is straight out of some painting, and I don't know how or why I'm here and not in my dorm. I see Sally lying down beside me on the beautifully carpeted ground. She's wearing a pretty dress, which looks lovely on her, but it's not nearly as expensive as the clothing of the strange man.

Jake and Hamdan are leaning against the beautiful tiles of the wall, right beside the door. Jake is wearing baggy black trousers with a long red shirt down to his knees. On top of the shirt is a long overcoat tied at his waist. On his legs rests a magnificent Karabela sword in a black sheath. Beside him sits a headdress made of what appears to be white felt. If worn, it would stretch down his back.

Hamdan's clothes are eerily similar to the peculiar man's who is still standing over me.

I look down at my clothing. They are easily the most extravagant. I'm wearing black trousers, black inner robes with a red outer gown that has exquisite gold trimming. On my head is a magnificent white and gold turban.

I look over at the room one more time. It's magnificent. There is a massive bed at the corner under a window that looks out to a view of a city I've never seen. The ground is covered by a wonderful carpet—a Turkish carpet.

I look at the man and this time I speak in Turkish.

"Who are you?" I ask.

He looks puzzled, but still answers. "I am Zaganos Pasha, my shehzade. Are you alright?"

Shehzade means *prince* in Turkish. He thinks I'm a prince. I chuckle and ask, "So, who do you think I am?"

He again looks at me in bewilderment.

"You are Shehzade Mehmet, son of Sultan Murat, the second of his name," he responds.

Now, I'm the one in shock. How can he think I am Mehmet the Conqueror? This has to be a prank.

"What is the date?" I ask the man claiming to be Zaganos Pasha.

He stares at me for a moment, clearly with the look of a concerned parent. He answers and it takes a minute for his words to sink in.

"Shehzade, it is the sixth of February, in the year 1451."

5. Mehmet

"February sixth, 1451." I repeat, looking towards the man called Zaganos Pasha for affirmation.

He nods, flashing the same look my mother gives when she's worried about me. I walk towards the window overlooking the city off the hill.

What's going on? The man doesn't seem to be lying at all. If he truly believes that I'm Fatih Mehmet, then somehow, we have travelled over 550 years back in time.

How's that even possible? It should make zero sense, but the sick thing is that there's a small voice in my head telling me he's correct. Why else would I be in a room like this?

Maybe I'm dreaming again. That dream I had earlier today felt so...real.

I look at the man claiming to be Zaganos Pasha. He's still staring at me, unsure of what to do or say.

Okay, first, I must find out if he is telling the truth. I do know history. That is my greatest weapon right now. I know that Fatih Mehmet was sent to Manisa, a city in the Aegean Region, after his father, Sultan Murat II, and his Grand Vizier, Çandarlı Halil Pasha, removed him from the throne in 1446.

I look out at the city from the window. "We are in Manisa, correct?"

"That is correct, Shehzade," he replies.

Okay, so we *are* in Manisa. That's cool.

"And am I the Governor of Saruhan?" I ask worriedly.

"Yes, my Shehzade." He sounds slightly concerned.

Cool. Cool. Cool. Definitely not in freak-out mode right now. I hope.

I pause for a moment, take a deep breath, and gaze out into the city of Manisa. I look into the late afternoon sun, trying to listen to the noise in the city. People should be returning home from work, meaning I should be able to hear some traffic noise.

I listen for a bit.

Nothing.

Alright, so there's a chance he's telling the truth. I must find out for sure.

Ugh... What do I remember about Zaganos Pasha from my studies? The man standing before me looks so different from the actor who portrays him in the docuseries I watched earlier this week. For starters, this man looks twice my age and is extremely tall. Perhaps even taller than Jake.

Okay, so what I *do* know is that Zaganos is Fatih Mehmet's righthand man—his advisor and protector. He sided with Fatih Mehmet following his removal from the throne. He's also a former janissary soldier.

I focus my attention on his perplexed expression and ask, "How did you become a vizier?"

He impatiently rattles through the answer. "As you know, sir, I rose through the ranks of the janissary corps after being recruited from Albania. I impressed my superiors and became a military commander, which granted me the title of Pasha. Sultan Murat took notice and appointed me as a vizier. However, when you were forcibly removed from the throne by Halil Pasha, I chose to join you as your Lala. Hamdan Pasha also accompanied us to Manisa. We await the moment that you shall ascend the throne again, my shehzade."

"Unbelievable," I murmur in English.

His answer was more detailed than I expected. I had no idea he left the capital to be Fatih Mehmet's Lala, meaning he's the one who teaches Fatih Mehmet how to be a politician.

Why are Sally, Jake, and Hamdan not up by now? I wish they were.

For some reason, I believe this dude might actually be for real. I mean, why would he lie? He's kept a straight face throughout.

But how is it even possible? How is it possible to go over 550 years back in time? This has to be another dream, even if it does feel ultra-real.

I start to pace around the room, figuring out what to say next. After a minute, Zaganos stops me and asks, "Are you feeling okay, my shehzade?"

I pause again for a moment, take a deep breath, and lie, "Yes, I feel wonderful Zaganos Pasha. I just had a particularly strange dream. In this dream, I entered Constantinople, and our banner is raised over the city."

I pray that he buys my white lie—Zaganos is known for his intelligence as well as his ruthlessness.

"*Inshallah*, one day we shall see this dream come true, my shehzade," he replies.

"Why have you disturbed me, Zaganos Pasha?" I ask, trying to be authoritative, while hoping that he leaves, so that I may talk to my friends.

"I heard a loud, disturbing noise from this room. When I got to the room, I noticed Hamdan Pasha, the janissary soldier, and *this girl* unconscious next to you, so I woke you up. Besides, I have important information for you," he accounts.

Ah, so Jake is a janissary, elite warriors, who in peaceful times, *can* be special police, like the RCMP and the FBI, or even bodyguards. If I'm supposed to be Mehmet II, I *could* assign him the position of my head security guard.

I won't be able to call him Jacob because janissary soldiers are supposed to be Muslim, and Jacob isn't a Muslim name. So, what should I call him? Ali? Nope, that's too basic. Great historical figure, but a very common name.

Maybe Umar? Nah, that doesn't suit him.

Khalid? He was the greatest Muslim general, but Jake is only a soldier right now.

Oh, I've got it! Jacob is the Christian name for the Prophet Yakub. The name fits perfectly.

But who's Sally? Zaganos referred to her with some disdain. Is she my teacher? Sister? Wife? I know that Fatih Mehmet was married the same year he was forced to leave the throne at the age of fourteen. I remember that because it's so weird, from my twenty-first-century perspective.

"The information can wait. First, tell me, do you know what Hamdan Pasha, the janissary soldier, and this girl, are doing in my room?" I ask Zaganos.

"Shehzade, that's not important. I implore you to listen to me, I must tell you something right now," he urgently replies.

"Just answer the question."

He sighs. "You went for a walk with Hamdan Pasha, taking the soldier with you as a guard. I do not know who this girl is, where she comes from, or why she is in this room."

My brain goes into overdrive, creating a proper backstory for Sally, just like the rest of the group. Her name can be Salmana, a name I find to be very beautiful, plus it's close enough to Sally, so it should be easy for me to remember. Her last name is MacLeod, which, from when I watched *Outlander* and became obsessed with Scottish clan history, is the name of a Highland clan. I have no idea if she is Scottish. She doesn't look like a stereotypical Scottish girl, but I am just gonna pray that everyone buys my lie.

Noticing Zaganos starting to get impatient, I want to give him a story—any story. "Hamdan Pasha and I went for a walk. Before leaving, I asked this soldier named Yakub to be my head bodyguard, to which he promptly agreed. During our walk, we met this lady named Salmana. She is the daughter of a Scottish laird from the clan MacLeod. She came to our land to embrace our wonderful religion and meet this amazing prince named Mehmet, the man who shall one day lead our armies to capture the Red Apple. She is a guest, Zaganos Pasha."

"Alright, my shehzade," Zaganos says. I'm not convinced he's buying the lie. "I do not really care about that right now; I have important news that you must absolutely hear right now."

"Okay, okay, just tell me what's so important that you must tell me straight away."

"I apologize, my Shehzade, but your father, Sultan Murat, has passed away. I received the letter right before I heard the commotion in this room." He doesn't look too sad that his sultan has died. "We must get to Adrianople, immediately, so that *you* are the one to ascend the throne."

This is the only thing that hasn't shocked me. I know that Mehmet the Conqueror ascended the throne in 1451.

"Prepare for our departure immediately. We must leave as soon as possible. We have also got to rally as much support as we can and bring them with us so that Halil Pasha cannot stop me from taking my rightful place as the sultan," I say as authoritatively as possible. "Leave me alone for now, so that I may gather my thoughts."

Zaganos nods and leaves immediately, lowering his head out of respect.

Man, it's been such a weird day.

I am now Mehmet the Conqueror.

That's such a crazy thing to say.

It is possible that this is all a dream, but there's something telling me it isn't. I slap myself twice, pinch myself, and blink a few times.

Still here. So, this is my new reality, I guess.

Okay, what am I supposed to do now? How do I get back home? How do I survive here? No idea.

For now, I guess I'm going to remain calm and act like Mehmet the Conqueror. I must I get to Adrianople as fast as possible, so I can claim the throne. History must be preserved.

I'm about to be the sultan of the Ottoman freaking Empire.

Unbelievable.

I walk towards Sally. She's still unconscious. I lightly shake her for about twenty seconds.

"What on earth...," she croaks as her eyes open.

"Quiet," I whisper. "Help me wake up these two."

"What's happening?" she mumbles as she rubs her eyes.

"Just help me wake up these two," I answer.

I tap Jake's head twice, and he starts to wake up.

"Quiet," I whisper.

Sally shakes Hamdan a bunch of times, which doesn't wake him. I smile. He's always been a heavy sleeper. I slap him three times on the face, and he finally wakes up.

"What the heck are you doing!?" Hamdan exclaims.

"Shush," I hiss. "If you're quiet, I can explain."

"Explain what?" Hamdan says.

"Look around the room," I say to the three of them. "Look at your clothes."

They do as I say. Their expressions turn to shock and fear.

Jake speaks first. "Where are we?"

"Manisa—a city in Turkey. Probably in the Manisa Castle." I try to sound calm.

If I start to freak out in front of everyone, there's no way we all make it to Adrianople alive. I might remain alive if we are discovered, but Zaganos will probably use me as his puppet sultan. I'll have to be the leader for us to survive.

"Manisa?" Sally asks. "How'd we get here? Why are you wearing such fancy clothes? Why am I wearing this dress?"

"Well, um, I don't know how to say this, but somehow, we're in the year 1451. Manisa is part of the Ottoman Empire."

"Ha, ha, nice prank, Mehmet," Hamdan says. "Is this payback for when I hid all your sticks before a game last year? This is kind of high budget though. I mean, is that gold on your robe? What's with this hat on my head?"

"Hamdan, I'm serious," I say. "Please, believe me, we don't have much time. We leave for Adrianople later today."

"At least show me proof," Hamdan proclaims.

"I will if you shut the hell up!" I'm angry and need to be strict. I look towards Sally and Jake, who are watching us argue, still looking worried about the current predicament.

"Anyway," I continue, "a man called Zaganos Pasha came in here earlier and woke me up. I thought I was dreaming. I mean, I still think I am, but he thought I was Prince Mehmet, son of Sultan Murat the Second, and heir to the Ottoman throne."

"Sure," Hamdan huffs and rolls his eyes.

I ignore him. "Hamdan, he claims that you are a vizier called Hamdan Pasha. Jake, he just called you a janissary soldier. The janissaries are elite, professional soldiers. When they aren't fighting enemies of the state, they could be police officers or bodyguards. I made up a story about you being my new head bodyguard. Also, your name is now Yakub, a Muslim name. Sally, Zaganos didn't know who you were, so I made up a story... You are a wealthy aristocrat from clan MacLeod, which is a real Scottish clan from the Highlands. I told him you accepted Islam and your name is now Salmana. I know this sounds crazy, but I really do believe the guy."

"That isn't proof, Mehmet," Hamdan says.

"Look," I say to Hamdan, "Babaanne once told me this palace in Manisa is supposed to be in ruins, but it's not right now! If that's not proof, look out the window. There isn't *any* sound of traffic. Also, when have I ever lied to you?"

He takes a deep breath, and I know I got him there. I never lie to Hamdan.

"Okay, fine," he relents. "Maybe I believe you. But how are we here? Why are we here? What do we do?"

"I was getting to that," I say. Looking over to Sally and Jake, I ask, "Do the two of you believe me?"

"Surprisingly, I do," Sally says, which makes me smile.

58

Jake takes a moment. "Look, man, I believe you think we are in 1451. I'm not sure yet, but if we are in 1451, I'll find proof soon enough. I trust you, and I'll follow whatever you suggest for now."

"Okay," I say, flashing a smile. "We've got two things to worry about. First, how to survive without anyone detecting that we aren't who they think we are. Second, we need to figure out how to get back to the twenty-first century."

"So how do we live in this time without anyone finding out we are from the, um, future?" Sally asks.

"Well, we stick to what the guy thinks we are. We're leaving for Adrianople later today because Sultan Murat the Second died. I'm going to have to ascend the Ottoman throne as Sultan Mehmet the Second," I answer. "Hamdan will be known as Hamdan Pasha and will be my advisor. We have to call Jake Yakub, and he will be my head bodyguard. Sally, we've got to call you Salmana. I don't know what your role will be just yet. Also, we should all remain silent unless we absolutely have to speak. Basically, avoid speaking at all costs."

"Great plan. Only, there's one *huge* problem," Hamdan says. "Only you speak Turkish."

"Crap! Well...y'all keep quiet and let me do the talking."

They all nod.

"Okay, let's get ready to go to Adrianople," Sally says.

We walk around the fortress looking for Zaganos. For some reason, I know exactly which way to go. It feels like I've already been in these halls. I lead the group to his study. Along the way, we're stopped by a lot of individuals working in the fortress.

"So sorry for your loss, Shehzade!" or "You're going to make a great *hünkar,* Shehzade!" are phrases we consistently hear along the way.

"Mehmet... I can understand everything that they're saying," Sally reveals. "What's going on?"

"That's strange," I say. Looking at Hamdan and Jake, I ask, "Same for you guys?"

They nod, and Jake says in English, "Well, there's the proof we needed. We are in the year 1451. How?"

"We'll focus on that later," I say. "Can you guys speak Turkish? Repeat what you just said in Turkish."

Jake repeats in Turkish, "Well, there's the proof we needed. We are in the year 1451. How?" Hamdan and Sally also add their comments in Turkish.

How on earth...!

"That's amazing!" It is shocking, but I gotta keep my composure. "Well, now you guys will be able to communicate on your own," I say. "We'll figure out what's happening on the trip to Adrianople."

We turn to the corridor where Zaganos' study is located.

There, we see a young woman sitting on a bench, wearing an exquisite blue and gold dress. She has a medium skin tone with brown hair that flows to her waist. She stands up, and I see that she's nearly as tall as me. She's exceptionally beautiful. She walks towards us and wraps her arms around me in a hug.

"My husband," she starts, "I just heard of your father's passing from Zaganos Pasha. I know you didn't get along with him, but I'm incredibly sorry."

She really doesn't seem that sorry. I hug her back anyway, just so she doesn't feel weird. The smell of her perfume is so strong that I struggle to breathe. I try to remember what her name could possibly be and the name Gülbahar Hatun comes to me.

"Um, thank you, Gülbahar Hatun," I stammer. "I'm kind of busy right now, preparing to leave for the capital..."

"Our son and I will accompany you," she says.

Great, I woke up today expecting to watch Sidney Crosby and Mitch Marner play hockey, and instead I've travelled hundreds of years back in time to be the heir to the Ottoman throne. If that's not wild enough, I've also got a wife and child as an 18-year-old.

Absolutely terrifying.

What's his name? Bayezit II is the name of the Sultan that succeeded Mehmet II, so I assume that's my son's name. My gut tells me I'm right.

"That's wonderful," I say. "You and Bayezit should prepare for departure immediately."

"We will, my Shehzade," Gülbahar says. She looks at Sally and crossly asks, "Who is this?"

I look at Sally. "She's a recent convert to Islam. Her name is Salmana, and she's from Scotland."

"Okay, I don't really care about her name or where she's from," Gülbahar says. "Why is she with you?"

She's got me there. I have no answer. I don't know what Sally's role is in this 1451 universe. I'm Fatih Mehmet. Hamdan is a vizier, a part of the political elite. Jake is a soldier, so it's easy to explain his presence. I don't know what role to put Sally in.

So I mutter, "I asked her here by my side."

"She shouldn't be by your side," Gülbahar says. "She must serve me."

"She isn't a slave," I say. "She's a guest."

"I would like her to be in my service," Gülbahar requests.

I pause for a moment; I can't think of anything to say that wouldn't raise suspicion.

"Okay," I respond. "She will serve you, but she is to be your *friend*, not your servant."

"Of course," Gülbahar slyly says, then she turns to walk away. To Sally, she says, "Come along, Salmana Hatun. We have a lot of work to do."

Sally glares at me but doesn't object as she follows Gülbahar.

Hamdan nudges me. "Is it wise to send her on her own?"

"Sally's smart, you don't have to worry about her," I say to reassure him. "Besides, I didn't really have another option. Gülbahar Hatun is about to become one of the most powerful women in the Ottoman Empire and the world. I must keep her happy."

"Whatever you say, Mehmet," Jake says. "Let's stop worrying about that right now. We've got to leave for the capital at first light, so let's get cracking."

Jake, Hamdan, and I walk into Zaganos Pasha's study. It's a massive room. The walls are covered with picturesque tiles of the most beautiful colours. There's a magnificent matching Turkish rug on the ground. Hundreds of books line the shelves, which Zaganos is looking over to choose what to take. He looks at Hamdan and says, "Ah, glad you have finally joined us, Hamdan Pasha. I could have used your help making the necessary preparations for our departure."

"I was, er, otherwise disposed, Zaganos Pasha," Hamdan replies.

Zaganos continues, "My Shehzade, I am glad to see that you are doing better."

"As am I," I say. "Fill me in on the preparations."

"You do not have to worry about that, my Shehzade. I will take care of everything. Why is the soldier in the room?"

"I trust him, and he shall be in all my meetings. Just answer my query."

"Of course, my Shehzade," he awkwardly replies. "I've got all the cooks preparing food for our journey. I've got servants working to pack our important belongings. Other servants are preparing the horses for travel. I have spread the word to people around the castle that they may join us on the road to the capital."

"How about the janissaries?" I ask, interrupting him. "How many of them will be joining us?"

"I have yet to ask them," Zaganos says. "All will join, when asked."

"The soldiers that accompany us will be placed under the command of Jake—I mean Yakub. When we reach the capital, they shall join the janissary forces there," I command, hiding my nerves. "Now, Hamdan Pasha and Zaganos Pasha, make all the necessary preparations to leave right after Fajr prayer in the morning."

"Of course, Shehzade," Zaganos says as he lowers his head and exits the room.

"Go, follow him," I order to Hamdan. "Don't speak unless it's absolutely necessary. When you get back, tell me everything he does."

He grudgingly follows Zaganos out the door.

"You don't trust Zaganos Pasha?" Jake asks.

"I'm not sure who we can trust yet, aside from the you, Hamdan, and Sally."

We walk towards Fatih Mehmet's study, which is adjacent to Zaganos Pasha's study. It's an even more beautiful room, with wonderful patterned and colourful mosaic art on the walls. The carpet matches the walls.

Two walls are covered in books from floor to ceiling. I go through them, looking for anything useful. There are a lot of books on Islamic, Persian, Greek, and Roman history. A few detail the history of the Ottomans, although they seem to be recent. There are books on religion, philosophy, astronomy, art, math, science, and fiction. While a majority of them are written in Turkish, there are quite a few in Arabic, Greek, Latin, Serbian, and Farsi. Remarkably, I can read and understand all the languages. Jake is also able to read the Turkish and Arabic books and can perfectly understand both languages.

I find some diaries written in by the original Shehzade Mehmet, which help me learn about the man behind the title of Mehmet the Conqueror. He absolutely loved the Roman Empire and wanted the Ottomans to be more like the Romans. He was obsessed with his legacy, as well as the legacy of his empire.

I believe that Professor Rizvi was correct in stating that Fatih Mehmet is similar to me. We both love academic topics such as political theory, history, and philosophy. Although, I wouldn't want the Ottomans to be like the Roman Empire. Sure, the Romans were brilliant. But they relied on slavery as the foundation of their society and actively suppressed cultures and faiths they didn't endorse. One example would be how the Romans repressed Christianity, until they decided it was good, and in my opinion, they restructured it from the religion that preaches equality and love to a tool that serves the elite—no offence to Christians.

My hope would be to lead the Ottomans towards a future where they are more like the rightly guided caliphs or the early Abbasids. I want the empire to be accepting of all faiths and people while leading the world in arts, commerce, and science, representing Islam positively.

I find maps and battle plans for different invasions, some of which have happened and some that are planned for the future. It's clear that Fatih Mehmet has been planning to conquer Constantinople for years. He hopes to improve the dynasty's legacy, so that when people think of them, they see the Ottomans as equals of the Roman Empire. He believes that to start the process, he needs to conquer the great city of Constantinople.

I find a diary that has nothing written in it, aside from the first page. On the first page, there is only one sentence: "To fully understand history, you must experience reality from all perspectives."

Oh, my lord, it's the same diary that Professor Rizvi gave me, only it's not so ancient. It's brand new. Engraved on the cover is the saying, *"We are not going to conquer lands, but hearts."*

"Hey Jake! This is the diary Professor Rizvi gave me this morning!"

"What?" he asks. "What does this mean?"

"I don't know," I answer. "But I think it has something to do with us being here. Professor Rizvi told me that the diary took the first-person perspective of Fatih Mehmet, a vizier, a janissary soldier, and a female servant."

"So? He remarks. What use is this knowledge to us?

"I think we are now those four people," I say. "I'm Sultan Mehmet, you're the janissary soldier, Hamdan is the vizier, and Sally is the servant, which, um, sucks for her."

"Okay..." he replies. "How does that help us now, though?"

"Again, I don't know," I reply. "That scares me."

"So why tell me?" Jake asks.

"Because I believe each of us will have to play a key role in the most pivotal battle in Ottoman history. I believe that we will witness the conquest of Constantinople."

Jake and I work through the night, gathering the most important books, documents, and maps. I pocket the weird diary, which I'm sure is the same one Professor Rizvi gave me. I also collect all the other diaries belonging to Fatih Mehmet. We overlook all other preparations. When Hamdan and Zaganos return, they tell us to get a couple hours of sleep, prior to departing.

I go to my room and change into sleeping robes already set out for me. Even my pajamas are fancier then anything I had in the twenty-first century.

Being rich is weird.

I sleep for a couple hours and dream of home. I see Anne,

Babaanne, my dad, and me sitting in the dining room of our apartment. We are eating lasagna, my favourite food, and Babaanne is telling stories. My father is joking around. Anne is just happy that everyone is happy.

Will I ever see them again?

I feel someone shaking me. I wake up to see Hamdan and Jake. I look around the room, hoping to see my dorm room. Unfortunately, I'm still in the year 1451.

A bath is drawn for me by servants in a marble bathing room so large it might be bigger than three dorm rooms from Victoria Hall. The beautiful arches and decorated pillars make for a nice, cozy, and relaxing aesthetic. When I get out, there's a comfortable pair of baby blue and red travelling robes laid out for me.

Wow, I'm literally being treated like a king. It's still doesn't feel real.

There's also a dagger in a sheath laid out on a desk. The handle is black and gold. I pull it out of the sheath and examine its blade. The steel is sharp, with wide grooves and silver inscriptions. Beside the dagger lies a sheathed sword. I pull it out of its brown cover. The sword has a hand-and-half brown handle. The steel is tinted gold. The one-edged blade bends and laps in the middle to make it incredibly sharp.

"The Ottoman kilij," I murmur to myself.

I get dressed, pray Fajr, and head out of the room to see Zaganos, Hamdan and Jake waiting for me, each bearing their weapons.

"Assalamu Alaikum!" I cheerfully say.

"Walaikum Assalam, my Shehzade," Zaganos answers.

"Everything is ready for our departure," Hamdan says.

"Good!" I say. "Let's leave now."

"My Shehzade, I think it would be wise for you to say a few words of encouragement to your supporters," Zaganos suggests.

"Um, okay...,"

Who does he think I am? I can't speak off the top of my head like that.

We walk out to the courtyard, where over 300 people are waiting. Most of the men are on horses, while the women and children are set to be travelling in nice-looking carriages. In addition, there are a dozen or so camels carrying people's belongings.

300 people are here.

Just for me.

Unbelievable.

I see Sally standing next to Gülbahar. I flash her a smile, hoping that I look confident.

There are probably one hundred janissary corps soldiers standing by the entrance of the fortress. I tell Jake to get them organized around the perimeter of the travelling party.

Zaganos, Hamdan, and I walk towards our horses by the head of the crowd. I'm to ride a gorgeous white Arabian horse, the very one I saw in my dream. A servant sets my saddle and waits for me to get on.

I've never been on a horse before. I pray that I don't embarrass myself.

"Help me!" I quietly plead to the servant who placed the saddle on the horse.

Shockingly, I get up on the horse quite easily and instantly feel comfortable, as if I've ridden a horse a hundred times before. I somehow know exactly what to do. I look at Hamdan, and he seems to know what he's doing as well.

68

"I'll call you Snowstorm," I whisper to the horse.

I turn to Zaganos, and he indicates that I should start speaking.

I look at the crowd. It's so intimidating. I blink twice, hoping that this is just a dream. I take a deep breath and start to speak.

"My brothers and sisters of my empire! Yesterday, I got the unfortunate news that our ruler, my father, Sultan Murat the Second, has passed away. I pray that he reaches the highest level in paradise. We all know that he worked relentlessly to secure this realm. Not only Sultan Murat, but our forefathers worked tirelessly to secure this kingdom that we now hold, at the cost of many struggles and very great dangers. They have passed this burden along in succession from their fathers to their sons, and now, this responsibility is being handed to me. I promise each and every one of you that I shall not take this obligation lightly. I swear that I will work, day and night for each of you. I will work hard so that no man, woman, or child, shall go to bed hungry. I promise that our kingdom will reach new heights and shall become the most dominant and crucial force in the world. Together, we shall forge a golden era for ourselves. I set out now to grasp my duty and face it head on. Let those who love me follow me!"

With that, I grab the reigns of Snowstorm and turn to leave the fortress. I hear Zaganos, Hamdan, and the Janissaries leading the thunderous roars of approval. With a smile so bright it'd light up streets, I lead the procession out the city.

6. Mehmet

I've always felt like an afterthought, like a face in a crowd. In high school, I was a guy who was just there, just one of the lads. On my hockey team, I was a body in the lineup, who showed up, worked hard, and performed. At home, my family didn't even care if I did a great job on something. Being great was just expected from me, and they just always emphasized that I can't be a mess-up. I've always been able to do whatever I want, and no one's ever batted an eye; I'm a fairly responsible person. No one has ever really cared about what I think or do.

Until now.

I'm going to be the Sultan of the Ottoman Empire in a matter of days. Everything I do or say matters.

Earlier today, during my address to supporters at Manisa, I could see everyone holding onto every single word I uttered, judging each expression to determine if I have what it takes to be their *hünkar* (ruler).

It's pretty surreal.

It feels incredible.

Riding Snowstorm, on the other hand, is extremely tiring. I hated long road trips back in the twenty-first century, but it's even worse in the middle of the fifteenth century. In a car, I detested cramming into a confined area. On a horse, I have fresh air, but I feel every single bump, which makes me exceptionally sore.

We've been travelling slowly since dawn and have yet to take a break. I look up at the sun which appears to be at its zenith.

Ugh, I wish I had my phone so I could know what time it is. Crazy how we always took these things for granted.

I look over at Zaganos and Hamdan. "Shall we take a break? We've been riding for a long time."

"Yes, we should," Hamdan prompts. "It's time for the Zuhr prayer. We can pray and rest for a short while."

"We ought to stay on the road," Zaganos stresses while glaring at Hamdan. "Since we're travelling, we're able to combine both Zuhr and Asr later on."

I can already tell Zaganos and Hamdan are not going to get along.

"We'll take a short break, in which we can pray both Zuhr and Asr," I say. "I need it—I've only had a couple hours of sleep."

"Of course," Zaganos reluctantly says.

He leads us to an incredible valley with luscious green trees and hills. A pleasant spring flows through the valley, making it a comfortable place to rest.

I get off Snowstorm and feel stiff and struggle to walk, so I just collapse onto the ground. Hamdan doesn't fare much better. Zaganos stares at me in confusion. I guess the real Fatih Mehmet doesn't feel tired after riding a horse for over nine hours, or maybe he's just gotten used to it.

I struggle to my feet. I guess the worst part of being the future sultan is that I've got to be perfect all the time, especially in front of people.

"You're going to lead the *Namaz*," Zaganos informs me. "You must show that you are a leader."

"Okay," I nervously say.

I've led prayer hundreds of times before, and I have memorized the entire Holy Qur'an. However, I hoped I wouldn't have to lead prayer anymore—nobody but Hamdan knows that I am a hafiz (protector of the Qur'an).

It also makes me uneasy. I've never led prayer for a crowd this large. When we left Manisa, the group had around 300 people. Along the way, I have been told our numbers have grown to over 500. Leading 500 people in prayer is nerve-wracking.

I rest for another moment, and Jake comes running towards me.

"Why did we stop?" he asks in Turkish.

"Riding a horse is really tiring," I complain. "Besides, we need to pray."

"Mehmet, you may have forgotten already, but Sally and I can't pray," Jake points out.

"You've seen me do it a bunch of times. Just copy the actions for now," I tell him. "Besides, something tells me you already know how to pray, similar to how you can speak and understand Turkish."

"I might know the actions, but Sally may not," he states.

"I told Zaganos Pasha that she is a recent convert," I say. "She should be fine. If you're worried, just go tell her to follow what everyone else is doing."

"Isn't that supposed to be your job?" Jake asks irritably.

"I am doing my job," I harshly say. "Everyone's eyes are on me, not you. I'm tryna figure out how to get back home—and how to be a monarch. So, if you're worried about something simple like whether or not Sally can imitate the people around her, figure it out yourself."

Hamdan, who's sitting a metre away from us, gets up. "Mehmet, chill, man. Jake didn't say anything wrong."

I probably shouldn't have gotten angry. I guess the lack of sleep, the weariness of travel, on top of the stress of our situation, have gotten to me.

I take a deep breath. "Sorry, I shouldn't have gotten angry. Please make sure Sally is okay. Tell her we'll try to seek her out as soon as we can."

"Okay." Jake storms off.

"Let's go wash up for *namaz*, Mehmet," Hamdan urges. "We don't want Zaganos Pasha to get upset."

After Hamdan and I make *wudu*, we walk towards Zaganos.

"Ah, you're finally ready, my Shehzade," he says. "Let me find someone to call the *ezan*."

"No need to do that," I say. "Hamdan Pasha will give the call to prayer."

"Wait, what!" Hamdan exclaims. "I'm not doing that."

"You dare disrespect an order from your future *hünkar*!" Zaganos angrily states.

I put my hand up and say, "Relax, Zaganos Pasha, it was merely a suggestion."

To Hamdan, I say, "You have a beautiful voice, you should absolutely call the *ezan* if you want."

Hamdan looks at Zaganos and reluctantly says, "I'll do it."

As Hamdan and I walk towards a hill where he will give the call to prayer, he asks, "Why would you make me call the *ezan*?"

"Because you need to get experience in the spotlight," I explain. "Simple tasks like calling the *ezan* will grow your confidence for public speaking."

"Do I really need to?" he asks. "I'm only an advisor."

"If we're here for a while, you're gonna have to get used to it. The viziers are supposed to execute the plans of the sultan. You're gonna have to deal with a lot of people, and speak in front of crowds," I inform him. "With the conquest of Constantinople coming up, all of us are going to have to step out of our comfort zone."

"Wait, are you saying that we're gonna fight a war?" Hamdan is appalled. "A fucking war? There is no way I'm doing that."

"Possibly," I reluctantly say. "Two years from now. Hopefully, we're back home by then. Also, the war will be fought by us laying siege upon the city, which means the war will have low intensity and be a lot more like a chess match—well, a chess match with human pawns."

"Still, it's a freaking war," Hamdan says. "How will we survive?"

"Using this," I say, as I knock his head. "And this," I say while brandishing my *kilij*. "Now, don't worry about that. Call the *ezan*."

Hamdan turns to face southeast on the hill. He lifts his hands to cup his ears. In his loudest booming voice, he proclaims, "*Allahu Akbar, Allahu Akbar!*"

God is indeed the greatest.

After prayer, we continue on the road to Adrianople. I ride

alongside Zaganos, while sending Hamdan to ride near Gülbahar Hatun and Sally's carriage.

I think I really scared him by talking about the forthcoming war. It'll be two years before the siege even happens. I should just keep the group's focus on the present. However, I can't shake the feeling that the conquest of Constantinople has something to do with why we're here and is connected to how we get back. I've got to push that idea out of my brain and find another way outta here.

I look over at Zaganos. I don't think I've seen him smile even once. He's so serious and keeps a fierce expression. So, I try to lighten his mood by telling a Greek mythology joke that I've heard. The only problem is... I'm not very funny.

"What did Poseidon say to the sea monster?"

He unenthusiastically replies, "I don't know, what?"

"What's Kraken?" I say, chuckling to myself.

"Is that supposed to be funny?" he asks. "What even is a Kraken?"

"I thought it was funny," I say. "A Kraken is a mythological sea monster from Greek and Norse mythology."

"Since when have you cared about mythology?" Zaganos asks.

Ever since I read Percy Jackson, as a kid... is the answer I want to give. Instead, I lie and say, "I do not."

"Good," he says. "We should only be dealing in reality, not fiction."

"It's just a joke," I say. "To lighten the mood."

"We ought to remain focused, my Shehzade," he declares. "We must focus on our plans after you get the throne."

"We don't get to the capital anytime soon," I say. "We've got more than enough time to discuss our plans.

"Are you freezing me out, my Shehzade?" he abruptly asks. "I've noticed you talking a lot more to Hamdan Pasha the past couple of days."

"I'm not freezing you out, Zaganos Pasha," I say. "You **are** my right-hand man. Hamdan Pasha is also amongst my most trusted men. He isn't going to replace you, but he adds to our collective knowledge."

"That's fair," he mumbles. "I'd just prefer to be involved in all of your meetings."

"You will be in all the important ones. You and Hamdan Pasha will have to work together for our empire to be successful and to accomplish our great plans. Do you understand that?"

"Yes, my Shehzade. Have you decided on who your Grand Vizier will be?"

I remain silent for a moment. I had assumed that Çandarlı Halil Pasha would automatically retain the position of the grand vizier. I know that Fatih Mehmet did not trust him or particularly like him. In fact, he even executed him following the conquest of Constantinople. However, he must have had a reason to retain Halil as Grand Vizier.

Then again, I don't think I'm nearly as cunning as Fatih Mehmet.

Do I preserve history? Or do I weed out someone who may potentially stab me in the back?

I honestly don't know what to do. This decision could set the tone of my reign.

"I'm going to need time to decide," I inform Zaganos. "Regardless of what I determine, you're going to play an integral role in the future of our empire."

"Thank you, my Shehzade," Zaganos says. "You know that I will always accept whatever you may decide."

Somehow, I don't believe that, but I nod and fall silent, tired from riding Snowstorm for so long.

Over the next week, we continue to travel towards the capital. We've gone through many beautiful cities, forests, and valleys. The Anatolia region of the Ottoman Empire is incredibly beautiful, despite the fact that it is still winter. It's a shame that so much of the beautiful land, created by Allah, eventually got cut down to create space for different human pursuits. There must be some decree I can pass for lands to be preserved.

I've become accustomed to our daily travel routine. We set out at dawn, after praying Fajr, stopping early afternoon to pray Zuhr and Asr. At sunset, we make camp and pray Maghrib and Isha. Our procession is making slow progress as we're continuously stunted by the growing number of supporters joining our march to the capital. I guess rumours have spread about the death of Sultan Murat, despite no official confirmation from the state. Zaganos claims that our caravan is approximately 800, mainly consisting of young men and women, with a few seniors and children sprinkled in. The bulk of them are on foot.

I'm generally at the forefront of the procession alongside Hamdan and Zaganos. At times, we're joined by Jake, whom I rely upon to relay my orders to the janissary soldiers. Jake and I have organized them around the perimeter of the group.

I've put all men carrying weapons under the command of Zaganos, who's placed them at visible edges of the procession to make our party seem more threatening. Those on horses are dispersed throughout the caravan. The dozens of camels with us are in the middle of the group, along with the women, children, and elderly.

Every night, I make sure to go see Gülbahar and Fatih Mehmet's son, Bayezit. I know that Bayezit is going to be the sultan one day, but it's hard to imagine this cute, cuddly, three-year-old as one of the most powerful rulers in the world. Every time I see him, or walk by him, his face lights up, and he exclaims, "Assalamu Alaikum, Baba!"

A little kid calling me "father" is the weirdest damn feeling in the whole world. I always thought that wouldn't happen, at least until I hit the age of thirty.

Talking to Gülbahar is extremely difficult. I can tell how much love she has for me, believing I truly am Mehmet the Conqueror. Talking to her makes me feel like a fraud, which I am. I absolutely hate deceiving her and Bayezit.

These visits are also an excuse to see Sally. Unfortunately, I've haven't gotten the opportunity to talk about anything important with her. I can't stand that fact that I'm unable to freely talk with her.

Every night, after we make camp, I give short addresses to the supporters travelling with us. As my first public address back in Manisa was a hit, I've got to keep delivering powerful addresses to ensure that supporters think I'm capable. Every night, I sift through Fatih Mehmet's diaries looking for words I can say during these short speeches.

All my addresses follow a similar pattern. I start by honouring

Sultan Murat and our forefathers for working hard and establishing this wonderful dynasty. A great way to do this is by telling stories of their successes. Next, I stress that our ancestors have passed along the responsibility of continuing and improving on their achievements to us, their sons and daughters. Finally, I promise to take up the mantle of being the next Ottoman hünkar. I vow that our empire shall prosper during my reign. I pledge to bring about a golden age for the dynasty. I swear to bring the empire's enemies to their knees.

Following my speeches, I spend an hour addressing people's grievances. Dozens of people stand in front of me with their concerns. I try to give out practical solutions to the simple problems, but I've been forced to learn how to deflect and promise to do better on more difficult matters.

With each passing day, I'm starting to get used to this unique situation. I've been somewhat uncertain on decisions, forcing Zaganos to be proactive leading the caravan. However, I think I've accepted the responsibility that I have over the future of this empire.

It's easy, since I'm being treated like a sultan. My clothes are laid out for me in the morning. I can ask anyone to do anything, and they see it done. Anytime I eat, Zaganos insists on making the cook taste my food to ensure it has not been poisoned. I hate that he does it, but I know that it's possible someone may try to kill me to create unrest.

Every night, I switch tents with Zaganos or Hamdan to ensure that no one knows where I sleep. Each tent is protected by seven janissary soldiers, while Jake sleeps in my tent to ensure my safety.

It's Friday evening, February 14, 1451. It's been about eight days since Jake, Hamdan, Sally, and I travelled back in time to the year 1451. We should reach Adrianople on Tuesday, February 18... If Zaganos is correct about everything.

Right now, I'm in my tent, trying to sleep. Sleep has been hard to come by. I constantly worry about the future. I don't know if I have what it takes to be a sultan. I don't think I can handle the civil unrest that can occur with a new sultan on the throne. I doubt that I'm ready to be the padishah (emperor) of the Ottomans—I mean, I haven't prepared for this my whole life like Fatih Mehmet has. I'm worried that my friends and I won't be able to get back to our lives in the year 2019. Anytime I close my eyes, every possible anxiety pops into my head. I feel hopeless, even if there are some nice perks to being a sultan.

After struggling to sleep for over an hour, I finally give up, light a candle (*Who knew I'd actually miss a simple-ass thing like lightbulbs?*), and take out the diary that is uncannily similar to the one Professor Rizvi gave me.

Ever since I discovered this diary in Fatih Mehmet's study back in Manisa, I've been contemplating its significance. I'm convinced this diary has something to do with why my friends and I are here. I'm disregarding the gut feeling that's telling me that our existence in this timeline has something to do with the conquest of Constantinople, because I *must* believe we'll get home before that, which is why I keep focusing on the diary. As I told Jake last week, I believe each of us have become the four individuals in the ancient diary.

At the time, I had no idea how this was possible.

Now, I think each person characterized in the diary is one of our ancestors. Fatih Mehmet is my ancestor, Hamdan's ancestor must be the vizier, Jake's ancestor is the janissary soldier, and Sally's ancestor is the Ottoman female slave. Basically, I believe we have become our ancestors. Time travel may only have been possible when all four of us were alone the same room.

Since we've assumed the identity of our ancestors, we may have also attained their knowledge, which explains why I understand Ottoman Turkish, as well as all the other languages Fatih Mehmet spoke. It also explains why my friends can comprehend and speak Turkish.

What happened to our ancestors? I don't have an answer to that. I mean, my body is exactly the same. I also believe that our ancestors' knowledge is hidden in our subconscious and only surfaces when we really need it. For example, Hamdan and I are able to ride horses because this ancestor, whose identity we've assumed, had the ability.

I know this theory is wild, however, it's the only plausible one that makes even a little sense to me. There is no common sense about this situation, and I still can't figure how my friends and I travelled over 550 years back in time.

I open the diary and read this line over and over again: "To fully understand history, you must experience reality from all perspectives."

Perhaps I'm hoping that something might come to me. After reading it about twenty times, I give up and pull out my Kilij. I begin to wield it and I'm able to use it effectively, despite having no prior experience, further validating my hypothesis. However, it's clear that I need further training as I appear rusty. I start attempting different sword movements and slowly increase the difficulty and speed. Within a few minutes, I'm drenched in sweat, despite the intensity of the crisp winter air. While practicing different sword slashes and lunges, I continuously think about the sentence on the first page of the diary.

All of sudden, it just slaps me across the face. I've figured out how we were transported to the year 1451.

Y'all.

It's the blasted diary—the diary brought us to the year 1451.

Back in my dorm when I first read the line— "To fully understand history, you must experience reality from all perspectives,"—
the room violently shook. At the time, Jake shouted that it was an
earthquake. However, I remember a light emitting from the diary
right before I blacked out. Maybe if I recite that line out loud with
Sally, Hamdan, and Jake in the room, we'll get back to the twenty-first century.

"JAKE! WAKE UP!" I shout.

Jake immediately jumps up, hand reaching for the hilt of his kilij.

"What happened? Are you okay?" he asks.

"Yes, I am," I exclaim. "I might have figured it out!"

"Figured what out?" Jake mutters.

"First, get Sally and bring her to Hamdan's tent," I order. "If anyone asks, tell them Hamdan Pasha has summoned her. I'll go with
another soldier to Hamdan's tent. Go now!"

"Alright, alright," Jake grumbles and then he leaves.

As he disappears, I grab a dark-black outer robe. I go outside the
tent and find a tall, muscular janissary.

"Salaam," I whisper, "I'm Shehzade Mehmet. Take me to Hamdan Pasha's tent, then return here immediately."

"Yes, my Shehzade."

We walk for a considerable amount of time. Hamdan's tent is on
the other side of the valley we are camping at tonight.

"*Jazakallah khayr*," I say as we reach Hamdan's tent. "Now, get
back to my tent."

"Yes, my Shehzade," he says as he lowers his head. He turns to
walk away.

I enter Hamdan's spacious tent and find him snoring in the corner. I light a couple candles and pull off his blanket, but it isn't nearly enough to wake him. Stifling a laugh, I grab a jar of water that is sitting by his bed.

"Hamdan," I plead. "Get up, GET UP! I have good news."

"Just two more minutes, Mom!" Hamdan moans.

"I ain't your mother!" I exclaim, as I splash all the water on his face.

"What the heck!" he says. He strikes my jaw with his fist.

"Ow!" I grab my jaw. "Why would you do that?"

"I apologize, my Shehzade," he sarcastically says.

"Why are you calling me that?" I ask. "Nobody else is here."

"I apologize, my Shehzade," he says again in a mocking manner.

"Why are you being such a prat?"

"I apologize, my Shehzade," he repeats.

Finally, I give in. "What did I do wrong?"

"Nothing, my Shehzade," he says.

"If you don't tell me what I did, how am I supposed to fix it?"

He sighs and relents, "I just miss home."

"As do I."

"Yeah, but I also miss having you as my friend," he sullenly says.

"WHAT? I am your friend," I assure him. "We're together nearly every moment of the day."

"It's not the same," he says. "Over here, you're effectively my boss—an extremely powerful boss who can do anything you want. If I act normal around you, people frown. I have to agree with everything you say, at least in front of everyone. It doesn't feel like a friendship."

"Dang, I didn't really think about that," I say.

"Well, I wouldn't have *expected* you to," Hamdan says with some snarl still left in his voice.

"You know, I'd probably be going crazy right now if it weren't for you. I'm glad to have Jake, Sally, and particularly you, by my side."

"Jeez, you don't have to be so corny," he says. "I'm sure you'd do just fine."

"Yeah, I probably would," I chuckle. "Hey, I promise I won't force you to do anything you're not comfortable with."

"Don't make promises you can't keep," he says. "Just look at what's happened to your friend Sally. You didn't know what to do, and now she's condemned to serving your wife."

"Gülbahar isn't my wife," I insist. "She's Fatih Mehmet's wife, and I'm just an imposter. As for Sally, I'm going to make sure she doesn't serve Fatih Mehmet's wife for long."

"Yeah?" he snorts. "How are you gonna fix that?"

Right then, Jake and Sally pull aside the covers of the tent and step inside.

"Finally!" I exclaim. "What took so long?"

"HOW ON EARTH IS THAT THE FIRST THING YOU SAY AFTER ONE WEEK OF FORCING ME TO SERVE YOUR WIFE!?" Sally screams.

"Um, Jake, you should probably send the soldiers to my tent," I mumble.

"YEAH, GO DO WHATEVER THE *PRINCE* WANTS YOU TO DO!" Sally bellows.

Jake looks back and forth at the two of us, and quietly says, "I-I'll tell them to go."

"Thank you," I say. "Sally, please sit down."

84

Begrudgingly, she sits down in the darkness on the far side of the tent. We wait in awkward silence for Jake to return.

"Sally, I'm so sorry. I didn't mean for any of this to happen," I say.

"Maybe you didn't want me serving Gülbahar," she hotly says, "but still, you can easily solve the problem, and I don't know why you haven't done so already. You've got hundreds of subjects here who'd do anything you ask without raising an eyebrow."

"Those subjects may not say anything in front of me, but they're always judging me behind my back."

"So?" Sally replies. "Why should you care what people think? You're about to be the head of the Ottoman Empire, so screw them. You're a good person and you've already shown you are more than capable."

Jake chimes in. "Sally, a ruler is reliant on their subjects' support. If Mehmet's own supporters think he is irresponsible, he isn't going to last long."

"Why would anyone judge Mehmet for forcing Gülbahar Hatun to release me from her service?" Sally asks.

"Nobody is going to judge Mehmet for releasing you from Gülbahar Hatun's service," Hamdan says. "The problem is what's going to be your role after he does that?"

"I don't need a position in the empire," Sally declares.

"Really?" I ask. "How will any of us be able to see you?"

"You're going to be the *hünkar*," she explains. "You can come to me anytime you want."

"Sure, I may be able to do that," I say. "However, don't you think people will wonder why the sultan of the Ottoman Empire, a married man, goes out of his way to visit an unmarried woman? I mean, it's still technically the Middle Ages! People will call me irresponsible, possibly immature."

"Screw what they think," Sally says. "You're the sultan of an ENTIRE empire. That has to count for something."

"It does," I counter. "I have the ultimate authority, which is a God-given privilege that I must respect."

Sally looks at Jake, Hamdan, and me for a moment. "Are y'all saying I'm gonna have to suffer being treated like a servant for the rest of my life?"

"Hopefully not," Hamdan says, looking towards me. "Mehmet claims he can solve our problems."

"I didn't say that exactly..." I mumble. "But I think I've figured out how we got here."

Everyone is quiet and looks at me. Honestly, now that I have to say my theory out loud, it feels even wilder. I take out Fatih Mehmet's diary.

I start to explain my bizarre notion. "The very morning we travelled back in time to the year 1451, I went to Professor Rizvi's office to pick up an ancient diary."

"Sorry, who's that?" Hamdan asks.

"Our history professor," Sally, who has calmed a bit, answers. "Continue."

I nod. "He gave me an old diary on the conquest of Constantinople—"

Hamdan interjects. "Is that the siege you were telling me about last week? The one that's supposed to happen two years from now?"

Jake nods. "It's supposed to be the most important and pivotal battle in Ottoman history. You already told me this idea last week."

"Yeah, I know," I say. "Though, it's a lot more detailed now."

"Continue on, then," Sally says.

"Okay, no more interruptions," I command.

They all nod.

"Okay, so this ancient diary takes on the perspective of four individuals from this time period—Mehmet the Conqueror, one of his viziers, a janissary soldier, and a female servant. Somehow, when the four of us were in my dorm, all the words vanished from every page. The thing went blank... Except the first page, which only has this line: 'To fully understand history, you must experience reality from all perspectives.' Back home, when I read that sentence, the room violently shook, and I can now recall a shining light coming from the diary. Next thing we know, we wake up in the year 1451. As I told Jake last week, I believe we've become the four people from this ancient diary. I'm Sultan Mehmet, Jake's the janissary, Hamdan's the vizier, and Sally's the servant."

"That's impossible!" Sally cries out. "We all look the same as we always have! Even in 2019."

"Is it truly impossible?" I ask. "Think back to that fateful day. Now think of how we're in the Ottoman empire, each taking on the same roles as the folks in the diary."

Sally scowls at me. "Perhaps there is some validity to this idea," she whispers.

Jake looks at me and says, "This is exactly what you told me last week. What's different?"

"Let me finish," I plead. "Now, I believe each person in the diary is one of our ancestors. I know it's crazy, but it makes sense—at least to me. Sultan Mehmet the Second is my ancestor, Hamdan's ancestor must be one of his viziers, Jake's ancestor may be a janissary. Sally's ancestor might have been an Ottoman slave. This is why I believe time travel may only have been possible with the four of us in the room."

"Now you've gone bonkers!" Hamdan exclaims. "My family is from Pakistan. Both Jacob and Sally are white. Did you forget that?"

"Hey!" Sally hisses. "Half-white. My Mom is Punjabi!"

Hamdan raises an eyebrow. "Still, Sally, it doesn't make any sense to me."

"Your ancestors could've been a part of Mehmet the Conqueror's court," I urgently say. "I'm not going to waste time explaining this. Do you guys trust me?"

"Do we really have any other choice?" Hamdan asks.

His tone crushes my heart. If Hamdan doesn't trust me, why would anyone else?

I grunt and look away, not knowing what to do. After a moment of awkward silence, I feel Sally's hand on my shoulder. "I believe you," she whispers into my ear. Hearing her say those words slightly raises my spirits.

"Thank you," I murmur.

I look towards the group again with increased confidence. Leaving out my theory on how each of us has gained knowledge through our ancestors, I focus on how I think we can get home.

"I may have figured out how to get back," I confidently say.

"How?" Jake excitedly asks.

"Using this," I say, displaying Fatih Mehmet's diary.

"A notebook?" Hamdan asks.

"It's *the* diary," I say and roll my eyes. "I believe it's the same one that Professor Rizvi gave me, only it's brand new. Only a page has been written on. It has one line, which is that same line I saw in the ancient diary."

"Okay," Sally tentatively says. "How do we get back home?"

"I open the diary and just say the line out loud."

"That's it?" Jake asks.

"Seems way too basic," Hamdan says.

I shrug. "I know it's a longshot, but it sounds nice in my exhausted head."

"It's worth a shot," Sally declares.

"Let's do it," Hamdan says.

The four of us gather around the diary, feeling like a part of a cult. Hamdan casts his arm around my shoulder; Sally grabs my hand and squeezes it.

I open the diary and close my eyes. I hear rustling leaves outside the tent. The brisk night air attacks my chest, leaving it with a feeling of refreshment. The sounds of heavy breathing from Sally, Jake, and Hamdan ricochets through my eardrums. My heart beats ferociously against my chest.

I open my mouth and chant the words, "To fully understand history, you must experience reality from all perspectives."

The wind starts to churn viciously and aggressively with the tent flapping in our direction. The cool air strikes my body again, leaving it immobilized while I attempt to maintain my confidence. A few moments of agony follow, and then I open my eyes.

The four of us are still sitting in the tent, and absolutely nothing has changed.

7. Mehmet

"Why didn't it work?" Sally cries.

"Did you really expect that half-baked idea to work?" Hamdan asks.

The look on her face tells me that she believed my idea would work. It crushes my heart. I probably shouldn't have raised her hopes just because of my desperation to get back home. It's already been difficult enough for her.

"I'm incredibly sorry, Sally," I say. "It wasn't a great idea."

"It's alright," she says. "I know you're doing the best you can."

I smile and start to pace around the room, deep in thought.

"What now?" Jake asks.

"I guess we get used to living here," Hamdan answers. "It isn't that bad. We're treated like royalty."

"Um, it *might* be nice for you and Mehmet," Sally begins, "but this kinda sucks for me. I'm sure it isn't much better for Jake. He's literally a slave."

"You sit in a carriage all day!" Hamdan objects.

"I don't feel like a slave," Jake responds. "The janissaries are in a social class of their own. The people respect us. Or are scared of us, at least. Also, it helps being around Mehmet all the time."

"Zaganos Pasha basically treats you like a robot," Hamdan points out.

I stop to add, "Zaganos is a former janissary soldier. Janissary corps soldiers aren't like the slaves that populated the Americas. They're paid wages and live a relatively comfortable lifestyle. The only problem is how they are recruited."

"Are you defending slavery?" Sally asks, bewildered.

"Nope, just stating a fact," I say, as I continue to pace around the room.

"Point is, I'll get used to living here," Jake states.

"Mehmet's the luckiest," Hamdan says. "He's an *emperor*. No one can openly contradict him."

Ugh, that comment is annoying, but I gotta ignore it because it's true, even if I don't feel lucky. I've got a lot of hard decisions to make in the near future.

Should I let Sally know right now about my gut feeling that the conquest of Constantinople is the reason we're here, and may be linked to how we get home? I already have hinted at this to both Jake and Hamdan. But I don't know anything yet. I don't know what the conquest has to do with our existence here. I only know that there is a correlation. I am speculating—nothing else. I can't make sense of anything, and that is pissing me off.

Before I get a chance to think on it any further, Hamdan asks, "Mehmet, you aight, fam?"

"Yeah, I'm fine," I reply. I stop pacing and sit down.

I must have a seriously dejected look on my face from all the overthinking. Sally sits next to me and quietly says, "None of this is your fault."

"I just feel bad for raising everyone's hopes with such a stupid idea."

91

"Hey, don't worry about that," she says. "We'll get used to living here."

"I don't want to," Hamdan moans. "Why would I want to be a political advisor for my whole life?"

I ignore him and tell Sally, "I have a feeling the conquest of Constantinople has something to do with why we're here and is linked to how we get back to 2019."

"Why didn't you say this before?" she asks.

"I dunno," I mumble. "I didn't want everyone to be hopeless. Wishful thinking, I guess."

"You already told me that we may have to fight a war," Hamdan says. "I've been mentally preparing for it ever since you said that."

"Same," Jake adds.

"You guys don't get it," I say. "A war is brutal, and sieges are incredibly sluggish. They've got long hours of battle, multiple attacks, guns blasting the city walls all day, starvation, people torn apart by sharp swords, and thousands of people dying."

"We can avoid all that with you as the sultan," Jake declares.

"We can't," Sally objects.

We all look at her in shock. Sally suggesting that we embrace the impending doom of a sluggish war? Insane!

"Why not?" Jake demands.

She takes a moment and gives a detailed answer.

"The sentence from Mehmet the Conqueror's diary says, 'To fully understand history, you must experience reality from all perspectives.' In the future, that same diary is now about the conquest of Constantinople. I think the diary wants us to fully understand the conquest. It brought us here to experience it from four perspectives, which means that we must conquer Constantinople to return home."

"So, if I've got this right, a piece of paper wants us to kill thousands just so we can return home." Jake raises an eyebrow. "You've gone bonkers as well."

"Hey, Sally's absolutely right!" I cry out. "The line makes perfect sense to me now. How did I not think of that first?"

Sally smiles. "Because I'm smarter than you."

I grin and sarcastically reply, "I'm sure..."

Jake interjects, "So, you're okay with sentencing thousands of people to death?"

"I'm not condemning anyone to death," I object. "They'll be sacrificing their lives for the good of their empire."

I don't really believe it, even as I say that. However, I do believe the conquest is inevitable, integral to the rise of the dynasty, as well as the fact that history ought to be preserved.

Jake looks as though he wants to argue, but Hamdan jumps in. "Hey, guys, it's really late and we've got a long day of travel tomorrow. According to Zaganos Pasha, there isn't going to be a break either. I need to sleep; you guys should go to bed as well."

I nod in agreement. "I've said everything I wanted to. I hope we're all on the same page."

Hamdan and Sally nod while Jake merely grunts.

"Let's go," Jake orders both Sally and me.

"See ya later," I say to Hamdan as I walk out of the tent.

Jake, Sally, and I walk towards Gülbahar's extremely large tent, which she shares with Sally. Jake walks a ways behind us, which provides Sally and me the opportunity to talk.

"So, how are you doing?" I ask, hoping to raise her spirits.

"That's a dumb question," she says. "Everything sucks right now."

"Well, the fact that we've travelled over 550 years back in time is pretty darn cool."

"Yeah, it might be if I weren't a servant of a grumpy queen," she says. "You're lucky to be royalty."

"Gülbahar seems to be nice. She's always so cheery whenever I talk to her."

"That's because she's in love with you," Sally explains.

"She's in love with Fatih Mehmet," I counter. "I'm just a fraud taking his place."

"Don't say that!" Sally exclaims. "You're just as capable as he is."

"In my opinion, Mehmet the Conqueror is the greatest Ottoman sultan. I don't think I'll be able to replicate his accomplishments."

"You're incredibly smart and talented, Mehmet," Sally says. "You've just gotta believe it. Your first speech back in Manisa proved to every single person how capable you truly are. You got me to believe that everything will be okay."

"If I'm about half as competent as Fatih Mehmet, I'll be ecstatic."

"Don't worry," Sally says. "You'll prove to be just as clever as he's supposed to be."

"I hope so," I say. "Okay, so I've got a decision to make—my Grand Vizier. It's between Çandarlı Halil Pasha and Zaganos Pasha. Halil is the current grand vizier, and he's got a boatload of experience, but he might literally just stab me in the back. He's so incredibly powerful that he got Fatih Mehmet to abdicate the throne five years ago. On the other hand, Zaganos is Fatih Mehmet's right-hand man, however, he may think that he pulls my strings and that I'm his lapdog, which is why I don't trust him."

"And what do your instincts say?" Sally asks.

"That I should keep Halil as Grand Vizier," I reply. "He has experience that can prove to be an asset. It's risky. He may lead to my downfall, but I feel uncomfortable going against what Fatih Mehmet did. It'll also show Zaganos that I'm in control."

"Trust that feeling," Sally says. "It makes a lot of sense."

I nod as Gülbahar's tent comes in view.

"Ugh," Sally exclaims. "I wish I didn't have to spend my whole day with her."

"Is she really that bad?"

"She's just really grouchy when you're not around," Sally replies. "I understand it, though. It's difficult being with someone you love for only five minutes a day..."

"It's so hard for me to be around her," I protest. "I feel so awful when I'm with her."

"That wasn't a jab at you," Sally says. "Your ancestor barely spent any time with her."

"I'll correct that mistake," I say. "I'll make time for her."

"Please do."

As we reach the entrance to Gülbahar's tent, I turn to Sally. "I'm gonna make sure Gülbahar treats you better."

"She treats me fine," Sally stresses. "Just get her to stop being cranky."

With that, Sally removes the cloth from the tent entrance and says, "See ya later, Mehmet," as she punches me on the shoulder and goes in.

I wish she could be my Grand Vizier rather than Zaganos or Halil. I've got to find a way to elevate her position in the empire.

Jake and I walk towards our tent, which is a short stroll away from Gülbahar's.

As I get ready for bed, Jake says, "I overheard your conversation with Sally."

"So?" I ask as I pull on my covers.

Jake quietly whispers, "We all believe in you. Trust yourself to make the correct choices."

After I feign sleep for over an hour, Zaganos comes into my tent to wake me up for Fajr.

"Today is going to be an exhausting day, my Shehzade," Zaganos says. "Especially since you didn't sleep all night."

"How do you know about that?" I ask in shock.

"I saw you and the soldier heading into your tent a while ago," Zaganos says.

"The soldier has a name that I'd like you to use," I say. "Also, I just had a difficult time sleeping, so I went for a walk."

"You needn't explain it, my Shehzade," Zaganos says. "Going for a walk at night is something you do regularly. There have been times this week you've acted like a completely different person, so I'm glad that there is a small sense of normalcy that has returned."

"How have I been acting different, Zaganos Pasha?" I nervously ask.

"It's the small things, my Shehzade," he explains. "You've been slightly uncertain on matters, almost as though you didn't expect to make these choices."

"You do realize my father has just passed away, Zaganos Pasha?"

"Yes, but you've always disliked him," he says.

"You don't realize how much you love someone until they're gone," I glumly express thinking about Anne, Babaanne, and my father.

"I've always loyally followed you, my Shehzade," Zaganos starts. "The reason for my loyalty is that you possess the ability to make difficult decisions in challenging times. You ought to showcase that ability now to gain the loyalty of the people you wish to serve."

"Are you threatening insubordination, Zaganos Pasha?" I harshly ask, raising my voice to divert the conversation from myself. "Are you questioning my competence?"

"N-n-no, m-my Shehzade," he stammers out. "It was merely an observation and a suggestion."

"You want me to make tough choices?" I ask. "Here's one. I will retain Halil Pasha as my Grand Vizier. You will be the second vizier, *but* continue talking like this, and you may fall to the third vizier."

Zaganos looks appalled for a moment but recovers. "Why? How is this wise? After all that we have suffered at Halil Pasha's hands? Do you not remember that *he* is the one that got you kicked off the throne and exiled to Manisa?"

"You shall understand my decision soon enough. Every decision I make is for the betterment of our empire. You may question my decisions, Zaganos Pasha, however, don't *EVER* question my intelligence or competence."

"Yes, my Shehzade," Zaganos meekly says.

"I'll be riding with Gülbahar today, so make sure to ready a horse for her to ride."

"Of course, my Shehzade," he says.

"Now, let's go pray Fajr."

It feels like the five daily prayers are the only times I have to my-self. It's time to reflect, clear my mind, ponder, and communicate with my Creator. Prayer is stress-relieving and feels like the only sense of "me" that's left.

During today's Fajr prayer, I recite verses of hope to reassure myself. In the first unit of prayer, I recite the last verse from second chapter of the Qur'an.

"Allah does not require of any soul more than what it can afford. All good will be for its own benefit, and all evil will be to its own loss." *(2:286)*

In the second unit of prayer, I recite the ninety-fourth chapter, which is fairly short. I recite,

"Have we not uplifted your heart for you (O Prophet), relieved you of the burden which weighed so heavily on your back, and elevated your renown for you? So, surely with hardship comes ease. Surely with (that) hardship comes (more) ease. So, once you have fulfilled (your duty), strive (in devotion) turning to your Lord with hope." (94:1-8)

Due to my ancestor's ability to speak Arabic, I'm able to under-stand every Quranic word I recite, which might just be the most marvelous feeling in the world.

Today's prayer reminded me of so much.

It might be hard to remember, but Allah doesn't abandon anyone, let alone His believers, and He doesn't burden a soul beyond that it can bear. The Prophets went through more difficulties than anyone in the world. The Prophet Yusef wrongfully went to prison for years. The Prophet Muhammad, peace and blessings be upon him, was an orphan who lost nearly every family member during his lifetime, including six of his seven children. He witnessed the persecution and deaths of many companions. He was forced out of his hometown, Makkah, and harshly exiled from Taif. Yet, he still achieved his goal in delivering the message of Islam, the religion of peace, to humanity.

I can bear this hardship that's been dropped on me. I can't abandon who I am, because of the blessings or difficulties that Allah has placed upon me.

I may not be able to see my family ever again. I may not be able to do a lot of things I love. I may have lost my identity and name. I may have hundreds of enemies who wish me dead. However, I can't let that stop me. I've now got power, prestige, wealth, and the opportunity to do good and help those who are less fortunate.

I find Zaganos in front of the crowd of supporters nearly ready to march. Snowstorm is saddled and standing next to a brown Turkoman horse. I nod at Zaganos as I get on Snowstorm and lead the brown horse towards Gülbahar's carriage.

"Gülbahar Hatun!" I call out. "Are you here?"

"Yes!" she responds. "Give me one second."

"Okay!"

After five long minutes, Gülbahar steps out of her spacious bronze carriage. Bayezit and Sally sit on a wonderfully cushioned seat by the door right behind her. She's dressed extravagantly, yet somehow still comfortably enough for travel. It's wild how effort-lessly beautiful she is.

Y'all, this is my wife... but also my ancestor, so how does this work?

"My Shehzade, what are you doing here?" Gülbahar asks.

"Would you like to ride with me today?" I awkwardly ask. "I'd like that very much."

"What about Bayezit?" she asks. "He'll be alone all day."

"Don't worry, Sally, er, I mean, Salmana Hatun can take care of him."

She cautiously looks at Sally for a minute and says, "Alright." Mouthing *sorry* to Sally, I help Gülbahar onto the brown horse. "Shall we set off?" I ask.

"As you wish, my Shehzade," she whispers and we ride off to-wards Zaganos, who motions towards a janissary. The soldier starts to play the thunderous marching music as Gülbahar Hatun and I lead the procession out of the valley.

The two of us ride awkwardly in silence for a while as we head towards the narrowest point of the Dardanelles Strait, from which we will pass into Rumelia, the European (and Thracian) portion of the Ottoman Empire. After we cross into Rumelia, Zaganos believes we'll be able to pick up our pace, as many of the people who've joined our march to the capital won't be able to cross the narrows. If only he hadn't insisted on allowing all of them to join us.

Gülbahar loudly clears her throat, grabbing my attention, and asks, "My Shehzade, why have you asked me to ride with you if you aren't even going to talk to me?"

I warily look at her. I have no idea how to talk to her. I know next to nothing about her. I guess Fatih Mehmet doesn't know her too well either. Nothing about her is popping into my head.

I simply say, "I asked you to ride next to me simply because I enjoy your company. I desire your presence, Gülbahar Hatun."

"You do, my Shehzade?" she asks while grinning.

"Of course I do, Gülbahar Hatun."

"Why must you always say Hatun after my name? You do not need to, my Shehzade."

"Why do you always call me Shehzade?" I counter.

"Out of respect," she says. "Shall I not call my husband a prince out of respect, especially since he is a prince?"

"Shall I not give my wife the respect she deserves? You are an amazing lady, and I shall honour you with the honourific Hatun," I say. "You should know I hate being called prince. I'd prefer you call me Mehmet."

"Okay, Mehmet," she playfully says. "You may call me whatever you desire, just make sure it isn't Hatun by itself. That makes me feel like an old lady."

"Of course, Hatun," I tease.

"Please don't, Mehmet," she cries out. "I'm not an old woman yet."

"Sorry, Hatun," I say as I grin at her.

Gülbahar shakes her head and asks, "Why don't you like being called a shehzade?"

"Because I'm just a regular guy. Just because I've been elevated to a high status doesn't mean I don't have the same hopes and dreams as every other guy."

"But you do have an elevated status," Gülbahar Hatun says. "You may as well acknowledge your blessings and wear the name proudly."

"Well, I'm not going to be a shehzade for long. Just call me Mehmet."

"In a few days you'll be the sultan," she says. "Then I'll call you *hünkar* or *padishah*."

"Mehmet sounds a hundred times better."

"I agree," she says.

"How are you feeling about the move?"

"I'm excited," she replies. "We've been waiting five years for this. I'm just a bit nervous to meet your stepmother and Gülshah Hatun again."

"Who?"

"Your stepmother, Mara Hatun, and your wife, Gülshah Hatun," Gülbahar says.

I register everything she says, and the information magically takes root in my brain. (Yeah, I'm definitely right about having Fatih Mehmet's knowledge in my subconscious).

Mara Hatun, also known as Mara Brankovic, is the daughter of a Serbian monarch and one of Sultan Murat's wives. Fatih Mehmet and she are extremely close, so much so that he considers her a second mother.

Gülshah Hatun is the second wife of Fatih Mehmet. I honestly don't know how a guy gets married twice by the time he's eighteen, but hey, he's a Muslim prince in the middle of the fifteenth century. They married in the year 1449 and have a son named Mustafa, born in early 1450, before she left to live with her family in Bursa, a city in northwest Anatolia.

"Gülshah Hatun does not live in Adrianople," I say to Gülbahar. "You will not have to see her."

"She will probably come to Adrianople after you ascend the throne," she replies.

I highly doubt she comes anywhere near the capital until her son gets older. She likely doesn't want to see Bayezit and Mustafa become friends; she probably wants *her* son to be the future sultan. I grimace and look away. I feel bad for Gülbahar. Fatih Mehmet is *indeed* permitted to have multiple wives under Islamic law, however you're only allowed to do so if you're able if you're able to equally fulfil each wife's right upon you, which is enormously difficult to do. I highly doubt Fatih Mehmet was able to do that. He may have been an incredible politician, but his personal relationships probably suffered.

I divert the conversation. "How do you like Sal...mana? Are you getting along with her?"

"Sort of," Gülbahar responds. "She's very quiet, but I can tell she pays attention to everything I say."

"Yeah, she's good at that."

"What?" she exclaims, wearing a worried expression. "How would you know?"

"I have talked to her once, you know," I say. "She seems like a great person."

I think she buys my lie; her expression goes back to normal.

"Like I said, she doesn't talk much, so I wouldn't know," Gülbahar says.

"You should try to get to know her," I suggest. "She's new to this land—help her fit in. By doing that, I'm sure that you two will get along well."

"As you wish, my husband."

For the next hour or so, we ride on as Gülbahar tells me stories

103

of what Bayezit has been up to during our journey to the capital. Apparently, Sally and Bayezit get along well. Sally and Gülbahar are teaching him his alphabets, how to count, about nature, and animals. Sally and Gülbahar spend the long days playing with Bayezit and telling him great stories. Gülbahar notes that Sally's stories are very different and that she's never heard of them. Thankfully, she attributes that to being from Scotland and not from a different time period. Then again, I doubt anyone here has ever thought about time travel.

I pay attention to everything Gülbahar says. I don't really get a chance to talk—she's super-talkative and I still feel slightly shy around her. She's incredibly sweet, and I don't want to take advantage of her ignorance. Also, is she not my bloody ancestor? Like, what on earth am I supposed to do? Everything in this reality is so murky. Nothing is black and white. Everything is grey. Nothing is clear.

As we near the point where we intend to cross the Dardanelles, Gülbahar says, "You know, it's rumoured that the ancient city of Troy is located a bit southwest of our current location."

"How do you know that?" I ask in astonishment. I'm 100 percent sure the location of ancient Troy has yet to be discovered.

She shrugs. "I think an old teacher of mine told me. It doesn't really matter—it's only a rumour. It's my first time here, so I guess it just popped in my head. The Trojan War might be one of my favourite stories, so it's very nice to be here."

"Why's that your favourite story?"

"Well, the war was fought over the love of a woman," she replies.

"I highly doubt it was actually fought for ten years over a lady," I say. "They probably just used her elopement with Paris as an excuse to fight a war the rulers already wanted. Helen of Troy may not have been a real person."

"Why do you have to be so serious, Mehmet?" Gülbahar asks. "It's just a tragic story that I like."

"I do like the ending. The Trojan horse is the most brilliant military tactic of all time, although I have no idea how the Trojans were so naïve."

"Yeah, in hindsight the Trojans were a little foolish there," Gülbahar says.

I realize that the area we are passing might be close to the city Çanakkale, which was originally built as a fortress by Fatih Mehmet.

"I'm going to build a powerful fortress near this area one day," I abruptly say.

"Why?" she asks.

The reason Fatih Mehmet builds his fortress is to control the traffic passing through the Dardanelles. However, I respond, "To honour this pleasant moment with you." To which Gülbahar gives me the brightest smile I've ever seen from a woman.

For the rest of the day, she and I continue to talk about history and mythology. We tell each other stories and jokes. I honestly didn't expect this, but talking to her is surprisingly fun. She's funny, cheerful, loving, and smart. As the day wears on, I find it easier to talk to her.

She isn't my wife, but perhaps I ought to make it a habit to regularly hang out with her.

Then again... that might just prove to be tough.

8. Mehmet

After crossing the Dardanelles Strait, I marched day and night towards Adrianople with my supporters. Today is Monday, February seventeenth, 1451. Following our entry into Rumelia (Europe/Thrace), our group numbered around 500. Over the last couple of days, the number has ballooned, with many men from nomadic tribes joining our caravan.

We're camped at a plain field slightly over ten hours from Adrianople. Zaganos has ensured us that the security around me is airtight. My tent is surrounded by fourteen janissary corps soldiers. The only people allowed to visit me are Gülbahar, Hamdan, Jake, and Zaganos. Hamdan and Jake are also supposed to spend the night in my tent for extra protection, but they're just about as talented with their weapons as I am, so I told them it wasn't necessary.

A strange thing has been occurring over the past couple of days. Every person I talk to—with the exceptions of Gülbahar, Bayezit, Sally, Jacob, Hamdan, and Zaganos—doesn't dare look at my face while speaking to me. I've spoken to many janissaries, and many civilians. All of them lower their heads and look at the grass beneath my feet.

I've asked Zaganos why this phenomenon has been occurring, and he claims that people do it out of respect, that it's apparent to everyone now that I'm going to be the next sultan. Fatih Mehmet is the only member of the Imperial family powerful enough to ascend the throne. He has a half-brother, named Shehzade Hasan, who's extremely young. He also has a cousin by the name of Orhan, who's being kept hostage in Constantinople by the Byzantines. The Ottomans pay a tribute to keep him alive. I'll be ascending the Ottoman throne tomorrow, so people are starting to treat me with the respect they would give a sultan.

I, however, don't think people lower their gaze out of respect. Rather, I believe it is done out of fear.

I absolutely loathe that fact. I mean, I don't want people to be scared of me. However, I get why my subjects fear me. In this time period, many rulers believe that they can either be loved or feared by the masses.

Some believe it's better and safer to be feared than loved. As the Italian diplomat and philosopher Niccolò Machiavelli says in his 1532 publication, *The Prince*, "it is much safer to be feared than to be loved, when one of the two must be lacking."

This could be because many rulers find warfare necessary, and in this century, war may actually be necessary for the Ottomans to survive.

I, however, believe it's possible to be both loved and feared. I want my citizens to love my accomplishments as sultan. I'll have to gain a reputation as someone who's extremely just, but to survive as a ruler in the mid-fifteenth century, I've got to have people fear my potential wrath and ensure my enemies fear the fury of our empire. The best way to do that is by winning at war. I must press the Ottoman military to subdue our enemies and use the wealth that we gain to invest in the citizens and grow the domain.

I lie down and take out one of Fatih Mehmet's completed diaries. This one is about his plans after he gains the throne. The first task is to consolidate power, the second is to build up the military and navy, and the third is to conquer Constantinople.

Fatih Mehmet's papers don't have a lot of details on his plans. This seems to have been written immediately after Fatih Mehmet was removed from the Ottoman throne back in 1446. There's a lot of anger. He doesn't consider the Ottomans to be an empire yet. He believes that they are a modest, nomadic frontier principality, and that conquering Constantinople will make the Ottoman state a true empire.

I completely disagree with that. To me, the Ottomans are presently an emerging empire, who are a major thorn in the side of the other major empires. I believe that conquering Constantinople will actually make the Ottoman state the most powerful empire in the world.

Fatih Mehmet planned to ensure that all the bureaucrats in the Ottoman court fell in line. He believed that the sultan should be a more exalted position than it currently is. He also feared the rise of powerful families, like the Çandarlı family, and considered them to be a threat to the imperial family. He believed that the padishah should stay distant from the public and should be rarely seen for him to be seen as greater.

I don't necessarily agree with everything he believes, but then again, I'm viewing everything from my twenty-first-century perspective. Professor Rizvi would always remind us to look at history in its own context, from the perspective of those living through it. Everything is just so darn overwhelming right now, but I am trying my best.

As I continue to go through the diary, I hear a noisy disturbance outside my tent. I grab my dagger that's right next to my long black robe and unsheathe it.

Zaganos' really got me fearing for my life. My heart's pounding rapidly, almost as if I've been running suicides after soccer practice. I nervously grip the black and gold hilt of my dagger.

The commotion continues for several seconds. I hear janissaries shouting, relaying instructions to each other so quickly that I can't catch what they're saying.

With each passing moment, my heart slows. Perhaps it's some sort of training exercise. Maybe the soldiers are sparring, though they aren't supposed to be doing that.

All of a sudden, I hear someone enter my tent from the side.

"Hamdan?" I call out as I see a tall dark figure in the darkness. "Yakub? Is that you?"

"No!" a harsh voice replies.

A huge lump grows in my throat as the tall, dark figure walks towards me. I freeze, afraid of dying a miserable death alone.

The figure laughs a laugh so vile it leaves me shuddering.

"Enjoy your final moments, my padishah," he declares.

The man charges towards me with intense speed and force, but suddenly, almost magically, my instincts take over. I step to the side, duck under the slash of his kilij, press forward, stab once at his stomach, once at his chest, and once at his neck.

The man falls, and blood pours out of his wounds. After a moment of utter shock, my body shakes violently before I gasp, drop my dagger, and check his pulse.

Nothing.

Oh, my God. I've just killed a man.

A killer.

Me.

"HAMDAN!" I desperately cry as my brain scrambles.

A janissary steps into my tent.

"C-call Hamdan and Zaganos P-Pasha. And do *not* say a word to anyone."

"Of course, my Shehzade."

After a moment, Zaganos walks into my tent. His eyes dart around the room until they find the body. His face reddens in an intense fury, making it look even more fierce than usual.

"You!" he barks to the janissaries outside the tent, forcing them to step in. Zaganos growls, "How could you let anyone into this tent?"

"I a-apologize," a soldier stammers. "There were six other attackers in front of the tent."

"How could you let this one slip by?" Zaganos hotly asks.

"I don't know," the soldier says.

"Who's the officer in charge of this group?" Zaganos demands.

"I-I am, my pasha," one mumbles.

"Get. On. Your. KNEES!"

The soldier reluctantly does so. In one effortless stroke, Zaganos pulls out his kilij and chops the soldier's head off clean.

I want to scream, cry, and throw up, but I can't because I know the Ottomans brutally punish failure. Fatih Mehmet and Zaganos were known for this.

Zaganos starts to howl at the rest of the soldiers. He gets two of them on their knees and is about to deliver them the same fate as the other soldier.

"STOP, ZAGANOS PASHA!" I bellow out.

He lowers his kilij and looks at me.

"Do. Not. Punish. Anyone else!" I declare. "Let the death of their fellow brother teach them that failure is not an option!"

Zaganos looks as though he wants to argue, but after a moment of glaring at me, he nods and sends the soldiers out of the tent.

"You may sleep in my tent, my Shehzade," he offers.

"I doubt I'll sleep tonight, Zaganos Pasha," I say. "Who do you believe sent these attackers?"

"I have three to four parties in mind, my Shehzade," he replies. "It could either be the Romans, the Hungarians, the Serbians, or even Halil Pasha."

"I doubt Halil Pasha would try this," I say. "He's the one who sent the letter informing us of my father's death. I don't think he'd attempt anything this bold. I also doubt the Serbians would attempt anything without the backing of the Pope. They've pledged their allegiance to us. Also, Mara Hatun is the daughter of the Serbian monarch. Durad Brankovic wouldn't do anything that could possibly hurt her."

"Halil Pasha would definitely try this!" Zaganos exclaims. "Have you forgotten how he incited a rebellion by the janissaries to get your father back on the throne?"

"My death wouldn't serve his interests," I reply. "He has yet to see how I even intend to rule. If he didn't want me on the throne, they would have already named my half-brother, Shehzade Hasan, the sultan."

"He's only two years old," Zaganos says. "No one in their right mind would make him sultan."

Gosh, I'm stupid.

"I meant to say they would name my cousin, Orhan, the sultan," I say. "I'm sure the Romans would have obliged."

"So, you're saying it's either the Hungarians or the Romans?" Zaganos asks.

I shrug. "Are any of the attackers alive?"

Zaganos shakes his head.

"Then there's no way to know who tried to kill me," I say. "Get rid of this body. What happened here tonight doesn't get out. Understand?"

"Yes, my Shehzade."

At that very moment, Jake and Hamdan walk into the tent.

Zaganos turns to Jake. "How could you leave Shehzade Mehmet alone in his tent?"

"I-I..." Jake stammers.

"You must be put to death as well!" Zaganos declares as he brandishes his kilij.

"Calm down, Zaganos Pasha. I ordered Yakub to remain with Hamdan Pasha until he came to my tent. Put away your kilij."

He hesitates, then places it back in the sheath, lowers his head, and leaves to get rid of the bodies.

"What happened here?" Hamdan asks.

"I'll let Zaganos fill you in."

We're approximately ten minutes from Adrianople. Last night's events weigh heavily on me. I know that I hold an enviable position—that many people want me dead. It just hadn't sunken in until last night's assassination attempt.

I also know that the Ottoman regime is supposed to be strict, that no one escapes punishment regardless of their position in the empire. Failure is not an option. Men are regularly executed for failure and insubordination. Kanunî Sultan Süleyman, the great grandson of Fatih Mehmet, was known as the Possessor of Men's Necks, due to the fact that he would execute anyone, even his highest officials, for failure and insubordination.

I shouldn't be surprised that someone would be executed following a nearly successful assassination attempt on the future sultan.

But I was.

I'm now responsible for the death of two men. The assassin and the executed janissary.

Yes, the assassin's death was out of self-defence, but it doesn't make it any easier. Any time I close my eyes or stop talking to someone, I see his dark brown eyes and crooked smile. I can hear that haughty laugh.

I'm living a nightmare.

I'm about to be responsible for hundreds of thousands of lives—if not millions. I'll have blood on my hands for thousands of deaths.

It makes me feel incredibly sick, but I must push through and focus on the moments ahead.

I'm about to ascend the Ottoman throne. I'll be proclaimed Mehmet II, even though I'm not him. Or maybe I am. I don't even know. I just feel like an imposter, a pretender.

After Fajr today, the most elaborate clothes were laid out for me. Scarlet trousers and inner robes with an incredible gold design. My outer robes are black with gold trimming and buttons. It's tied down with a type of black belt. On my head, I'm wearing a black hat wrapped in white cloth. It's an especially cold morning, so I'm wearing a fur scarf and thick black gloves.

Not too bad for a leader of a "modest nomadic frontier principality" as Fatih Mehmet and the Europeans think we are.

Zaganos and Hamdan are also wearing great clothes. The two are matching with black inner robes and a red outer robe. As we approach the walls of Adrianople, our party is around 400. Zaganos instructed me to leave everyone behind who doesn't carry weapons. Gülbahar, Bayezit, and Sally also wait a short distance outside the city, with a small band of men staying behind for protection.

Gradually, robust walls with an enclosed and spiked gate protected by soldiers at the heart of the walls come into view.

"Who wishes to pass these gates?" a booming voice calls out.

"It is your padishah, Mehmet, son of Murat," I grandly respond. "I demand you let me in this very moment. This delay is wasting my precious time."

A minute later, the gates swing open. These walls of Adrianople are going to be in ruins 550 years from now. Currently, they are sturdy and should hold during a siege, but then again, the conquest of Constantinople will prove that even the mightiest of walls can fall.

Crowds are gathered along the side of the path watching us head towards the palace. None of them seem happy. Many look incredibly sad—an entirely different mood than what I've gotten accustomed to throughout our journey.

Zaganos warned me of this. People loved Sultan Murat II. He was an excellent *hünkar* and an even greater *ghazi* (warrior)—very big shoes to fill. People will doubt my abilities. During Fatih Mehmet's first reign, as a 12-year-old, the Ottomans had to fight off a

Crusade, followed by the janissaries revolting against the throne, which forced him to abdicate at age 14. The living conditions during his first reign may have been awful. The people won't love me yet; they don't know if I'm up for the job or if I'll be able to follow up the great work Sultan Murat, a man who'll be known as "The Great." I'm going to have to prove myself, and it won't be easy.

After riding for over twenty minutes, we reach the iron gates of the Adrianople Palace, built on a former hunting ground. The palace is massive, although it's incomplete. Sultan Murat had only begun construction at the start of last year. A considerable amount has been completed, but it definitely needs further construction.

A modest crowd has gathered behind us, probably hoping to see if I receive a warm reception at the palace gate. Zaganos indicates that I should probably give a short address. I feel a lump in my throat. I look up at the noon sun, thinking about what I should say. I don't want to give the same generic speech I've been giving for twelve days. So, I bellow out the same words the Prophet Muhammad, peace and blessings be upon him, said upon his first entry into Madinah.

"*Oh, people, spread the* salaam, *feed the hungry, be good to your family, pray at night when everyone is asleep, and you will enter paradise with peace.*"

I continue with a few words of my own.

"I say to you the same words the blessed Prophet Muhammad, peace and blessings be upon him, first uttered upon entering the great city of Madinah. These are words that every single person should strive to live by if we are to be prosperous. I now enter the great city of Adrianople, and these are words I pledge to live by as **your** *hünkar*. Now, my father was a great and honourable man. He was an excellent padishah and has accomplished many great triumphs. I pray that his abode is in the highest levels of heaven. He's helped transform our land to the wonderous state we see today—a state where children can prosper, a state where Islam prospers. However, he had a lot left to accomplish. He had dreams he had yet to fulfill. We have yet to spread the beautiful message of Islam to the whole world. We have yet to become a dynasty that will be talked about for centuries to come. The dream of our forefather, Osman, has yet to be realized. I vow to each one of you that I will follow in my ancestors' footsteps and with your help, I shall bring forward a golden age for our people."

My words don't have the same effect as they did in Manisa, and it's actually disappointing, as I've gotten used to the thunderous applause.

I do, however, get a polite round of applause and a few nods of approval.

Turning around to see the gates of the palace opening up for me, I ride in with Zaganos, Hamdan, and the soldiers. Everyone else remains outside the palace gates.

Right ahead of me I see a short man with a greyish beard and sour expression. He's got a long and slightly chunky face, and he's wearing similar clothing to Hamdan and Zaganos.

This is the infamous Çandarlı Halil Pasha. He's accompanied by three other viziers, whose names—Aslan, Mahmut, and Ishak—immediately come to mind. All are significantly taller and younger than him. They're wearing similar outer clothing to Hamdan, Zaganos, and Halil Pashas, but with different brightly coloured outer robes.

Behind him is the defterdar, who is the Ottoman state treasurer, sort of like the Minister of Finance. He's old, significantly taller than Halil, and has a long white beard. He wears brown outer robes and yellow inner robes. I can't recall his name, so he must not be some-one Fatih Mehmet deemed important, or he's a recent appointee.

Next to the defterdar stands the kadi'asker, the chief judge re-sponsible for legal matters. He also has jurisdiction over soldiers, which is why he can be referred to as the military judge. His name pops into my head as Mawiz ibn Hasan. The Kadi'asker is a mid-dle-aged man with a thick brown beard. His robes are baby blue and red.

Next to him stands the Agha, commander, of the janissaries. He's a massive man who looks as though he's over the age of 60. His name is Yusef. He never actually served as a janissary soldier but was named the Agha at the start of Sultan Murat II's reign. I'm definitely going to name Jake his second in command. A former janissary corps soldier should lead the force. Also, I trust Jake to not rebel against me.

Behind everyone walks a small man with a very pointy chin, sporting a fashionable mustache that has been curated to perfection. He's even shorter than Halil and appears to be around the same age as Zaganos. His name pops into my mind as Adham ibn Eymen. He's the Nişancı, which means he's the official court scribe. His job is to seal all official documents with the official *tughra* (seal) of the sultan. He is also the head of the government secretariat.

Accompanying the eight men are fifty janissaries. If it comes to a fight, we easily outnumber them. I lead Snowstorm all the way to Halil and stop less than a metre in front of him. Behind us, the gates of the palace close, shielding the view of the public.

"Halil Pasha," I boldly say. "It's been quite some time since I last saw you."

"I'm sorry that it's under such appalling circumstances that we meet again," he responds.

A wild idea jumps into my head. I turn Snowstorm to the side and climb off him.

I stand in front of Halil and look down at the short man.

I take off my glove, hold out my right hand, and say, "Grand Vizier!" motioning at Halil to kiss my hand.

I feel the atmosphere tense up. Everyone looks on anxiously as if they are expecting fireworks to erupt. At that very moment of silence, Snowstorm forcefully neighs. You can almost hear the tense music rising as if it's a scene in a movie.

Halil nervously looks around at the men by his side. He gets down on one knee and holds out his hand. I place my hand forward and he grasps it, kisses my knuckles, and presses my hand against his forehead.

After Halil grovels for a moment, I pull my hand away.

That was... unpleasant.

He stands up, folds his hands behind his back, and glances at my face once before lowering his gaze. He then loudly proclaims the two powerful words I've been waiting to hear: "My sultan."

The eight hours following the events of the morning were dreadfully boring, but I completed a lot of necessary tasks.

Halil and I spent hours arguing over the rest of my appointees to the Imperial Divan, which is a council of senior ministers who meet informally to discuss matters of the state, or in other words, my political cabinet.

Fatih Mehmet is the Sultan who formalizes the divan, so I figure I'm going to have to do the same thing. It's wild that the Ottomans have been so successful with their senior ministers never having formal meetings. That must be changed.

Anyways, after a serious round of debate with Halil, he and I finally agreed on my new appointments:

Halil Pasha- Grand Vizier

Zaganos Pasha- Second Vizier

Mahmut Pasha- Third Vizier

Hamdan Pasha- Fourth Vizier

Aslan Pasha- Governor of Saruhan

Ishak Pasha- Provincial Governor of Anatolia

Yakub- Deputy to the Agha of the janissaries

Ishak Pasha will be governing from the city of Ankara. Ishak Pasha will also marry Sultan Murat's widow and mother of Shehzade Hasan, Sultan Hatun. Halil insisted on this. In return, Jake is now the appointed deputy to Yusef Agha.

I've decided to retain every other senior official in their current role. I don't know if that's what Fatih Mehmet did, but I don't think it's a bad move. Sultan Murat must have had a reason to appoint all these men. If they prove to be disloyal or incompetent, I can always replace them.

Following my initial meeting with Halil, I met with Nişancı Adham Ibn Eymen to confirm that I will be keeping the exact same *tughra* my ancestor held during his first reign. Halil, Adham, and I drafted a letter with my official *tughra* to send out to all regions, provinces, and allied states, announcing the death of Sultan Murat II and my ascension to the throne. Halil and I debated the wording of the letter, but in the end, I was able to get my way.

Next, I met with each senior minister, informing them of their roles. Each person presented me with a customary gift. I received a lot of gold, more than I've ever seen in my life. Zaganos presented me with a chest of gold and other trinkets, while even Hamdan gave me a handful of gold and silver.

The Agha of the Janissaries, Yusef Agha, did not present me with the customary gift, which worries me. He also doesn't seem to be pleased with Jake's appointment as his deputy. However, he's got more than enough time to send the customary gift. I haven't even been inaugurated as the Sultan yet.

Halil is the only other senior official yet to present me with the customary gift. He's probably going to delay it as long as possible. His disdain for me is clear.

At this moment, it's late evening, I'm sitting in study of the sultan, which overlooks the palace courtyard. I'm exhausted. Unfortunately, I still have to pray Isha and be officially inaugurated as the Sultan of the Ottoman Dynasty.

In less than an hour, my name is going to be Sultan Mehmet, the second of his name.

It still feels ludicrous.

I go through the desk of Sultan Murat and don't find anything besides official documents, which I pile up at the side of the desk.

There's a knock at the door. I look up to see Hamdan and Zaganos.

"Do you wish to see your father one last time, my padishah?" Zaganos asks.

"He hasn't been buried yet?" I ask in shock.

"No," Zaganos responds. "You know that it's custom for the new sultan to first see the body of the former sultan and pay his respects."

"Oh yeah, of course. Please, lead the way, Zaganos."

In my opinion, Sultan Murat should have been buried the day following his death, to let his body rest in peace. However, I'm not going to get in the way of this Ottoman tradition.

Zaganos leads the way through the halls towards the body of Sultan Murat while Hamdan and I walk slowly behind him.

"Hey!" Hamdan hisses. "How are you doing?"

"Fine," I mumble. "Where did you get all that money from?"

"Dude, I've got a mansion a short walk away from the palace," Hamdan whispers. "There's a huge safe in my office filled with gold, silver, copper, and jewels. I grabbed a handful. Zaganos Pasha said that we were gonna have to give you a gift."

"That's cool," I say as I try to suppress a yawn. "Have you seen Jake or Sally?"

"Yeah. Jake went with the Agha and the rest of the soldiers to the garrisons," Hamdan says. "I last saw Sally with Gülbahar Hatun and Bayezit heading to the harem."

The harem. The word means forbidden. It's a secluded area of the home set aside exclusively for women. The imperial harem is home to the sultan's mother, wives, daughters, other female relatives, as well as his concubines (I've no use for those).

The problem is that I won't be able to see Sally for quite some time. If I summon her, everyone will believe that she and I are... well, they'll just assume I favour her, which will open her up to hate and

121

jealousy. Gülbahar will especially detest her, but this is an issue for another day.

We reach the room where Sultan Murat's body lies. He's prepped for burial. I look into the casket. He looks surprisingly similar to my father, with the same long face, sharp nose, thick brown beard, hair, and eyebrows.

This is a man that most historians often ignore. His reign is sandwiched between Mehmet the First and Mehmet the Second, two very influential Ottoman rulers. Sultan Murat's reign brought stability to the empire. All of Fatih Mehmet's achievements wouldn't have been possible without him.

"To Allah we belong, and to Him is our return," I declare in Arabic. Turning towards Zaganos, I ask, "When will he be buried?"

"Ishak Pasha leaves for Bursa tonight following your inauguration, my padishah. Your father will be buried alongside your ancestors and brothers."

"Very well. When is my inauguration?"

"Right now, my padishah." He motions for me to follow him.

We head towards the Imperial Hall. On the way, Zaganos asks, "Do I have permission to do what we both believe is necessary following your ascension to the throne, my padishah?"

That's an extremely vague statement. What he's talking about? Nothing's coming into my head. I blindly nod. "Of course, Zaganos Pasha. Make sure to take Hamdan Pasha with you."

He nods as we reach the doors of the Imperial Hall.

"Wait here," he instructs. He and Hamdan slip into the room.

The buzz in the room seems to be incredible, with sky-high anticipation. I impatiently wait a couple moments and then I hear a voice behind me. "Wonderful! You are here, my Padishah!"

I turn to see Halil right behind me.

"Shall we go in?" I ask.

He nods and the door to the Imperial Hall opens. The room isn't as vast as I imagined it to be, yet it still fits many people. The hall has many pillars and arches that help make it seem like a true Imperial Throne Room. It is decorated with all the beauty of the Ottoman Empire, with carpets, stone, cushions, curtains, paintings, windows so beautiful it melts your heart. At the centre of the hall on the ceiling, a marvelous candlelit chandelier brightens the room. It is packed with senior ministers, a whole host of men I have yet to meet. Jake is standing behind the Agha of the Janissaries. Hamdan is standing right by the throne alongside Zaganos and Mahmut Pasha. Halil hurries to join them.

The throne is a wide seat made of solid chestnut. The cushions on it are of the finest cloth, and the colours match the red aesthetic.

Next to the throne is an imam reciting a prayer for Sultan Murat. He also prays for my success and the success of the empire. I slowly make my way towards him. The voices behind me propel me forward. He asks me to pledge on the Qur'an. Honestly, at this point, I'm so exhausted and I just repeat everything the imam says without actually knowing what I'm vowing. It's some sort of variation of things I've already promised throughout my various addresses.

Next, I'm handed the kilij that I've carried ever since we left Manisa. It now has Fatih Mehmet's *tughra* and his title, "*Sultan Mehmet Khan, The Second of His Name, Sovereign of the Sublime House of Osman, Sultan of Sultans, Khan of Khans, Padishah of Anatolia and Rumelia,*" engraved on the blade.

I smile knowing that Fatih Mehmet's titles will greatly improve in the coming years.

After that, I'm presented with the kilij of Osman, the father of the Ottoman dynasty, bound by his belt. It may use the same steel as the original, but it's much too small to have been used in battle. This kilij is plated in gold and jewels.

I humbly accept it, and the imam wraps it around my waist.

Carrying the kilij of Osman is the equivalent of wearing a crown. It means that I'm officially the sultan of the Ottoman Empire.

I turn to look at people gathered in the room. I gaze towards the back of the room and see Gülbahar standing next to a group of women who look to be in their late thirties to early forties.

I smile at her and take a seat on the Ottoman throne.

Three weeks ago, I was stressing over a history essay. Today, I'm sitting on the Ottoman throne as the leader of a budding superpower.

Absolute fucking lunacy.

Halil motions for everyone in the room to be quiet. He takes out his kilij and declares, "All hail Sultan Mehmet Khan, the Second of His Name, and the man who shall lead our realm to countless victories!"

What happens next is super wild. Every single man gets up, brandishes his kilij, and chants: "All hail Sultan Mehmet Khan, Sultan of Sultans!"

9. Sally

Trapped.

Trapped in the year 1451.

Trapped serving the sultan's wife and her son.

I mean, my job is literally just to be friends with Gülbahar and to babysit her son. It isn't fun, but it could have been worse.

Upon entering the harem yesterday—yes, *harem*—some slaves started to usher me towards the female slave quarters, but Gülbahar stepped in. She told them I wasn't a slave and that I would be sharing her quarters.

Let me say this... The imperial harem is stunning. It looks exactly how you would imagine a palace to be. Like something out of a Disney movie. I don't think I've ever been in such a fancy place, but then again, I've never lived in a palace before.

The harem is tucked away in a secluded section of the palace. It's a world with green and blue tiled rooms trimmed in gold and filled with luxurious furnishings, cushions, carpets, and curtains. It's the full-on Ottoman Turkish aesthetic, and it's marvellous. As I walked through the place with Gülbahar, she pointed out the sisters, aunts, and stepmothers of Mehmet the Conqueror. The harem is also the base for about fifty slaves, which again reminds me that I'm living in the middle of the fifteenth century.

At the centre of the harem, there's a massive courtyard with a pool for bathing, as well as a garden. It's a quiet and nice place to relax.

It's not a harsh lifestyle, yet I still feel trapped.

I can't do whatever I want. For example, I would have loved to have ridden a horse rather than sit in a carriage on our journey to Adrianople. However, I was forced to sit in Gülbahar's carriage. Tonight, she went to see Mehmet ascend the throne. She insisted that I stay behind to watch Bayezit. I would have loved to see my friend ascend the Ottoman throne, but of course, I can't tell her that Mehmet's my friend. She's under the impression that my friend Mehmet Osman is Mehmet II, a former prince, current sultan, and her husband. She also believes I'm the daughter of some Scottish laird from the clan MacLeod. It'd come as a huge shock if I revealed that Mehmet and I aren't who we say we are.

Every day, I think of the decision that changed my life. I really went to Mehmet's dorm for help with my history paper, and all of a sudden, I wake up in the mid-fifteenth century with a made-up identity and a completely different lifestyle.

I've got to give Mehmet *some* credit for his quick thinking that created a false identity for me. I don't think I look Scottish, nor have I ever told him about my Scottish heritage. I've never even acknowledged it myself. I know that my father is apparently a descendant of some laird from the Scottish clan MacLeod, but he lives on the other side of Canada and has told me next to nothing about our ancestry.

While Mehmet may have come up with a brilliant fake identity, I'm a hundred percent sure that I could've come up with a better one. I mean, why didn't he think to use my Punjabi heritage? Now, Mehmet and his friends, Jake and Hamdan, are important members of society in the mid-fifteenth century world. I, on the other hand, don't really have a role in this new world. Or is this the same world, but a different life?

Point is, I'm going to have to fight my way to the top. That's difficult for a woman in the twenty-first century. It's going to be even *more* difficult in the fifteenth.

Right now, I'm lying down next to Bayezit trying to get him to sleep. He fell asleep about twenty minutes ago but if I get up, he wakes up and starts to whine. At this point, Gülbahar's been gone for over three hours.

I'm extremely bored. If this were my actual life, I could be binging Netflix, or at least finishing my midterms. Instead, I'm lying here just babysitting and staring at this gorgeous room.

For at least twenty minutes, I lie down in silence, with my eyes getting heavier. After what feels like a few seconds, I feel Gülbahar shaking me awake.

"My Hatun..." I drowsily say. "How was the ceremony?"

"It was amazing!" she exclaims. She walks over to her overly large bed. "The actual ceremony was fairly short. Mehmet simply took an oath on the Qur'an and received the kilij of Osman, officially making him the padishah of the Ottoman State."

I get up to sit by her bed, knowing that she's only just getting started. She never stops talking.

"Right before he sat on the throne, he flashed the biggest smile in my direction," she gleams. "He looked so relieved. He's been waiting for this moment for years."

No, he hasn't, I wanna scream.

"The celebrations after went on for so long. You should have seen it."

I roll my eyes. *She's* the reason I missed the celebrations.

"I think I got along well with Mara Hatun," she continues. "She's probably the person Mehmet gets along with the best in this world. He loves her like a mother."

I nod and smile. Mehmet Osman doesn't even know Mara Hatun.

"I really want to get along with her and perhaps a couple of his sisters. You should try to be friendly with them as well."

I nod again, waiting for her to finish.

"Of course, it's possible that she gets married again. Every prominent man will ask for her hand in marriage."

"Uh-huh," I say.

"The feast was so good. There was soup, meatballs, kebabs, and salads and more laid out on the tables. For dessert, we had baklava and *kunefe*, and that's just what I had. Dancers performed, music played throughout the evening, and soldiers sparred for our pleasure."

I sleepily nod hoping that she finishes soon.

"During the feast, Mehmet was so serious. He's always been a serious person, but he generally pretends to be happy in the presence of others. He didn't even try today."

"Mhm," I say, knowing Mehmet Osman is very serious, and he doesn't hide the fact that he is.

"He didn't look happy all night," she points out. "I don't understand. He seemed relieved, but not happy. It doesn't make any sense to me."

I uneasily wait, unsure of what to say.

"I thought he might ask me to stay with him tonight, but he didn't even acknowledge me after the feast. It's been almost an entire month since I've spent the night with him. The only proper conversation we've had recently was during our journey here on the day he asked me to ride alongside him. I really hope he isn't getting bored of me."

I remain silent. Truthfully, I don't want to hear this. I hardly know Gülbahar. This is something a person would tell a close friend. Yet I find myself feeling incredibly sorry for her.

"Why are you always so quiet?" she asks.

I hesitate. "I-I'm just not a chatty person, my Hatun."

"You should talk more. I don't wanna be the only one talking."

"Alright, my Hatun."

"Now that we've got that cleared up, tell me about Scotland. I've never been outside the Ottoman state."

I pause. "It's um... very green. Uh... cold as well."

She gives me a puzzled look. "A teacher once told me that Scotland is a very beautiful place."

"Uh, yes, it is," I tentatively say.

"Why did you decide to come to this land?" *Why's she asking this now?*

"I became Muslim," I lie. "I needed a fresh start and coming to a land ruled by Muslims seemed a good idea."

"Why not Al-Andalus?" she asks and slips under her duvet. Wouldn't that have been a lot closer to Scotland?"

Why's she interrogating me?

I vaguely remember Mehmet saying something about Islamic Spain back at school. He kept referring to it as Al-Andalus. I probably should have paid attention. I think he said something about Muslims and Jews getting kicked out of Spain during the Reconquista in the 1490s, only a few decades from now.

"I prefer to live in a more stable and stronger land," I lie. "The, er,

Ottoman State is a much more powerful territory, and I heard that living in this realm is outstanding."

"Of course, our realm is amazing," she exclaims. "Mehmet's going to make it even better. By the way, how did you meet him?"

"Mehmet?"

I don't know what Mehmet told Zaganos Pasha. So, I am quick on my feet. "I sorta got lucky. I got lost and bumped into him. I told him that I came all the way from Scotland, and he invited me to the fortress back in Manisa."

"Hmm, Zaganos Pasha told me that Mehmet said that you came to Manisa just to meet him," Gülbahar says. "That's why I insisted that you serve me back in Manisa."

That's probably the dumbest thing Mehmet has ever said. I shake my head and continue to lie. "I just told him that because it would've been embarrassing to say that I was lost."

"Oh." She's not convinced. "I'm sure he wouldn't have embarrassed you."

"I know... I just panicked when he asked me." I smile. I'm pretty sure that I've successfully pulled off the lie.

"Well, I'm glad you're with me now. Mehmet is right. You do seem like a magnificent person."

I blush. "I'm glad that Sultan Mehmet thinks so."

"I've just got one more question," she says. "What about your family? Aren't you going to miss your parents? Aren't they going to miss you?"

I think about my mom and little sister Rani. They're probably worried sick. They probably think I'm missing, or even worse, dead. My dad, who lives in Saskatchewan for work, may have come back home to help them. They probably don't know that I'm okay. They also may not realise how much I miss them.

"Of course I'll miss them," I say. "Don't you miss your family? We can't live with them forever. Life goes on."

"Uh-huh," she yawns. "I'm sorry, it's been a long day. I need some sleep."

"Of course," I say as she lies down on her bed.

I start to change into an off-white embroidered night-gown.

I look around the room and realize there isn't a bed set out for me. "Um, where am I to sleep, my Hatun?"

Turning over to look at me, she asks, "Didn't they set out a bed for you?

I shake my head.

"Well, I guess you'll have to share mine," she says. "Just don't move around too much."

I climb into the bed.

Gosh, this may be the coziest bed I've ever been on. Another benefit of living in a palace.

"Good night," she says as she turns away.

"Good night," I say as I turn to my side of the bed.

I pleasantly smile as I try to sleep. I know that I didn't want this life. I'd rather be out and actively working to make a living. I don't want to spend my life in the Imperial Harem, but if my life is condemned to being a lady in the Ottoman court, I'll need to learn how to play the game to rise to the top.

I'll have to be both liked and envied, and I'm fairly sure I've just made a powerful friend and ally.

10. Jake

Soldier.

Deputy commander.

That's my new life.

My new reality.

When I left home for Queen's, I thought being a business analyst was my future, but now I'm a leader in the Ottoman Empire.

Crazy how life works, huh?

Following Mehmet's inauguration ceremony, he requested that all senior ministers meet him in his office. Yusef Agha, the leader of the janissaries, insisted that I accompany him.

There, Mehmet announced his changes to the government. He instructed those assigned to new positions, such as Aslan Pasha and Ishak Pasha, to rush to take over so that there is no power vacuum.

He announced that the imperial divan is to meet five days a week with the exception of Fridays and Sundays, between the hours of Zuhr and Asr prayers. A meeting can't take place without the permission of the sultan and the attendance of the grand vizier.

He ordered Yusef Agha to ensure his soldiers are prepared to be deployed around the realm to keep the order of the state. That's a very Donald Trump thing to do, but I guess politics in the mid-fifteenth century is bound to be conservative. I just hope Mehmet doesn't lose sight of himself while ruling the empire.

After announcing there will be an imperial divan tomorrow, he dismissed everyone and wished Aslan Pasha and Ishak Pasha a safe journey to their new places of governorship.

Right now, I'm in Mehmet's study, watching him go through government documents. A few awkward moments of silence pass. Then he says, "I hope you don't mind that I've named you the deputy commander of the janissaries."

"I probably would have preferred to remain in the background," I say. "It'd be easier to adjust to this new lifestyle out of the spotlight."

"This is the best way for me to ensure your safety," he responds. "As the deputy commander, you won't be deployed on campaigns. You lead the reserve forces. So, unless it's absolutely necessary, you won't have to fight."

"So, you only named me deputy commander to keep me safe?"

"Partially," he replies. "You're also extremely smart, so it'd be useless for you to be just another soldier."

"I'm not that smart," I contend.

Mehmet smiles. "Do you remember when we played capture-the-flag during orientation week?"

"Yeah…" I wonder where he's trying to go with this.

"Remember how we won the game?" he says. "We each led our side to victory. The two of us came up with the strategy. You led the offence; I led the defence. That's when I realized how smart you are. It also helps that you're a freaking math genius."

"I'm pretty sure you came up with the winning strategy," I say. "Also, capture-the-flag and running an empire have no correlation."

"Not true. But I'm just using that example to illustrate how smart you are," Mehmet says. "Look, it's fairly simple. I named you the deputy commander of the janissaries because you're intelligent,

133

trustworthy, and I want to keep you by my side as a leader, not as a soldier deployed on the front lines."

"Well, thanks, I guess... For the promotion."

"No problem," he says. He gets back to looking at the government documents.

"What do you hope to find in those?"

"I don't know. Perhaps the direction Sultan Murat planned on taking the empire. Maybe I'll find the exact military strength of the Ottoman State."

"Why don't you go to sleep?" I suggest. "It's been a long couple of days. You won't be able to get anything done without sleeping."

Mehmet stares at his desk for a moment and whispers, "I can't."

"What do you mean?"

"I just don't want to, okay?"

"You look pretty tired, dude."

"Nah, I don't," he says.

"Mehmet, you've pulled your beard in four different directions. Go to bed. I need to as well."

He sits still for a moment. I've honestly never seen him look this tired. He takes a deep breath. "I've been having trouble sleeping ever since...well, you know, since we travelled back in time. After what happened last night... never mind. I don't want to sleep, alright?"

I stand up, unsure of what to say. I've never seen Mehmet like this. He's usually quite calm and collected.

"I'm just trying to tire myself out so that I can fall asleep," he says. "It should work."

"Look, I know this situation is difficult. Heck, I can't imagine being an inch from death. You've got to know that Hamdan, Sally, and I will work through this together with you. We've got your back, man. Now, you're not Superman, so get some sleep."

Mehmet meekly smiles. "Superman hasn't even been created yet. Take that in. We can literally create his story if we want to, and no one could call it plagiarism."

"Yeah, I bet we could."

"Usually, when I can't sleep, I listen to music and watch hockey highlights," he says. "I wish I could do that right now, but of course ice hockey doesn't even exist, and I ain't calling an entire orchestra or whatever form of music they got right now to put me to bed."

"I wanna play some FIFA," I say. "I still haven't won a series against you."

"And you never will!"

I scoff. "Lemme take you to your room."

Mehmet yawns and says, "Aight."

I lead him down the dark hall of the palace. It's so dark that it's difficult to see. We walk past the vast imperial harem and find Mehmet's room adjacent to one of the harem doors.

We head into the darkened room, and he throws the belt of Osman and his kilij onto a desk and jumps into bed. The room is gigantic. It's decorated with large renaissance-type paintings, beautiful carpets, and plush furniture that's all sorta hard to see in the dark. It also seems surprisingly homey for a large room.

"Hey!" Mehmet exclaims. "You don't have to stay. Take your own advice and go to bed."

I yawn. "Alright, man, see you tomorrow."

After leaving Mehmet's room and ensuring there is adequate security outside of it, I head towards the janissary garrison stationed a short distance behind the palace. It's a massive fort with hundreds of soldiers within it. As I enter the battalion, it's mostly empty. Most men are either asleep, stationed in the castle, or out patrolling the streets at night.

I head to the bath and take what's possibly the longest bath ever recorded. I prefer showers, for the record, but they aren't around here. It's been forever since I've been comfortable. I haven't had a chance to relax since travelling back in time with Mehmet and his friends, Sally and Hamdan.

The long bath provides me the opportunity to truly think. Gosh, I miss my family so much. It's been some time since I've seen them. I miss talking to my dad, watching basketball with my mom, and even hanging out with my little sister, Nicole. I wish they had some way of knowing I'm safe, but they don't, and that worries me.

Most of all, I miss my girlfriend, Priya. I miss her long and flowing hair, the lovely dimples in her bright smile that lights the world on fire, and the sparkle in her beautiful brown eyes. I haven't gone this long without talking to her since we met back in sixth grade, when she moved from India to Simcoe to live with her adoptive family. I wonder what she's thinking right now. I just hope she isn't moping around worrying about me.

I get out of the bath, dry off, and change into some casual robes. Worst thing about this current predicament is that I'm always wearing some sort of robes. Not that my current fit isn't fire, but I actually do miss my jeans. Heck, I'd rock a Canadian tuxedo over always wearing robes.

I walk towards the common area of the garrison, hoping to bump into someone who can tell me where to sleep. I see three sizable men sitting by a table in the corner. Each of them looks to be at least ten years older than me.

I walk over to them. "Mind if I join you?"

"Of course not, brother," one of them replies in a rough voice. "Join us."

"Ah, this lad here looks like a pup," another says. "Looks as though he just left his ma's lap, don't it?"

The third laughs and says, "Looks as though he has yet to be taught how to shave. Look at that tosh growing on his chin."

"Don't mind the two scoundrels," the first guy says. "The name's Arslan. These two duds are Baver and Demir."

"Nice to meet you," I say. "My name is Yakub."

The three men stare at me for a moment. Demir breaks the awkward silence. "How on earth are you the new deputy commander? You're just a pup, a rookie."

"Um, it's actually my third year as a janissary soldier," I lie. "Not exactly a rookie."

"Still, our sultanate hasn't fought a major battle since the Battle of Kosovo back in 1448," Baver says. "I doubt you fought in that."

Somehow, as soon as Baver mentions the Battle of Kosovo, brutal images of battle flash through my mind, causing me to shiver. Intestines ripping out from the stomachs of soldiers, chopped limbs littering the fields of battle, men begging for water as their souls are ripped from their bodies.

These images must be from the Battle of Kosovo. Perhaps Mehmet is right. Maybe I have become my ancestor. How else could these images pop into my mind? My ancestor must have fought at the Battle of Kosovo. The real question is, was my ancestor's name Yakub? If not, how has no one called me out?

"I did fight in the battle," I hoarsely whisper. "My very first one. Wet my blade with the blood of men for the first time on the fields of

Kosovo, fighting on the frontlines alongside my janissary brethren, fending off the Hungarians, Wallachians, Poles, and Moldavians."

"What makes you so special?" Arslan asks. "There are plenty of men with a lot more experience."

I shrug. "Just lucky, I guess."

"You must've made a good impression on the new *hünkar*," Demir says. "What do you think of the guy?"

"Um, seems like he'll be a great *hünkar*. I can see him being an exceptional leader."

"I've got no love for any of the imperial scoundrels," Baver says. "I still remember the day they took me from my mother in Sofya."

"I mean we do live better lifestyles than we would have if we remained in our homelands," Demir says. "I'd be working all day on a farm in Serbia if I weren't recruited for the janissaries."

Baver scoffs. "Recruited? We are forced. It may not be slavery, but it is definitely forced labour."

"Where are you from, Yakub?" Demir asks.

Now that's a difficult question to answer. Canada as a country doesn't even exist yet. My family has lived in Canada for generations. My parents were born in Canada. My grandparents were born in Canada. Their grandparents were also born in Canada. I'm not exactly sure where my family is originally from. I think Brannan is an Irish name. I've also got red hair, which is what Irish people stereotypically have. Yeah, I should claim I'm Irish.

"Are you still with us, Yakub?" Arslan asks.

"Uh, yes," I reply. "I was born in...Ireland."

"How the hell did you get all the way here?" Demir asks.

"Long story."

I mean, it's not totally a lie.

138

"See what I mean?" Baver asks. "I want to see the new *hünkar* scrap the Devshirme practice. No more forcibly recruiting people into the corps. It's plain evil."

"At least we're paid," Demir says. "The empire doesn't treat us like a slave army. Honestly, the European empires are even worse."

"As long as Sultan Mehmet isn't an arrogant snob like he was last time. If he treats his people and us with respect, I'll be alright," Arslan declares.

My mind grows weary. "Well, it's been a great talk, brothers, but I need to hit the hay. Do you guys know where I'm supposed to sleep?"

Arslan gets up. "I'll show you the way, brother."

After saying *salaam* to Baver and Demir, I head with Arslan towards my sleeping quarters. We go up at least five flights of stairs before we get to a big blue door.

"This is where all the most experienced janissary soldiers sleep," Arslan says. "As the deputy commander, you also sleep here."

"Thank you," I say as I step into the cold, dark hall. I find the empty quarters of the deputy commander. In there, I find a desk, a large bed, different weapons on the wall, a large chest filled with clothes, and a small bookshelf. I pull out a pair of ragged robes to sleep in and jump into bed.

While trying to sleep, I think back to something my father said right before I left for Queen's. "Worrying about your past is stupid— it's history, and you can't do anything about it. Worrying about your future is dumb—it's all up in the air. Do whatever you can to make the most of the present. It's the only thing you can control."

That makes a lot of sense to me now. I miss my family and Priya. However, there's no point dwelling on how my friends, and I got here. Worrying about what may happen in the future makes no sense. I truly don't know what's going to happen. Mehmet says that there is to be a major war in the near future, yet I can't do anything to control that. The only thing I can control, is the present moment, and I intend to be the best at whatever is thrown at me.

11. HAMDAN

Waking up in a mansion is pretty dope.

However, Zaganos waking you up is the exact opposite.

Today, he somehow got through my security (*yes, I have personal security*), came into my bedroom, pulled off my blanket, and used my pillow to beat me until I got out of bed.

"GET OUT OF BED! GET OUT OF BED!" he shouted. "We've got important tasks to do today."

Yeah, the guy is wild.

Also intimidating. So, I didn't object.

Right now, he's in the lobby of the mansion, waiting for me to get dressed. A bath is drawn in the remarkably large bathroom right next to my bedroom. The elaborate bathroom is easily the size of the upper floor of my parents' house back in Mississauga.

Simply enormous.

After I finish bathing, I head into my room to find black and baby blue robes laid out on my bed by servants. A black Turkish hat sits on top of the robes, and it's wrapped in a white cloth. My kilij has been polished and placed in its sheath attached to a belt. There's also a dagger next to my kilij, but I leave that on the bed as my servants help me get dressed.

I think about my current position.

Ever since I got to the capital, bits of my new identity have magically become clear.

The person that I am now initially ran an extremely successful clothing business in Adrianople as a 12-year-old.

A 12-year-old—running a successful business—unbelievable.

The business was successful enough to get him noticed by the *defterdar*, the minister of finance, so he began to work for him.

When the original Shehzade Mehmet initially became sultan, he took notice of the young assistant who worked for the *defterdar* and elevated him to the very position of *defterdar*, causing a lot of uproar in the Ottoman court. A couple years later, the O.G. Sultan Mehmet, desperate for supporters, elevated him to the position of vizier and gifted him the wealth and lands of a former vizier who had recently passed away. This move again caused a significant uproar and pushed Halil Pasha to get Sultan Murat reinstated as the *hünkar*.

When my best friend, Mehmet, suggested that we have possibly become our ancestors, I probably shouldn't have slammed the idea. I mean, what other explanation could there be for us being in the year 1451 and able to speak Turkish? Not to mention details about the person everyone assumes that I am constantly popping into my head. Also, my appearance hasn't changed at all.

I can't think of another explanation.

I don't get it, but Mehmet's view somehow makes some sense, despite a few glaring holes.

Over the past couple weeks, I've stopped worrying about what's happened to my friends and me. It really doesn't matter anymore. The important thing is to figure out how or *if* we can get home. For now, though, I've got to learn how to be a God-damn government official.

Truth be told, I'm extremely uncomfortable with my new life. I detest being so formal all the time. I'm someone who loves art. I'm a creative, free-flowing person. I can't be super-formal all the time.

It feels stifling.

Suffocating.

Zaganos is so rigid. I'm not that way. I don't think time is going to solve this problem.

I don't think I'll ever feel comfortable with this new lifestyle.

It makes me so mad...but I've got to try.

After I get dressed, I head down to meet Zaganos Pasha by the front door. He grunts to acknowledge my presence and motions to follow him.

He's a weird dude. Like...take it easy, bro. Shit ain't that deep.

I look up at the sky, and it appears to be around noon, so a couple of hours before Mehmet's first imperial divan meeting.

"Are we going to meet Sultan Mehmet?"

"No," he firmly responds. "He hasn't left his room yet, according to the guard posted outside his quarters."

"Is he alright?" I ask. Mehmet is generally an early riser. He doesn't sleep in unless he's sick. In fact, as far as I know, he hardly sleeps at all, which is definitely gonna be a problem.

"Of course he is," Zaganos answers. "He just hasn't left his room yet."

"So, where are we going?"

"To execute the wishes of our padishah."

"What does that mean?"

"You'll see." Now he's sounding shrewd. We walk through the castle gates. "We're to meet Ali Bey by the entrance of the harem."

"Who?" I'm fairly sure that I'm supposed to know all of the important Ottoman officials.

Luckily, Zaganos doesn't say a word about it. Instead, it seems like he didn't expect me to know who Ali Bey is, as though he thinks I'm stupid.

"Ali Bey is the son of Evrenos Bey, one of the greatest generals in our state's history," Zaganos drowsily explains.

"Oh, okay... um, why are we meeting him?"

"Well, you'll see," he says again. We enter the hallway leading to the imperial harem. At the end of the hallway, we find Ali Bey. He's a tall, muscular man, who looks to be in his early forties.

"*Assalamu alaikum*!" Ali Bey calls out to us.

"*Walaikum As-salaam*," Zaganos responds. "Is everything ready? Has Sultan Hatun been summoned?"

"Yes," Ali Bey replies. "She should be here any second."

"Uh...what's going on?" I ask.

"We're ensuring the tranquility of the Ottoman State," Ali Bey answers.

"Oh, okay," I say. I have no idea what he means by that, but I don't wanna seem stupid, especially since I'm supposed to play a significant role in this state's governance.

After waiting over five minutes, a middle-aged woman, whom I assume to be Sultan Hatun, steps out of the harem doors.

"Why have I been summoned?" she demands.

"Sultan Hatun," Zaganos says, "your new padishah wants to meet you."

"Really?" she asks. "Why?"

"I am only the messenger," he answers. "He did not tell me why."

"Am I to go see him right now?"

"Yes, I'll take you," Zaganos says. She follows him away from the harem.

I start to trail behind him, but Ali Bey grabs my arm. "We have work to do, Hamdan Pasha."

I nod. He enters the imperial harem, which is really weird. I'm fairly sure that all men, aside from the sultan and his sons, are not allowed to enter. However, I stupidly follow him inside.

Immediately, I am filled with awe. The harem might just be the most beautiful section of the palace. There are fountains, pools, gardens, lounges…, and many hot women. Like, what is this paradise? I find Ali Bey jogging down the courtyard towards a child playing by the pool. I hurry towards him and see Sally out of the corner of my eye.

"Hey!" she shouts.

I quickly wave at her while running towards Ali Bey.

When I get to him, he looks around to see if anyone's looking, then grabs the child.

"Let's go!" he hisses.

As we sprint out of the imperial harem, I whisper, "What are we doing? Who's this kid?"

"How are you so dense?" Ali Bey exclaims. "We're making sure that our state doesn't plunge into civil war."

"What does this kid have to do with war?"

"He's Sultan Mehmet's half-brother," Ali Bey exclaims. "This is Shehzade Hasan Çelebi."

As we enter a palace hammam (bathhouse), I ask, "So what is it that we're doing?"

Shehzade Hasan starts to cry, and Ali Bey tries to soothe him as he twists the faucet to fill up the tub.

Ali Bey plainly answers. "We're going to drown him."

I stare at him in disbelief. There is absolutely no way in hell that he's serious. Or is he?

After just watching him fill the tub for a moment, I whip out my kilij. "Let Shehzade Hasan go!" I shout. "Padishah Mehmet would not want this!"

I mean, there is no way he would. Perhaps Mehmet the Conqueror would be okay with murder, but my best friend, Mehmet Osman, would absolutely detest this. He would never condone the murder of a small child!

"I thought the padishah told you everything, Hamdan Pasha," Ali Bey states as the bathtub completely fills up. "I'd put the kilij away if I were you. There is no way you'd beat me in a duel."

"Test me!"

Ali Bey sneers. "You do realize that our *hünkar* ordered this, right?"

"No way!" I yell as over the boy, who is wailing.

"Clearly Padishah Mehmet doesn't trust you," Ali Bey says. "He explicitly ordered Zaganos Pasha to do this."

Ali Bey grabs Shehzade Hasan and throws him into the water, holding him down by the throat.

I drop my kilij, and it loudly clutters against marble flooring.

No.

No.

No.

There is no way Mehmet ordered this.

I get on my knees, pick up my kilij and scream, "Stop! Stop! Please stop! Take Hasan Çelebi out of the water! By Allah, if you don't pull him out right now, I'll chop off your head!"

That gets his attention. He pulls the boy's body out of the water and kicks him on the marbled floor of the hammam as if he were Gronk scoring a touchdown.

I desperately start to give the shehzade CPR, but I know it's futile. Several minutes fly by in the matter of seconds. I check for his pulse.

Nothing.

I look into his lifeless eyes and start to sob.

I have just witnessed the death of a child—a baby—for no reason.

Standing up, I wipe away my tears, place the kilij in its sheath, and storm outta the hammam.

Time to go knock some sense into Mehmet Ahmet Osman.

12. Mehmet

Lying down in the world's most comfortable bed isn't helping me fall sleep.

In fact, I've never felt so awake.

Upon entering my room, I crashed onto the enormous bed. Only, I realized I had yet to pray the Isha prayer, so I got out of bed and prayed.

Since then, I've been tossing and turning.

I just can't sleep.

Nothing's working.

I try blinking my eyes at an extremely fast pace.

Doesn't work.

I try relaxing my face and body, taking deep breaths, and thinking of a relaxing place. Unfortunately, that's difficult to do. I try to think of something relaxing, but each time I do, my mind turns to what happened last night. I see myself thrusting my dagger into the assassin's stomach, chest, and throat as his body goes limp, falling to the dirt, with my hands sodden with his blood.

Don't even know how I did it.

That's not even the worst image I see. When I close my eyes, I also see the head of the dead janissary soldier, detached from the body, eyes open with a look of fear that will remain for the rest of time.

Trust me, it's not something anyone ever wants to see.

After another hour of twisting and rolling in my bed, I give up and slide out the bed.

I know I need sleep, but it ain't happening.

I walk over to the desk in the room and light a couple lamps. I pull out the kilij of Osman and examine it.

It's beautiful, even if it is smaller than the one I use. The feel of the hilt is ideal, although it's only fit to be used by a single hand, which is not my preference. The belt it's attached to is exceedingly heavy, which is going to be a pain in the ass to wear. The kilij is useless in battle, so I shouldn't need to wear it. I wrap it and the belt of Osman in a white cloth and tuck it underneath my bed.

I sit down at the desk for a moment, unsure of what to do. Usually, when I'm unable to sleep, I go on my laptop and watch hockey while listening to The Weeknd, Bruno, Drake, Taylor Swift (don't ask), J. Cole, and 6LACK, or binge on some stupid Netflix show.

I can't do that, so instead, I pull out a quill, ink, and a diary. I've never used a quill before, so this is um... cool, I guess.

I generally abhor writing. It's something I just don't do for fun, but I have nothing else to do, so I decide to write down everything I know about Fatih Mehmet's reign.

I mean, it feels like a smart idea. Recording everything that's supposed to happen will prevent surprises. Of course, I can't be a hundred percent accurate.

I start from the beginning. Fatih Mehmet was born in 1432 to Hüma Hatun. Not much is known about her, and he hardly ever spoke of his mother. Mehmet isn't the eldest son of Sultan Murat, but I believe that everyone older than him has died or aren't a threat

149

to the throne. I don't write about his first reign—I'm already fully aware that everyone was unhappy with the child sultan.

Now, everything I'm about to write has yet to actually occur in the world I'm now living in. I don't know if my knowledge of what happens could potentially change the future, but that would suck.

I know that Fatih Mehmet's first major European campaign is the conquest of Constantinople, but I have a hard time believing that was his first course of action as sultan. It would be way too risky to conduct such a challenging expedition as his first move. Instead, I write that it's possible that Fatih Mehmet initially led a campaign in the east, which is probably why European scholars ignore it.

Next, I write a bit about the conquest of Constantinople. The preparations for the siege are probably just as important as the actual conquest.

Fatih Mehmet intended to choke out the Byzantines. To do that, the Ottomans had to gain control of the waterways. They already controlled the Sea of Marmara. To gain control of the Bosphorus, the Ottomans built the Rumeli Hisarı (nicknamed Boğazkesen, meaning the Throat Cutter), a fortress on the European side of the Bosphorus, in conjunction with the Anatolia Hisarı, the Ottoman fortress on the Asian side. The intention was to prevent Byzantine ships from going through. Fatih Mehmet heavily invested in the Ottoman navy, which was virtually nonexistent at the start of his reign. He also invested in the newest and biggest cannons in order to breach the great walls that have stood for over a thousand years.

On April 6, 1453, Fatih Mehmet began the siege of Constantinople, accompanied by an army of 80,000 men. If you include the navy, it's possible that the number of men on the Ottoman side neared 100,000. Somehow, Ima have to gather 100,000 men in the next two years. I don't know how Ima do that, but let's not think of it right now.

In the initial stages of the siege, the Ottomans took control of all Byzantine holdings surrounding Constantinople to ensure they wouldn't be attacked from behind. The Ottoman navy parked itself in front of the Golden Horn to prevent aid from reaching the city. For weeks, Fatih Mehmet blasted the powerful walls of Constantinople with his massive cannons, making little progress. There were minor skirmishes that were mainly unsuccessful for the Ottomans. It would have been accurate to say that the battle wasn't going well for the Ottomans, after three ships sent by the Pope or Venice (I can't remember) managed to break through the Ottoman naval blockade.

The tide of the battle shifted when Fatih Mehmet maneuvered to get his Ottoman ships filled with cannons into the Golden Horn, which was guarded by a massive chain. The only problem is... I can't remember how Fatih Mehmet got his war galleys into the Golden Horn.

Ya Allah.

I can't remember the turning point of the most important conquest in Ottoman history.

I should absolutely know this.

I sit still for around twenty minutes, just vacantly staring at the diary, trying to figure out how he got his navy into the Golden Horn. I know it had something to do with the Genoese colony of Galata, but I just can't figure it out.

"Ugh!" I exclaim as I slam my fist on my desk.

"Ow!" I shout. Probably shouldn't have done that, but I'll come back to how Fatih Mehmet turned the tide of the battle later.

Anyhow, after Fatih Mehmet got his ships in the Golden Horn, he offered the Byzantines peace. He made numerous offers, but the Byzantines refused each one. Constantine XI, the Byzantine emperor, refused to give up the city.

After facing the pressure of his men deserting ranks and some civil unrest back in the Anatolian province, Fatih Mehmet launched a full-scale assault on Constantinople on May 29, 1453.

First, the Ottomans fired their cannons. Then, Fatih Mehmet sent a wave of his second-rate, lesser-armed troops. Next, he sent better-armed troops to supplement the others. The Byzantine defenders gave it their all, looking as though they may just hold the Ottomans for another day, until Fatih Mehmet unleashed his final wave of soldiers, the greatest standing army in all of Europe, the elite infantry troops, the valorous, daunting, and triumphant janissaries. After that, the Byzantines were unable to defend the city, which fell to the Ottoman state.

Following the conquest, Fatih Mehmet ruled for another twenty-eight years, establishing a new order for the Ottoman state, one that elevated the sultan's power. He formalised the imperial divan, worked to resettle Constantinople after the population had been significantly diminished due to the long Byzantine decline. Fatih Mehmet built *masjid*s, hospitals, schools, and monuments to showcase the Ottomans' strength.

Fatih Mehmet would continue to go on conquests. Most were to gain the upper hand on trade and expand the Ottomans' wealth and influence throughout the world.

I drop my quill on the desk and admire my work. I hear the ezan called from a distance, so I quickly wash up and pray Fajr. Then I crash into bed to think about what I've written.

All in all, I've written about five pages. I probably know more about him than most teenagers in the twenty-first century. However, I still don't know enough.

Not even close.

True, I've read a considerable amount about him, but I don't have any of my books or notes with me.

Unfortunately, I can't remember everything.

I don't know enough.

People may call me Sultan Mehmet II, but the truth is, I don't know what I'm doing.

I've got no training and no experience.

I'm the Ottoman sultan, leader of the dynasty, and I don't know what I'm doing.

For some reason, this puts my mind at ease. I close my eyes and lie down in peace.

I'm *not* Fatih Mehmet. I may hold the same title as the greatest Ottoman *hünkar*, but I'm a different person with different views, principles, and goals. I can lead the Ottoman state as I see fit.

I may follow in my ancestor's footsteps, but Ima do it my own way.

I am Mehmet Ahmet Osman. I may not be a brilliant historical figure. I may have lost my identity, but I'm still the son of Ahmet and Dalia Osman. They've raised me to be a great person, a great leader.

And a great leader I'll be.

I'm riding Snowstorm, leading a large force of men through a plain open field. I must have fallen asleep because this has to be a dream.

The dream quickly shifts, and I find myself sitting on the Ottoman throne. Standing next to me are my viziers, Halil, Zaganos, and Hamdan. We're receiving some sort of ambassador. Our expressions turn to anger on hearing his message. Unfortunately, I can't hear the conversation.

Again the scene shifts, and I'm sitting next to Sally in my room. She's wearing an utterly stunning sky-blue dress. She looks incredibly magnificent, like a queen. Does she have an elevated status? I don't see how that's possible. Regardless, it's clear that she's content. We appear to be having a joyful conversation as she jumps on me and gives me a huge bear hug. I don't know if I've ever felt happier.

All of a sudden, the scene shifts again. I see Zaganos in front of Sally and myself pointing his kilij right at me while my back is on the ground beneath him. I'm utterly helpless.

Next, the scene shifts to a room that I don't recognize. I'm sitting next to Gülbahar. She's leaning on my shoulder, crying as I try to comfort her.

Then, I'm standing next to an old man over what seems to be a grave outside the walls of Constantinople.

Next, I'm standing by enormous cannons, witnessing Ottoman soldiers getting impaled.

After that, I'm riding Snowstorm, kilij in my hand, and I'm rallying support from the massive Ottoman army in the middle of the night.

I feel someone shaking me. I ignore it and try to focus on the dream, but the shaking becomes unbearable, so I open my eyes. Hamdan and Zaganos are standing over me.

I sit up and rub my eyes, as the two bicker over something.

What was that dream? The future? Is that even possible? Am I really gonna be leading the Ottoman army? Do I have to? Why was Sally hugging me? Why was Gülbahar crying? Who's the old man?

Their argument gets louder, snapping me outta my thoughts. Along with Hamdan and Zaganos, there are two Janissary soldiers and an extremely large man. His name, Ali Bey, pops into my head.

"What's going on?" I mutter, as I pull at my beard and stretch my arms. "Why are you two arguing?"

"HOW COULD YOU?" Hamdan screams. "HOW COULD YOU KILL A CHILD?"

"SHOW SOME RESPECT TO YOUR *HÜNKAR*, HAM-DAN PASHA!" Zaganos growls.

"Wait, what?" I exclaim. "What are you talking about?"

Hamdan lunges towards my bed as though he wants to strangle me.

"Mehmet, don't you act like you don't know what I'm talking about," Hamdan says as his eyes flare up with fury.

I anxiously look at him. Honestly, prior to us travelling back in time, I hardly ever saw him angry. Now, it's the second time in a matter of days that he's gotten pissed at me. He looks as though he wants to kill me. I've never seen him so pissed off, and it scares me.

"Hamdan Pasha," I say as I try to hold my nerve, "I really don't know what you're talking about."

He jumps onto my bed as though he wants to grab me. I see the

155

janissaries reach for the hilt of their karabela swords. Zaganos and Ali Bey look as though they're about to jump in as well.

I really hope Hamdan doesn't do anything stupid right now. It's been less than a century since the Ottomans have had a sultan killed or his successor abducted. These guys are not gonna let anything happen to me.

"Hamdan Pasha!" I exclaim. "Please, calm down! Please, tell me what I've done."

"You ordered the death of Shehzade Hasan," he says.

I clasp my hand against my mouth. Of course.

How could I forget about Fatih Mehmet's fratricide law?

When Fatih Mehmet came to power, he enacted it. Once someone becomes sultan, they must kill their brothers to prevent civil conflict.

Now, Fatih Mehmet is only legislating something that was started by Bayezit the First who strangled his brother, Yakub, immediately after being anointed sultan during the Battle of Kosovo in 1389.

I understand why Fatih Mehmet enacted the law. Both his grandfather and father had to fight long battles against their brothers and family members to secure their positions. This threw the state into civil conflict. Fatih Mehmet reasoned that if the sultans simply killed their brothers, there wouldn't be any more civil conflict.

Of course, this would prove to be wrong.

So, while Fatih Mehmet's logic for the fratricide law may be valid, it still doesn't make it correct. I can't allow this terrible practice, but what can I do to stop it?

I look at Hamdan, who's just glaring at me. The rest of the people in the room are waiting for him or me to do something.

"Zaganos Pasha," I authoritatively say, "take everyone out of the room. Hamdan Pasha and I need to talk."

"Are you sure, my padishah?"

"Did I stutter? Do as I say."

"Of course, my padishah."

After Zaganos leaves the room with the rest of the men, Hamdan says, "What the hell is wrong with you! How could you kill a child?"

"I didn't—"

"You may not have physically drowned him, but you may as well have! I've seen how everyone fanatically follows everything you say."

"Hamdan! Do you really think I ordered the murder of Shehzade Hasan? Do you really think I'm that cruel?"

"Well, I wouldn't have this morning," Hamdan says. "When Ali Bey said you ordered the death of Hasan Çelebi, I didn't believe it."

"So, why are you accusing me of the deed now?" I ask as calmly as possible. "What could have possibly changed your mind?"

"Zaganos or Ali Bey wouldn't kill a shehzade without your permission," Hamdan states.

I stare at him for a moment. He's right. They wouldn't kill Hasan Çelebi without my permission. However, I can't recall ordering Zaganos to murder the child.

"Hamdan, I'm telling you I didn't order Shehzade Hasan's death. Wallahi, I could *never.*"

Hamdan's face relaxes, but he still doesn't let up. "Why would they kill him without your permission?"

"I think that Zaganos thought he had my permission," I reply.

"How's that possible?" Hamdan asks. "You either ordered them to kill him or you didn't."

"Zaganos and I have been discussing how we wish to proceed

157

with consolidating my power within the realm for a while," I say. "Whenever Hasan Çelebi's name was mentioned, he always claimed that we'd already discussed what to do with him."

"Holy crap!" Hamdan exclaims. "You're saying that Fatih Mehmet and Zaganos have been planning the murder? I thought these were good people."

"They are good people, I think. The mid-fifteenth century world is vastly different to the world we've grown up in. Zaganos and Fatih Mehmet believe they are preventing civil war. The Ottoman Empire has recently gone through several civil conflicts."

"So, the plan is to kill everyone in their family who doesn't become sultan?" Hamdan asks. "That's so stupid."

"In theory, yes," I reply. "Fatih Mehmet enacted a fratricide law after he became sultan. Sultan Mehmet the Third executed nineteen of his brothers. His son, Sultan Ahmet, banned the practice after he became sultan."

"That's crazy!"

"I know," I say. "I still don't get why Zaganos went ahead and killed him today without even asking me."

Hamdan falls silent, before he suddenly exclaims, "He did ask you for permission!"

"When?" I curiously ask.

"Last night," Hamdan replies. "Right before your inauguration, he asked for permission to do what's necessary. You *gave* him permission and told him to take me with him."

Crap.

How on earth could I be so stupid?

My words matter.

I can't blindly agree to anything.

I'm the reason a child is dead.

What am I to do now?

"Well, I can't bring Shehzade Hasan back from the dead," I say as I bury my face into my hands. "I don't know what I'm supposed to do now, but I'm going to have to figure something out."

After a minute of awkward silence, Hamdan says, "I'll let Zaganos know that he can come in."

"Only him. I don't wish to see Ali Bey."

"Alright," Hamdan says as he walks towards the door.

I get out of bed, pick up my kilij and walk towards the window. I gaze out and see a bunch of janissaries training on the green fields. Wonder if Jake is among them. He's probably adjusted perfectly. That guy can become friends with anybody.

I hear Hamdan and Zaganos quietly talking next to my bed.

"Zaganos Pasha!" I exclaim. "What are we going to say about the death of Shehzade Hasan Çelebi?"

"Pardon me, my padishah," he replies. "What do you mean?"

"Shehzade Hasan is dead!" I angrily say. "How do you plan to justify the death of a two-year-old shehzade? Are we going to say he died of natural causes? Are we going to call a two-year-old child a traitor? Did you think about that before you had him strangled?"

"I did, my padishah," Zaganos Pasha says. "Shehzade Hasan may only have been two, but as long as he's alive, there's always potential for an open rebellion by the powerful families of Anatolia."

"I know that!" I bellow. "Your reasons for doing so might be noble, but people will see me as a power-hungry tyrant. It's on *you* to ensure I'm not seen that way!"

"Of course, my padishah," Zaganos Pasha replies.

"Now, how long do I have until the imperial divan?" I ask.

"A little over an hour, my padishah," Hamdan replies.

I let out a grim smile and turn around. Hamdan calling me his emperor is incredibly weird.

"Okay, I need to get dressed," I say. "Make sure my clothes are laid out for me when I get back from my bath."

Hamdan scowls and says, "Of course, my padishah."

After thirty minutes, I've bathed, prayed, and changed into a snazzy pair of black trousers and inner robes. My outer robes are Slytherin green with silver trimming and buttons. I slide my newly engraved kilij into its sheath that's attached to my belt. I also throw on a fur scarf to combat the cold February day. Of course, on my head is a beautiful turban.

I really detest wearing the turban, but I guess I'm supposed to.

Clothes are a status symbol in the Ottoman Empire, which is why they're generally bright. The sultan owns the fanciest and most colourful clothes. Although, Fatih Mehmet does also own a lot of black clothes.

I look at myself on a reflective metal. I definitely look slimmer and more athletic than I did on my last day in the twenty-first century. Sorta how I looked when I was winning provincial championships in soccer, hockey, and table tennis with my high school team. I guess travelling hundreds of kilometres on horseback and practicing sword moves at night pays off.

I walk out of the room. Hamdan and Zaganos are waiting by the door of my room.

"Let's go to the imperial hall," I say.

"My padishah," Zaganos says. "Perhaps you should go through the harem. I'm sure everyone will want to congratulate you on becoming sultan."

I look at Hamdan and he nods, encouraging me to go through the imperial harem.

"Of course, Zaganos Pasha," I say as I walk towards the entrance of the harem next to my quarters. "I'll see the two of you in the imperial hall."

I step inside the harem and am instantly filled with awe. The harem has an enormous courtyard with an open roof, garden, and pool. To the sides are living quarters.

It's a cold day, so no ladies are out in the courtyard. From a distance, I see one lady sitting in the courtyard, but I don't approach her. Instead, I walk by the rooms.

After I pass three massive rooms, a woman who looks to be in her early forties walks out of a room down the hall wearing an indigo dress. She's got dark-brown hair down to her waist and has a darker complexion than Gülbahar. As she walks towards me, I notice that she's nearly as tall as me. She's also got fierce dark eyes. Her name, Mara Brankovic, pops into my head.

The great Mara Brankovic. She might be one of the most beloved women in Ottoman history, despite not being Muslim. Fatih Mehmet may not have had a valide sultan (queen regent), but she was as close as one could be to that position.

I'm standing in front of greatness. Mara Brankovic commands my respect, but what am I supposed to call her? In history books, she's referred to as Mara Brankovic, Sultana Marija, and Mara Hatun. I feel like *Mara* is too informal, but Sultana Marija is too formal. Mara Hatun sounds best in my opinion.

"Good morning, Sultan Mehmet!" she joyfully exclaims. "Congratulations! The title of sultan suits you well."

"*Jazakallah khayr*, Mara Hatun!" I brightly say.

"I know you've been waiting for this moment for a long time," she says.

I shrug. "Um, yeah, sure, I guess..."

"I also know you didn't get along well with your father," Mara Hatun says, "but you should know what he said right before he died."

"What?"

"That he regrets placing you on the throne when you weren't ready for it. He told me he's extremely proud of you and knows that you're now ready to take up the mantle of being a sultan."

"I've been ready for years," I say, knowing that Fatih Mehmet felt he should never have been removed from the throne. "He should have had confidence in me all those years ago."

"He did," she insists. "It was just hard for him to remain on the sidelines."

"I would have never kept him on the sidelines. He should have had confidence in me. It doesn't matter anymore."

"It does," Mara Hatun exclaims. "Who knows what Halil Pasha would have done if your father hadn't endorsed you in front of everyone? He could have tried to place your cousin Orhan Çelebi on the throne."

She's right, I think. If you listen to Zaganos speak about Halil, you'd be surprised that he hasn't maneuvered to rob me of the throne.

Halil would be much more powerful if I weren't on the throne. Right now, he knows I trust Hamdan and Zaganos more than him.

Of course, Halil doesn't know I'm not Fatih Mehmet. He doesn't know that I don't have any beef with him. I'm going to keep an open mind, but Zaganos has convinced me to be wary.

"Well, I'm glad my father came to his senses," I say. "I will prove him right. I WILL be the greatest *hünkar* the world has ever seen."

"I know you will," Mara Hatun says. "Now everyone wants to congratulate you."

I hadn't realized that a crowd of women had gathered around us. Among them are Fatih Mehmet's aunts, stepmothers, and sisters. Of course, there are also female slaves who are hoping to impress me. I noticed some flashing me huge smiles and flirtatious looks throughout the feast last night.

For five minutes, I listen to the women congratulate me and offer their condolences for the death of Sultan Murat. I don't see Gülbahar or Sally amongst the group of women, so I quickly thank them and run off.

Out of the corner of my eye, I see a lady wearing a shiny emerald dress, sitting on a bench in the courtyard reading a book.

I slow down to see who it is, and I instantly recognize her.

"Salmana!" I call out as I walk over to her.

Sally looks up and her face instantly brightens.

"Mehmet!" she exclaims. In English, she says, "What are you doing here?"

"Zaganos made me walk through the harem," I reply, also in English. "I've been wanting to see you. It feels like it's been forever."

"It's been, like, five days…"

I shake my head. "It's just that so much happens in a short period of time here. That makes five days feel like forever."

"I guess... yeah."

"Walk with me. I gotta get to the imperial hall for my first imperial divan meeting."

"Alright."

"Watchya reading?"

"A book on the founders of the Ottoman Empire," Sally answers. "Stories about Ertuğrul Ghazi and his son, the founder of the Ottoman Empire, Osman Ghazi."

"That's so cool! Is it historically accurate?"

"Gülbahar Hatun swears it is," she says. "Although some of the details seem farfetched."

"They're Turkish and Ottoman heroes," I say. "There isn't a lot written about them in English. I'd be interested in reading that book."

"Lemme finish it first!" Sally says. "Actually, I'm sure you can get another copy from somewhere else. I'm sure someone will get it for the *sultan*..."

"Yeah, I guess so..." I say as we walk out of the harem.

"So, what's it like being the sultan?" She playfully pushes me. "I thought you'd be wearing a crown all the time, unless that turban is your crown."

I grin. "It hasn't even been a day yet, but I guess it's pretty dope. Also, sultans don't wear crowns."

"Really?" Sally asks. "How would people identify you as the ruler?"

"I was presented with the kilij of Osman yesterday," I say. "That's my crown."

"That's his sword, then?"

"No," I say, as I take the kilij out of the sheath and hand it to her. "It's mine."

"Woah!" she exclaims. "I've never held a sword before."

"Look at what's engraved on the blade," I say.

She flips it over and reads, "*Sultan Mehmet Khan, the Second of His Name, Sovereign of the Sublime House of Osman, Sultan of Sultans, Khan of Khans, Padishah of Anatolia and Rumelia.*"

She hands it back to me, and I place it back in its sheath.

"Pretty neat, huh?" I say.

"Absolutely," Sally says. "This is just really weird."

"What?"

"That you're a sultan with all these impressive titles," she replies. "That we're standing in a palace."

"Well, yeah," I say. "How could it not be?"

"When I sat next to you in history class, I never would've guessed you'd be an emperor in a few weeks."

"Well, yeah," I say. "But you can call that day the best day of your life."

Sally scoffs and punches me on the shoulder as we reach the imposing black and silver doors of the imperial hall.

The butterflies in my stomach flutter. I'm going to have to seem awfully majestic in the divan. I'm going to have to be a boss to ensure my imperial cabinet has confidence in me.

"Don't worry, dude," Sally says. "You'll be fine in there."

"After what happened this morning, I'm not so sure."

"Wait, what?" Sally asks. "What happened?"

"You don't know?" I see Mahmut Pasha walking down the hall towards us out of the corner of my eye.

Sally shakes her head. "What happened this morning?"

"Uh... you'll find out soon enough," I say as I look towards Mahmut Pasha. "Just know it wasn't my fault. Nah, I mean it technically *is* my fault, but I didn't order it."

"You didn't order what?"

"The murder of Shehzade Hasan," I answer. "I would never."

Her jaw drops. She composes herself and says, "Gülbahar told me that some sultans have killed their brothers to secure their position on the throne. I just didn't think you would do it."

"Please believe me when I say this. I didn't intentionally order the murder. Zaganos sorta did it on his own."

She glares at me for a moment, as though she's tryna scan my brain to see if I'm lying.

"Okay," she says. She starts to walk away. "Mehmet, take a deep breath. Relax. You'll impress in the divan. I know you will."

I smile at her as she walks away.

As soon as she's five paces from me, I hear Mahmut Pasha call out, "*Assalamu alaikum*, my padishah."

"*Walaikum As-sala*am, Mahmut Pasha," I reply. "Shall we go in?"

"After you, my padishah," Mahmut Pasha gracefully says.

"Alright." I push open the gigantic doors.

As I walk down the beautiful red carpet towards my wide, cushioned seat, I see that all of the senior ministers are present. The four viziers, defterdar, kadi'asker, Agha of the Janissaries, as well as Jake, the Nişancı, and the Governor of the Rumelia Province.

I slowly make my way across the room to my throne. *My throne.*
Gosh, that's weird.

The sun shines brightly through the window. I squint as I reach the throne. I turn around to see that everyone's head is lowered out of respect.

I shake my head and take my seat.

"Halil Pasha! Let us begin, in the name of Allah, the most compassionate, most merciful."

13. MEHMET

Halil stands up. "Welcome, all, to the first imperial divan of Sultan Mehmet's second reign."

He's immediately interrupted by a short and awkward round of applause. I notice that Hamdan is the first to clap, then a couple of people follow to save him from the embarrassment.

I stifle a laugh and continue on listening to Halil.

"Thank you, thank you, Hamdan Pasha, for the generous applause," Halil cheerfully says. "Now, please don't interrupt the adults while we're speaking."

Hamdan looks as though he's about to insult Halil, but Zaganos grabs his arm and glares at him, stopping him from further disruption.

"We are honoured to be joined today by the Provincial Governor of Rumelia, Turahan Bey," Halil continues. "We are in the presence of the honourable Yusef Agha, commander of the janissary corps. Would either of you like to say anything before we begin?"

The Governor grabs a large crate resting next to him and walks towards my throne with his head lowered. He's an older man with a long white beard tied in the middle with a bead. He's fairly overweight (putting it lightly) and limps while he walks.

He stops about two metres from the throne, kneels with difficulty, then opens the crate. It is filled with silver, jewelry, a shield, and daggers.

Still kneeling, he says loudly, "My padishah, I present you with this small token in hopes of building a long and excellent relationship, working together for the good of the Ottoman State, Rumelia, and furthering our interests in Europe."

"Arise, Turahan Bey!" I proclaim. "*Jazakallah khayr* for the impressive gift. Now, for what reason are you present here?"

"Pardon me, my padishah," Turahan Bey states as he gets on his feet. "I do not understand your question."

"Why are you present at the imperial divan?" I ask. "Is there something you require?"

"I have every right to be present, my padishah," Turahan Bey replies. "The capital of Rumelia is right here in Adrianople, which makes it easy for me to attend. Although I do have an issue I wish to address."

That's strange. I would have thought that the capital of Rumelia was Sofya, the capital of present-day Bulgaria.

Halil clears his throat. "Your concerns are at the top of the docket for today, Turahan Bey. You may as well state them for the divan."

Turahan Bey nods and looks towards my throne with his head and gaze lowered. "My padishah," he starts, "a couple weeks ago, rumours of your father's death circulated the streets of Rumelia, with the acknowledgement that you would succeed him as the *hünkar*."

"Yes," I say, "please get to your point, Turahan Bey."

"Of course, my padishah," Turahan Bey says. "These rumours have emboldened certain individuals across Rumelia."

"Which individuals do you speak of, Turahan Bey?" Zaganos asks. "What do you mean?"

"I mean that the news of Sultan Murat's death has encouraged people who wish to be rid of our rule," Turahan Bey replies. "People in Sofya, Thessaly, Thessaloniki, and even some in Adrianople."

"What, exactly, do these people want?" Mahmut Pasha asks.

"It's what they always want," Turahan Bey answers. "The return of the old days under the rule of Christians such as the Bulgarians, the Serbians, the Wallachians, or the Greeks."

Greeks? Does he mean the Byzantines? I thought the Ottomans refer to the Byzantines as the Romans, as shown when I—er, Fatih Mehmet—call myself the Caesar of Rome after conquering Constantinople. I know the Byzantines speak Greek and are culturally different from the Romans, but I still thought they'd be known here as Roman. Perhaps the Ottomans use both.

I look at Turahan Bey. "That's exceptionally foolish," I state. "Our realm is significantly more powerful than the Serbians or the Wallachians. The Bulgarian Empire couldn't compete and collapsed during the reign of my great-grandfather. The Romans can barely hold what they presently have. These people are much better off under our rule. They live far more comfortably."

"Of course, my padishah," Turahan Bey says. "The problem is that these voices have grown substantially since your father's death. I fear these individuals hope to take advantage of a young, new, and inexperienced leader."

Hamdan interrupts him. "Are you suggesting that our padishah is incompetent?"

This gets an audible murmur across the room. People seem to disagree with Hamdan's tone. I smile and shake my head. Hamdan's always got my back, but it's unnecessary in this situation. Turahan Bey isn't trying to disrespect me.

"I believe that Turahan Bey is trying to say that I'm unproven," I state as Hamdan gives me a flustered look. "Our empire may be prone to uprisings, trying to take advantage of a new leader. My father was an excellent and powerful *hünkar*, so there was no opportunity for a full-out rebellion. Now, the important question is, how much attention should we pay to these alleged voices? Is there likely to be a rebellion, Turahan Bey?"

"I don't fear an uprising from people within our lands," Turahan Bey says. "Rather, I fear that the Serbians and Wallachians might try to repel our influence and potentially gain some of our lands in Rumelia—"

"They are in no position to do so!" Zaganos exclaims. "They are much too weak to challenge us. They'll have to ally with other empires, particularly the Hungarians, the only empire in the Balkans that can dare *hope* to challenge us. They'll almost certainly need Pope Nicholas to call another Crusade. There's too much that needs to happen for them to be successful. It's pointless to discuss this, we should be focusing on the first steps that this government is going to take. The best way to ensure the security of our people and territory is to continue to advance into Europe. That is my only suggestion to you, my padishah."

"I implore you to take this threat seriously, Zaganos Pasha," Turahan Bey pleads. "The Christian European powers can unite against us. I think we all vividly remember this happening a few years ago. When that happens, people across Rumelia who are unhappy with our rule will rise up and spread trepidation across our realm. It is possible that they will try to create unrest within our own borders."

"I agree," Halil, who's been eerily quiet, asserts. "This happened during the first year of your first reign, my padishah. It could easily happen again."

There are a few grumbles of agreement across the room.

Yusef Agha speaks up. "In my experience, the Christian kingdoms won't rest while we maintain a presence in Europe."

"That may be true," I acknowledge, "but what exactly is it that you want me to do, Turahan Bey? What are you suggesting?"

"I'd like to know that as well," Zaganos declares.

"My padishah," Turahan Bey expresses, "my request is simple. Send the janissaries to cities and outposts across Rumelia to help keep order throughout the province, and to intimidate those who may wish to attack us in Serbia or Wallachia. I can coordinate with Yusef Agha, and the soldiers can be placed under my control, where they are most needed."

Yusef Agha stands up. "I am on board with this plan."

"Seems reasonable to me," Halil proclaims.

He's got to be kidding me. There is no way Halil agreed to that. Handing over the janissaries to a powerful bey is absolutely dumb. Turahan Bey and Yusef Agha could easily go to Constantinople and throw their support behind Orhan Çelebi, and I'd be screwed.

When I say screwed—I mean dead.

This is an attempted power grab, and *Hamdan* sensed it first.

Zaganos and Mahmut Pasha also seem to understand. They fire back.

"That is simply not a good plan," Mahmut Pasha states. "It's utterly unreasonable as long as there is no active threat to Rumelia."

"I completely agree," Zaganos asserts. "There is no need to turn over the janissaries to you, Turahan Bey. You already have the largest force in the entire realm. It's absolutely unreasonable. I simply don't see an active threat on the borders of Rumelia from the Serbians, Wallachians, Hungarians, or the Romans. Now, if you came with a reasonable plan, I'm sure our padishah would be more than happy to accommodate your request."

"I have to agree as well." The defterdar, whose name I learned last night as Titrek Sinan Çelebi, interjects. "This plan is going to cost the state too much. I see negligible gain at best."

"If we disperse the janissaries across Rumelia, we're opening ourselves up to threats from the east," Mahmut Pasha states. "The Karamanids may invade our territories in Anatolia."

"Did you guys forget what happened in 1444?" Halil angrily asks. "The Christian powers across Europe think our *hünkar* is weak. They will take advantage of him, just as they did last time!"

"Are you suggesting this will be a repeat of years ago?" Zaganos hotly asks. "It's been seven years, and I *still* remember how often you and Yusef Agha undercut our padishah's plans. It was despicable, and we will not tolerate it this time."

"Whatever I suggest is for the good of this realm," Halil angrily says. "We need to protect ourselves from the rest of Europe."

"Turahan Bey's suggestion is simply not the way to go," Zaganos fires back. "It seems to me, my padishah, that Turahan Bey, Yusef Agha, and Halil Pasha have no confidence in our *hünkar* and are looking to snatch his authority."

That last statement by Zaganos causes a ruckus across the room. Halil and Zaganos start to bicker. The defterdar, Titrek Sinan, and the kadi'asker, Mawiz, argue with them. Jake is paying full attention. Nişancı Adham looks flustered trying to write everything down while still being involved in the debate.

It's a full-blown clown show in here. It's hilarious to watch these men fight while still trying to be as cordial as possible. They're call-ing each other by their formal titles and not interrupting anyone while they're speaking. However, everyone's voices are rising, and I can hear the veiled insults.

My head starts to spin with the rising volume of the room, so I frantically look towards Hamdan who mouths, *Do something.*

I shake my head, stand up as straight and tall as I can, and bellow, "SILENCE! I DEMAND SILENCE!"

That gets everybody's attention. They take their appropriate places to the sides of the room and lower their heads out of respect.

"Good!" I proclaim. "All this bickering is not helping our realm. My divan needs order. The Ottoman Sultanate needs order. If we disagree on a subject, we will orderly debate over the issue, and each of you will present the facts, and I will make the final decisions. Do you understand?"

Simultaneously, the room erupts with declarations of agreement.

"Good! Now, Halil Pasha, Zaganos Pasha: I demand you apol-ogize to me and the rest of the room for the unpleasant disruption."

A sense of shock goes across the room.

Yes, it may be a shocking demand, but I need to stamp my au-thority on this room.

Zaganos walks towards my throne, places his right hand on his chest, lowers his head, and says, "I apologize to you, my padishah, and to my fellow colleagues for the disruption that I've caused."

Halil reluctantly walks towards the throne, lowers his head and whispers the same thing.

"Halil Pasha," I loudly say. "I can't hear you. Please repeat what you've just said."

Out of the corner of my eye, I see Zaganos wearing the world's largest smile. Even Hamdan has a smug expression as Halil goes red and loudly repeats the words.

"Now I think it's time to hear my suggestion on what we should do regarding Turahan Bey's request," I say.

The room gets unnervingly hushed, and everyone waits for me to continue. I don't think I've ever felt this nervous before. The butterflies are jumping in my stomach. This sorta feels like the overtime penalty shot I had to take in last year's high school hockey provincial quarter finals. Only, this is so much more important.

I take a deep breath. "Turahan Bey, Halil Pasha, and Yusef Agha's concerns are legitimate. It is possible that certain European empires may try to stoke unrest within our lands. It is certainly possible that they will try to take advantage of our new government, but I agree with Zaganos Pasha. The European empires surrounding our borders are not nearly strong or organized enough to truly threaten us, but that does not mean that we're to take them lightly. While I intend to take the potential threat seriously, Mahmut Pasha has correctly pointed out that there is no active threat, which is why I'm not granting Turahan Bey's request for dispersing the janissaries across Rumelia under his command."

As soon as I reject Turahan Bey's request, Halil, Yusef Agha, and Turahan Bey immediately start to protest.

"My padishah!" Halil cries out.

I raise my hand and calmly say, "Halil Pasha, I have yet to finish. May I continue?"

Halil lowers his head and says, "Of course, my padishah."

"I believe I have a better plan to keep order within the Ottoman State and to ensure there isn't an attack on our lands. I have decided to move Rumelia's capital from Adrianople to Sofya."

"What does that accomplish?" Turahan Bey asks. "That's moving a key capital closer to the borders of Serbia and Wallachia—a key capital they could easily attack."

"It's a bold move," I say. "Currently, Serbia and Wallachia's leaders rule in part because we allow them to. They are essentially bound to us militarily and economically. This move showcases our strength. It tells them they have little authority."

"I like it," Zaganos states. Mahmut Pasha and Hamdan grunt in approval.

"There is no point in having the provincial capital and the imperial capital in the same city," I say. "Dispersing our strength across the province is a good thing."

My words get a resounding acclaim across the room.

"Shifting the capital to Sofya will be costly," Sinan Çelebi states. "However, I think that is a worthy investment. I can envision Sofya as the long-term capital of Rumelia as we continue our westward expansion."

"When do you expect me to make the move, my padishah?" Turahan Bey asks.

"You will not be moving to Sofya, Turahan Bey," I declare. "Mahmut Pasha will be taking over as the Provincial Governor of Rumelia along with his duties as my vizier. You will head to Thessaly to govern the region for me."

"Why am I being demoted, my padishah?" Turahan Bey aggressively asks. "Have I not served this realm and province well throughout the years?"

"You have, Turahan Bey," I calmly say. "You have served this realm well. This is not a demotion. I'm allowing you to govern Thessaly semi-autonomously. As long as Thessaly pays taxes, abides by

Ottoman laws, and provides military support, you are free to govern the region as you see fit."

"That is unacceptable!" Halil Pasha exclaims.

"Halil Pasha, I have now dispersed our strength to the corners of our realm," I say. "Is that not what you wanted? Ishak Pasha and Aslan Pasha in Anatolia. Mahmut Pasha and Turahan Bey in Rumelia. Each one is loyal and commands a substantial force of men that can mobilize quickly. If any are attacked, I easily can send support from the capital."

"That's all fine," Halil says. "However, I can't understand Turahan Bey's demotion. He's served this realm gallantly for numerous years."

"Exactly," Turahan Bey vehemently says. "I don't get it either."

"It isn't a demotion, damnit!" I respond. "Turahan Bey, I've got a great plan for my reign of the Ottoman State. I *will* be the man who conquers the great city of Constantinople. This requires patience, calculation, and perseverance. It's like a chess match. Turahan Bey, you and your sons are my opening move. You will play a substantial role in the greatest conquest the Ottoman Empire will *ever* see."

"Yes, my padishah," Turahan Bey says as the men in the room whisper to each other about my declaration.

"For far too long, Constantinople has been a thorn in our side. I hope to completely isolate the Romans in Constantinople," I declare. "If we go on an expedition, it will be to ensure that a crusading army will not invade our lands. I will neutralize all threats, so that Constantinople does not slip through my fingers. I intend to use the present state of peace we find ourselves in to build a powerful navy and a potent army, one so robust that it shall be talked about for centuries to come. It will take us some time, but we will break through the resilient walls of Constantinople and take out the painful thorn in our side. The Red Apple *will* fall to us!"

The divan members roar in applause—everyone but Halil, who sullenly stands next to Zaganos.

"Now, what else is on the docket for today?" I ask when the ruckus calms down.

Halil clears his throat. "Right before the imperial divan, I received news that you ordered the execution of Shehzade Hasan Çelebi. Would you like to address that, my padishah?"

Son of a gun. Why does he have to bring that up now? I don't know how to justify it.

There isn't anything in the world that can justify killing a child. But I guess I'm going to have to try.

"And what about it?" I lazily say seeking to dismiss the topic.

"Why did you order his death?" Halil asks.

"For the good of the realm," Zaganos answers in annoyance.

"How does killing a child help our realm?" Halil asks.

"Do you not remember baby Mustafa leading an army against Sultan Murat?" Zaganos asks. "It hasn't even been fifty years since our realm was split by the powerful sons of Sultan Bayezit. Sacrificing the life of Shehzade Hasan is a necessity for the tranquility of the Ottoman State."

"There is legal precedent for this," the kadi'asker, Mawiz Ibn Hasan, says. "The precedent was set by Sultan Bayezit, and each sultan has followed by killing their brothers for the good of the realm. Of course, most waited for their brothers to betray the throne."

"See," Zaganos Pasha says, "we have no legal problem here. This is a nonissue."

Across the room, there's a murmur of agreement.

How is this even possible? How can people just dismiss the fact that a child was murdered today?

"I just have one suggestion," Mawiz ibn Hasan states. "We should legislate that the next sultans of the Ottoman Empire must kill their brothers for the interests of the state. This would ensure that there is no more civil conflict."

No, it won't, I wanna scream out, but there's a resounding grumble of approval across the room.

"Sounds perfect to me," Zaganos says.

"I have no objections," Halil says as everyone turns to see if I approve of the kadi'asker's legal suggestion.

Hamdan glares at me, probably to indicate I should put a stop to this, but what do I suggest? If I go against the consensus, I'm invalidating one of my first moves as sultan. It would be extremely stupid to do that.

However, I can't endorse the law.

What would Anne think of me?

What would Babaanne think of me?

What would my father think of me?

They would all be so disappointed if I endorsed this law.

What's Sally going to think of me?

She'll never wanna speak to me again.

In the Qur'an it is decreed that *"whoever takes a life, unless as a punishment for murder or corruption in the land, it will be as if they have killed all of humanity. (5:32)"*

This proposed law is completely unIslamic.

Countless people will die because of this law.

And it will be all because of me.

Hasan Zia

I'll be responsible for each death. I shall bear the sin for each one caused by this awful law.

As the awkward silence continues, I find myself drawing a blank on what I should do. I stroke my beard, twisting it in different directions.

I'm going to have to agree with the suggestion.

By Allah, I will find an appropriate solution to this problem.

A better solution.

An Islamic solution.

It just won't be today.

"Ibn Hasan's suggestion makes a lot of sense," I say. "I have no objection. Let's legislate the Fratricide Law."

There's a unanimous buzz of approval as the words slip out of my mouth.

I officially hate myself.

14. Mehmet

Today is Tuesday, March 11. My day starts with my new routine. My new normal. I generally fall asleep after Fajr prayer. Today, I slept about two to three hours before getting up to work out.

Yeah, I work out. I hate it, but I don't have much else to do. Obviously, I work out without weights in my quarters, but it still sucks.

After an hour or so, I finish, wash up, change into cobalt and silver robes, and head towards the field where the janissaries are training. While they train as a unit, I usually sit on the side and observe. Today, I'm joined by Fatih Mehmet's stepmother Mara Hatun, the daughter of Durad Brankovic.

"How are you, Mehmet?" she asks, "I haven't seen you since the day after you became sultan. What's it been—three weeks?"

I slowly nod as I marvel at the swiftness of the soldiers. They are really intimidating and marvelous.

Mara Hatun continues. "You never go that long without speaking to me. Even when you were in Manisa, you'd write to me all the time. Is everything alright?"

"Uh... everything's great," I say. "Everything's just perfect, awesome, splendid."

Mara Hatun scoffs. "Say it one more time and I might believe you."

"Trust me, everything's fine." I watch Jake lead a training exercise. He seems to be adjusting well.

"The chatter across the palace is that you hardly leave your quarters. When you do, it's only to train with the janissaries or to sit in the divan." She looks at me knowingly. "You haven't visited anyone in the harem, you haven't had philosophical discussions with your ministers or friends. You haven't seen your wife or child. I think you're grieving your father, and that's completely okay. Every man would grieve for their father."

"I've just been busy. I've got no time for fun. That doesn't mean I'm devastated by Sultan Murat's death. I didn't know him."

"What are you saying?" Mara Hatun asks.

Oh crap. Of course, Fatih Mehmet knew his father. I gotta switch the topic.

"I've got something to ask of you."

"Okay," she says. "What do you want?"

"Advice."

"That I can give. Ask away, my padishah."

"Don't call me that."

Mara Hatun rolls her eyes. "I can call you whatever I want."

I smile. "I wish to place a loyal man in your father's court. I don't know who it should be. It needs to be someone in front of whom your father will be comfortable discussing important matters."

"How would you even do that?" she asks. "You can't just place someone in another man's court."

"I'll just force him," I counter. "Your father can't stop me."

"He may not have the forces to capture lands from you, but he can easily kick you out of his country if he is able unite Serbia and align himself with Hungary," Mara Hatun declares.

"That's a huge *if*. There is no way he'll be able to."

"My father is an excellent ruler," she says. "He'll be able to do so. Now, if he dies, my brothers aren't close to capable of ruling Serbia, but last I checked, he's in excellent health."

"That's the whole reason I want to place a man in his court. I can't have him attacking us with the Hungarians, Wallachians, and other European powers while I chase the Red Apple."

"So, you're set on conquering Constantinople?" she asks.

"Why wouldn't I be?"

"You've dreamt about conquering the city for so long," Mara Hatun says. "Ever since you learned about the failures of your father and great-grandfather. Not to mention the hadith in which the Prophet Muhammad prophesied, *"Verily you shall conquer Constantinople. What a wonderful leader will he be, and what a wonderful army will that army be!"*

I smile at her. Man, the Prophet, peace and blessing be upon him, accurately prophesied everything, which is one of the reasons I believe in his message.

"Then you understand why I can't have your father as an enemy. I need to be sure that he isn't a threat."

"Yes, of course," Mara Hatun says. "But you need to go about it in a smarter way. Don't send in a man my father isn't going to trust."

"That's why I'm trying to find someone he will trust."

"So, send me," she says.

"What?" I exclaim in astonishment. "I need you here."

I mean, I thought Mara Hatun stays in Fatih Mehmet's court as an advisor. I'm fairly sure she does. I remember reading that she brokered peace between the Ottomans and Venetians, so how can I possibly send her away?

"Look," she says. "You need someone in his court, someone who's loyal to you and only you. I'm that person. You know how much love I have for you. You're like the son I never had."

"But I need you here! I need your wisdom."

"You don't," she calmly says. "Look at the past three weeks. You haven't visited me. That's because you have confidence. I will be able to serve you better from my father's court."

I think about that. She is sorta right. I haven't seen her in three weeks, but that has nothing to do with confidence. It has more to do with the fact that I don't know her. If anyone is going to figure out that I'm not Fatih Mehmet, it's her. But if she truly is loyal to me/him, I see no reason why I shouldn't send her. Her father won't suspect she's a spy. Now, how do I ensure that she'll be genuine to me?

"What if your love for your father trumps your love for me? What if you wish to marry again?"

"I don't ever want to marry again. Your father is the last man that will ever share my bed," Mara Hatun states. "As for my father, I love him and always will. Nevertheless, I love you just as I would love my own son. I also know what's to happen after my father's death. I know that my brothers will fight over his seat. I know that my homeland won't be able to resist your rule. I also know that you will be a just *hünkar*, so I have no problem with Serbia joining your realm. My loyalties lie with you while you chase your lifelong dream, because I *know* that the Red Apple will fall to you."

I fall silent. I don't know if I should send her. Her loyalty seems too good to be true. I mean, how convenient is this? But what other choice do I have? Everyone else, suggested by Hamdan, Halil, and Zaganos, just don't fit the bill.

"Alright. You can go live with your father, but I expect you to write me as much as possible, not just about what your father's doing and planning, but also how you're doing. I expect your letters to be detailed. Okay?"

"Of course!" she says. She sounds excited. "When am I to leave?"

"Whenever you want," I say. I get up to stretch as the janissaries finish up their group training. "Of course, you will have an entourage escort you whenever you wish to leave. I'll personally see that only the best men escort you."

"Thank you!" Mara Hatun exclaims. "Now, I wanna see how good you are with that kilij."

"I'm alright," I declare. I turn towards Jake and the rest of the janissaries, twirling my curved blade to show off.

For the next couple hours, I duel with Jake and his friends Arslan and Demir. I've dueled with about 25 different janissary soldiers over the past three weeks, but the only one to defeat me so far is Baver. Of course, I suspect that most of them are toying with me and that pisses me off, but Baver is just massive. He's probably as big as LeBron James, only he's a trained soldier, so he's a lot more intimidating. Dueling him is as fun as scoring a goal in the final seconds of the third period with your goalie pulled for an extra attacker.

Simply electrifying.

The biggest issue for me is that I have knowledge in my brain that comes from Fatih Mehmet, which makes me an excellent swordsman, but my body struggles to complete the moves. I'm a fraction of a second slow on my parries, slashes, feints, stabs, and blocks. That's why it frustrates me that some of the soldiers are letting me win—I need to get sharper. My body needs to learn how to fight, or I could easily die in battle.

After defeating Jake, Arslan, and Demir, I turn to Baver and shout, "YOU! Let's duel."

Everyone comes over to encircle us, excited for the spectacle. Baver smiles and walks over, flexing his muscles and stretching his legs.

I smile at him, place my right hand over my heart, and vehemently yell, "Begin!" just as I grip my kilij with my left hand.

I'm not a lefty, but for some reason my left arm is a lot stronger than my right. I've always played hockey with a left-handed stick, and I bat left in baseball. Gripping the kilij with my left hand also makes it easier for me to swing. I grip with both hands, my left on the top and my right on the bottom.

Baver and I circle each other a few times. I have to let him come to me, since he's bigger than me and his kilij is longer. Hopefully I can force him to fight me in tight, limiting his strokes. The purpose of the duel is to disarm the other person. Of course, a few cuts are allowed, and Baver has yet to show any restraint in cutting me.

Baver bites and charges towards me. I stand my ground, allowing him to get as close as possible. He slashes my stomach with his extremely long reach, so I lunge forward to parry his sword away and attempt a disarming maneuver. I feint a thrust at his hip, so he moves his kilij to deflect mine, only as soon as he does that, I flick my wrist to strike his sword, only he blocks the strike. Next, I try to use the flat part of my blade to smack his wrist, but he easily deflects, pushing away my weapon and leaving my chest exposed, so I leap back and take a breath. Baver smiles arrogantly.

Flustered, I charge him and attack with a flurry of slashes and stabs. He parries each strike with a level of focus and confidence I've never seen before.

186

We continue dueling for the next fifteen minutes. I can't seem to gain an advantage. My timing is simply off, yet he hasn't taken advantage of that. Perhaps he's going soft on me. I fucking hate that.

After yet another failed attack by yours truly, I leap back to catch my breath. This man is just toying with me. He's got to stop that.

I curse and go for broke by recklessly charging him. He smiles and charges towards me as well. He viciously slashes my left hip, cutting me. Then he smacks my chest with the flat side of his blade and punches me in the face with the other hand. Finally, he uses the hilt of his kilij to hit my wrist and then hack my kilij away from my hand. As it falls from my hand, Baver gives me one last shove, ensuring that I fall to the ground.

As I lie on the ground, He stands over me, smirking while Jake, Arslan, Demir, and the rest of the janissaries rush towards me. Baver kneels next to me and says, "Your feints are too obvious. You give them away with your eyes and body position. You gotta work on that."

I meekly smile at him. Jake crouches next to me. He takes a look at my leg and says, "We're never training with blades again. We're going to make replicas with wood."

"Aw man! It barely hurts. It's only a scratch."

"We'll get the doctor to check on you," Baver says.

I nod and lie down on the ground, exhausted. I smile and shut my eyes as the janissaries load me onto a wicker stretcher and take me inside the palace.

187

The royal doctor they take me to freaks when he sees the gash on my hip. I keep insisting it doesn't hurt, but everyone flat out ignores me. As far as pain goes, this doesn't even come close to some of my hockey injuries.

The doc curses in Farsi, disinfects the cut using boiled water and vinegar, and bandages the wound, demanding that I rest. He promises to come in the evening to check on the cut.

The janissaries offer to carry me to my room, but I insist that they let me walk to my study. They persist until I relent and allow them to carry me to my study. When we reach the office, I request that Jake remain behind to keep me company.

My viziers, absent Mahmut Pasha who's gone to Sofya, are gathered in my study.

"What happened?" Hamdan demands.

"Training accident," Jake replies. "He was slashed by a kilij."

"Are you stupid!" Hamdan exclaims before realizing his mistake. "I'm sorry, my padishah. I'm just worried about your wound. We need you healthy."

"Don't worry," I say. "It's only a scratch. The doc says I'll be fine with some rest."

"Good," Zaganos says. "Perhaps next time you will not be so reckless, my padishah."

I scoff as I lean my head against a cushion.

"Do I have your permission to go ahead with today's divan, my padishah?" Halil asks.

"No way!" Zaganos exclaims. "We must postpone."

"I don't think there's anything major on the agenda today," Hamdan adds. "No envoys visiting today."

"No, no," I say. "Halil Pasha, you have full permission to go ahead with the Divan. As I said on the day of my inauguration, we only need the sultan's permission and the presence of the grand vizier for an imperial divan to occur. You may go ahead with the divan, Halil Pasha, provided that anything decided is run by me."

"Thank you, my padishah," Halil says. He turns to exit the room. Zaganos angrily looks at me before turning to follow him.

"Tell me everything that happens, Hamdan," I whisper as he gets up to leave. "Just make sure Halil and Zaganos don't strangle each other."

"Aight," Hamdan sullenly says as he walks out of the room.

I sit in silence for a moment, when Jake shakes me and says, "So... what should we do?"

"Let's continue going through these books," I say, pointing to the stack of papers on the desk across the room. "If we don't have a clear picture of this world, how are we meant to rule it?"

I sigh and close my eyes, annoyed by the pain from my fresh wound.

Okay, I need to focus.

Since the first divan, Jake, Hamdan, and I have been researching the 1451 world.

So far, we've learnt that the Ottoman legacy is rapid expansion, fighting off constant Crusades from Europe, and civil wars caused by rivalling brothers. No wonder my divan is so pressed about a military threat, particularly from the Europeans. They constantly start shit, even if we do kick their asses for the most part.

My lands stretch from Sofya to Thessaly to Adrianople to Bursa to Manisa to Ankara. My people are multiethnic, multicultural, and multireligious. I rule over the most diverse empire in the world. Well, the 1451 world.

I rule over delicate situations with Serbia, Wallachia, and the Karamanid Dynasty. Constantinople has yet to fall and will remain a thorn in my side until it does. Oh, the Hungarians and Venetians also hate my guts and my empire.

My predecessors, Osman Bey, Orhan Bey, Sultan Murat I, Sultan Yıldırım Bayezit I, Sultan Mehmet I, and Sultan Murat II have done an excellent job securing this realm for me. It's been decades since the empire has been this stable. There will be no brother trying to steal my throne.

I am the undisputed leader of the Ottoman Empire.

Right now, the sultanate needs a decisive, cunning, patient, and resilient ruler. Can I be decisive? Can I be Intelligent? Can I be patient? Can I be resilient?

By Allah, I really hope so.

15. HAMDAN

Today is Sunday, March 30th.

I've been living in this bloody mansion for five weeks now. It's been about seven weeks since I left the twenty-first century with my best friend Mehmet Osman, who's now known as Sultan Mehmet the Second or "the boy padishah" or "ibn Murat" as I often hear him referred to on the streets of Adrianople.

Calling Mehmet a boy emperor is just so wrong.

True, he's only eighteen. Wait, is he nineteen now? His birthday is on the thirtieth of March.

Which is... today.

But he was born in 2001... And we're in 1451.

Does that mean he's negative five hundred and, uh, fifty years old?

I guess we're going to celebrate the fact that a prat will be born in 550 years. Oh, this also means that my birthday is tomorrow. Dope!

Anyway, Mehmet doesn't act like some immature ruler. Over the past four weeks, we've been receiving envoys from all over. We've hosted the Hungarians, Serbs, Crimean Tatars, Karamanids, Mamluks, Venetians, Genoese, and a few others.

Some of the envoys, like the Venetians, Hungarians, Wallachians, and the Karamanids, have been slightly disrespectful to Mehmet, sorta like Halil, to see how far they could push him. With each envoy, Mehmet spoke with complete confidence. It's kinda weird for me to say this, but he almost sounds majestic. I don't know much about politics, but Zaganos always seems overjoyed with all of Mehmet's dealings.

The most interesting meeting so far was with a man by the name of Vlad and his brother Radu. Vlad is the son of Vlad II of Wallachia, a man literally known as Dracul, which means *the dragon* in old Romanian.

Mehmet was passive-aggressive with him, but very friendly with his brother Radu. The two brothers with incredibly weird mustaches (and I mean it when I say that) came asking Mehmet for help taking Wallachia back from their distant cousin Vladislav II.

Mehmet sorta brushed the request aside. He was actually kinda disrespectful, which really surprised me. He pissed off Halil with his attitude, and when Halil confronted him, he wouldn't say anything. He wouldn't even say anything to me, which is so damn annoying. I mean, how can he expect me to advise him if he won't tell me anything?

Mehmet spends literally his whole day in meetings with his senior ministers mapping out strategies to improve the empire. He works in his office every evening with his boy Jake, who's now known as Yakub. I get along with him, but it's weird to see my best friend hanging out with some other dude without me.

I hardly ever see him without Halil, Zaganos, or Jake by his side. We hardly talk about anything apart from work. Well...work and Sally. Mehmet is always tryna find out how she's doing even if he won't visit her, which he certainly can, but doesn't out of an abundance of caution.

Mehmet genuinely cares about doing a good job. I mean, all he does is work. He's probably overworking himself, but today, he is finally taking the day off on the insistence of Halil, Zaganos, Jake, and myself, a rarity that the four of us actually agree on something.

I am presently in my office, working through the accounting books of my business with my partner Mazhar.

When I say business partner, I mean slave.

Mazhar has been helping run my clothing business, which has now expanded to include carpets and furniture, for nine years now, taking over for me after I became vizier.

Well, he's worked for the person that I now am, which Mehmet thinks is my ancestor.

By the way, I'm just going to claim my ancestor's history as my own. I tell myself that everything that happened to him, happened to me, only I suffered amnesia and don't remember it.

Anyhow, Mazhar is a fifty-something-year-old man of Bosnian origin. Bosnia isn't a Muslim country yet and isn't completely part of the Ottoman empire. He voluntarily fought against an Ottoman force attacking a fort in Bosnia and was captured as a prisoner of war fourteen or so years ago.

He was bought by a Genoese sailor and served him for five years, before I witnessed Mazhar being abused by that Genoese sailor nine years ago, when I apparently was in Galata, a colony of Genoa, on business with my elderly father as a nine-year-old (well...my ancestor's father, but I guess his father is also my ancestor).

Evidently, I was extremely upset at the treatment of Mazhar. So, I ran up and purchased him for a pound of gold, fifteen *akçe* (silver coins), and three silk garments. Mazhar still calls that an overpayment.

193

My father—I mean, my ancestor (gosh, this is confusing)—died later that year, and I took over the business with the help of Mazhar.

Five years ago, Mazhar accepted Islam not by force, but by learning. In fact, he really likes how slaves are supposed to be treated in Islam, which is a topic I still don't get. Perhaps I'll have Mehmet explain it next time I see him.

Now, this is the last year Mazhar is going to serve me. Apparently, he has an agreement with my ancestor to be freed after ten years of service. He showed me the very document, with my personal seal (so cool, right?) on it.

I really don't know anything about accounting, so Mazhar is pretty much doing all the work. What am I to do without him? Do I just sell the business?

"Mazhar," I say. "Can I just hire you as my full-time assistant? I'll pay you handsomely."

"What!" Mazhar exclaims. "You want me to stay, Hamdan Pasha? Why?"

"Why wouldn't I?" I ask. "I'm going to have to hire someone after you leave. I'm busy helping our sultan run the Ottoman state. Why not you?"

"I'm hoping to track down my family members in Bosnia after the year," Mazhar states. "I fear I won't be able to if I take up the position as your assistant."

"You are free to do whatever you like. Just know that if you were to stay, you'd be able to use my resources to track down your family and bring them here to stay at my estate. We will construct a place for you."

"Why would you do that, Hamdan Pasha?" Mazhar asks.

"I'm too busy running around with Zaganos Pasha handling the state's business to be concerned with my own. Also, I'm just giving you what you deserve."

I genuinely mean that. I spend all day with Zaganos doing exactly what Mehmet wishes. Also, this dude has been a slave for fourteen years. He deserves to live his own life with his family. Going by the numbers in my books, I can afford to pay him a fortune. Not to flex, but I'm really rich.

"I would very much like to be your assistant, Hamdan Pasha," Mazhar says. "Although I'm in shock you're willing to do all that for me."

"Mazhar," I say. I stand up and put my hand on his shoulder. "You are family."

He smiles at me, and I respond in kind.

"Do you want to iron out the terms of our agreement now or in the morning? I desperately need sleep."

"Whenever you wish, Hamdan Pasha!"

"Okay!" I exclaim as I walk towards my study. "I'm going to head to my quarters for the rest of the day. Please don't disturb me unless it's extremely important."

"Of course, Hamdan Pasha," Mazhar says as he lowers his head.

I walk through the large doors of my study and then stroll for about eight minutes to get to my bedroom. I lived in a fairly large house back in Mississauga, but this estate just gets a bit annoying. Back home, I lived with my two sisters and my parents. It made the place feel homey.

This mansion is empty.

Cold.

Lifeless.

I mean, I live by myself.

I do have slaves living on my estate, but they all have their own rooms.

Don't worry, I checked to make sure that they live in good conditions. Looks like my ancestors weren't cruel.

None of my ancestor's family are alive. His mother died giving birth to him. His father died when my ancestor was nine.

That leaves this house completely empty all the time. My slaves (do I have to call them that?) tend to avoid me, completing their tasks without getting in my way.

I'm not like Mehmet. I like being around a lot of people. Being by myself all the time is boring. It's okay sometimes, but I like to have fun with people. However, I'm not gonna complain, because I'm literally living like a king.

I walk over to the balcony in my room and gaze out at the field underneath it.

I see a few female gardeners working on my mother's garden. I see a couple of men working in the stables. I see a couple of my hired guards jousting by the gates of my estate.

What do I do now?

There are no video games, no TV shows, no Tik Toks or tweets to scroll.

What even is there to do in life but mope?

It's about a half hour after Isha. It's a slightly cool day, which feels refreshing as the air passes through the light grey *thobe* that I'm wearing. It makes lying in bed doing nothing feel slightly better than it actually is.

After counting all the tiles in the room for the third time, I hear a soft knock at the door.

I try to ignore it, hoping for the person to go away, but they continuously knock the door louder and faster. Angrily, I call out, "PLEASE! Come in!"

In walks a tall, beautiful slave with light-brown skin, who looks about the same age as me. She goes by the lovely name of Hafsah, and if Ima be honest, she's quite possibly the most beautiful and breathtaking woman I've ever laid eyes upon. Her dark eyes are beyond enchanting, her sleek wavy hair that goes down to her waist absolutely stuns me, and her face is utterly mesmerizing, and to my shock, she seems as though she hails from what is now Pakistan, the land of my ancestors.

"WHAT IS IT?" I rudely yell as Hafsah makes her way towards my bed.

Hafsah hesitates before stutteringly saying, "T-the s-sult-tan immediately r-requests y-your p-presence, H-H-Hamdan P-pasha."

Damn, I guess really spooked her.

"I apologize for my rude tone, Hafsah," I calmly say as I smile at her, which instantly relaxes her. "Please, why has Mehmet requested my presence?"

"His messenger did not say," she replies. "He only stated that the *hünkar* wants you at the palace immediately."

"Okay, thank you, Hafsah," I say. "Get someone to ready a horse for me by the gate of the estate. I'm just going to wash up and grab a bite to eat on my way out."

"Of course, Hamdan Pasha," she says.

I head to the washroom and quickly make wudu to freshen up. I throw on a black cloak and rush towards the kitchen. I quickly devour a *Simit* (bagel-like Turkish bread) and drink some milk.

I see Mazhar with the dark Turkoman mare that I use to go around the city of Adrianople.

I climb onto it, nod at him, and set off, wondering what could possibly be so urgent that Mehmet needs to see me straight away.

A palace guard leads me to Mehmet's quarters. It's not really a room. It's the size of an extremely large penthouse with the most luxurious furniture and items. There, I find him silently sitting at the desk staring at his diary.

I slap him on the back of the head then take a seat next to him.

Mehmet looks over and punches me really hard on the arm. He turns back to stare at his diary.

"So... happy birthday, brother!" I exclaim in Turkish. (We hardly ever talk in English anymore). "How's it being nineteen?"

Mehmet meekly smiles and says, "Today I learned that I share the same birthday as Fatih Mehmet."

"That's so weird! Like, what?"

"Yeah, it is." He sounds weak. "You should've seen the shock on my face when I woke up to Bayezit jumping on top of me with Gülbahar and Sally standing on side of the bed."

"Bet that was fun," I say. "Is this the first time you're seeing Gülbahar Hatun since becoming sultan? Did you get a chance to talk to Sally?"

Mehmet makes a face before returning to stare at his diary. As far as I can tell, it isn't the same diary that brought us here.

"What are you doing?"

"Just tryna remember something," he mutters as he pushes the diary. "It's gotta do with history."

"Well, uh… I don't think I can help with that, so why'd you ask me here? It sounded urgent."

Mehmet turns to look at me, and I can see the exhaustion in his eyes. He looks dismayed. Something is clearly bothering him.

"I wanna go out," Mehmet states. "Into the city."

"Dude, why'd you call me then? Yusef Agha or Jake are supposed to accompany you everywhere with a band of janissaries."

"You don't get me," he says. "I want to go out anonymously. I want to be normal for a night."

"You wanna leave the castle without security? Are you dumb? Someone has already tried to kill you. Zaganos will be furious when he finds out—and he's not gonna take his anger out on you, he'll take it out on me!"

"Chill, man!" Mehmet exclaims. "No one will find out. We'll take our swords to protect ourselves."

I stare at him for a moment. It would be fun to go out and not have to be a vizier for a night. Spending time with Mehmet is always pretty fun, too, I guess.

"Alright, let's do it. If something bad happens, it's your fault."

"Trust me," Mehmet says. "This night can't get worse."

We sneak out of the dark palace wearing black and carrying lanterns. We enter the stables to get a horse for Mehmet. He walks towards his white Arabian horse and starts to saddle it up.

"Hey!" I exclaim. "All of Adrianople has seen you on that horse. You can't go on that."

He makes a face. "You're right, I guess." To his horse he says, "Sorry, Snowstorm."

"You named your horse?" I ask in surprise.

"Of course," Mehmet says as he starts to saddle up a light-brown Turkoman horse. "Alexander the Great also named his. No reason that Mehmet the Conqueror's horse shouldn't have an epic name."

"It's an awful name."

"It's an amazing name." He climbs on the Turkoman horse. "Let's get going."

I get up on my dark horse and follow him out of the stables. When I say dark, I mean pitch black.

"Your name shall be Shadow," I whisper. "Nah... I don't like that. How about Furat? Yeah... that works."

Mehmet looks back at me and says, "Keep up, man."

"Where are we even going?" I ask. "I don't recognize this place."

"There's a low fence past the garrisons of the janissaries. We can jump that and head into the city."

After five minutes or so, we indeed reach a half-broken fence and Mehmet swiftly gets his horse to jump over it.

"How'd you do that?" I'm astonished.

"Practice, I guess," he says and looks back at me. "Get a running start and urge your horse over the fence. It'll come to you instinctively, as if you've done it before."

I stare at him for a second, then go back a few paces.

"Come on, Furat," I murmur as I beckon the horse forward into a canter. Furat starts to go faster. It looks like we're gonna hit the fence any second. All of a sudden, I seem to black out and Furat jumps over the fence. I don't know if she did it by herself or perhaps, I pulled her reigns up beckoning her to jump.

Yeah, that's probably what I did.

Mehmet continues to lead me around the perimeter of the palace until Adrianople comes into view.

"Looks like you've been preparing to escape the fortress for a while," I say.

"Every day," he says. "Sometimes I wish I could live as far as possible from this palace as Mehmet Osman with Sally by my side... as well as Jake and you, of course."

"Um... okay," I hesitate. "What do you want to do now?"

"Explore," Mehmet says. "I wanna see a mid-fifteenth century city at night."

"Alright. Let's go into the city."

We head south towards the streets of the city. We pass my estate, then slowly navigate our horses through a rather compressed residential area.

"This place looks so small compared to the palace," Mehmet whispers. "I feel guilty living in the palace while my people live in such small places."

"Dude, these houses aren't that small. They're just about the size of your apartment back in Mississauga. It looks small just because we've been living in these gigantic castles. There's just not a lot of space between the homes of these people."

"Yeah, I guess so," Mehmet murmurs as we continue through the streets. He looks around the streets in wonder. However, I can tell there's something wrong.

"Is there a mall or bazaar or something like that?" he asks.

"There isn't really a grand bazaar; most people work in agriculture," I reply.

"I know that," he says, "but is there a place where most of the businesses or vendors set up? Because there absolutely should be."

"Well, there is something like that in the centre of the city, near the old palace. However, vendors set up their stalls all throughout the city. It's sorta messy, if I'm being completely honest."

"Alright." Mehmet takes a deep breath. "Let's go there. Lead the way, Hamdan Pasha."

I shake my head and get in front of him. "You mentioned earlier that this night can't get worse. What's that supposed to mean?"

"Hmm... Forget about it," he replies.

"No, I won't," I angrily hiss at him. "How am I to be a good advisor and friend if you don't tell me anything? Like, seriously, you don't tell me what you're planning or keep me in the loop. I find out about everything from Zaganos."

"That can't be true," Mehmet says. "You're present at all the meetings and the divan."

"I wasn't briefed about the salary bump for the janissaries," I object. "Nor about Ali Bey leading a raid on a fort in Albania, or the support we're providing for the construction of hospitals and schools across Anatolia."

Mehmet falls silent for a moment. He slows his horse down and turns to look at me.

"You didn't need to be briefed on any of that. They had nothing to do with you," Mehmet replies. "I went over the books with Titrek Sinan. We found that there's space to increase the salaries of the janissaries, and I wanna keep them happy. There's a lot of work they're gonna have to do in the future. I also saw the space to provide funding for foundations that maintain or construct hospitals and schools. I had the option of giving them tax breaks or providing money. I gave them money on the advice of Titrek Sinan, and I agree. As for Ali Bey's raid, he protects the lands we control in Albania. He saw an opportunity to capture a key Albanian fort and took it. He sent a message to me about it. The messenger delivered it in front of Zaganos. I don't necessarily care about gaining lands in Albania, so... I don't know why it's such a big deal."

"I still wanna know what's going on," I say. "Tell me, why are you so troubled tonight?"

Mehmet takes a deep breath. "Halil and Yusef Agha both left the city tonight, heading towards Constantinople per my sources. I also haven't heard anything from Turahan Bey for the past couple of weeks. He usually sends his updates to Halil."

"Okay," I say. "Why are you so concerned?"

"I don't know if I should be," Mehmet states. "I sent Zaganos after them. I told him to take you as well, but he refused, saying that you should remain here with me. I need loyal people by my side. Mahmut Pasha is sending someone to Thessaly to check up on Turahan Bey as we speak."

"What's the worst-case scenario here?" I ask. "I mean, it's possible that Halil and Yusef Agha left for business purposes. I know that Halil has many business interests in Constantinople."

"All I know is that the two of them haven't given me my gift yet," Mehmet states. "The gift is sorta like a pledge of allegiance. What if they throw their support behind my cousin Orhan?"

"Wouldn't they have done that already? It's been over a month since Sultan Murat died."

"No point in discussing that now," Mehmet says with finality. "We'll wait for Zaganos to return before talking about this anymore."

"Of course."

We continue riding towards the centre of the city. The streets are mostly empty. It's well past Isha time. We sometimes ride past a vendor who still has his shop open on the side of the road. Mehmet stops to talk to each of them, then drops a couple of *akçe* from his pouch into their laps. After about fifteen minutes of this, we hear a baby wailing from a slight distance.

"Let's find out where that's coming from," he suggests.

"Alright," I say. We turn onto another street.

We don't have to go far. At the end of the street, we find a young lady sitting on the side with a baby wrapped in a blanket.

Mehmet walks over to her, and from a respectable distance, calls, "*Assalamu alaikum*, sister! Is there anything I can help you with? Are you and your child okay?"

If I were that lady, I wouldn't even respond. I mean, it's the middle of the night and two men that are strangers are approaching her. I'd be running.

However, the lady replies. "*Walaikum as-salaam*, brother! My daughter is crying because she is hungry. I haven't gotten the chance to get food for the past couple of days. My husband has been out of town longer than expected, and the money he left us has run out. I left my home tonight hoping to trade my wedding trinkets for some food, yet I can't seem to find a vendor that is open. My daughter started to cry, and I got tired of carrying her around, so I'm sitting here waiting for her to fall asleep before I get up to walk home."

Mehmet turns to me. "Go find food and pay for it with this." He takes out ten of his newly minted akçe and hands them to me.

I nod and lead Furat away as Mehmet gets off his horse and sits next to the lady and strikes up a conversation with her.

It takes me ten minutes to find an open food vendor. I purchase some rice, meat, and bread. I pay with the ten freshly minted coins. (I got to witness the coins being made. They have Mehmet's title on them in pretty cool calligraphy.) I rush back to find Mehmet and the lady.

I return to find Mehmet putting the baby to sleep as the lady peers over his shoulder, shocked that he knows how to take care of a baby.

I get off next to Mehmet and hand her the food. "Let's go home," I say to Mehmet.

"Are you dumb?" Mehmet replies. "We're not leaving Azka and Defne on the side of the road. We'll drop them at their place."

With that, Mehmet grabs the food from her and gives it back to me. He helps the lady, Azka, onto his horse then hands her baby Defne.

He takes hold of the food and doesn't get onto his horse. He grabs the reigns, asking Azka for directions. It takes us twenty minutes to get there. Luckily, her house is close to the centre of the city.

Azka gets off the horse and she asks Mehmet, "Who are you? I didn't catch your name."

Mehmet smiles and says, "I'm Osman, and this is my friend Naeem. We're glad to be able to help!"

With that, he gets on his horse, and we ride away.

"Are you done?" I ask. "Shall we head back to the palace?"

"One more thing," Mehmet states. "Lead me to the market."

"We're basically here," I say as we turn another street corner passing the old palace.

Here we find a slave market, and it's not a sight you ever wanna see. Trust me on that.

There are about a dozen or so male slaves with their necks, hands, and feet chained to a wooden platform. There are a few female slaves on the opposite sides who are also chained. Most of them appear to be European, although a couple of them appear to be from Africa.

It looks as though they haven't eaten or bathed in a few days. They look severely dehydrated. I absolutely hate this sight. No human being should be treated this way. There is no way that this is regulated. I mean, this can't be allowed. It shouldn't be allowed.

I quickly ride through the place. I look to my side for Mehmet, but he isn't there. Instead, he's on the ground giving a female slave water from his flask.

I ride a few paces back and say, "We've got to get going. We don't want the slaver to find us."

Mehmet ignores me and continues to give water to the others. I impatiently stare at him hoping the slaver doesn't show up. After a moment or two, I get off my horse and start to give water to some of them from my own flask.

I overhear Mehmet whisper, "Y'all shouldn't be treated like this," to a few of the slaves.

A moment later, a bit of light appears behind Mehmet. It's a man carrying a torch.

"Hey!" the man bellows out. "What are you doing!"

Mehmet stands up and says, "Are you the man selling these slaves?"

"Of course, I am!" he exclaims. "Who are you?"

"A man looking to buy some slaves," Mehmet answers.

What the hell! Why on earth does he wanna buy slaves? He already has so many in the palace.

"Perfect," the slaver says while rubbing his hands. "Which ones are you interested in?"

"All of them," Mehmet replies. "I wish to buy all of them."

Has he gone mad?

It's disgusting.

Appalling.

The slaver looks shocked. I can now see him more clearly. The guy is slightly fat, with a pointy beard and dark eyes, like he's wearing dark eyeshadow and mascara.

"You want all of them, sir?" he repeats.

"Yes," Mehmet says. "What will the cost be?"

The slaver looks at him for a moment and says, "All the slaves are able-bodied, and the females are young and lovely, it's going to be costly."

"I don't care," Mehmet says. "If you keep them like this, they aren't going to be able-bodied for long. Perhaps by tomorrow or the day after, everyone will see the men as weak. Have you even given them any food or water? What's going to happen if I inform the authorities? This treatment isn't legal in Islam, which means it isn't legal in the Ottoman sultanate."

"I haven't," the slaver states. "It would be bad for business, so go ahead and inform them, because they aren't going to say anything. Halil Pasha and his family are my biggest clients, and I treat my slaves just like all the other slavers across the realm."

"Slaves have rights, too," Mehmet growls. "Now. Name. Your. Price."

The slaver vacantly stares at Mehmet. I guess he's tryna see if Mehmet is for real. Mehmet smirks and places his hand on the hilt of his kilij as he takes a few steps closer to the slaver.

"Your Price! Now!" Mehmet authoritatively yells.

"There are nineteen able-bodied slaves. The cost will be six hundred *akçe* and the ring on your friend's finger," the slaver says.

Mehmet smirks and opens the pouch on his belt. He takes a bunch of coins out and counts them on the wooden platform. After counting out six hundred silver coins, he places them into the pouch of the slaver. Next, he demands the ring I was wearing on my finger and hands it to the slaver. He places it on his left pinky finger (it's a bit too small) and hands the key to the chains over to Mehmet. As the slaver walks away, Mehmet calls out to him, "If you asked for three times the amount, I would have paid it. Now go away. I don't wanna see you here."

The slaver slowly backs up and walks away, loudly cursing at Mehmet in Greek.

I turn to Mehmet and ask, "Now what?"

He ignores me and starts to unchain all the slaves.

After every slave has been unchained, he gets on his horse and announces, "I am Sultan Mehmet, the *hünkar* of these lands." He repeats this in a bunch of different languages. "Each of you is free to choose your own destiny. If you wish to be free, I am offering you clothing, food, coin, and prayers for safe travel. You shall be free to remain in the Ottoman Sultanate as free persons, or to return to your homelands. If you wish to serve me, however, I promise you will never go hungry. You will always be clothed. You shall earn a yearly stipend and you can back out of this agreement any time."

The slaves whisper to each other.

I'm in shock. Did Mehmet plan this? How much money did he even bring with him? How does he expect to feed, clothe, and pay nineteen slaves without anyone finding out?

"Those who wish to go off on their own, step to my right," Mehmet says. "Those who wish to remain with me, step to my left."

Nearly all the men and one lady go to Mehmet's right. Most of the women and a couple men go to his left.

Mehmet gets off his horse and helps a couple of women onto his horse. He grabs the reigns and motions everyone in front of him.

"Hamdan!" Mehmet calls. "We'll drop the ones that are leaving at your place, where you will feed and clothe them. They can sleep at your estate and leave in the morning."

I nod as we continue to slowly go through the narrow and dark streets of Adrianople.

After about half an hour, we reach my estate. I quickly find Mazhar and relay Mehmet's instructions.

After the former slaves enter the estate, I leave with Mehmet and the rest of the group, heading towards the Adrianople Palace. We enter through the same half-broken fence.

Mehmet walks over to my horse and loudly says, "You should probably take them through the front of the palace. Ensure that they are safely within the palace, and the women safely into the harem. Get Adham Ibn Eymen to write up a contract with all the terms I promised them and seal it with my tughra. Each will get 100 akçe per year, with the chance for more. All the money will come from the Enderun Hazinesi, the inner treasury. That ensures that the money comes from my own personal wealth."

"Of course, my padishah," I say out loud.

I then quietly ask, "Where are you going to go? I thought you didn't want everyone to know that you left the palace. How are you to sneak in now?"

"Don't worry about me," Mehmet says. "Just get them inside the palace, and see that they bathe, get warm food, and clothing."

"Of course."

He places his hand on my shoulder before getting on his horse and turning towards the stables.

"Mehmet, why do all this tonight?"

"I like helping people, man," he replies, stretching the *A* in man as he always does. "What I did tonight is similar to what Umar ibn al-Khattab would do as caliph. In Islam, slaves aren't supposed to be treated poorly. Every single person is equal, no matter their earthly status. The only thing that distinguishes a person is what's in their hearts. That's why I couldn't stand by when I saw those slaves tonight. Allah has blessed me, so the least I can do is help people who are suffering."

With that, he gives me a weak smile as he rides off into the darkness.

16. Sally

Uncertainty.

I think that's the best way to describe my days here so far.

Whatever I do, I'm always filled with uncertainty. I know I sound like a Debbie Downer, but let me explain myself.

My time in this palace has been surprisingly good. Most days are really enjoyable, few days are mediocre, but overall, I feel like I'm adjusting well to my new lifestyle and identity. I try to keep busy. I often start my day early, helping some of the slave girls that are around my age with their chores. All of them are from the non-Muslim lands the Ottomans have conquered, mainly what's now known as Eastern Europe. There are a few new slave girls, who were sent as "gifts" for Mehmet, to be used for his pleasure. They've been sent by other sovereigns, and they've recently moved into the harem. I try to be friendly to make them feel welcome.

Through helping the slaves, I've gotten the chance to explore the palace and even the city once.

I've cleaned the imperial hall on top of taking care of Gülbahar's room, helped cook in kitchens, and once even served food to Çandarlı Halil Pasha and Yusef Agha in Çandarlı Halil Pasha's office, which was particularly intimidating.

I've seen the dungeons located outside the palace. Let's not talk about that... It was freakish.

I've seen some of the Ottoman treasury stored in a large room within the palace. It was filled with heaps of jewels, piles of gold coins, mountains of silver coins, stacks of copper, glorious art pieces, an assortment of weapons, and a few books of financial records.

I was told by someone that the room contained the inner treasury, known as the *Enderun Hazinesi*. This means that all the wealth I saw is owned by the sultan. It all belongs to Mehmet.

Mind-boggling.

What's even more incredible is that Çandarlı Halil Pasha is apparently even wealthier.

I don't know exactly how wealthy Mehmet is, but I do know that the Ottomans are supposed to get a whole hell of a lot wealthier after the conquest of Constantinople, when they'll be able to exert more control over trade routes.

Anyway, there is also an outer treasury, called the *Birun Hazinesi*, outside the palace, but I haven't seen that yet.

I've gone through Adrianople once. I escaped the walled palace by climbing over a half-broken fence at the back of the fortress, a fence that should definitely be fixed.

Adrianople has narrow streets that are bustling throughout the day, despite not having a huge population. There is a lot of agricultural land outside the residential and social areas of the city. I actually got lost exploring, but luckily Jake found me roaming around and took me back to the castle. Unfortunately for me, he wouldn't tell me anything about what was going on with Mehmet or pretty much anything else, claiming he didn't know anything, which is total bullshit.

Okay, I'm getting way off-track. So, my daily routine. After I

help some of the slaves, I return to the chambers I share with Gülbahar and sorta do whatever I want. Most of the time, it's reading.

Prior to traveling five-hundred-something-years back in time, I
wasn't a huge reader. Don't get me wrong. I like to read, and I've read
all the popular book series—*The Hunger Games*, *Divergent*, Harry
Potter, Percy Jackson, and *Twilight*. I just prefer to do other things,
like play sports, ride my horse, sketch, and binge shows, especially
supernatural ones.

I kinda pretend I'm an actress here in this new world, or should
I say old world? Whatever... doesn't matter.

I'm trying to learn as much about this role as possible. So, I'm
being taught how to read the Qur'an by the remarkable Fatma Hatun, one of Mehmet's sisters, who as one of Zaganos Pasha's wives,
does not live in the harem, but visits every day.

She's not really his sister, but y'all know what I mean. It's actually
quite eerie that Mehmet and her look alike. If someone were to tell
me that Mehmet and Fatma Hatun were siblings, I'd believe them in
a heartbeat.

She's also been teaching me a bit about Islam, and I think I'm
solid on the basics. I know about the five pillars of Islam, which are
the *shahadah* (profession of faith), the *salah* (five daily prayers), the
zakat (alms), *sawm* (fasting the month of Ramadan), and the *hajj*
(pilgrimage to the holy Kaaba).

There are also the six articles of faith. They are the belief in the
Almighty God, the angels, the revelations, the prophets, and the Day
of Judgement. Finally, there is the belief in premeasurement, which
is that God has knowledge and control of everything that exists in
time and space. The key to this is that human beings still have free
will.

Fatma Hatun was kinda shocked I hadn't learned these things sooner, but she never really questioned me about it, which is a good thing as I probably would have spilled that I haven't converted, and I don't really know whether I believe in God. That would really shock someone from the fifteenth century, I think.

The books I read are mostly on Islam. I really do wanna learn more about it. I mean, it's the second largest religion in the world—perhaps the first in *this* world. I am curious why so many people have been swayed by the message.

What I have read so far has been overwhelmingly positive. Islam is a religion predicated on equality. Everyone is equal in the eyes of God, no matter their skin colour, gender, or social class. The only thing that distinguishes one person from another is their heart.

A wonderful quote by the Prophet Muhammad in his final sermon reflects this promise: *"An Arab has no superiority over a non-Arab nor a non-Arab has any superiority over an Arab; also, a white has no superiority over a black nor a black has any superiority over white except by piety and good action."*

He said this in seventh-century Arabia. It would have been outlandish then. In that same sermon, he also said, *"O People, it is true that you have certain rights over your women, but they also have rights over you. Remember that you have taken them as your wives only under God's trust and with His permission. If they abide by your right, then to them belongs the right to be fed and clothed in kindness. Treat your women well and be kind to them, for they are your partners and committed helpers."*

It definitely feels like the Prophet Muhammad was an early human rights activist.

The Prophet Muhammad came to a heavily polarized and ignorant society. Fathers killed their own daughters, there was constant war among the tribes, people disregarded the poor, and there were many enslaved people. In his twenty-three years of prophethood, he united all of Arabia, helped women regain their dignity, and minimized the gap between the poor and rich. Some of his greatest companions were the poor and slaves, as well as women.

His whole biography is incredible.

I don't know a lot about Islam yet (I mean I've only been pretending to be Muslim for less than two months), but I don't think I'm ready to change my opinion on God. I still don't know if there is any supreme being.

Okay, lemme get back to explaining this state of uncertainty I feel.

While I read, Bayezit and Gülbahar wake up and go about their day, but by that time, I have been away for hours. I then tidy up the room while she gets him dressed.

Next, she teaches him basic things like etiquette and stories. I don't know exactly what a three-year-old boy is supposed to learn, so thankfully Gülbahar takes care of that. More often than not, they're just doubling over in laughter.

While she works with him, I usually sketch or paint. Sketching might be one of my favourite things to do. I think I'm good at it. I recently sketched out Gülbahar playing with Bayezit, and she framed it and placed it on the drawer next to our bed. I prefer sketching supernatural beings like dark angels, devils, ghosts, and vampires, but she doesn't really appreciate that.

I never really painted much before, but it is something my mother loved to do, so I sorta paint as something to remember her by. A couple weeks ago, I tried to paint a portrait of my family from memory. The only problem is that I'm starting to forget some of their features, which is why I don't think it turned out great. I still keep the canvas safe in the corner of the room and look at it daily. Gülbahar seems to like it, but of course she's never really seen my family.

I'm also trying to learn Arabic calligraphy. Fatma Hatun and Gülbahar, who are extremely good at it, are teaching me. I kinda expected them to be illiterate as, uh... they're women in the fifteenth century. But it does seem like Islam stresses the importance of education of all Muslims, not just men.

In the afternoons and early evenings, all the women in the harem gather and pretty much hang out. Sometimes it's games, or everyone tells stories and poems, or they just talk.

The conversations seem to be about what Mehmet is doing. For the first couple weeks of his reign, the talk was about how he imprisoned Sultan Murat's wife, Sultan Hatun, killing her son and passing a fratricide law. People speculated on what his future moves might be. Almost all the older women were calling him an immature tyrant. Mara Hatun and Gülbahar were the only ones defending him. To be honest, I know Mehmet is a good person, but it is hard defending his first action. Mara Hatun made compelling arguments about how this prevents civil war from occurring. Also, in that short conversation I had with him, he claimed he didn't order it.

A little over a week ago, Mara Hatun suddenly left for Serbia, shocking everyone, including Gülbahar. Apparently, women don't leave the harem after the death of their husband. Sultan and Mara Hatun are the exception. Now, everyone is calling Mehmet cold. No one knows what he intends to do next. All anyone in the harem knows is that he doesn't care to visit his sisters, stepmothers, wives, or child. He doesn't care to, uh... I feel weird saying this, but everyone seems to think he's cold because he doesn't seem to want to be intimate with anyone, whether that's Gülbahar or any of his uh... concubines. He just spends the whole day with his officials, or the janissaries.

That's what I mean by uncertainty. Everyone in the harem is just guessing what Mehmet is thinking. I probably know him best in the harem (which is really saying something—I feel like I don't know him well), and I have no idea what he's thinking. I don't know how he's doing, what he's planning. I wanna be in the loop. I wanna help him out in some way.

I convinced Gülbahar to go with Bayezit and surprise Mehmet for his ancestor's birthday today. I also went along and with Zaganos Pasha's permission, we entered his room.

When we woke him, Mehmet made awkward and uncomfortable conversation. Of course, with Gülbahar and Bayezit there, I couldn't *really* talk to him. Even though he had a hard time talking to her, he did seem to be extremely comfortable with Bayezit. After half an hour, he asked me to leave with the baby so he could speak privately to Gülbahar.

She returned after an hour and was extremely giddy. I didn't ask her anything about what happened, but I don't know what Mehmet could have possibly said to make her so happy.

Good for her, I guess.

Me? Nothing has alleviated my uncertainty.

I don't like feeling uncertain. I feel like I need to have some sort of control over my life.

Unfortunately, I just don't have that here.

I'm in my shared bed, waiting for Gülbahar to fall asleep. She's been tossing and turning for an hour now. Some days, after everyone falls asleep, I slip out of the harem and go for a stroll through the palace grounds. Today feels like a nice day to do so.

I wait another twenty minutes until I hear absolutely nothing. I look over at her and she seems to be peacefully asleep. I lightly shake her to confirm, and she unconsciously brushes my hand away.

I quietly slip into a dark blue dress and throw on her black cloak as I leave the room. I walk through the extremely dark halls of the harem. Nearly everyone is sleeping, except for a couple slaves named Remi and Soha, both gifts from a ruler. Neither pay any attention to me.

I exit the gates of the harem and walk past Mehmet's quarters. There are no guards posted by the doors.

That makes no sense.

There are always guards posted at this time.

It's well past Isha, the night prayer. He's always in his room at this point.

I walk back to the door and knock, blindly hoping that Mehmet opens the door. I stand there for what feels like an eternity, only to be disappointed. I curse under my breath and walk away.

I sneak around the halls hoping not to be seen by any of the guards strolling through the fortress. I pass by Mehmet's study and there are no guards posted there. I pass Zaganos Pasha's study, which also seems to be empty. The same is true for Halil Pasha's study. As I sneak past Hamdan's study space, I see three janissaries quietly talking to each other. I quickly stroll away towards the staircase that leads to the field behind the palace.

I walk down the stairs and immediately hide behind a pillar. I hear voices from a distance. One voice is awfully familiar, except I just can't put my finger on where I know it from.

From the corner of my eye, I try to make out who's there. I see a few poorly dressed and bruised people being ushered inside...by Hamdan?

What on earth?

After Hamdan walks by with...those people, I quietly walk out of the palace, closing my eyes and taking the deepest breath I can. The cool night air feels so refreshing, sending goosebumps across the back of my neck. I look around for a second, trying to figure out which direction I should go.

I've only seen the stables once, and I absolutely love horses. I guess that's the move tonight.

I quickly run over to the stables and peer inside. It's empty, so I enter.

It's totally unfair how good these stables are compared to the ones back at the farm in North Dumfries. It's gigantic, tidy, and filled with so many different horses. I walk through the stables to the most majestic horse—Mehmet's white stallion from Arabia. It's so stunning, beautiful, gorgeous, and powerful. While I don't have the same emotional connection with his stallion as I do with my black Canadian mare, Betty, I am drawn to him by his strong aura.

I reach out with my hand and wait for him to embrace it. He does, and I gently stroke his head.

A horse this magnificent should have a majestic name. I wonder what Mehmet calls him.

"Should your name be Winter?" I ask. No... I don't think that's good enough. Knowing Mehmet, he's probably named the stallion after Alexander the Great's horse or something like that.

"Your name should be Pegasus," I say. Can't go wrong with that. This horse is just so awesome and pure, just like Pegasus. I'm also fairly sure Mehmet likes Greek mythology, so this definitely works.

I think back to the group of people being escorted by Hamdan. Who were they? Prisoners? They weren't wearing any chains though. Slaves? It's possible, but I don't see why the palace needs any more.

Suddenly, I hear a familiar voice from outside the stable. The guy seems to be singing? It's in a language I don't understand, which means it isn't English or Turkish.

The voice seems to be coming closer, yet I can't take the chance that it's someone I know. I climb into the stable next to Mehmet's stallion—the only empty stable. Thankfully, it's also fairly clean. I lie down on the hay and throw Gülbahar's cloak over myself.

The person rides into the stables. I hear a clatter of hooves coming closer, and the voice gets louder and louder. It isn't actually singing, but reciting what I am guessing is the Qur'an. The voice is way too majestic and stern to be singing. It is also so familiar, I almost wanna peer out from under this cloak.

All of a sudden, the clatter of hooves stops right in front of the stable I'm hiding in.

Crap.

I pull the cloak slightly down, to see who on earth could be bringing their horse into the stables so late at night. I see the familiar medium-length curly dark-brown hair swept to the side and the broad shoulders of... Mehmet Osman.

Oh my gosh.

This is just too perfect.

I listen to him reciting the Qur'an, simply sounding so perfect, as he slides off a light-brown Turkoman stallion and begins to unsaddle it. I creep over to the gate of the stable, with the cloak still draped over me. As soon as he turns his back to me, I leap over, thankfully making no noise. Mehmet continues to recite the Quranic verses as I tiptoe behind him, still covering myself with the cloak. He takes the saddle off the horse. As soon as he does, I grab his shoulder and in the raspiest voice I can make, I loudly say, "How are you, my padishah?"

He grips my arm, twists it, and pulls me out in front of him. He grabs my neck with one hand and pushes me against the wall. He unsheathes his dagger with his other hand.

"*M-m-m-meh*," I squeak as I squeeze and pinch his hand around my neck. He raises his dagger. My touch seems to make him hesitate, so I use my other hand to pull off the hood and reveal my face.

"Sally?" He looks at my face in shock and fear, immediately dropping the dagger and letting go of my neck, before dropping down to his knees in disgust.

I massage my neck and take a deep breath. He buries his head in his hands. I kick him and demandingly yell in English, "WHAT ON EARTH IS WRONG WITH YOU?"

He doesn't respond, so I kick him again, as hard as I possibly can, and yell, "ANSWER ME, IDIOT!"

He looks up at me, flashes the sweetest puppy eyes in the world and hoarsely whispers, "I-I'm sorry. I thought you were an assassin..."

Ugh, I hate how innocent he looks right now.

"I know that sounds stupid, but you did come out of the shadows, grab my shoulder, and use a super-creepy voice to a guy who was nearly assassinated," Mehmet sheepishly says.

"What!" I exclaim. "You were nearly assassinated?"

He gets up and goes back to his stallion.

"Wanna ride somewhere?"

"Of course!" I exclaim.

"Uh... What are you doing?" Mehmet asks. "You're riding Gülbahar's horse."

"Which one is that?"

"The one I just unsaddled," he replies.

The two of us race to saddle and sit on our horses, and of course, I win.

"I guess that's a drawback of having servants," I jest as I climb onto the light-brown horse. "You don't learn how to do anything."

Mehmet scoffs as he slowly mounts his horse.

"You better call him Pegasus. He deserves an awesome name."

"Who?" he asks.

"The horse, dummy!" I exclaim as we ride out of the stables.

"You mean Snowstorm?"

"That's what you named him? I kinda like it, but... it doesn't feel like a legendary name. Snowstorm deserves a legendary name."

"Snowstorm shall become a legendary name," he declares.

I smile. Then I turn serious. "Explain what you meant when you said you were nearly assassinated. No sane person exaggerates something like that."

"Maybe I'm not sane. Perhaps you're hanging out with a lunatic."

"Come on!" I exclaim. "Just be straight with me."

222

"You see that fence there?" he asks. "The one that's half-broken? Race you there."

"What...?" I ask in confusion.

"First one over the fence wins!" He holds up his hand up, looks at me, and counts down. "Five, four, three..."

"Oh, you're on!" I grab the reigns of my horse.

"...two, one, GO!"

I get a brilliant start right off the bat, yet he easily catches up to me. I urge my horse into a gallop, and Mehmet and I are basically stride for stride. Out of the corner of my eye, I can tell that Mehmet is heavily inexperienced, yet he refuses to fall behind.

This is so exhilarating. It's been a while since I've ridden a horse—a year since I last raced with someone.

I feel amazing, as though I'm flying, completely free.

Invincible.

I hear Mehmet shout, "This has to be what Connor McDavid feels like!"

"WHO?" I yell back.

"A really fast hockey player!" he replies. "One of the best in the world!"

Of course he thinks about hockey at this moment. It may be the only thing he likes more than history.

As we approach the fence, our horses are pretty much neck-and-neck. I ensure that the horse's strides leading into the jump are perfect, steadying the horse, getting him to slow a bit, before urging him over the fence, which is about four and a half feet tall.

"YES!" I shout as I get the horse to a full stop.

I look back to see Snowstorm majestically leaping over the fence.

"You better not have slowed down on purpose, Mehmet!"

223

"Does it look like I know how to?"

"How on earth do you know how to ride so well? You nearly beat me, and I've been riding for over thirteen years."

"How do you know Turkish?" he replies. "It's the same thing."

I guess he's right. Nonetheless, it still doesn't make sense.

"What do you wanna do now?"

"Let's just chill on this field," he suggests. "We can just relax and enjoy the night."

I tie Snowstorm and the Turkoman horse to the fence as Mehmet lays our cloaks on the ground. He lies flat on his back with his head resting on his arms.

I walk over and lie right next to him. He immediately shuffles over to make some space between us. I ignore that—he always seems to want space between us for some reason.

"So, tell me. You were nearly assassinated?"

"Don't worry about that," he replies. "How are you doing? What have you been up to?"

Ugh... He's so hopeless, dodging questions like a sports coach.

"I'm doing great," I softly reply.

"That's good to hear." He turns to look at me. "What've you been up to? I wanna know everything."

I answer in great detail, starting with how I help his slaves, reviewing the books I'm reading, including the Qur'an, my artwork, then discussing his sister, his wife, his son, and the rest of the women.

I don't, however, tell him about the uneasiness inside the harem nor my own uncertainty. I think I'm gonna use that to get him to answer my questions.

"That all sounds splendid," he murmurs. "I wanna see your sketches."

"You may do that when you next visit Gülbahar and Bayezit. I share a room with them."

Mehmet remains quiet for a moment. "I see them before Friday prayers," he says. "Now, describe my sister to me. I've always wanted a sibling. Her name is Fatma, correct? The one who's married to Zaganos. She usually isn't at the prayers."

"Yeah, that's her name," I reply. "Also, perhaps you should find out yourself. Why don't you meet her?"

He again falls silent for a moment. "What do they say about me in the harem? How's the morale in there?" he asks.

I laugh. "What do you think, Mehmet? You've imprisoned Sultan Hatun, killed her two-year-old son, sent your biggest supporter, the lady that Gülbahar looks up to, away to fucking Serbia. You isolate yourself from everyone, and no one knows what you're thinking or planning. They call you a cold, immature tyrant."

"Does Gülbahar think that?" Mehmet asks. "Does my sister think that?"

"They defend you. I don't think anyone really believes it when they say you're going to be the greatest *hünkar* the state has seen."

"And what do you think?" he asks. "Surely you don't think I'm cold or that I'm an immature tyrant."

"I don't think you're immature, nor do I think that you are a tyrant. Perhaps a bit cold at times though…"

"Are you serious?" he exclaims. "Like, you're not joking, right?"

"I'm only half-joking," I reply. "Does anyone know what's going on in your head? Do you let anyone know what you're thinking? I'm the one who knows you best in the harem, and I feel like I don't know you at all."

"There isn't much to know about me." He lies flat on his back again. "You know everything there is to know about me."

I scoff and say, "I don't even know when your birthday is—"

He interrupts. "Then why did you wish me a happy birthday today, on my birthday? Was that not your idea? I don't think birthdays are a big deal in the fifteenth century."

"You share the same birthday as your ancestor? That's incredibly weird."

"Well, he was born exactly 569 years before me, so it's not exactly the same birthday, but point taken," Mehmet says. "Your birthday is July 26, correct?"

"Yeah. I don't remember mentioning it to you."

"You did once," Mehmet replies. "Now, what else do you wanna know?"

"Who's your celebrity crush?" I jokingly ask.

"Are you serious?" Mehmet asks as he looks directly into my eyes. "*That's* what you wanna know?"

"I mean, if you aren't gonna answer my actual questions..." I sarcastically say.

"Growing up, Jessica Alba. Or maybe Tara Sutaria," Mehmet states. "I don't know, I don't really care much about celebs. Now, ask what you really wanna know."

Okay, why did I ask that? I guess I'm just trying to figure out his type. Doesn't help that I have no idea who Tara Sutaria is. Perhaps I should ask him more dumb questions.

"I probably wouldn't have guessed Jessica Alba, but who is Tara Sutaria?" I ask.

"An Indian actress Hamdan's always talking about," Mehmet replies. "Kinda looks like you, to be honest."

Looks like *me*? And that's his celeb crush? Does that mean... No, I'm not going to read into anything. I must change the topic.

"What's your favourite colour?"

He makes a bizarre face. "I kinda like baby blue, red, green, purple, but my favourite colour has to be...," he whispers, "has to be the colour of your eyes under the bright sun."

I nearly choke because he knows damn well what he's doing. I recover enough to ask, "Favourite music artists?"

"I swear, we've talked about this," he replies. "I have a first tier, which is Brett Young, Dua Lipa, Taylor Swift, Drake, J. Cole, The Weeknd, Niall Horan, Zayn Malik, and Bruno Mars."

"Some really good ones," I say. "Favourite song?"

"'Here Tonight,' by Brett Young," Mehmet replies.

"Ooh, I love that song!" I excitedly say. "How does it go again? I don't remember. Sing it!"

"You want me to sing it?" Mehmet asks. "No way!"

"Please!" I beg. "If you can recite the Qur'an so well, surely you can sing great as well."

"The Qur'an is not a song," Mehmet replies.

"Okay, but still..."

"Ask me the real questions!" he demands. "No more nonsense."

Man, he can sound like such a dad sometimes.

"Okay. Please tell me what you meant by saying you were nearly assassinated!"

Mehmet takes a deep breath, sits up, stretches his arms, adjusts the cloak under him, collapses back down, and turns his whole body so he's directly facing me. I look into his light-brown eyes, and he's gazing right into mine.

In a voice barely above than a whisper, he begins. "Over a month ago, the day before I was named sultan, an attack against my life was carried out in my tent. There were seven assailants. Six attacked the front of the tent, distracting the janissaries. One entered from the back. It felt like he came outta the shadows. He was tall, wore dark clothing, and had the harshest voice. He, uh... Do I have to describe it for you, Sally?"

"No, no, no!" I sit up. "You absolutely don't, unless you want to. No wonder you reacted that way when I snuck up on you!"

"I still shouldn't have," Mehmet replies. "It's unacceptable. I could have killed you just like I killed that guy. I gotta keep myself in check."

Um, so... Mehmet killed someone. Self-defence, but what the fuck?

"Give yourself a break. I probably would have reacted the same way. I still don't get how you pulled off those moves on me. Seems like you've been fighting for years."

"Again, it's just like how you speak Turkish perfectly," Mehmet says. "I do, however, train everyday with Jake and the janissaries. I trained daily before my injury. I'll start again sometime this week."

"What injury?" I ask, interrupting him. "I never heard you were injured."

"Seriously?" Mehmet asks. "No wonder y'all don't know that Mara Hatun asked to go to her father's court in Serbia. I seriously thought that all the news goes through the harem."

"Wait, what?" I ask. "Why'd she ask to leave? And what injury? Where did you get hurt?"

"My hip," he replies. "A sword cut my hip. Before you start freaking out like everyone else, it only was a minor injury. It doesn't even hurt anymore. Also—"

"Show me!" I demand, interrupting him again.

"It's on my hip," Mehmet says. "I ain't gonna show you."

"Let me see," I plead.

"It's not wrapped up anymore, but fine." He lifts up his dark-green thobe. He slightly pulls down his *şalvar* (baggy trousers) on his left side to reveal a cut that looks like it would have been nasty a couple weeks ago. The wound is beginning to scar. I trace the cut with my finger. Gosh, this must have hurt so much. I look towards Mehmet's face, and it's turned to a deep shade of red.

Oh, dang. I must be hurting him.

"Did that hurt?" I ask as he pulls his şalvar back up.

"No, I just don't wanna be touched. Er, I mean... ah, forget it," Mehmet whispers. "Now, to answer your question about why Mara Hatun asked to leave. It's because she thinks she isn't needed here anymore. She believes she can help me more from her father's court back in Serbia. We do write to each other. I got my first letter from her yesterday. I don't know why she didn't say that she asked to leave, but don't tell anyone. She probably had a good reason. She's incredibly smart, you know."

I slowly nod, processing everything he just said. It makes perfect sense why she didn't tell everyone that she asked to leave. They've been calling Mehmet immature. It would've seemed like he was losing one of his biggest supporters. Everyone would think that he did something to damage their relationship.

"Of course," I reply. "Now, tell me, what did you and Gülbahar talk about today? She seemed so happy after."

Mehmet laughs. "We played chess. She destroyed me twice. While we played, we talked. I let her air out her grievances with me. I told her my plans, and how I need her help to fulfill them."

"How's she supposed to help?" I demand. "No offence to her, but, like, we stay in the harem pretty much all day doing nothing."

"I asked her to run the palace for me," he replies. "That means she'll supervise the slaves and attendants, and oversee all other matters related to keeping the palace going. I'm hoping to host some political banquets soon, and I'm gonna need her to make sure the palace is in perfect shape. I'm sure you've noticed that it's incomplete. Also, I promised her that in exchange, I'll spend my Friday nights with her and that she can call out my missteps whenever she wants in front of me."

"Does that mean you're gonna be intimate with her?" I ask. "Isn't she your ancestor?"

Mehmet turns red. "Dear God! No! You're right. I'm fairly sure she's my ancestor, but I don't know how long it'll be before she realizes I'm not her husband. Also, let's not talk about this."

"Okay," I reply. "Now tell me what your plans are?"

"I've been tryna accomplish a whole lotta different stuff."

"Like...?" I ask.

"Well... Halil, Zaganos, Hamdan, and I have been debating the first steps of my government. By first steps, I mean military expeditions. Halil wants me to maintain the status quo. That means I allow powerful Anatolian families, like his own, to live relatively autonomously of Ottoman Rule. He maintains that European powers surrounding our borders will attack us, so we should spend our time preparing for the attack. He also advises that we maintain peace with the Byzantines, instead of looking to take the city. Halil's literally said, 'The Greeks are incredibly weak. The great city of Constantinople has become a rotten apple under their rule. Yes, it'll be excellent for us to take the city, but we shouldn't besiege the city, as it'll be a

230

waste of time and resources. The city will eventually fall under our control anyway. For now, we should pursue peace with the Greeks.'"

I laugh. He does a funny imitation of Halil Pasha's nasty and angry tone.

"Is his opinion any good?"

"Lemme finish," Mehmet pleads. "Now, Zaganos refuses to even see Halil's point of view. He believes that our state should annex Serbia, Wallachia, and take over the rest of the Byzantine strongholds to send a message to the world that we are a global power. After we do that, we turn to Constantinople, which will be completely isolated. Then we conquer the city."

"That sounds smart, but I think it's going to take more than two years. Also, are you really gonna attack Serbia while Mara Hatun lives there?"

"Let. Me. Finish. Please. Sally!" he demands. "Hamdan for the most part agrees with Zaganos' plan, but thinks we should conquer Constantinople first. My personal opinion is a lot more complex. I understand why Halil Pasha wants to maintain the status quo, but I'm not gonna do that. Fatih Mehmet and I agree on one thing. For a dynasty to survive, the imperial family needs to be the most powerful family in the state. I've thought long and hard about it, and there is no other way."

"Okay. I guess that makes sense. Of course, that isn't something people would accept in the twenty-first century."

"Well, it's the fifteenth century, and this is how the world works," he states. "The strong survive, and the weak perish. Nonetheless, the Ottoman dynasty must always reign supreme."

Okay... now that's something I never thought I'd hear out of

Mehmet's mouth. Perhaps in a movie, but not from his mouth. Then again, our lives are quite literally a movie, and I'm not exaggerating.

He wants to tell me more. "I want to default to whatever Fatih Mehmet did as a leader, but what if I don't want to? Let's say, for example, I wanna press eastward, not westward like my ancestor did. What if I wanna create an alliance with the Mamluks in Egypt and the Muslims in Al-Andalus? What are the consequences for history? Will the twenty-first-century world become a different place? A better place? Or will it be worse? If I do something different, will we be able to get back home? Will we ever get back home, even if I don't change history?"

"I don't think you're ever going to get those answers, unless you actually go ahead and do those actions."

"I know, and it's so darn frustrating!" he exclaims. "If I go with Zaganos' plan, Serbia is pretty much ripe for the picking by the Ottoman state. Wallachia's situation is a bit more complex. I think it's going to be difficult to conquer. They won't go down easily. I mean, I think the Wallachians could attack us if all the pieces fall into place, but hopefully that doesn't happen. Regardless, I don't want to go after them until Constantinople falls."

"Go after Constantinople and get us home. Isn't that what your ancestor wanted?"

Mehmet laughs. "Yeah, I guess so. It definitely feels like the safest option. History will remain intact, and the Ottoman empire will become the greatest power of the world, but let's see how things shake out. Jake and I are looking into all options."

"That's smart."

"Of course, conquest is only one avenue to strengthening the empire," Mehmet states. "As Dr. Rizvi always says, trade is what truly makes an empire."

"I miss that old geezer," I reminisce. "So, what are you doing on that front?"

"Not all that much, to be honest," Mehmet replies. "Just making sure that all my ministers and governors know that it's business as usual. Venice and the Karamanids attempted to switch up terms on me, so I had to ensure that our alliances remained intact—that there is smooth trade and commerce."

"Um, cool, but Mehmet, I find trade and business to be pretty boring."

He laughs. "I guess so... One thing I am trying to do is write a constitution. The problem is that I start it every night, but I know I'm too tired. And writing up something so important should be done when my brain is at full capacity."

"And the problem is that your brain never is," I jokingly say.

Mehmet smirks. "That's exactly what I was gonna say."

"Don't sell yourself short. You're extremely smart. You'll be able to write a killer constitution."

"No, I won't!" he insists. "*You're* going to write an incredible constitution."

"What!" I exclaim. "You want *me* to write the constitution? I don't know enough about the Ottomans to do that! Surely, you have an expert in law who can draw this up."

"But you're learning," Mehmet replies. "You're learning about Islam and the Ottomans. A constitution needs to be perfect. It needs to be written by someone who has the time to learn and perfect it. It needs to be written by someone who isn't ignorant of the plight of the common person. Also, your perspective is different than mine, which is a good thing, and it will only make the constitution better. As for the expert... I can ask my *kadi'asker*, Ibn Hasan, to write up the constitution, but thing is, I don't know what his values are. I think I know what yours are. Anyways, he'll still go through it before it gets ratified."

"Uh... I guess I can write it up," I uneasily say. "I'm not exactly sure how you want it."

"Perfect!" he exclaims. "The constitution must, of course, be in accordance with the shariah, which is Islamic law. Of course, it has to establish the rights of minority religions, and you'll find all those answers in the traditions of Prophet Muhammad, peace and blessings be upon him. There also needs to be a way to ensure that the House of Osman maintains control, while still ensuring the empire has a fair governmental system. Finally, you need to find a solution to the line of succession problem, and it—"

"Whoa, please slow down. You expect me to do all that? Have you gone mad? I'm an eighteen-year-old who wants to be a forensic anthropologist."

"And now you're writing a constitution for a 152-year-old budding superpower!" He gets up and starts to dust off his thobe. "Crazy how life works sometimes, right?"

I shake my head as he helps me up and dusts off the dirt from Gülbahar's cloak.

"I know I can do this, Mehmet, but why me?"

"Um, let me see..." he says as we walk over to the horses. "You're incredibly smart, definitely sensible, extremely humble, and did I say remarkable? Don't worry, you won't do this alone. I'll be by your side every step of the way. We can make this a weekly thing. Meet on Sunday nights to work and relax."

I smile at him as I get on the Turkoman horse. I lower my head and joke, "Thank you, my padishah, and yes, we should make this a weekly thing."

Mehmet smiles, pulls his hair back after settling down on Snow-storm, and then shouts, "Last one to the stables is a rotten egg!"

"Hey!" I shout, as urge my horse after him.

I've got no idea how Mehmet does it, but almost all the uncertainty I was feeling is gone. He really is the oddest person ever, but I now have an objective. Something to do to wipe away my uncertainty.

I don't know how he knew I needed something like this, but I can finally be helpful.

I now have a foothold in my new world.

I must take advantage.

17. Jake

"Ah!" Demir exclaims as I drop to one knee after receiving an excruciating blow. "Take that, Deputy Commander!"

"Please, tell me, Yakub!" Baver bellows. "How were you given deputy command? You can't even best a fool like Demir!"

That dig gets all the janissary soldiers in the surrounding area laughing. It's an insult to both me and Demir.

I struggle to my feet, raise my hands, and charge.

"Oh look, everyone!" Baver shouts. "The pup gets up for some more!"

"Aah!" I shout as I throw Demir a right hook. He ducks underneath and dodges it. As soon as I miss the punch, I raise my hands to brace for contact, quickly turning to face Demir, but I'm far too late. Next thing I know, he's driven his elbow into my jaw and knocked me to the ground.

Demir turns to face the swarm of janissaries. His arms are raised in the air with a sense of triumph.

I lie flat on my back, grabbing at the left side of my jaw. I must have let out a small whimper because Baver shouts, "Look at our amazing deputy commander! Whimpering like the little pup he is!"

This leads to another round of laughter as I try to find my bearings.

"Now, now! Why do you tease a lad ten years your junior, Baver?" Arslan proclaims. "Perhaps because you can't hope to beat a man your same age."

Thank God for Arslan. I'm still not used to the janissaries' banter. Luckily, Arslan always picks up the slack.

"Damn you, Arslan!" Baver thunders. "Do I have to remind you that I'm the only man here good enough to best our *hünkar* in a duel? None of you can hope to beat me. Not in a duel! Nor in a wrestling match!"

"Okay, you oaf," Arslan says. "Show us your physical prowess by ensuring everyone completes their chores before sundown. Training is over! Is that correct, Yakub?"

I grimly nod, and everyone groans as they head towards the garrisons. Except Demir and Arslan, who kneel down next to me.

"Are you okay, Yakub?" Demir asks. "I did not mean to strike you so forcefully."

I smile. "I wouldn't have it any other way, Demir. I'm completely fine. A little humiliated, but physically fine. Continue to train hard."

"Perhaps you ought to train with some other soldiers, Yakub," Arslan suggests. "Baver, Demir, and I are the strongest of all the janissary fighters. The elite of the elite. A young lad like you should fight people who are equal to you to build confidence."

"How am I to become a better fighter if I don't fight the best?" I ask Arslan. "How am I to command the respect of my soldiers if I'm not a great warrior?"

"Remember you were picked as the deputy for your potential and brains," Arslan says. "We don't need you to become a legendary gladiator. Rather the janissaries need you to become like Khalid Ibn Al-Walid, the Sword of Islam and the greatest of military generals."

I smile as he helps me up. It's kinda funny how they want me, a

Christian, to become like a man known as the Sword of Islam, the greatest Muslim general.

"Also, all the men here respect you, including Baver," Demir states. "You talked to Titrek Sinan about giving us soldiers a pay bump. You also have the ear of the sultan. It's more than what we can ask for from the deputy commander. It's a whole hell of a lot better than what Yusef Agha has been doing. He's basically ignored us since the death of Sultan Murat, argued with the sultan over control, and left the city without informing anyone except you."

"Do you really have no idea why Yusef Agha left last night, Yakub?" Arslan asks.

I shake my head. "I wish I did. Then, at least I could explain it to our padishah."

"Ha!" Demir says. "The boy padishah probably has no knowledge of the news. All he cares about are his books and besting Baver in a duel."

"Those books are what's really gonna make this empire prosper, Demir," I argue. "Sultan Mehmet does everything with precision."

"Whatever you say, Yakub," Demir replies. "Just know that the sword is what truly builds an empire."

I shake my head and turn towards the palace.

"I need to see our padishah," I state. "Make sure the garrisons are in tiptop shape by the time I return."

"Of course, Yakub," Arslan states as he and Demir run off to catch up with Baver and the rest of the soldiers.

"*Alif-Lam-Meem-Ra. Tilka ayatu alkitab. waallathee onzila ilay-ka min rabbika alhaqqu walakinna akthara annasi la yuminoon.*"

Mehmet's soothing voice reciting the Qur'an reverberates throughout hall. The door to his study is open, so I knock, walk in, and sit on a chair by his desk. Mehmet closes the Qur'an and asks in Turkish, "How was training?"

"Good," I reply. "What were you reading? It sounded really nice."

"Don't you know how the recitation of the Qur'an sounds like at this point, Yakub?" Mehmet states.

"I mean, which verses are you reciting?" I ask. "Also, why are you calling me Yakub?"

"Because it's easier to say while speaking Turkish." He walks over to the door and closes it. "I was reading surah Ar-Ra'd, the Chapter of the Thunder. Do you want me to explain the first few verses for you?"

"Sure," I reply. "The Arabic, it was...so poetic. Gentle. Thought-provoking. The verses get me thinking. I always figured the Qur'an would be harsher."

"The Qur'an is the word of God," Mehmet responds. "It's supposed to get us thinking. This chapter is about the power of truth and the weakness of falsehood. Allah reveals this through his signs. The intricate details of the universe, like the orbit of the sun and moon or the creation of fruits in pairs, are only some of the signs in this chapter. The fourth verse says, '*Surely in this are signs for those who understand.*' Those who "understand," take the signs to believe that there is only one God, who has no equal or child. I also don't know why you would presume the Qur'an is harsh! There are verses about hell and the wrath of Allah, but it is a book of mercy. Each chapter begins with a reminder that Allah is the most compassionate, the most merciful. Each time Allah's wrath is mentioned, it is accompanied by mentioning that Allah shows mercy to those who repent. That our sins will never outweigh his mercy."

"That's pretty similar to Christianity. Although we believe that Jesus is the son of God who has saved us from our sins. We believe that God is one, but in that there is God the Father, God the son, which is Jesus Christ, and God the Holy Spirit."

"So, it's like a trifecta?" Mehmet asks. "Is that what the trinity means?"

"Yes, at least for the denomination I follow. The trinity holds that there is one God in three divine persons."

"And there is the fundamental difference between our faiths," Mehmet asserts.

"Pretty much," I say. "Aren't there a lot of verses in the Qur'an that deal with killing and war? I don't know, but I have heard that from people who argue that Islam is not a religion of peace, love, and mercy."

"Well, those people are ignorant and live with hate in their hearts." Mehmet sounds angry. "One thing you'll hear Muslims say is that Islam is a way of life. The Qur'an and the Prophet's traditions go through different aspects of life—aspects like marriage, divorce, money, economy, law, and yes, warfare. Islam has rules for defensive battle, for offensive warfare, for retributive warfare, and when to engage and disengage. These verses were revealed when conflict arose in the early Muslim community. For example, verses of defensive warfare were revealed when the idolaters launched an offensive attack against the Muslim community in Medina. Or the verse that every Islamophobe likes to quote about killing the disbelievers wherever they stand, was revealed following a betrayal by a Jewish tribe

240

in Medina, where they broke their treaty with the Prophet and supported the idolaters waging war against the Prophet. The context matters, and these verses do not make Islam a violent religion, but rather a practical religion that deals with all walks of life. Anyways, speaking of warfare, let's continue discussing our strategies, Deputy Commander of the janissaries."

"Of course." We walk over to one of Mehmet's bookshelves. "Have you decided which territory to attack? I ask.

Mehmet remains quiet as he takes out multiple maps and books. I see the map of the entire Ottoman state and its surroundings. There are maps of Sinope, Trebizond, the Karamanid Sultanate, Wallachia, Serbia, and the Byzantine lands in Greece.

He spreads them across the four desks in the study, placing books on each territory as well as diaries with our notes to the right of each map. On top of them he places our estimates on the fighting men each realm can raise in the event of an attack, as well as our estimation of the required resources to conquer them.

So, I should probably explain what's going on. Mehmet and I have been looking into every possible conquering avenue, trying to figure out what exactly happened in history and what lands we should invade. So far, we've narrowed the list to uh... the lands listed above.

"I think we should rule out Wallachia," he states. "It's going to take too much time, too many men, and too much money. They are backed by Hungary, so we'd have to deal with them as well, and it simply isn't worth the cost. If I really want a better grip on the land, I may as well back Vlad and Radu for the throne and provide them with the resources. Only thing is, Vlad simply does not have any honour. I—"

"What do you mean no honour? How would you know? You've only met him once. Is there something you know from history that I don't?"

"If the situation arises that you need to know, I'll tell you," he icily replies. "Are we ruling out Wallachia?"

I pause. Why does Mehmet hide things from me? I'm only trying to help us succeed and get home.

I clear my throat. "Yes. There is little benefit to conquering Wallachia. Both sides will suffer massive losses. There will be too much killing."

"It's war, there will always be bloodshed," he states. "It's how the world works."

"Why must we conquer lands then, Mehmet? Surely a religious man like yourself does not wish for violence or bloodshed. Religion always strives for peace, which is why you and I should champion the cause."

Mehmet sits and stares at me for a moment, as if he's looking for an answer. "You're completely right," he says. "We should not be seeking violence. Peace is what Jesus and Prophet Muhammad would strive for."

"So why must we conquer lands? Why do you want to conquer?"

Mehmet gets up and moves to the desk with the map of the Ottoman state. He picks up a diary. "It is simply because we have to."

"What do you mean by that? Surely a strong empire should maintain peace. Are we not stronger than the Sinope, Trebizond, Karamanids, Serbs, Wallachians, or Greek empires? If we want peace, who are they to deny our wish?"

"I don't know if you've forgotten, but this is the fifteenth century. The headdress on your lap should remind you of that," Mehmet states. "Look at this map, we are the dominant authority in Anatolia and Thrace. We are also a significant force in the Balkans, along with Hungary. We hold this territory and influence because of our hard work and military might. The Serbs fear our military might, which is why they don't attack us. The same goes for the Hungarians, Wallachians, and Karamanids. The second they stop fearing us, is the second they attack us.

"I highly doubt the common man cares which dynasty rules over them. All this bloodshed and warfare... it just hurts the common person."

"I totally agree with you. The average person does not care which monarch rules over them," Mehmet states. "That is why I'm not going to wage war for the simple reason of acquiring land. Rapid territorial expansion may have been cool for Genghis Khan and Alexander the Great, but what's the point if you are not creating a better world for yourself, your people, and the people in the lands we conquer? That is what I want, and I believe that is what Fatih Mehmet genuinely wanted as well."

He hands me the diary. I look down and read the words engraved on the leather cover. *"We are not going to conquer lands, but hearts."* I open the book and look at the first page. *"To fully understand history, you must experience reality from all perspectives."* This is the diary of Mehmet the Conqueror—the same lost diary that Professor Rizvi gave me in 2019, only this one isn't lost yet.

"Okay. How do we conquer hearts? It can't be by conquering a place like Serbia, Sinope, or Trebizond, where people live comfortably in peace."

"I have a goal in mind," Mehmet states. "Uniting all of Anatolia under one rule is good for all who live in the region. It makes the land more stable with free-flowing trade and commerce. While Sinope and Trebizond are formidable powers, the only other major power in Anatolia is the Karamanid Sultanate. They have attacked and raided our realm numerous times in the past few decades. The last attack was only seven years ago, when the Crusaders marched to defeat us. We crushed them, and they now pay major reparations, so there's no way the people living in the territory are happy, which means the rulers will create a scapegoat to try and maintain power."

"And you think that scapegoat will be us? You think they are going to try to attack us?"

"Perhaps," Mehmet replies. "Or they could create a scapegoat within the realm, like a minority group or political opponents. It is literally what every ruler does to gain popularity. Trump with Mexicans, Muslims, and African Americans. Stephen Harper with Muslims and the Indigenous. Hitler with Jews and every other minority. The Chinese with Uyghur Muslims. The Athenians with Socrates. In Florence, the Albizzi and the Pazzi with the Medici. The Young Turk government with the Armenians and Assyrians. I could go on, but the point is made."

"And when they do so, there will be civil unrest. That means we use it as a legal reason to take over."

"Precisely," Mehmet exclaims as he sits down, grabs a red apple from the fruit basket on his desk, and takes a bite. "Now, in the meantime, we build up our army, gather intelligence, and devise a winning strategy."

"Perhaps we ought to include Hamdan, Zaganos, and Halil in this discussion," I suggest. "Now that we're set on a particular course, the experience of Zaganos and Halil could come in handy. Hamdan is smart and creative as well."

"Yes, of course," Mehmet says. "Saad!" A young male slave walks into the room. He can't be older than we are. "Summon Hamdan Pasha and Nişancı ibn Eymen. Ensure that they arrive immediately. Also, send someone to Zaganos Pasha's estate to inform him that I require him as soon as he is able. Do the same for Halil Pasha, but say I require him immediately."

"Of course, my padishah," Saad says as he lowers his head and hurries out of the room.

"Zaganos and Halil aren't exactly in town," Mehmet states. "When you told me yesterday afternoon that Yusef Agha left town, I found out that Halil left at the same time, heading in the same direction—the city of Constantinople. I sent Zaganos after them as a sort of spy."

I slowly nod. "Okay... Why summon the Nişancı?"

"He's basically the foreign minister," Mehmet says. "His input is valuable. Now, wanna arm wrestle?"

I smirk. "You're on crack if you think you can beat me."

"Who's to say I'm not?" He puts his right elbow on the desk presenting his hand to me.

I clasp it and exclaim, "Three, Two, One, GO!"

"Aw, man!" he exclaims as I slam his arm onto the table for the fourth time in a row. "This isn't fair! You know my right arm isn't as strong as my left. You have a clear advantage."

"It's not my fault you're WEAK!" I get up and straighten out my waistcoat.

"Let's wrestle then," Mehmet suggests. "You won't dare, cause you're a coward."

"I'm the coward?" I ask. "You're the one who doesn't have the balls to stand for peace instead of violence."

"Fam, I'm just joking. I don't think you're a coward." He gets into a fighting stance. "Also, I thought we discussed this. I'm not trying to be a violent bloodthirsty ruler. I'm trying to be realistic."

He lunges to begin the fight. I swiftly dodge and take a seat. In English, I reply, "I just don't want you or me to lose sight of who we are just because we lead a different lifestyle. I feel like we could use this position to create a better world. Imagine the fifteenth-century world with a progressive forward-thinking ruler who cares about his subjects and advocates for peace."

"I get what you're tryna say, Jake. And I truly care about the people I serve. Any good ruler has to, but the truth is, every state in history looks to expand its territory. So, just shut up and fight!"

I don't know if I agree with him exactly, but I trust him. Still, if I see him step outta line, I'm gonna call him out. I'm never gonna change who I am.

"I wonder where Hamdan and Adham are," I say. "I swear, it's been almost half an hour."

Literally at that moment, the door opens and Hamdan steps inside.

"Speak in Turkish," Hamdan warns. "I heard you guys from the hall, and Adham should be here any minute. I saw him enter the palace gates on my way up here. By the way, Zaganos was with him."

"Really?" Mehmet replies in Turkish. "Hopefully, he knows about Halil and Yusef Agha's whereabouts."

Mehmet takes a seat by his desk and Saad opens the door.

"My padishah," Saad says as he completely lowers his head, "Zaganos Pasha and Nişancı Adham Ibn Eymen have arrived. Do they have your permission to enter?"

"Of course, Saad," Mehmet says. "Did I not ask you to summon them?"

"Yes, my padishah," Saad says. "I'll send them in it at once."

"Get us snacks and something to drink," Mehmet calls out as Saad leaves the room.

A second later, Zaganos and Adham walk in. Zaganos takes a seat directly across from Mehmet. Hamdan sits on the chair next to me. That leaves Adham without a chair. He takes out an ink bottle and places it on the desk with the map of the Karamanid region.

"Zaganos Pasha, please get a chair for Ibn Eymen," Mehmet says in his most authoritative voice. "He is an extremely important part of this discussion."

It's still really weird watching Mehmet act like the sultan.

"Of course, my padishah," Zaganos says. His face turns to a deep shade of red. I guess he isn't used to Mehmet bossing him around. Or perhaps he thinks getting a chair for Adham is beneath him.

Zaganos places the chair next to Adham. Adham starts to take a seat, and Mehmet asks, "Did I tell you to put it there? I didn't. Place it right next to me."

"Of course, my padishah," Zaganos states. He seems flustered with embarrassment.

He places the chair to Mehmet's left and takes his seat again. Adham smiles and takes his seat, placing his ink, pen, and parchments on the desk.

"Good," Mehmet says. "Ibn Eymen is an honourable and smart man. I value his opinion, but I don't feel like he gets a fair chance to add his perspective to the dialogue within the divan and elsewhere. Perhaps that is because Ibn Eymen does the most underappreciated work for this state. He helps everything run smoothly, but today; I'm giving him the chance to add his respected input. Now, let's begin our work."

Mehmet looks down at the desk, where the map of the Ottoman empire is laid out. On the map are our notes within a diary (in English so no one besides us and Hamdan can read them), the military fortresses throughout the realm, with the number of soldiers each fortress holds, the number of men and resources each governor has, as well as the men, coin, and other resources we can raise for a full-scale attack.

"Wait, I forgot to ask you, Zaganos Pasha, but were you able to track down Halil Pasha and Yusef Agha?" Mehmet asks.

"You wish to speak about this in front of all these people, my padishah?" Zaganos asks in reply.

"Yes," Mehmet says. "I trust everyone in this room equally. Now, please answer me."

"Halil Pasha should be returning extremely late tonight," Zaganos says. "Perhaps after the banquet at my estate. It's truly a shame he's going to miss it. He does love the food served by my cook."

"But where was he?" Mehmet asks impatiently. "That's more important information."

"He stayed in a tavern eight leagues from Constantinople," Zaganos replies.

"Doing what exactly?" Hamdan asks.

"I can't be too sure, but it seems like he was meeting Loukas Notaras."

Mehmet blankly stares at Zaganos. I wonder if he knows who Loukas Notaras is. I certainly don't.

"Why on earth is he meeting Constantine Palaiologos's Grand Duke by himself?" Adham exclaims. "He can't be conspiring with them, can he?"

"If we question Halil Pasha, he will deny it," Zaganos replies. "He's always been good friends with Notaras. Now, Halil Pasha could also have gone to the tavern to drink some alcohol and hump some wench. We all know he's a man with no morals."

"You said he'll be in the city tonight, correct?" Mehmet asks.

"That is correct, my padishah," Zaganos confirms. "Likely after the banquet at my estate being held to honour the arrival of my first wife and daughter from Manisa. You will be attending, my padishah, correct?"

"Um, yeah," Mehmet says. "As soon as Halil Pasha arrives, take a band of janissaries and bring him to my study. And how about Yusef Agha? Did you find him?"

"No, my padishah, I did not."

"Then why are you here, Zaganos Pasha?" Mehmet asks. "I asked you to track both Halil Pasha and Yusef Agha's whereabouts and return with them. It seems you've only completed a quarter of the task."

"I do have more information, my padishah," Zaganos replies. "Yusef Agha has left the capital numerous times without informing anyone in the past month. Last night was the first time we've noticed. Perhaps someone, like the deputy commander, isn't doing their job."

Why is he trying to deflect blame onto me? Although this could explain why I hardly see Yusef Agha. And why was he sitting in my room waiting for me before leaving yesterday? Is it possible Yusef Agha knows I'm not from here? Is that why he's being so secretive? Or does his contempt for the other/real Sultan Mehmet make him this way? And what's he so secretive about?

Mehmet stands and says, "The blame does not lie with Yakub, Zaganos Pasha. We don't know why Yusef Agha has been disappearing, but it is problematic. The problem lies with the informal culture this administration has. There needs to be serious reform. From now on, every governor, vizier, and administrative official needs to inform the Sultan and Grand Vizier of everything. If they leave the city, if they draft a new bill, and any other intricate detail. Ibn Eymen, ensure that you get Ibn Hasan to draft legislation that legislates this wish of mine. I also want you to draft a letter to every governor, commander, minister, and fortress, saying that if Yusef Agha arrives there, he is to be sent back to the capital immediately."

"Of course, my padishah," Adham ibn Eymen replies in his squeaky voice as he immediately starts drafting the letters.

Zaganos smiles, folds his hands, and places them behind his neck.

Mehmet starts to walk around the room, then stands at the desk with the map of the Karamanid Empire.

"And now, the real reason you all are present in my study," Mehmet states. "I wish to inform you all of my plans for territorial expansion."

250

Hamdan shuffles over to his chair. Adham drops his pen, and Zaganos' face immediately brightens.

"I wish to maintain peace with all territories that surround our borders."

WHAT! I thought Mehmet said that there is no way that he will be able to maintain peace?

I hear Zaganos mutter, "So incredibly naïve." I look at Hamdan who's smiling ear to ear. Adham immediately picks up his quill and starts to write.

"I want to build up our army and wealth, gather intelligence, and wait for the right time," Mehmet states. "I think the opportunity will present itself against the Karamanid state. The people seem miserable, and the political bureaucracy isn't addressing their quality of life.

"My padishah," Zaganos says as calmly as possible, "you're being naïve. You and I have always believed that the Ottoman sultanate must consistently expand to keep our enemies off balance. I know you have your ideals. I know you consider yourself to be a man of the people, but surely you understand there are no friends on the other side of our borders. There are the powerful and the weak. The powerful impose their authority, while the weak cower in fear. Those who pretend the world does not work this way are caught in between. They get ripped apart by the powerful until they are weak. Empires fear our military and our quick growth. They don't tolerate us out of love; they hate us and pray for our demise. They fear us. The second they stop fearing you, they'll attack."

"Hate begets hate. Violence begets violence," Mehmet declares. "Don't get me wrong, Zaganos Pasha. I will subject our enemies to my will. If the Karamanids attack, we'll crush their army and seize their lands. We will mediate any civil conflict. In the meantime, we maintain peace with Europe. I don't need another Crusade invasion."

"I respectfully disagree, my padishah," Zaganos says. "Our European neighbours will take advantage of us!

"I'd like to see them try!" Mehmet dares.

"An army invading our territory will just hurt more people," Adham points out.

"Ibn Eymen, that is why you and I must ensure peace is kept with our European neighbours," Mehmet replies. "But I really don't think we need to worry about an att—"

At that moment, we hear a sharp knock on the door.

"Ignore it!" Mehmet commands. "Now, let me present my vision for the next ten years."

The sharp beating of the door persists.

"Come in!" Mehmet growls.

In walks Saad with a tall, middle-aged man with bulky shoulders. He is well-dressed and has a long, thick, light-brown beard.

"What are you doing here, Saruca Pasha?" Zaganos asks.

Pasha? Does that mean he's a general or a high-ranking governor?

"Is everything alright?" Mehmet asks.

Saruca Pasha waits for Saad to leave. "I was sent to deliver this letter from Mahmut Pasha, my padishah."

He hands the sealed letter to Mehmet, who immediately opens it. Mehmet's face hardens as he takes a seat and glares at the letter like a hawk.

"What is it, my padishah?" Hamdan asks.

"No." He falls silent, deep in thought.

"What does the letter say, my padishah?" Adham asks.

252

"Mahmut Pasha has received intel suggesting that an army is gathering at Târgoviște, the capital of Wallachia," Mehmet answers.

JESUS...

He continues. "It will be composed of soldiers from Wallachia, Transylvania, Moldavia, Poland, and Hungary. They will march towards the port city of Varna in two weeks' time, along with a naval fleet from Moldavia. With no delay, they will be at Rumelia's border in three weeks, heading straight for Varna. If they conquer the city, they intend to use Varna as a launching pad to steal significant portions of Rumelia."

WHAT. THE. HECK.

I guess there won't be any peace now.

"Who will be heading the army?" Zaganos asks. "Will it be the Hungarian bastard, Jànos Hunyadi?"

"Not that we are aware of, Zaganos Pasha," Saruca Pasha replies. "It seems like the force will be led by Vladislav the Second."

"How large will the force be?" I ask.

"As of now, we believe the force is 20,000 strong," Saruca Pasha replies. "Of course, Mahmut Pasha and I believe that the force will be around 35,000 strong by the time it reaches our border, excluding the naval force."

Mehmet loudly curses in English, which causes everyone, particularly the non-English speakers, to stare at him.

Without realizing or even caring, Mehmet orders, "For now, we can raise the same number or perhaps more men without forcing my other governors and generals to leave their posts. Saruca Pasha, you will carry my letter back to Mahmut Pasha at first light, along with the sixty percent of the janissaries. Yakub, ensure that every soldier is ready to march. Make sure the fiercest soldiers are among the sixty percent. Ibn Eymen will write to Ali Bey and Turahan Bey for a relief force, which will arrive in time. I want Ali Bey to personally lead a large relief force, while Turahan Bey's son, Ömer, should join a smaller force. Other leaders will be sent to Varna to defend the city. I'll speak to them at your banquet, Zaganos Pasha. Also, I want you to summon Vlad and Radu, the sons of Dracul, immediately. *Inshallah*, I will speak to them following the banquet tonight. Are my orders clear?"

Everyone lowers their heads, places their right hands over their hearts, and says in unison, "Yes, my padishah."

"Now, please leave!" Mehmet exclaims. "Do what I've asked each of you to do. Time is of the essence. Use it wisely." To Zaganos, he whispers, "We can reconvene at the banquet. I need some time to think."

Zaganos turns to leave, and I turn to follow him.

Mehmet immediately grabs my shoulder. "Bring three of the most trustworthy soldiers to me. I want to see them before the banquet."

"Um, okay," I reply. "Why?"

"You'll find out soon enough. Also, I want to know if you're mentally prepared for—"

"For?" I ask.

"If Yusef Agha does not return by first light, you will be leading the janissary corps."

I vacantly stare at him. He sits back down next to Adham, and they begin strategizing.

This can't be.

I've got no battle experience.

254

And now, I've gotta command the most elite infantry corps in the world.

18. Mehmet

Slow motion.

Time is moving in slow motion.

Ever since I read that letter, each second feels like a minute, a minute feels like an hour, and an hour feels like a day.

This is a nightmare. I've got no military experience, let alone experience in military command. My highest-ranking military advisor, Halil, isn't even here, and he's potentially conspiring against me. The experienced commander of my elite infantry troops, Yusef Agha, is missing, and I have no clue as to why. Worst of all, I don't even know how this plays out in history. No book I've read had anything about an attack by the neighbouring European powers this early in Fatih Mehmet's reign. I did say to Sally last night that I could see Wallachia attempting to attack us, but I believed it was highly unlikely, and I was *utterly* wrong.

I'm going into this blind, without the historical cheat sheet I've been using.

How did the Ottomans manage to conquer Constantinople while fighting a significant military campaign two years earlier against a European kingdom? Perhaps this never happened. History could be changing due to our presence here.

Why couldn't that cursed diary of my ancestor transport us to the actual day of the conquest if it wanted us to understand it?

Anyways, lemme stop venting and start explaining what's been going on since I got that letter.

Within minutes of receiving it, I also received a letter from Mara Hatun, informing me that the Serbs had also been asked by Hungary to join the coalition. She says that Durad Brankovic has not committed but is in the process of gathering his resources just in case.

I can't have that happening, but how do I stop them from doing so? The European territories clearly wanna push out the Ottomans out. Why? Because they think we're a threat—which we clearly are. They believe they must invade or be invaded, which is the same philosophy Zaganos holds.

I guess I also hold that view. Yet, I overestimated Europe's fear of the Ottomans. They don't *truly* fear us yet. Or perhaps they do, and they weren't going to allow the sultanate to live in peace. Either way, they were never gonna allow us to focus on the east before turning back west. That's why they attack right now. They believe I'm weak and inexperienced, and they think *this* is their best chance to repel us.

Halil was right. I am seen as weak and inexperienced, and you know what? Perhaps it's an accurate assumption, but *this* is my chance to prove them wrong. If I come out a winner, I'll be able to accomplish most of what I want. If I don't, who knows if I'll ever be able to conquer Constantinople?

But how do I come out of this situation a winner? What equals a win? If we repel them, but lose valuable manpower and resources, is it truly a dub? I don't think so as it's going to take the Ottoman Empire far too long to recover and I can't have that happening.

The most important question is, what do I want? Somehow, after talking to Sally last night, I was convinced to let events develop until a practical and easy conquering avenue showed up. I wanted to walk the middle ground between peace and warfare. Perhaps that's why I feel like I've been confusing myself and others. I don't believe I can do that anymore. I need to take a side.

I must do whatever possible, including violent actions, to maintain peace with Serbia and Wallachia. I should also make peace with Hungary.

Exactly how, I don't know.

I guess Jake's words got to me.

"My padishah, my padishah, my padishah, are you still with us?" Adham Ibn Eymen's waving his hands in front of my face.

I slowly nod. "Of course. Why wouldn't I be?"

"You've been going through the maps of Rumelia and Wallachia for the last hour," Hamdan says, "without paying attention to us. Do you need help?"

"Just give me a moment."

"Of course, my padishah," Ibn Eymen affirms.

The truth is, I'm not exactly comfortable airing my opinion in front of anyone unless I know I'm right. Not in front of my ministers, nor even Hamdan. I don't want people to lose confidence in me, and I feel like that's about to happen. I don't know if I'm right, yet I have to make a quick decision.

I wish I had time to talk to Sally. I always feel like I get clarity after talking to her, and she doesn't even have to say much. But now I've kinda screwed her over. Creating a constitution for the Ottoman Empire is going to be incredibly tough. I guess I just want an excuse to talk to her regularly; perhaps that's the real reason I gave her the task.

For now, I guess I'm stuck revealing my battle plans to Ibn Eymen and Hamdan, who are gonna start to implement them.

No pressure, I guess.

"Ibn Eymen, Hamdan Pasha, come gather around this map," I order. I wait for the two. "Ibn Eymen, can I trust you not to reveal certain details of this meeting to anyone? Not to Halil Pasha, to Zaganos Pasha, not even your wife?"

"Absolutely!" he excitedly replies.

Of course he'll be loyal. My father, Sultan Murat, cemented the importance of his post, and I've expanded it to include being the official foreign minister, so he's most definitely grateful to my father and me.

"Thank you!" I exclaim. "Now, my plan is simple. We simply sue for peace with Serbia, Wallachia, and Hungary."

Ibn Eymen and Hamdan just blankly stare at me as if I've gone mad.

"What?" I ask. "Are you guys not going to ask me how?"

"No," Hamdan states.

"It is impossible, my padishah," Ibn Eymen declares. "They would never go for peace. Everyone will see it as a sign of weakness, and our enemies will pounce us."

"But what if we sue for peace from a position of strength?" I suggest.

"How on earth is that possible, my padishah?" Hamdan aggressively asks.

"Ibn Eymen, Hamdan," I say, coldly smiling about the plan formulating in my brain. "The two of you are going to save this empire."

Getting your hair cut in the late Middle Ages is really annoying.

First, the room is quite dark. The only light comes from the sun and a torch in the corner.

Second, there isn't a mirror.

Third, this Persian dude from Tabriz who's cutting my hair, doesn't have a machine to properly cut the sides of my hair, so he's using a very sharp blade and an even sharper set of scissors to trim my hair and beard, which are both growing outta control. I don't mind having longer hair, but when my curly hair gets too much to handle, it's time for a trim.

While Armin (the barber's name) cuts my hair, I try to strike up a conversation with Hamdan, who is also about to get his shoulder-length hair trimmed.

Hamdan hasn't said a word in three hours, and he's been by my side the entire time, just grunting or shaking his head to acknowledge my questions.

In English, I somberly say, "Hamdan, I'm so incredibly sorry."

He turns to me, and in English, he harshly replies, "Sorry for what exactly, Mehmet?"

I clear my throat, but before I reply, Armin interjects, and, in Farsi, asks, "Excuse me, my padishah. What language are you and Hamdan Pasha conversing in? I don't recognize it as Turkish, Arabic, Latin, Greek, or Farsi."

"Do you fluently speak all of those, Armin?" I ask in Farsi.

"Yes, I do, my padishah," he replies. "I grew up speaking Farsi and Arabic. When I moved to Bursa ten years ago, I learned Turkish and Greek. I then learned Latin for fun around the same time."

"That is an incredible feat," I exclaim. "The language we are speaking is called English. It is the language spoken by people living in the Kingdom of England, a land ruled by King Henry VI. Now, Hamdan Pasha and I learned it from an English sailor in Manisa a couple years ago. Also, may you please trim the sides a bit more? You mustn't tell anyone that Hamdan Pasha and I speak English. Perhaps one day, I may just teach you."

"Of course, my padishah," he replies.

To Hamdan, I say again, "I'm incredibly sorry for putting you in this situation."

"Then why do it, my padishah?" Hamdan asks, while sneering.

"I absolutely had to," I insist.

Hamdan falls silent.

Armin asks, "How short would you like the top of your hair, my padishah?"

"I don't want my hair to go over my ears."

Armin nods and starts to snip some of the long curls off the top of my hand.

Hamdan breaks his silence and whispers, "You broke your promise, you know."

"What promise?"

"On our way to Adrianople, the night of the failed attempt to return home, you promised you wouldn't force me to do anything I'm uncomfortable with. I am extremely uncomfortable with this upcoming mission, Mehmet."

I am silent as Armin continues to snip my hair. I don't know what to say to him, because if I did make that promise, I completely forgot about it.

"Hey, man, if you don't wanna do it, just say the word," I say. "I'm not gonna make you do anything you don't want to do."

Hamdan takes a moment to consider. "I'll do the task, but not for you. I'll do it for the Ottoman sultanate. I'll do it for the territory I now represent."

"Wait, so you're willing to risk your life for a state you're not really from? A state where you have to conceal your identity? A place where you have to live a lie to survive? Why?"

"Look around at this place, man. Look at what your ancestors have built. The streets are filled with Muslims living in near harmony with Christians and Jews," Hamdan explains. "You can hear the *ezan* calling Muslims for Isha or Fajr. The *masjids* are beautiful, and all the Muslims close their businesses and drop what they are doing to go pray *namaz*. It's honestly beautiful and it's probably brought me to an Iman high. It's lovely to live in a Muslim-majority and Islamic empire..."

"Well, it isn't entirely correct to call the Ottomans an Islamic empire," I say, interrupting him. "They're Islamic in the same sense that the French are a Christian empire. The government primarily cares about its own advancement, rather than the advancement of Islam."

"Will you shut up and let me finish, you nerdy idiot?" Hamdan mutters. "I understand that the Ottoman state isn't an ideal Muslim state. The slaves we saw last night were mistreated, and it seems like the government doesn't care. The devshirme recruitment process is horrifying, as is the fratricide law, and I'm not even getting into the fact that some commanders have committed horrific war crimes that are completely unacceptable in Islam."

"Are you going to get to the point?" I impatiently ask. Armin finishes up with my hair and starts to line up my beard.

"Yes, I am," Hamdan states. "While the Ottoman Empire has nowhere near the Islamic adherence the early Muslims had, I see the potential of an unbelievably amazing state for Muslims, Jews, Christians, as well as others from different backgrounds. You have the potential to go down in history as one of the greatest Muslim leaders after the Prophets and the initial caliphs. With you leading the Ottomans to greatness, the world can become a better place. I truly believe that."

I smile and say, "Thanks, brother. Although, there's no way I'll be greater than scholars like Imam Abu—"

"Don't get me wrong," Hamdan interrupts. "I'm scared shitless for this mission. There are a thousand ways this can go wrong. I may never see you again after tonight's banquet. I may never see my mother again after this operation, and it's all because you don't value me."

"That's not true!" I exclaim as I push Armin away from my face.

"Sorry, my padishah," Armin states in Farsi. "But I have completed the job. Are you satisfied?"

"Yeah, yeah," I say, brushing him off as he switches to cut Hamdan's hair. Switching back to English, I say, "Hamdan. I completely value you."

"If you truly did, you would send Zaganos or Halil in my stead," he replies. "But you won't because you think that they are smarter than me. The military campaigns you planned? You planned them with Jake because you think he's smarter than me. In high school, when nearly all your other friends abandoned you, who stuck by

263

you? That was me, yet you never acknowledged that either. It was all doom and gloom for you, but somehow everything was supposed to be perfect for me? Still, I never complained because I knew you did nothing wrong. But all you seemed to care about was running off to university, as if I never existed. You can be a heartless bastard at times, you know that?"

"Okay, what is this all about, man? Stuff that happened in high school?" I exclaim. "*High school*? Dude, I get that you're angry, but this is just stupid. I value you completely, *levels* above anyone else in this 1451 world."

"Then why don't you send Zaganos?"

"Because I need him with me," I angrily reply.

"More than you need your best friend?" Hamdan asks. "Your *supposed* brother?" I open my mouth to reply, but words fail me. Armin continues cutting Hamdan's hair until Hamdan raises his hand, informing him to stop. Hamdan gets up, brushes off his robe and says, "Exactly what I thought, Sultan Mehmet."

With that, he storms outta the room, with his ink-blue robes flailing behind him. He slams the door, with the echo of his last words reverberating through my brain.

19. Mehmet

A cold and heartless bastard.

The words burn my brain. Apparently, that's what I am to the people I truly care about. Clearly, I'm doing something wrong. I mean, a person doesn't just say stuff like that.

I can understand why Sally thinks I'm cold and heartless. We only knew each other for a month before we were sentenced to live here. I'm a sultan and she's basically a slave. She already said, literally over a month ago, that I should be able to use my position to get her a better life, which I haven't done. Perhaps it's out of selfishness, because I don't wanna be away from her, but I've basically abandoned her to this fate. I've kept her in the dark for a month. Hopefully, with the monumental task I've given her, she doesn't feel like she's in the dark anymore.

Ugh, even that sounds stupid. The job is so damn hard for a scholar, let alone someone who has little understanding of law, this region's history, or Islam.

With Hamdan, I don't get it, though. I realize that the task I put him up to is difficult, perhaps even life-threatening, but where is this idea about me not valuing him coming from? I don't know, and I don't get why he thinks I am a heartless bastard.

I have to find out why and make things right with him. There is no point in being sultan if I neglect those I care about most.

The door to my carriage swings open. In walks Gülbahar, wearing a lovely lavender dress with exquisite silver trimming and some fancy jewelry in her hair. She smiles and takes a seat right next to me. She tightly grasps my hand. Sally enters behind her wearing an absolutely marvellous sea green dress. She's clearly done something with her hair to make it very sleek, and I know I'm supposed to keep my gaze low, but Sally looks drop-dead gorgeous. She takes a seat across from me, and when she notices my attention, she flashes a beautiful smile right at me, rocking my whole world and giving me butterflies.

Gosh, I gotta get a hold of myself.

Gülbahar nudges me and softly murmurs, "You look extremely handsome today, Mehmet."

I smile and look down at my own clothes. I'm wearing an extremely nice aqua *mintan*, a cross between waistcoat and short jacket with gold buttons and designs. Underneath, I'm wearing a long black shirt with a matching *şalvar*, and my dagger is on my belt. On my head, I'm wearing my fanciest turban.

I look at Gülbahar, smile brightly, and say, "Thank you, my love. You look absolutely stunning yourself, Gülbahar."

She beams with delight. I turn to Sally and quickly say, "As do you, Salmana Hatun."

I give the signal for the coachman to set off. All this is very weird to me. I don't think I've truly felt like a member of high society until now. I feel as though I'm on the set of a Turkish version of *Downton Abbey* as I ride through the countryside. It's much rougher and bumpier than it seems on TV, though.

Gülbahar immediately starts talking, as she always does, and I truly do try to pay attention, but it's so difficult. My mind is preoc-

266

cupied with the looming war, Halil and Yusef Agha being missing, the rough road, and with what Hamdan said today.

I note the hint of concern that comes up in her voice every time I nod or grunt in response to whatever she's saying. Even Sally looks at me with concern.

Just as Zaganos' estate, which looks like the castle of an evil lord, enters our sight, I decide to tell them. The carriage stops and I adjust my turban and the ladies fix their dresses.

"Before we enter," I say, "I wish to let you know why I've been so quiet, Gülbahar Hatun."

She looks at me with full concern. "Okay, go on then, Mehmet."

She motions for Sally to leave, but I say, "No, please let Salmana Hatun stay. I think it's important for her to hear this since the two of you will be working together."

Sally remains seated, and I inform them of the disastrous news. Both their faces turn to shock.

"Are you going to march out to meet the enemy?"

I look at Gülbahar sadly. "No."

"Then how will we defeat the invading army, Mehmet?" she asks. "Will Mahmut Pasha lead our army, or are you sending Zaganos Pasha or Halil Pasha?"

"Mahmut Pasha will be leading the Ottoman army on the battlefield," I inform her.

"You must be the one leading the army, Mehmet. People can't see you as a coward. If Mahmut Pasha prevails, it will be seen as *his* victory, not yours. We all know you're an excellent warrior and the best commander. Now you must show that to the whole world and bring about victory for the Ottoman sultanate."

"Victory for me means that no battle takes place," I counter. "I wish to be the victor before the invaders lift a single kilij against us. The pen is my true weapon."

"What do you mean?" Sally asks.

"I seek peace, not bloodshed," I say. "I don't waste time and resources fighting a futile battle at the border. Instead, I want to resolve these disputes with my mind and my pen. I intend to sue for peace. Now, don't tell anyone I said this; the only people who know my true intentions are the two of you, Hamdan Pasha, and Nişancı Adham Ibn Eymen."

"Why tell us?" Sally asks. "Why don't you just tell your ministers and advisors?"

"Because I wish to impose peace from a position of strength," I declare. "Hamdan Pasha and Ibn Eymen are completing a task for me. If they are successful, there will be peace. For it to be official, I expect the invading leaders to come to Adrianople to sign my peace agreement, meaning that the two of you will have your work cut out for you then. For now, I will make plans with my military leaders."

"Alright," Gülbahar agrees. "Can we go in now? It's much too cold out here."

"Of course, my wife," I answer, summoning the driver to open the door to the horse-drawn carriage.

I step out in front of the gate leading into Zaganos' estate, helping Gülbahar down the steps. Sally slips out behind us.

Gülbahar grabs my hand, and strangely, I welcome it into mine, feeling comfort in its warmth as my mind immediately focuses on what's next.

Something tells me this night is about to be wild.

We walk towards the mansion in the crisp spring cold for about five more minutes. Suddenly, a friendly voice calls out, "Gülbahar

Hatun! Salmana Hatun! Mehmet!" We approach the grandiose door. "You're here!"

Gülbahar releases my hand and excitedly exclaims, "Fatma Hatun!" She runs in her dress, and she jumps to hug the woman at the front door.

So... this is my sister. She's nearly as tall as me with curly hair that's royally set down to her waist, and large eyes. She has a short, pointy nose, a smaller version of mine, and I don't want to presume, but she looks at least eight to ten years older than me. All in all, honestly, we look kinda similar, and that scares the crap outta me.

I wonder if Fatih Mehmet and her shared the same mother.

As soon as Gülbahar releases her embrace, my sister immediately wraps me up in the tightest bear hug.

"T-too tight," I grunt. Zaganos steps out of the mansion with his other wife. Her name, Sitti Nefise Hatun, pops into my head.

"Now, now, Fatma Hatun," Zaganos happily says as Nefise Hatun warmly smiles at me. "We want our beloved *hünkar* to be able to breathe."

Fatma Hatun sheepishly backs away and whispers, "Sorry... it's just that we just haven't had the chance to share words since the death of our beloved father."

"We will never go that long without speaking again, my sister," I promise. "You do look lovely tonight, Fatma."

"Now, let's go join the banquet," Nefise Hatun says.

"After you," Zaganos directs the women.

They file into the mansion, heading straight for the main area, where the banquet takes place. They are all immersed in conversation and laughter.

Zaganos and I begin to follow, but he immediately pulls me

269

back, right by a room that looks like a study. We're right next to an extremely long and steep staircase that actually looks sorta scary. The aesthetic here is very dark.

The curtain behind me ruffles, but before I can turn to look closely, Zaganos asks, "Have you come up with a plan to deal with this invasion, my padishah?"

I hesitate to answer. He adds, "I need to know before we enter the hall, my padishah. If not, it makes it difficult for me to facilitate your plan, both tonight and in the future. This is the way you and I work."

Again, I hesitate. I know full well that he wishes to eliminate the enemy, and I do not.

"Whatever I decide, you will follow, Zaganos Pasha?" I harshly say, intending it to be both a question and an order.

"Of course, my padishah," he replies. "I may question sometimes, but I will always follow. Do not ever doubt that, my padishah."

"Alright, Zaganos Pasha. I wish to sue for peace."

He starts to say something, but I hold up my hand and add, "I know it is not what you want, Zaganos Pasha, but I do have a plan that will help the Ottoman state reign supreme in the Balkans and eventually, the rest of Europe."

"And what is that, my padishah?"

"Zaganos Pasha," I say. "Hamdan and Ibn Eymen will be presenting my letter of peace to Durad Brankovic in Serbia, which he will be forced to accept. If he doesn't, he will face our wrath as we invade his kingdom. I will also provide Vlad and Radu of Wallachia the resources to attack the invading army as soon as they leave Târgoviște. The battle will take place at Silistra, and it will be the invading army's only hope for success. Mahmut Pasha will lead our force along with

Saruca Pasha, Ali Bey, and Ömer Bey, but *inshallah*, there won't be a battle if Hamdan Pasha and Ibn Eymen complete their mission—to go to enemy camp at the death of night, forcing the Hungarian leader to secretly sign a peace agreement—taking out the legs of this invasion. While all this is happening, Hamza Bey and Baltoghlu Süleyman Pasha will go to Varna to protect the city from the sea. Now, do you think I'm being stupid, or is this a solid plan?"

"The plan will succeed because we are mightier, my padishah," he reluctantly answers. "However, I will say this, if I may." I nod. "Idealists never succeed in politics; they get ripped apart and spit on by the ruthless, setting themselves up for destruction."

Is this dude really telling me that nice guys finish last?

"There is no point in my family ruling this sultanate if we don't try to be idealists, Zaganos Pasha," I say. "We must make life better for our people and for the whole world. That is our responsibility."

"I worry, my padishah, that we are only pricking the enemy," he counters. "There is no use in that. I believe we should either befriend them or crush them. There is no in-between."

"I am not willing to do either, Zaganos Pasha," I reply. "Now is absolutely not the time for that."

"Sometimes, my padishah, a man must do evil in order to bring about goodness."

"I understand," I say, "but again, now is just not the time. Now, I thought I was invited to a banquet, and I can hear the sounds of celebrations from right here."

"Of course, my padishah," he says. "The entrance to the hall is right behind this staircase. I ask you to patiently wait here so I may announce you as our guest of honour."

"Announce my presence?" I abruptly ask. "There is no need."

"You *are* gracing us with your presence, my padishah," Zaganos states. "Taking time out of your busy day to honour my family and our guests—that is deserving of a grand entrance, and you will always get that at my house."

"Thank you, Zaganos Pasha," I reluctantly say.

"Please wait here, my padishah," he orders. "Enter on my cue."

He leaves me standing there stupidly as he vanishes behind the dark staircase. A moment later, I hear him loudly saying, "Welcome, Welcome..."

I set my left foot on the first stair and start air-boxing. I can literally never sit still.

As I throw my first punch, I hear rustling from the curtain once again. Worried, I turn around to a pretty girl sneaking out from behind the curtain. She looks right around my age and is reasonably tall with dark and thick wavy hair that's beautifully set, and an olive skin tone. She's dressed in an exquisite white and gold dress. Her appearance is striking, yet it all appears effortless.

As soon as the girl realizes I'm staring directly at her, she freezes and looks right back at me at with her beautiful hazel eyes that make me want to talk to her.

Again, I absolutely need to settle myself down.

"*Assalamu alaikum*," I say. "Why were you hiding behind the curtain?"

"I'd love to talk, my padishah, but my father just finished introducing the sultan of the Ottoman empire," the girl says. "If you don't enter the room immediately, it is going to be...very awkward."

So, she is Zaganos Pasha's daughter. She does look Albanian, which is where Zaganos was recruited through the *devshirme* system.

"It would be funny if you walked through the doors instead of me," I say. "But I will save the embarrassment from your father here today."

I warmly smile at her, and she responds in kind. I then swiftly turn and walk towards the banquet hall, finding the room, taking the deepest breath, and entering. Immediately, I'm filled with awe. The room is decked out in candles, chandeliers, the grandest of carpets, curtains, paintings, and cushions. I am greeted with thunderous applause led by Zaganos. A true and proud standing ovation.

He proudly proclaims, "All hail Sultan Mehmet! The young lance that shall lead our realm to glory!"

That gets even more cheers as I am ushered down the room to sit on the largest red cushion.

As soon as I sit down, the rest of the room take their seats, with the men and women sitting separately. Immediately, I look around the room for familiar faces. I see Hamdan behind a group of men. Ibn Hasan is standing next to the sons of Dracul, Vlad the Impaler and Radu the Handsome. Standing behind Zaganos are two men I haven't met before, but my brain recognizes them as Hamza Bey and Baltoghlu Süleyman Pasha. Out of the corner of my eye, Zaganos' daughter sneaks into the back of the room, taking a seat next to Sally, who is sitting behind Fatma Hatun, Gülbahar, and Nefise Hatun.

"Now, let the fun and games begin!" Zaganos exclaims.

For the past hour or so, dancers and musicians have been performing in the centre of the room. They are primarily women, perhaps even slaves, who are inadequately dressed. They are meant to be dancing for my pleasure or in my honour or whatever.

I don't even wanna get into how much this annoys me. Look, I'm not anti-fun, as all of you probably think at this point, but this just goes against the basic Islamic principle of modesty, for both men and women. I may not be the perfect Muslim, but this outward display makes me uncomfortable.

Thankfully, Zaganos notices my uneasiness and stands to announce, "I think we've had enough music and dancing for now, so let us now turn our attention to dinner. The cooks have worked long and hard to prepare the most marvelous feast."

As he says that, servants rush into the room, placing food on low tables set up on both sides of the room. The men gather around the food on one side, reclining on comfy cushions on the ground, and the women do the same on the other side of the room. This time, maids place a barrier between the men and women.

I sit at the head of the table. To my right are Vlad and Radu. To my left are Baltoghlu Süleyman Pasha and Hamza Bey, the top Ottoman admirals. Zaganos sits opposite me, with Hamdan and Saruca Pasha right by him. Ibn Hasan, Ibn Eymen, and Sinan Çelebi also sit close to Zaganos. In between are a bunch of men I don't know. Judging by their clothing, they are mostly low-level commanders and a few businessmen.

Everyone awkwardly waits, not even attempting to go for the food at all. They are not even looking at it. I look down the table to view the options, and there is flatbread, soup, stew, meatballs, kebabs, salads, fruits, veggies, and so much more.

I look around hoping someone to take food first. I'm never one to go first. I mean, I'm young, and manners dictate allowing elders to go first. Also, going first is quite embarrassing, yet no one attempts to go for the food. I look around, finally resting my eyes on Hamdan, and he motions for me to take the food.

My lord, of course... They are all waiting for me to go first. How am I always so stupid?

I reach for the bread in front of me, breaking it into two pieces, handing a piece to Hamza Bey and another to Baltoghlu Süleyman Pasha. I pick up some more, break it into two pieces again, and hand them to Vlad and Radu.

I'm literally breaking bread with the man who refers to himself as Dracula. My mind wanders as I leer into his eyes. He has the pointiest nose and the sharpest chin, as his eyes are especially dark and sullen.

"My sultan," Hamza Bey says. "Are you alright? You appear to have lost colour."

"No," I reply. "I am completely fine. Now, *bismillah*! Let us eat!"

Everyone immediately rushes for the food on the table. Hamza Bey senses this and quickly fills up a plate and hands it right to me, saying, "You're a young man, my sultan, and a young man must eat to his full, burning the fat he gains through training and battles!"

I kindly smile at the fifty-year-old admiral and say, "Jazakallah khayr."

I start to eat, only to be disturbed by the long-haired and weirdly mustached Vlad the Impaler.

"Why have you asked us here, your excellency?" he asks in his harsh tone.

I look at his sixteen-year-old brother Radu, who also has long hair and the whisps of a mustache. I remain quiet and continue to eat. Radu amusingly smiles at my silence, knowing that it's getting to his brother.

"Ahem, ahem!" Zaganos loudly and annoyingly clears his throat. "Perhaps we ought to inform the men gathered here about the...upcoming event."

"At your behest, Zaganos Pasha," I grandly say. "Let everyone in on what's going on."

"Today we have received intel about an army approaching the borders of Rumelia, heading towards Varna," Zaganos announces. "The army is led by Vladislav of Wallachia and will be composed of several nations."

I tune out most of what he says, instead focusing on people's reactions. The merchants seem worried about how the impending conflict will impact their businesses, so they'll be very happy for a peaceful resolution. The lower-level military commanders seem eager, probably hoping for an opportunity to prove themselves and receive promotions. Perhaps they do care about defending the Ottoman sultanate as well. The admirals look very concerned. They are ill-equipped for a long siege for a port city. They are the true underdogs in a naval battle. Vlad the Impaler looks especially keen, obviously, believing that this is his chance at regaining the throne that he believes is rightfully his.

Zaganos concludes by announcing, "There is no need for concern, however. We will repel the invaders, and with the help of Allah, we will be victorious."

"Zaganos Pasha is correct," I declare. "No Ottoman subject needs to worry. The invasion will be absolutely halted."

"How exactly will that happen?" one of the low-level military commanders asks.

"It is not your place to ask," Zaganos says. "When the plan is fully developed, you will be informed."

That immediately shuts the guy up. Thankfully.

To Baltoghlu Süleyman Pasha and Hamza Bey, I whisper, "The two of you are going to have to set your ships in Varna in order to defend the city."

"By when, my padishah?" Baltoghlu Süleyman Pasha, the grand admiral, asks. "When?"

"In two weeks," I reply. "Your ships will be transporting resources into the city as well. Now, how many ships do you command?"

"Thirty in total, my padishah," Hamza Bey replies. "Only eighteen are war galleys. The rest are used for transportation."

"Is that really all the ships we have?" I ask with a hint of astonishment. I knew the Ottoman navy was small, but not that small. "Also, do the two of you command *all* the ships?"

They both look perplexed. Baltoghlu Süleyman Pasha replies. "I am the grand admiral. Hamza Bey is my deputy. Each boat has a captain, but they are all subservient to me, and yes, we really have only eighteen war galleys. Unfortunately, my padishah, we just aren't a serious naval force. The ships we have are nowhere near as good as our enemy's ships."

"I promise you I will rectify that. We will vastly improve the naval standard of the Ottoman state."

"Thank you, my padishah," Hamza Bey replies.

"What do we do for now?" Baltoghlu Süleyman Pasha asks. "Surely the enemy's fleet will be larger and more supreme than ours."

What kinda attitude is that? How can my grand admiral have such an attitude? I thought that in the Middle Ages, soldiers would die for their lands. I mean, that's what they've signed up for.

"You fight. Till your very last breath, Baltoghlu," I authoritatively say. "For Varna. For Rumelia. For the Ottoman Empire. More important, you fight for yourself, for your honour. You fight for your children that Allah has blessed you with. You fight for your women, so enemy hands will not lay a finger on them. Last but not least, you fight for your forebearers, who gave their blood so that YOU may prosper. Is that clear?"

"Yes, my padishah!" both say in unison.

"One more thing," I say. "The two of you will work together with the city guard and the janissaries to coordinate the city's defence. Mahmut Pasha will be facing the main invading force at the fortress of Silistra. Baltoghlu Süleyman Pasha, you will be leading the defence of Varna."

"It is an honour, my padishah," he says before biting off a piece of bread.

I start to eat again, but again, I'm immediately interrupted by the Dracula.

"Why have you called us here?" Vlad the Impaler asks.

"You're a smart man, Dracula," I say.

"You want us to help you stop our cousin," Vlad replies. "Why should we even raise a finger to help you? What have you ever done for the sons of the Dragon?"

Radu grabs his brother's arm as if he's tryna get him to shut up, but I smile and gracefully reply, "The fact that you peacefully live in our realm should be reason enough, Dracula. You *are* aware that your cousin requested your head on a pike upon my ascension to the throne, right?"

"Why not comply with the request?" Vlad asks.

"Well... there are a few reasons, Dracula," I answer. "The first being, your cousin didn't offer enough money. Secondly, why should I listen to a usurper? There is no need to kill a man peacefully living in my realm."

"The third reason is that you want control over Wallachia," Vlad adds. "To gain control, you must place me as Voivode of Wallachia."

"That's why he wants us to help him, Vlad," Radu says. "We help defeat Vladislav and he supports your claim as voivode. A true win-win, my brother."

"Is that right, your excellency?" Vlad inquires. "We help you in exchange for you helping me gain my rightful place?"

I quietly continue eating. Of course, these are the terms Vlad the Impaler wants. Yet, I can't promise that. If I want peace, Vladislav likely won't lose his title as voivode.

"You ought to realize that you need me more than I need you," I say. "You will help me because you wish to remain in my good graces, Vlad. You need that to live comfortably in the Ottoman state. If you remain in my good graces, I will help the sons of Dracul regain their positions in Wallachia *when* the time is right."

Vlad sits quietly a moment, looking disgruntled.

"And when is that, your grace?" Radu asks.

"Perhaps right after this battle," I answer. "Maybe a year, or a couple. I don't know exactly."

"Why not now?" Vlad asks. "Why can't you provide us with the resources to take our realm back now?"

"Like I said, Dracula, you are a smart man. I'm sure you can figure that out yourself."

"You must not be willing to sacrifice the resources," Vlad says. "It's a shame, your excellency. I've always known you as a bold man, not a cautious one."

"Trust me, Dracula," I haughtily remark. "You have no idea how bold I am."

"What do you mean?" Vlad the Impaler asks.

"How many men can the sons of the Dragon raise on short notice? A hundred each? A couple hundred? How much cavalry?"

"Within two weeks, we can raise five hundred men, your grace," Radu says.

"Half will be cavalry," Vlad adds.

"Well, I only need your cavalry," I assert. "And you must gather them within a week."

"One week?" Vlad exclaims. "But Zaganos Pasha said that Vladislav doesn't march for two weeks!"

He proclaims this so loudly that everyone at the table turns to look at him.

"Continue eating and conversing," I say. To Vlad, I whisper, "I will supply you with five hundred *akinji*, light cavalry. They are elite fighters trained to intimidate opponents before battle, to demoralise them."

"I don't need you to tell me what *akinji* are, your excellency," Vlad replies. "Why do I need them? Do you intend to use us as an advance force?"

"Precisely," I answer. "As soon as Vladislav leaves Târgoviște, you and the 700-strong cavalry forces will set upon the army, using attack-and-retreat tactics, harming them as much as possible while driving them towards the fortress of Silistra. This will force them across the Danube. At Silistra, Mahmut Pasha will be waiting for Vladislav's forces. Your cousin will have no chance at success. He will be pressured to sue for peace."

"That is certainly an...intriguing plan," Radu asserts. "Very bold. It can go wrong very quickly, but Vlad and I will succeed."

Vlad the Impaler frowns, however. "Peace?" he asks. "Why? That's not going to help me regain my rightful throne!"

"Patience, Dracula," I say. "My plan will succeed, helping both our causes."

Vlad begrudgingly says, "Okay, your excellency."

"Immediately after the feast, meet with Ibn Eymen and Hamdan, who will provide you with the details as well as a letter to give to Mahmut Pasha prior to entering Wallachia."

"Of course, your grace!" Radu eagerly says.

"Now," I exclaim. "Let's continue feasting."

The banquet continues deep into the night, as gossip, stories, business talk, politics, and games are the themes. Not going to lie, I'm having a lot of fun. Zaganos and I even dueled to please the guests. I've tried to have words with Hamdan for a while, but he keeps swerving me.

After a couple hours, I step out into the hall to get some fresh air.

I walk through the mansion, trying to find a place to relax. I walk up the staircase, closely examining everything to ensure that I remember my way back. As soon as I reach the top of the staircase, an extremely large window overlooking the estate grounds stares right back at me. I pull aside the curtains and open the window, removing my turban and placing it on the ground next to me. I stupidly stick my head out of the large window. It's a beautiful night with a light breeze striking my face and a full moon. One of my favourite things about living in this era is that I don't have to go three hours out of the city just to see a clear night sky, with all the beautiful stars that look like silver glitter on a beautiful canvas lighting up the world. I take one more deep breath before pulling my head back in, feeling completely refreshed. As I do that, a sweet voice from behind me says, "Gorgeous view, isn't it, my sultan?"

Out of surprise, I flinch, and nearly stumble onto the figure behind me. It's Zaganos Pasha's daughter, and she's standing right behind me, her hand fiddling with her white and gold dress.

"Do I scare you, my padishah?" she asks.

"Do you enjoy sneaking up on people?" I reply.

"I didn't," she says. "You're just standing right outside of my bedroom."

"Your room?" I ask. Sure enough, there is a bedroom right by the staircase. Judging by the doorway, it is a very large bedroom.

"I just thought that if the banquet is too boring for the sultan of the Ottoman state, it must be too boring for an honourable lady such as myself."

"Um...okay," I uncomfortably reply. "I really wasn't bored. I just needed a breath."

"Because it felt congested in there," she says, completing my thought. "You're absolutely correct. It really was, and I saw you were uncomfortable the whole time. You don't have to hide it."

I sheepishly nod. "What's your name?" I ask. Her name hasn't popped into my head like everyone else's.

"You really don't know?" she asks.

282

"Sorry?" I mutter, unsure what to say.

"You needn't apologize," she squeals. "We've never really spoken before. Besides, you're the sultan."

"So, are you going to tell me, or...?"

"Hatice," she answers while brightly smiling. "Sitti Hatice Hatun, if you wish to be formal."

"Okay, Sitti Hatice Hatun. I'm Mehmet."

"Yes, I know," she says. "Everyone here knows who you are."

"Oh. Yeah, that's true... I forgot," I say, smiling at her. "I guess it still doesn't feel real."

"How on earth does it not, my padishah?" Hatice asks. "You've been a prince all your life. Your father basically hand-picked you to be the sultan when you were twelve. This has always been in the cards."

I smile. "I guess... You don't have to call me padishah, sultan, or hünkar. I prefer Mehmet."

"Okay, Mehmet," she happily says. "Now, why are you so anxious?"

"The possibility of an upcoming conflict with Hungary and Wallachia." I sit down. "It weighs on me."

"It shouldn't place a burden on you; you've got nothing to lose," she says as she sits across from me.

"How do I have nothing to lose?"

"I know you don't wanna hear this, Mehmet, but no one has high expectations of you."

"What?"

"Each reign is a fresh chapter in the history of the dynasty. Each sultan authors his own chapter. Mehmet, you get to author the seventh chapter of the Ottoman dynasty. You control the story. You get the chance to write the most crucial chapter. If you don't, not one person will care, besides you, as long as you don't burn the previous six chapters."

I sit silently for a few moments. "You should know that you're a very wise woman, Hatice Hatun."

"I know I am." She smiles at me. "Now, shall we go back to the banquet?"

"Oh, yeah. Zaganos will send out a search party for us if we're gone for a moment longer."

"Yes, my father can be a bit... extreme," she giggles.

We both get up and set off quietly for the hall, limiting our noise levels to only small bits of laughter. As I re-enter the hall, I see Zaganos staring at me and Hatice, so I rush back to my red cushion, and she rushes back to Sally's side. As I sit back down on my spot, Zaganos gets up and proclaims, "Now that our honoured guest has re-joined us, it is time for the closing *dua*."

Supplication? Okay...

A man walks through the doorway with grand footsteps. He's got a long white beard and is wearing cheap clothes. The murmur throughout the room increases. Some of the whispers are angry, others are pleasant.

As he walks straight towards me, his name instantly pops into my head. I know exactly who he is. He's the old man from that strange dream I had the day after I became sultan. This is so strange.

"We're honoured to have the scholar, poet, and shaykh, Ak Shemsettin!" Zaganos proclaims. "The lala and advisor to our exceptional *hünkar*, Sultan Mehmet the Second!"

Ak Shemsettin sits next to me. In his noble voice, he grandly says, "*Assalamu alaikum*, Mehmet!"

"*Walaikum as-salaam*, oh, teacher!" I gracefully reply.

All the men gather around us, and the women gather around the back.

Ak Shemsettin throws his hands in the air and joins them in prayer.

Everyone else in the room, with the exception of Vlad, Radu, and one Jewish guest, do the same.

"Oh, Allah," AK Shemsettin exclaims, starting the *dua*.

My mind loses focus straight away, which is a bad thing, yet I can't stop thinking about how we went from scarcely dressed women dancing for the men to group supplication. The Ottoman court culture is hella weird, even for a Muslim Turkish descendant of the dynasty.

The night is still young, and I just have a weird tingling that it's about to get crazier.

20. Mehmet

"My padishah, I've received a report that Halil Pasha has re-entered the city and is resting at his estate," Zaganos whispers as everyone starts to leave. We are presently standing at the grand doors of his mansion.

I motion to Gülbahar and Sally to wait for me in the carriage that's at the bottom of the front steps. As I watch them head down, I whisper, "Detain him, and I shall speak to him tomorrow morning during the divan."

"In front of everyone?" Zaganos asks.

"Why not?"

"Talking to him privately might be the best next step, my padishah," Zaganos explains. "It provides you with a better opportunity to confront with him, without having to monitor your tone."

"Sure," I reluctantly say. "Bring him to my chambers in the palace then."

"I can bring him here if you wish, my padishah," Zaganos says. "Surely it'll be easier for you."

"Okay," I tiredly reply. "Where am I to wait for him?"

"In my study, my padishah."

He calls out to one of his maids and instructs her to guide me to his study space. I wave at the coachman, motioning for him to the ladies back to the palace. From the corner of my eye, I see Ak Shemsettin setting off with Ibn Eymen towards the palace, where I've requested he stay until further notice.

I walk back through the doors of the mansion with the maid, and she takes me straight to his study. At the top of a lengthy staircase sits Hatice, calmly reading in the candlelight. She looks down at me, so I smile and nod, and she smiles back, waving at me as I walk into the study.

Man, it's insanely dark. The maid lights three candles and two lamps, but even still, it remains dark. I'm about to ask her to light the hearth, but she leaves the room. So, I'm stuck in a very dark and creepy room by myself. What to do...

I really want to get to know Zaganos better, and I mean the person, not just the politician. Perhaps going through some of the office may help.

I walk towards the bookshelf. When I pull out various volumes, I find lots of philosophical and educational stuff, similar to what's on my bookshelves in the palace. I see the works of great thinkers like Plato, Aristotle, Cicero, Ibn Rushd, Al-Farabi, Al-Ghazali, Al-Kindi, Khayyam, Ibn Arabi, Ibn Sina, Ibn Khaldun, and Rumi, telling me is that he is a man who loves knowledge. He probably critically thinks about the world, or at least has created his view of the world through reading and understanding diverse works by great scholars on top of his personal experience.

I think Zaganos is a pessimist, which is honestly how someone might describe me. He seems to believe that if we don't try to conquer our way to becoming the most supreme empire on earth, the Ottomans will fade away, and honestly, I can understand that view.

I look at the different books until I find some stacks of papers and folios. I pull one out of the shelf and open it. The book is a diary. I'm looking at another man's diary. And…it's about me. Well not me, exactly. It is from seven years ago, so it's about Fatih Mehmet. I quickly put the diary away and look for the current one.

I take out at least eight different diaries until I find one that is dated 6 February 1451. That's the day we got here, so I open it.

Gosh, I'm acting like Joe Goldberg from that Netflix show *You*, like a full-on stalker. I swear to God I'm not a psychopath like him.

On the opening page it says, *"Sultan Murat has died, and now his son, Sultan Mehmet the Second, takes the throne. This is my chance to regain honour and create a better name for my family."*

I flip through the pages. So far, it seems to be about how he needs to help Mehmet succeed as sultan, the challenges we may face, and how to solve them. Stuff I don't really care about right now.

After a few pages, I find this: *"He seems to be grieving his father's death a lot more than I expected. Mehmet appears to be hesitant, or rather surprised, as if all of this is new to him. It's very strange. Perhaps his father's death has shaken him. It is not of concern yet, but this can't persist."*

The passage makes my heart race, so I check the date again: 20 February 1451. Two days after I officially became sultan. I breathe a sigh of relief. Okay. That makes sense. Zaganos has already voiced this opinion to me.

I keep flipping the pages. Zaganos has opinions on a range of things. He praises certain actions I've taken, like raising the salaries of the janissaries. He likes that I remain silent during divans to allow debate until I decide on what to do. He likes the way I deal with foreign ambassadors, which is by trusting Zaganos and Halil to receive them, speaking as little as possible. When I do speak, I speak authoritatively.

All this was written within the first three weeks of my reign. This is all good. It seems I am keeping the second vizier happy.

Zaganos spends the next few pages developing his conquering plan. I flip through the pages without truly reading the words until I reach a page without a lot of words that is titled 31 March 1451. Today.

I carefully read the blurb. It says, *"So far, Mehmet the Second's reign has gone smoothly. However, I have one major concern. I believe Sultan Mehmet is not the same man he was before the death of Sultan Murat."*

I let out an audible gasp and nearly drop the diary. My heart rests in my throat.

I keep reading. *"Sultan Mehmet the Second is a smart man, and that has not changed. He still knows how to deal with people. He still loves his books, and his love for Allah has not wavered. To those who don't truly know him, he may seem to be the same person. I, however, know Mehmet the Second better than anyone in this world. If I were to voice my concern to anyone else, they would brush aside my issue. They would argue that he is just like any other young man. But Mehmet the Second is not like anyone. This concern has been an issue since the sixth of February. It has been nearly two months. The sultan seems to be searching for his love of this realm. He, at times, acts like a foreigner. It is as if he's never lived in these lands. As though he doesn't truly resonate with the land. He is unsure of who he is, as if he's searching for a purpose. Finally, he seems unsure how to proceed in his new role. It is almost as if he has forgotten his lifelong training. At times, he contradicts himself as if he lacks confidence. Some of his ideas seem to have changed. He wanted to place the Ottoman Empire as the successors of Rome. His appetite for that seems to be gone. He now wants peace, which is a naïve idea that he will never achieve unless we impose our authority, which he seems unwilling to do. The Mehmet I knew two months ago had none of these problems. He was a confident man who wished to create a dynasty so strong the Romans would be jealous. He was self-assured. I don't know what's changed. All I know is that Mehmet the Second is no longer the man I knew two months ago. He is a different man. There is no question about it. I must find out what has changed."*

I shut the diary and place it on the pile under some papers. I arrange the rest of the diaries. Once I'm sure that the room looks unchanged, I sit down on a comfy cushion near the unlit hearth.

Zaganos is onto us. Well... onto me. He suspects there is something different about Fatih Mehmet. It's only a matter of time before I slip up and he finds out.

No. I can't think like that.

He won't find out. I mustn't let him.

I can't let him.

I hear movement outside the hall. I get up and walk to the window and see a band of janissaries outside. I keep my back towards the room as I look out the window as I hear people shuffle into the room. I hear the muttering and anger of Halil and some others as the footsteps stop right behind me, followed by two loud thuds.

"On your knees, you miserable wretches!" Zaganos orders.

Plural? I thought I would only be speaking with Halil.

"My padishah, I found Yusef Agha and Halil Pasha relaxing at Halil Pasha's estate," Zaganos informs me as my back is still to them.

"And is that against the law, Zaganos?" Yusef Agha nastily spits out.

"SILENCE!" I thunder as Zaganos starts to angrily snap at him. Still with my back towards the room, I roar out, "Everyone! Leave the room! That includes you, Zaganos Pasha!"

"My padishah, I a—"

I hold my hand up into a fist and bellow, "Leave!"

Zaganos falls silent, standing there for a moment before turning to leave with the soldiers.

That should be decisive enough for him.

Once I hear everyone's footsteps walk out the door, I take a deep breath and turn around. Halil and Yusef Agha are right in front of me. They're on their knees, heads lowered, so I only see their turbans. In front of them are two open bronze trunks filled to the brim with precious valuables.

"I hope this token pleases you, my padishah," Halil says.

"A-as do I, m-my-y p-padishah," Yusef Agha says in his old raspy voice.

"I'm sure the two of you would like to know why I've summoned you here like this," I say.

"Yes, we would, my padishah," Yusef Agha asserts.

"Shut up, you buffoon," Halil angrily mutters.

I smile and calmly take a seat on Zaganos' desk, absolutely leering into the eyes of the two men sitting before me. "Where have you been for the past couple of days, Halil Pasha?"

"I wa—"

"Look at me while you're speaking," I demand as the grand vizier still bows to the cold floor.

Halil looks up directly into my face. He gives this steely answer: "I was attending to some business, out of the city."

"Where exactly?"

"Kirklareli."

That town is a short distance from Adrianople. On horseback it is a half day's ride. Furthermore, it isn't towards Constantinople at all. That means Zaganos is lying. Or Halil is lying. Either way, one of my two highest-ranked advisors is lying to me.

"What possible business could you have there?" I ask. "It's a small town."

"Slaves," Halil replies. "I went to purchase slaves and workers for my business."

"Is there a slave market at Kirklareli?"

"There are slave markets all across the realm, my padishah," Halil asserts. "Perhaps you'd like to see the slaves I've purchased?"

"No, no, no." I pause. "What exactly is your business?" Somehow, I don't know the answer to my own question, which is a serious problem.

"Mining," he replies.

"Such a profitable business," I sarcastically say. "Perhaps one of the most profitable in the entire realm. *And* you're the *grand vizier* of the Ottoman Empire. What good fortune!"

"Allah has blessed me, my padishah," he exclaims.

More like your family has profited over a conflict of interest, I want to say. No, the entire family isn't corrupt. They are a political family, and the immense wealth came after. Perhaps during Sultan Murat II's reign. Çandarlı Halil Pasha is the corrupt one.

"And you, Yusef Agha?" I say. "Where have you been exactly?"

"With Halil Pasha, my *hünkar*."

A blatant lie. By the both of them. I'm sure of it. Halil didn't need to go to Kirklareli to purchase slaves, and Yusef Agha probably wasn't with him.

"You've been leaving the capital consistently for the past two months," I say. "Where have you been going?"

"To visit the young janissary recruits living across Rumelia," Yusef Agha replies.

"And this is something you do without informing anyone? Even your deputy commander?"

"Yes, my padishah."

Okay, I think I know that both of them are lying, and if I let them go, Zaganos will know for sure that Fatih Mehmet has changed. Not only that, these two will think I'm weak.

Perhaps I am.

Maybe I should just out myself as a fraud.

No. No. No.

I pace back and forth. Probably looking like a mad man. Who gives a damn? I'm about to be outed.

No. I can't be.

This isn't just about me. It's about Hamdan, my brother. It's about Jake, who's become like family. And Sally, who's my... friend, a good friend.

I can't give it up, and I can't give up our identity. I need to be decisive and harsh, but... I have no evidence to truly punish Halil Pasha or Yusef Agha.

So... what should I do? Get angry.

"The two of you came here with two chests of treasure and a

bunch of half-baked truths and you expected me to be okay with that?" I bellow, spitting in their faces out of disgust. "I AM NOT MY FATHER!"

"My padishah, by Allah, I'm telling the truth!" Halil implores.

"Perhaps," I say. "But doing things without my permission is where I draw the line. HOW COULD YOU LEAVE THE CITY WITHOUT MY PERMISSION? AND SIMPLY TO PUR-CHASE SLAVES?" Silence. "You know, I have intel suggesting something else," I add. "I was briefed earlier that neither of you were in Kirklareli."

Yusef Agha starts to protest, but Halil hisses, "Shut up, you old oaf!"

"Now you see my dilemma, gentlemen," I say in a cold, calculating voice. "My source can't bring evidence to refute your claim, and you can't bring evidence to refute his claim. Or... can you?"

They remain silent. Just as I expected.

"Really? No bill of payment, Halil Pasha? Surely buying slaves is expensive. Human life... truly priceless, isn't it?"

Again, silence.

"Okay, Halil Pasha, Yusef Agha," I say. "Since I have no proof of your dishonesty, I can't punish you for that, because I never punish anyone without a burden of proof."

Yusef Agha lets out a sigh of relief. Halil nudges him with his elbow.

"I can, and I will, punish each of you for insubordination though," I declare. Halil grimaces. "Halil Pasha, your business must be shut down or sold within the next ten days."

"My padishah, you can't just shut down the most successful mining business in the Ottoman state," Halil Pasha says. "What about the workers?"

Of course. He's really gonna hide behind his workers. Rich asshole.

"That is why you must sell your business," I repeat. "Otherwise, it becomes a crown corporation, or it shuts down and you pay all the workers who earn a wage from your own pocket."

"My padishah, the Ottoman government does not interfere with the market," Halil Pasha counters. "You are interfering with the market here, forcing a businessman to sell his business on the cheap."

"No, I am punishing a politician for a conflict of interest," I declare. "You have two choices."

"What are they, my padishah?"

I slowly pace around the room.

"You sell your mining business within the next ten days," I state, "or I strip you of your title as grand vizier. You and your family, aside from your son, Ibrahim, will be banished from this realm."

"So, my business, or my honour?"

"Precisely, Halil Pasha," I say. "As sultan, I need your cunning mind, not your wealth."

He takes a deep breath. He exhales and looks around, clearly dejected. "Okay, my padishah. I will sell my business."

"Good. Now, Yusef Agha, you must pay a fine of 3,000 *akçe* to the state."

Yusef Agha looks at me bewildered, then says reluctantly, "Of course, my padishah."

"Now, Halil Pasha, I hear you are good friends with Loukas Notaras," I say. "Is that correct?"

Halil Pasha turns icy white. "That's correct, my padishah. Why do you ask?"

"I want you to go negotiate a treaty with the grand duke of the Byzantines."

"A peace treaty? Why?"

"Zaganos Pasha will fill you in. I want a written agreement of free trade and peace between our realms. As soon as possible, you must leave Adrianople for Constantinople and get me my signed agreement."

Under his breath, Halil mutters, "Of course, my padishah."

"Yusef Agha, you will be briefed by Yakub on the present happenings," I say. "You will be marching to Sofya tomorrow morning with sixty percent of the janissaries. Understood?"

Yusef Agha places his right hand over his heart.

"Rid yourselves from my sight now. I don't want to remain in inferior company."

They immediately get up and basically bow to me, before scurrying out of the room, as I let out a huge sigh. Was all that anger an act? Or am I a ticking time bomb? I sit down on a cushion near the unlit hearth and bury my head in my hands to reflect, only to come up with no real answer.

My life is just confusion.

After about thirty minutes, the door to the room opens. I look up to see Zaganos at the doorway with cookies and juice. I walk up to him and sit on his desk. He places juice and cookies down.

I take a sip, and it's apple juice? That's literally my favourite. I gulp the rest and devour three gingerbread cookies. I wipe my mouth with my sleeve before realizing that Zaganos is just staring at me.

"What? Apple juice is my favourite."

Zaganos smiles and says, "You did well, my padishah."

"You heard all that?"

"Yes, my padishah."

"Is alienating Halil Pasha smart?" I ask. "Am I right in making him my enemy?"

"My padishah, he has always been against you. He is your true enemy."

I meekly smile.

"Stay here tonight, my *hünkar*," Zaganos asserts. "It's been a long day, and it'll be better for you to rest away from the ruckus at the palace."

"Thank you for your hospitality," I say, "but I don't want to be a burden on your family."

"That, you are not, my padishah," Zaganos says. "It is an honour and a blessing upon my household. Besides, Fatma Hatun would love to see you in the morning."

"Alright, Zaganos Pasha. Show me to my room."

I'm dressed in a black and grey sleeping robe, which is pretty comfy and dope. I usually sleep in some baggy *şalvar* and an undershirt, but this sleeping robe actually rules, as long as no one looks at me. Right now, I'm lying in bed reading the tales of Nasreddin Hodja, a very funny Turkish folk character. He apparently lived in the thirteenth century and is a real person, but these stories must be exaggerated. For some reason, he's always riding his donkey backwards.

A soft knock at the door interrupts me, so I place the book to the side and throw the covers over me. I really don't wanna talk to anyone right now.

The knocking persists, so I angrily exclaim, "Come in!"

The figure opens the door and probably walks in. With the covers still over me, I drowsily mutter, "Go away! I'm sleeping!"

"You're not, Mehmet," a sweet voice murmurs. "You're not even close to being tired."

Who on earth...?

I feel her sit at the foot of my bed, and she starts to crawl towards me

What the...

I take the covers off my face and sit up to see... Hatice? On all fours!

"What are you doing here?"

"What do you think, Mehmet?" she says as she moves closer.

"What do I think?" I repeat. "I think that you're in the wrong room."

"I'm exactly where I want to be," she says as she removes the covers creating a distance between us.

"Okay, what exactly is going on here?"

"I wish to spend the night with you," Hatice declares. "I'm here to lie with you, to be truly intimate with you."

I burst out laughing as if I'm at a Dave Chappelle comedy special, and her face turns red and she looks disgusted.

"You're joking, right?" I ask. "You don't really want to be intimate with me!"

She throws a cushion at me and mutters, "Not anymore!" She gets off my bed and turns towards the door.

"Wait!" I call out. "Please wait!"

Hatice turns her back to me.

"Please forgive me if I offended you," I say. "I'm just surprised. I mean, why would such a strong, smart, and beautiful woman show a flicker of interest in such a rubbish lad like myself?"

"You really are..." She looks at me in disgust. "A rubbish lad."

"Well, I'm a rubbish lad who is incredibly sorry for offending you, my hatun," I say with all the charm I have. I am truly disgusted at myself, but I can't afford to piss off the daughter of the second vizier.

Hatice smiles. "Don't think of yourself too highly, Mehmet. While you are a very nice and charming man, I would never have come here tonight without the direction of my father."

"What? Your father told you to lie with me tonight?"

"Uh-huh."

Of course. He wants to find out what the hell is different about me. I thought I dismissed those concerns already, but clearly I have not. He saw me enter the hall with his daughter and now he's pawning her off on me to figure out if I am truly the same man he's known. He wants to know that I, meaning Fatih Mehmet, haven't changed, but man this Ottoman court culture is so wack.

"Earth to Mehmet, earth to Mehmet," Hatice says. She waves her hand in front of me.

I blink twice. "Were you okay with your father's order?"

"I have absolutely no quarrels with it." She smiles at me. "I'm okay with it, if that's what's stopping you."

What would Fatih Mehmet do? I truly don't know. He is a reli-

299

gious man, as Zaganos explains in his diary. He talks a lot about how Allah, the Prophet, and Islam are a huge influence on his life.

Then again, he did kill a two-year-old.

"You do realize that this is morally and Islamically incorrect, right?" I ask. "Like, I would never do this, and honestly can't believe Zaganos Pasha or you would be okay with it."

"Like I said, I would never have come here without my father's insistence, Mehmet. I know it's not correct, but I also don't want to disobey my father and mother."

"You know you're allowed to politely disobey your parents if they ask you to do something wrong, like adultery," I say. "It is a major sin. I also happen to be married. To two women."

"I-I don't like to disobey my parents, my padishah," she says.

Oh crap. I think I'm patronising her.

"I apologize for my impoliteness," I say. "You may sleep here tonight, and you can tell your parents you did what they asked in the morning.

I take my pillow and slide off the bed and walk towards a corner of the room where there are a lot of cushions laid out.

"What are you doing?" she asks.

"Giving you the bed," I reply. "I can make myself a bed here with these cushions."

"You are the sultan of the Ottoman Empire. You deserve the bed. You must have it."

"The second caliph of Islam would give sermons and people would notice that his clothes were riddled with patches. Once, a Persian noble came to visit him in Madinah, demanding to see him in his palace, and that noble was directed to a tree, where Umar was sleeping."

"What's your point, Mehmet?"

"That I don't deserve the bed or wealth due to my status," I say. "The greatest men and women in the world have struggled and lived in poverty so the world can be a better place. Allah raised their status, and His love is all anyone needs."

"My father did say you were religious," she says. "Abdurrahman Ibn Awf and Osman Ibn Affan were both wealthy men that dedicated their lives to Allah. You don't have to deny yourself wealth to serve Allah. Just know that you will be questioned more on the day of judgment for it."

I smile at her as she sits down. "I know. I'm just not used to all this wealth."

"What do you mean? You've literally been a wealthy shehzade your entire life. Sultan of the Ottoman Empire at the age of twelve and governor of Manisa at the age of fourteen."

Oh crap, my fat mouth might just get my friends and me killed.

"If you don't mind me asking, how old are you?"

"You really don't know? I'm seventeen. I turn eighteen in a couple months. On the thirty-first of May."

"That's nice," I say. "My birth-"

"Your birthday is on the thirtieth of March, and you're nineteen. I know, my *hünkar*."

"Oh yeah," I sheepishly say.

"Now, I see you were reading Nasreddin Hodja, Mehmet, and I do love his stories. They brought me through childhood."

I smile at her, and we jump into a conversation about the stories, as she recounts her favourite ones, and we read them together. As we read, she interrupts me to explain the philosophy and genius behind the stories, revealing her intelligence and wisdom. We continue to do this for well over an hour, perhaps even two. We talk history, literature, and art. She insists that I read *The RIhla*, a book by the fourteenth-century Muslim explorer Ibn Battuta, recounting his travels through the Iberian Peninsula, Africa, Anatolia, and Central, Southeast, and South Asia, as well as China. He travelled more than any other explorer in history.

As the hours pass, I realize that I sorta really like Hatice, and I hate myself for having to lie to her.

"Hatice, I have to come clean to you," I say. I'm about to do the dumbest thing.

"What do you mean?" she asks.

"I've been lying to you and pretty much everyone in the sultan-ate."

"What about?" she hesitantly asks.

"I am not Mehmet ibn Murat, and I'm not the son of Sultan Murat, but rather, I am Mehmet Ibn Ahmet, or more commonly known as Mehmet Ahmet Osman."

"Okay, I believe that you have gone mad," she laughs. "Halil Pasha was literally present the day Hüma Hatun gave birth to you. There is no way she could have given birth to another man's child."

"What if I told you my mother's name isn't Hüma Hatun?" I ask. "My mother's name is Dalia Osman."

"Okay, you're delirious." She backs away from me. "We should get some sleep."

"I haven't even gotten to the crazy part, Hatice," I say with a poker face. "I am Mehmet ibn Murat's descendent, born in the year 2001, which is almost exactly 550 years from today."

She studies my face, looking extremely concerned. "You believe you're telling the truth, don't you?"

"That's because I am, Hatice," I say. "By Allah, I am not lying to you. I know the year Mehmet Ibn Murat dies. I know he will be known as Fatih to the entire world. That he will be the one to put the final nail in the coffin for the East Romans. In a few decades, the Muslims living in Al-Andalus will be kicked out by a man known as Ferdinand and a woman known as Isabella. That same year, the Europeans will discover lands that will be known as the Americas. That land has precious resources, and the European powers will fight over them, killing and destroying the lives of people native to the Americas. The Ottoman state will become the most powerful empire in the world within the next hundred years, but my family's dynasty will fall in the early 1900s, and the House of Osman will be kicked out of the realm. During the twentieth century, there will be two world wars, wiping out millions of humans. Out of the rubble of the wars, a state known as the United States of America will become the most powerful empire in the world. Humankind will take their first steps on the moon. That's right, a human being will walk on that moon you see out the window. Technology will evolve to the point where I just need to pick up a handheld device and tap a screen to be able to talk to a man on the other side of the planet. That is the world I'm from. I am from the twenty-first century."

One minute, two minutes, three minutes, four minutes, five minutes pass, and Hatice silently sits in front of me, contemplating the weight of my words. Eventually, all the sand in the hourglass behind her eventually reaches the bottom.

"Say something, Hatice," I plead. "Something please, because anything is better than this."

"I don't know why," she whispers. "But I believe your words.

Something in my head tells me you are a truthful man, speaking the truth..."

I breathe a sigh a relief.

"But why tell me, Mehmet ibn Ahmet?" she asks. "I promise to defend this secret with my life, but a secret like this is dangerous. It may get you killed. But wait, first tell me, how did you get here?"

"By accident. My friends and I came here by accident. Through a diary given to me by my teacher."

"Your friends?" she exclaims. "What diary? And what happened to Mehmet ibn Murat? I'm sorry that I have so many questions."

I smile. "The diary is in my office. As for my friends, I came with three of them. I will not reveal their identities—that is their secret to tell. As for Mehmet Ibn Murat, or Fatih Mehmet, I don't know what happened to him. All I know is that I woke up and everyone thought I was him without my appearance changing at all."

"And why tell me, Ibn Ahmet?"

"I need your help," I say. "Your father suspects there is something different about Mehmet the Second. I can't have him find out. Will you help me?"

"Why would I betray my father?"

"Because he will never have the evidence to prove I'm a fraud," I answer. "If he does accuse me, I will have no choice but to execute him. I'm sure Halil Pasha would love to see that."

Does this count as emotional manipulation, because what on earth am I doing?

"Okay, my padishah," she replies. "I agree to help you out, however, you must answer my questions."

"Ask away, Hatice Hatun."

"Tell me, if the House of Osman was thrown out of the realm, where did you live?"

"Get me pen and paper. Let me draw a map of the twenty-first-century world and tell you about a land called Canada."

21. JAKE

"Are you alright, Yakub?" Demir asks. We are all sitting in the common room after preparing for our departure. "You do look slightly pale."

"He is perfectly alright, Demir," Arslan reassures him. "He's always pale. I mean, it's in his Irish blood."

I don't even know if I'm Irish, I wanna scream.

"Well, he's a Turk now," Baver states. "But he does look paler than usual."

"You'll be fine commanding on the battlefield," Demir assures me. "The Hungarians don't stand a chance."

"You do realize that three other powers are also attacking us," Arslan points out.

"Yes," Demir replies. "The true power behind the attack, however, is the Hungarians. The fact that Vladislav of Wallachia is leading the force makes it a joke. The Hungarians are testing our sultan."

"And I'll say that the sultan's reply is genius," Arslan says. "The three of us along with Vlad, Radu, and the *akinji* will batter the army as soon as they leave Târgoviște. When the Hungarians and Vladislav eventually reach Silistra, it'll be no match for Mahmut Pasha, Yakub, Ömer Bey, and Ali Bey."

"Why are we coddling the deputy commander?" Baver angrily asks. "He should be comforting us! We have to pretend to be *akinji*.

306

The sultan has also tasked us with killing the Wallachian brothers if they show a hint of betrayal. Our task is much more difficult. I've never even ridden a horse to battle before."

"You're completely correct," I say. "I don't need you lot to worry about me, so just get some sleep."

"The three of us don't sleep the night before a military campaign," Baver says.

"Why not?"

"The excitement," Baver replies.

"The anticipation," Demir asserts.

"The tension," Arslan whispers.

"You lads enjoy battle?"

"Of course!" Baver exclaims. "We literally live for battle."

He is right, I guess...

I know that I don't. I've been sick to my stomach all day, unable to grasp the reality that I'm going to have to lead a few hundred elite fighters. Yes, the janissaries are elite, but I've only had a little over a month to train with them, so I don't know all the formations. Mehmet insists that everything will come naturally, but I just don't believe it. I just wish he didn't order my three closest janissary friends to disguise themselves in the ranks of the *akinji* to ensure that Vlad and Radu won't step outta line. They'll essentially be the true leaders of the *akinji*. I look over at the three men, who have become like blood brothers.

"Back in 1448, the battle of Kosovo," Baver states. "Amazing battle that was. Wasn't it, Yakub?"

"Uh-huh."

"Ah yes!" Arslan exclaims.

"The twentieth of October 1448 remains in my dreams to this day," Demir asserts.

"Hunyadi's shock when our army appeared out of nowhere was priceless!" Baver cries.

"He didn't think we would be ready for his attack," Arslan calmly adds. "He believed he could get 30,000 men through Serbia, while plundering it, without the sultan knowing."

"The cowards tried to attack us in the middle of the night," Baver says. "And they FAILED MISERABLY! We sent them back to the arms of their women with their heads hung in shame! Missing some very important limbs!"

The three thunder with laughter, as my mind drifts to the one person I've been thinking about all day--Priya. I desperately wanna get back to her and hug her once again.

I don't know exactly how it's going to happen. I don't know how we're gonna get back. Perhaps it has something to do with the conquest of Constantinople, but I *will* get back to her. See the dimples on her face when she smiles, the twinkle in her lovely brown eyes when she laughs, the look that nothing could ever deter her, and the genuine energy with which she carries herself.

I will see her again.

I had pushed thoughts of her and home to the back of my mind for over a month, but I simply can't anymore. I need to get back. I've been feeling sick all day because of what I might have to do to get back to her.

And what I might have to do is kill. Kill another man. *Men*, in fact. Christian men who are loyal to their realm. Along with catastrophically destroying the environment. All to defend a land I knew nothing about two months ago. I keep telling myself it's all self-defence, that I'll do it to stay alive, so I can get back to Priya, my family, and friends, but my mind just isn't getting wrapped around that. It just doesn't feel right, no matter what I tell myself.

"Yakub, why are you so quiet?" Arslan sounds like a concerned mother.

"You've been sitting like a statue all night," Demir states.

"You can't seriously be scared?" Baver asks.

Ugh... I hate how the three of them talk one by one, as if they're interrogating a prisoner.

"The only one who shall be scared is he who dares to step in front of my kilij!" I holler as arrogantly as I possibly can.

"Those bastards won't know what hit them!" Baver exclaims as the three hysterically laugh in reply.

"Yakub, you'll be an excellent commander," Demir proclaims. "The best the Ottoman dynasty has seen!"

"Perhaps you'll even rise to the office of grand vizier," Arslan asserts. "You *are* close friends with the *hünkar*, and once you prove yourself in battle, your path shall be clear."

I smile kindly at my three friends. I wanna tell them that I have no aspirations for such a high office, but before I can open my mouth, I hear an old and raspy voice from behind me. "Already looking to replace me? I've only been gone a couple days."

I quickly turn around.

Yusef Agha stands right behind me in his yellow and black robes as his untamed white beard displays the weariness of travel, and somehow, not one of us noticed his arrival.

"How long have you been listening to us, Agha?" Arslan asks.

"Long enough to hear this foolish conversation," Yusef Agha replies. "Baver, Arslan, Demir: leave. I wish to speak privately with my deputy."

The three of them start to go. "Perhaps it is best if we speak in your office, Agha?" I ask.

Yusef Agha narrows his eyes, surveying me. "Of course, deputy commander," he whispers.

My three friends sit back down, and I follow Agha back to his cozy house, which is right outside the palace grounds.

I feel like a kindergartener sent to the principal's office.

I'm sitting on a small chair, directly across from the Agha, who's sitting behind an exceptionally large desk on a grand and elevated seat, which makes him seem more menacing.

Agha's study is located in a windowless and cold section of his house. To call it a study is generous, as the only items in there are a desk, three chairs, armour, a Karabela sword hanging from the wall, a spear, and a shield.

That's really it.

There are no books, documents, pens, or paper.

The massive and angry Agha looks down at me. He hasn't stopped glowering since he snuck up on me twenty minutes ago.

These past twenty minutes have been...unpleasant.

Agha's wife steps into the cold room and sets down tea on the desk. He pours a cup of each of us and adds two spoons full of sugar into each one. He sips his.

Any time now, I wanna say.

He takes another sip. He looks directly into my eyes, narrowing his eyebrows.

He takes another sip. He keeps looking directly at me, licking his lips.

Agha takes yet another sip of tea. This time, I go for mine, taking an extremely large gulp and it's scorching hot tea.

Pro-tip, never do that. I feel as though I'm gulping fire. I wanna scream, yet I keep my mouth shut and bear the pain.

Agha quickly smiles before getting stern as he takes yet another sip.

"My Agha," I quickly say as my tongue goes numb. "Time is of the utmost importance. An invading army will be at our borders within weeks."

"I know."

Huh? "How do you know, Agha?" I ask. "Were you briefed by the *hünkar*?"

"Yes, I was," he slyly says. "Well, not exactly by him, but I did learn that you betrayed my trust."

What? "How did I do that? By informing Sultan Mehmet of your absence when he asked me to summon you?"

That's a fat lie. I pretty much ran off to snitch on him. I have no reason to keep his secret.

"I told you not to tell the sultan!" he thunders. "I am working hard to help the janissaries and the realm!"

"Is consistently abandoning the corps you are supposed to lead truly helping the realm?" I ask with as much confidence as I can muster. "The soldiers need you here to ensure they don't get complacent. They need you to represent them to the sultan. The realm needs you to keep him safe."

"Whatever I do, I do for my soldiers and the realm," he mutters. "That's the only reason I've been leaving the city. Now, answer me. Zaganos Pasha mentioned the Hungarians are trying to push us back, using the smaller realms to help. Thousands of troops led by Vladislav of Wallachia approach. Not a bad test for the sultan. What is he planning?"

"Sixty percent of the janissary troops will be marching to Sofya with Saruca Pasha," I say. "From there, Mahmut Pasha will coordinate how to distribute our force. The invading army is trying to reach Varna, but we will cut them off at Silistra, where the battle will take place."

"How can we decide the location of the battle weeks in advance?" he asks. "Vladislav hasn't even left Târgoviște."

"That's where the next part of the plan comes in," I explain. "The sons of Dracul will lead an advanced force of *akinji* into Wallachia, attacking Vladislav's army, forcing them to Silistra."

"What's to stop the sons of Dracul from betraying us? Heck, even if they don't betray us, what's to stop the invading army from transporting their main force by the Black Sea, which borders Wallachia?"

"Well, they won't. The enemy is gathering at Târgoviște, and they won't reach the coast. Vlad won't let them, and I refuse to believe he'll betray us. Even if he does, Demir, Arslan, and Baver will be with the force with orders to kill him and Radu at the first sign of betrayal."

"Then, who shall lead the force after the brothers are gone?" he demands. "See what I mean? Our *hünkar* has a lot to learn. The *akin-ji* will scatter without a leader, and Vladislav will march unimpeded to Varna, while we'll be sitting like fools at Silistra."

I remain quiet.

He's right. How did Mehmet not think of that? Perhaps he was sure of Vlad and Radu's loyalty, but I don't see why they wouldn't just support their cousin.

"Now that I'm back, you won't have to march with the corps," he adds.

"I guess I'm stuck here then?" I ask in a fake-somber tone.

"You will join Demir, Arslan, and Baver," he orders. "You will march with Vlad and Radu and take charge if, or when, they betray the Ottoman Sultanate."

No! I wanna roar, but instead, I sit in the prison-like office, as if I'd just been sentenced to death.

"You need the experience," he explains. "This is a difficult task, but the janissaries always have to do the difficult tasks."

I slowly nod.

"With so few brothers around, it is important to know what you're fighting for," Yusef Agha states. "Do you?"

I pause, but the answer is clear. I'm fighting to get home, to get to Priya. There is no question about it. Priya is my home, and I must get back to her.

Before I can say anything, Yusef Agha says, "I don't need to know what *you* personally are fighting for. While we collectively fight for the Ottoman Empire and the prosperity of Muslims and all people of the book in the land, the cause is different for every man. Just know that if what you fight for matters more than anything in the

313

universe to you, you should be willing to do anything. Is that the case for you, Yakub?"

"Definitely."

"Then I fear for the life of the man who dares to face you on the field of battle."

22. SALLY

"Salmana Hatun! Salmana Hatun! Salmana Hatun!"

I open my eyes and sit up to see the three-year-old Bayezit struggling to climb onto the bed. I help him up, while looking over to my left to find Gülbahar's side vacant. I feel the bedsheet, pillow, and covers. They're cold, so she's been gone awhile.

"Where's your mother, my shehzade? Were you up before she left?"

"She gone right now, Salmana. Gone."

"Where to?" I patiently ask.

"She gone right now."

I sigh and rub my eyes. Kids... so useless. I look at him sometimes and think, *is this kid really going to be sultan someday?*

I go over to a basin close to the bed, quickly wash up, and put on a simple blue dress. I grab Bayezit's hand and try to get him dressed, but... that is not easy. I struggle to get the three-year-old shehzade washed up. He just keeps splashing water on my face. Eventually, I prevail. After that, I try to dress him in clothes that are much too fancy for a three-year-old.

Yes, I really am jealous of a three-year-old boy.

As I try to grab him so I can wrestle him into a *şalvar*, I hear someone walk through the door. It's Gülbahar, dressed eloquently in a long pink and gold dress.

"Good, you're up," she says. "It's Friday. Before Bayezit wears that, he should bathe, and you should do the same, Salmana."

I feel my face turn a shade of pink. When she acts like my mother, it flusters me. Being told to shower by someone who is just as old as I am, is sorta weird.

I nod. "Of course, my Hatun."

"Quickly, Salmana!" she says urgently as she grabs her son. "It is nearly time for Jummah (Friday prayers) on the grounds! I can't believe you woke up so late! You ought to turn your mind away from those books!"

I lower my head and rush towards the hammam, and thankfully, it's mostly empty.

The hammam is filled with robust pillars, each with a beautiful, coloured arch, connecting to the next one. The ceiling is beautifully domed, and it seems to be accompanied by smaller domes, but I have no idea how that works. The floors are adorned with beautiful porcelain tiles, and the bath is the greatest I could ever hope to experience.

I go to a secluded corner and set my clothes down. I step into the water, comfortably sit, and breathe a sigh of relief, and I feel the drowsiness slip away. I was up late last night working. I guess that kept Gülbahar up as well.

I don't think Mehmet mentioned how hard my job would be. Instead of a constitution, I'm thinking of making a rulebook. I mean, the Ottoman Empire is an absolute monarchy. There's no point creating a constitution that would be voided as soon as Mehmet dies, or as soon as he figures out how to get us home, because hopefully, he doesn't die here.

If I create a rulebook, hopefully, Mehmet—and I mean Mehmet Osman, not Mehmet the Second, although I suppose they are the same person now—will be bound to the rules, creating precedent that other rulers will follow. The difficulty lies in the fact that I don't know the land, nor do I know its laws. I'm just a guest here, despite the fact that I feel like a permanent immigrant, so I need to be sensitive. But the thing is, how can I be culturally and religiously sensitive when I know very little about the culture, religion, or time period?

Every day this week, I've been trying to figure out why Mehmet would give me this task. Surely, he doesn't think I'm smart enough to create an excellent constitution for an empire I knew almost nothing about two months ago, and I still don't know much about it. I mean, I'm just a first-year anthro student. I did take a grade 11 law class in high school, but I mostly slept through it.

Mehmet has clearly put me on a pedestal, as someone who is great, and he shouldn't do that, because what if I mess up? Or what if I'm not who he thinks I am? He'll be disappointed. I don't ever wanna disappoint him.

Perhaps that's not a good thing, but it's just how I am.

Anyway, that's why I've been studying a bunch of books, and that's why I am—

"Salmana!" Gülbahar angrily calls out. "Ten minutes till prayer! What are you doing?"

Oh, crap, I finish washing up, dry myself off, slip into the simple blue dress, and run towards my shared quarters, so I don't risk getting yelled at again.

I understand why Gülbahar is upset. Fridays are a blessed day in Islam. Jummah, the Friday prayer, held in congregation, is the most important one of the week. All of the prayers are important, and it is highly recommended that men pray in congregation at the *masjid*, but the Jummah prayer comes in place of the *zuhr* prayer on Friday afternoons, and there is a sermon too. On top of that, Fridays are one of the few days Bayezit gets to see his father.

I enter my room to find it abandoned. Of course she left without me. I touch my hair and it's extremely wet. I look out a window to see some women walking towards the place for congregational prayer, so I grab a pretty embroidered towel type of cloth and try to dry my hair as much as possible and change into a long-sleeved, silky white dress with bronze trimmings and design that go down to my ankles. I take out a matching *hijab* and wrap it around my head to the best of my terrible abilities. I rush out, grabbing a cloak as I leave the door.

I run past the Imperial Hall, offices, the quarter-built library, the incomplete banquet hall, until I reach a half-completed side entrance.

I shudder as the cool breeze hits my body and wet hair. It probably wasn't the best idea to wear a silky dress right after the bath on a cool and cloudy morning. I reach the shaded half-built outdoor *masjid* on the palace grounds. Mehmet demanded its construction after Yusef Agha and Halil Pasha said he couldn't go to the city's *masjid* for security reasons. Because he can't go for prayer, Mehmet requests that all in the palace attend the Jummah prayer on the grounds. So, every Friday, the government officials, attendants, Muslim slaves, and women attend the Jummah at the makeshift *masjid*.

I sit in the third row of the ladies' section, which is located behind the men's section, with Gülbahar, Fatma Hatun, and the friendly daughter of Zaganos Pasha, named Hatice. As I sit down, Hatice smiles warmly at me.

"You know, I can teach you how to wear the hijab properly if you want, Salmana Hatun," she whispers. "All the different hijab styles too."

"Thank you," I reply in a hushed tone. Fatma Hatun clears her throat, glaring at us as she points towards the front, where Titrek Sinan is finishing up the *ezan*.

Ak Shemsettin gets up and starts to give his sermon. "Praise belongs to Allah, we praise Him, and we ask for guidance and forgiveness. And we seek protection in Allah from the malice of our own souls and the evil of our actions..."

My mind drifts from the sermon. I scan all the faces and there are considerably fewer men than last week, which is to be expected with a lot of the janissaries and a few ministers gone. I locate Mehmet in the first row with Bayezit dangling from his shoulders. I warmly smile before Ak Shemsettin pulls my focus by saying in his old, noble voice, "Today, his excellency, Sultan Mehmet, has asked me to speak about integrity in the face of adversity."

He smiles directly at Mehmet and Bayezit. "As Muslims, we have the greatest of examples, the greatest of role models, the greatest person that has ever, or ever will grace this beautiful planet Allah has caused to come about from nothingness—the seal of prophethood, Muhammad, peace and blessings be upon him. His whole life was filled with adversity, from being born an orphan, losing his mother and grandfather at a young age, seeing his followers persecuted by the idolaters, he himself being on the receiving end of persecution. Injustice. Yet, through it all, his integrity, his character, his faith, never wavered."

He spends the next several minutes going into some of the hardships that Prophet Muhammad and his early companions faced. Two of his stories truly stand out.

The first is the story of Belal, an Ethiopian Muslim enslaved to a noble. When his slaver found out about his acceptance of Is-

319

lam, Belal was dragged through the scorching hot and sandy streets of Mecca, with a burning hot rock on his chest and was publicly whipped. All to prove a point. His slaver promised to stop only if he renounced his new faith, but Belal did not. Nearly all Muslims, lacking earthly prestige and being impoverished, were powerless to stop the mistreatment. He kept being tortured until word finally reached Abu Bakr, the Prophet's closest companion, who rushed to purchase Belal's freedom. Eventually, Belal became the first Muslim to give the call to prayer.

The next story that sticks out is the story of the boycott of the Prophet, his clan, and the early Muslims. During the seventh year of prophethood, the Idolaters from Quraysh enforced a social and economic boycott of the Muslims, as well as the Prophet Muhammad's clan, Banu Hashim. No one was allowed to trade with them, sell anything to them, or assist them. No one was allowed to marry their sons or daughters to them. This lasted three years. In the tenth year of prophethood, the boycott finally ended. When it ended, the prophet lost his uncle, Abu Talib, who passed away a few months after the boycott, leaving the Prophet without protection to continue his preaching. A couple months following that, his wife, Khadijah, passed away. After the deaths of the two most beloved, he went to a city called Taif, seeking protection. Not only did they reject his request, but they pelted him with stones and garbage on his way out. God sent him the Angel Gabriel, known as Jibril in Islam, with the Angel of the Mountain, so that if the Prophet wills, Taif would be crushed within the mountains that surround the city. The Prophet instead prayed for the city, hoping that one day, the children of Taif would turn away from ignorance.

Ak Shemsettin summarizes the point of these two stories. "The first generation of Muslims faced incredible adversity. The Seal of Prophethood faced more anguish, misfortune, and hardship than any other man the world has ever seen. Yet, they persevered, displaying honour, courage, and integrity. Never did they resort to the tactics of their enemies. Never did they lose their character. The idolaters would plot the death of the Messenger of Allah, yet they would entrust their gold and silver with the Prophet, peace and blessings be upon him. Such was his integrity. He was the praised and the trustworthy one. The idolaters could never slam his character. Not even to the Byzantine Emperor, Heraclius. This is how we should be, brothers and sisters. When hardships come our way, we must not despair. We must not lose our character or integrity. Allah promises that after every hardship comes ease. So, brothers and sisters of Islam, if any difficulty comes your way, take the example of the greatest generation of Muslims. Persevere. I promise you; no, Allah promises, that there is light at the end of the tunnel for those of good character and faith."

He then gives a concluding supplication in Arabic, before everyone gets up to pray, standing in equal, straight rows, foot to foot, shoulder to shoulder. A Muslim congregation of prayer is truly beautiful.

The content of the sermon was so... optimistic. I may not be acting super positive these days, but that is how I strive to be. There is so much beauty, even within the struggle of this world, that there is no point focusing on the bad stuff. I know everyone has their mental health struggles, and that is not a sign of weakness, but remaining upbeat is my way of pushing through, and gosh, there have been many struggles in my life. Not nearly as many as the Prophet Muhammad, but struggles nonetheless.

My family has gone through difficult times. We nearly lost our farm, like five or six times before I was ten. When I was eleven, my father separated from my mother, not divorced, just separated, and moved to Prince Albert, Saskatchewan, a city known as the Gateway to the North, where a college buddy of his runs a uranium mining company. My mother was a mess for well over a year, and we struggled during that time, but my mom and I grew super close, so I take a silver lining out of that.

My father returned after what felt like decades, but in reality, it was only fifteen months. He and my mom got back together. He promised to visit as often as possible and send money consistently. Only problem was that my mom would get super-sad whenever he had to go back. I had to remain upbeat to keep her spirits up.

A year or so later, when I was nearly thirteen, my little sister, Rani, was born. While my mother worked, I had to take care of Rani. The next year, despite my father and mother both working their asses off, we struggled to pay the bills. Our family was forced to sell almost all our land, the stables, and our three horses. That was tough. We never wanted to let the land or the horses go. The people who purchased the land, stables, and horses, realizing how sad I was, offered me a job, saying I could buy back my horse through my work and earn some extra cash.

At fourteen, I was taking care of my sister for half the day, training horses, and maintaining the stables, on top of school, riding competitively, and being on the school soccer and archery teams.

Yeah. I work damn hard, and I worked hard when my mom suffered a stroke during grade 12. Taking care of her and my little sister, being forced to drop archery, soccer, and the equestrian teams to work two jobs, while getting killer grades to receive a scholarship to go study at Queen's.

Then all this shit happened, so yeah, the message of this sermon resonates with me. There has to be a light at the end of the tunnel for people who are truly good. There just has to be. This Islamic lesson makes a ton of sense, and I understand why so many are enamoured by the message.

But...I still don't think I believe in a Supreme Being. A God.

If there truly was a God, why would God put so many good people through hardship and struggle? I'm not talking about my family. I'm talking about how there is so much injustice and inequality in the world. Why put good people through all that?

I need these answers. I want these answers, but I don't know where I'm going to get them from.

Ak Shemsettin (finally) concludes the prayer, looking to his right and left, saying, *"As-salamu Alaikum wa rahmatullahi wa barakatu."*

Everyone behind him does the same, and the Friday prayer is complete. The men encircle Mehmet and Ak Shemsettin as they make their way to the front gates of the palace, to the Imperial Gate, where I assume a large group is gathered, as they do every Friday, trying to get their messages through to the sultan. The Imperial Gate has a platform where the sultan gives his public addresses. Mehmet also has his guards, usually Jake, and his viziers, usually Zaganos Pasha and Hamdan Pasha, collecting letters and requests directed to the Sultan.

I look around for Jake and Zaganos Pasha, knowing that Hamdan is gone completing some task for Mehmet. I find Zaganos Pasha next to Mehmet, who's swinging Bayezit around and is surrounded, as he usually is, by a ring of janissaries. I don't see Jacob at all.

"Who are you looking for?" Hatice asks.

"Um, no one..." I reply as I'm literally scanning every single janissary around Mehmet.

"Well... do you have any idea what Mehmet is going to announce to the city right now?"

"Yeah, I probably shouldn't say this yet, but since he's about to announce it, I guess it doesn't matter anymore," I accidentally say. "There is an invading army approaching these lands."

Hatice studies my face, I guess trying to figure out if I'm telling the truth. She looks away, whispering to herself.

Okay... that's weird.

Mehmet lets Bayezit go, handing him to Titrek Sinan. He steps onto the platform where he will give his address. Now that my focus is on him, I can see a slight hint of weariness, frustration, confusion, and anger on his face.

What on earth is going through his mind?

The Imperial Gate swings open, and three lines of soldiers rush out and stand guard, to ensure no one crosses into the fortress.

Mehmet begins his address. "My brothers and sisters of this blessed realm. I come to you today with news of utmost importance. So, listen to every last word that I utter." He clears his throat. "For the past few days, rumours have been swirling through the roads of Rumelia that the Ottoman army is gathering to prepare for an attack. I am here to confirm this."

A huge uproar comes from outside the gates. I can't really tell the tone of the crowd from here though.

Mehmet holds up his hand up, until everyone falls silent. He then continues passionately. "I have received news of an invading army approaching the city of Varna, where many of our brothers and

324

sisters are located. The Ottoman army advances to intercept and defeat them. By Allah's will and grace, by the time I next speak to you, the Ottoman Empire WILL HAVE VICTORY!"

The crowd again roars, this time in support, I think.

"Now, I'm sure every single one of you is worried about your safety and security," Mehmet proclaims. "No Ottoman subject will be harmed. The only ones who shall be harmed are those who bring corruption to our lands! Each of you shall carry on with your lives comfortably, but for now, the people of Varna need our support, so I ask you to support them. I will personally provide the City of Varna with 300 bags of grain, as well as other necessities! Varna needs our help. I pledge to help! I ask the same of you!"

With that, he jumps off the platform and walks back to the palace. The rest of the ministers are with the janissaries, collecting the requests and letters of the people.

I follow the women back to the harem, and they all talk about Mehmet's address. Rabiyah Hatun, a half-sister of Sultan Murat, asks Gülbahar, "Did Sultan Mehmet mention any of this to you?"

She nods.

Rabiyah Hatun asks, "Do you know of his plan for battle?

"Does he plan to march out to battle?" another woman asks.

"I do, Rabiyah Hatun," Gülbahar says. "It is a very clever plan that I am not at liberty to expose."

"And is he going to march out?" Rabiyah Hatun asks again impatiently.

Gülbahar reluctantly mutters, "No. Mahmut Pasha will command the force."

"He's a stupid boy who lacks the courage of his father!" Rabiyah Hatun proclaims. "He needs to prove his prowess in battle!"

"A coward!" another woman shouts.

"How is a coward meant to lead our realm to glory?" a third proclaims.

A few laugh, and I honestly can't believe this. Aren't most of these people related to him? Well, a few *are* enslaved to him, but I bet those he purchased and freed earlier this week would be defending him if they knew more Turkish.

I look at Gülbahar who seems unsure of what to say. Fatma Hatun is out on the palace grounds, and Hatice is silently observing the chaos. No one is here to defend him. No one but me.

Naturally, I stupidly open my mouth. "Mehmet is far from a coward! If he isn't personally marching out to lead our state's defence, there must be a very good reason!"

Everyone stares at me. I don't usually speak unless I have to, which is one of the first things Mehmet advised us to do after we awoke in Manisa.

"Salmana Hatun is right," Hatice says from behind me. "I've known Sultan Mehmet my entire life. He is a cunning man, a brave man, and my father is his favourite advisor. He must have a great reason for not marching with the army. Even the Prophet, peace and blessings be upon him, did not personally lead every battle. Nor did Abu Bakr, Umar, Osman, or Ali. Nor did Ertuğrul Ghazi, Osman Ghazi, Orhan Ghazi, Murat the First, Yıldırım Bayezit, Mehmet the First or Murat the Second."

The women start arguing over the validity of her words. To me, Hatice quietly whispers, "You don't want them to think you know Mehmet, right? Stay quiet."

I plainly stare at her in confusion as she walks over to Gülbahar. Does she know who I am? She can't know who I *truly* am, there is no way. Perhaps she thinks that Salmana Hatun, the convert Muslim girl from Scotland, wants to gain the sultan's favour.

Either way, she can't know my secret.

She can't know Mehmet's secret either.

But if she does... Gülbahar isn't far off from knowing our secret.

23. Sally

"Breathe, aim slightly above where you want it to go, keep your arm still, and calmly release the bow string with confidence."

Mehmet takes a deep breath. Well, a few, and he aims the arrow above the target I've created about twenty feet away on a tree. As he steadies his arm, he takes another deep breath.

"Good. Now, release."

He nods. His arm's quivering. I hear the snap of the bowstring, the woosh of the arrow, and a thud against the tree. It misses its mark by over a foot. I've been counting: this the twentieth arrow on this path. Only five have hit the target, none anywhere close to the bullseye.

"Gotta do better..." he mutters. He walks off to collect the arrows.

"Hey, you know this is your first time touching a bow, right?" I yell. "You're not expected to be the Green Arrow in one day. It takes time. Also, you're a natural. The fact that you're anywhere near the target after only an hour of practice is amazing."

Mehmet's hardly said a word since we met at the stables over an hour ago, not even when I mentioned that since the date is April 6, we've lived in the Ottoman Empire for exactly two months.

He goes back to his mark, rotates his shoulder, takes a breath, and cocks an arrow on his magnificent Turkish bow, which kinda looks like a U with its sides curled outward. He takes another deep breath and raises his arm to aim, before stopping to take another deep breath. He tries to steady himself, before firing the arrow at the tree, missing by a mile.

"Your arm moved!" I exclaim.

He grabs another arrow, notching it on the bow. He raises up and fires at the target without even aiming. The arrow barely grazes the tree.

He prepares another shot. Again, he quickly raises his hands.

"ENOUGH!" I shout as I take hold of his arm.

This gets his attention. He looks visibly unnerved, embarrassed, and angry. This is a side of him I've never seen, and to me, this is coming out of nowhere.

"Talk to me," I insist, still gripping his arm. "What is going on?"

He pulls his arm away. "I should be able to do this."

"What makes you say that? You have no experience. You said that yourself only an hour ago."

"You wouldn't get it..." he mumbles and turns away.

"What makes you say that?"

"Fatih Mehmet could.... Expertly, according to Zaganos Pasha."

"Okay... but you aren't him."

"You don't have to remind me..." He drops his bow and quiver and walks off to collect the arrows.

I grab the bow and sit against a tree, waiting for him to show up again. What the hell is going on in his head?

I wish I knew.

I trace my fingers across the bow. This is not like any other bow I've used. I use a mechanical one, but this is wooden. I *have* used a long bow before, but this is much shorter with its ends curled. Perhaps I'm not the ideal coach. Either way, he can't seriously expect to pick up archery in a day, but he seems to think he can, and I have no idea why.

Also, what is with his attitude today?

I close my eyes and think back to the day I met him. He was awkward to say the least, almost like he didn't know what to say or do. Pretty nervous as well. Super lovely, though, and polite almost to a fault. He's handsome with those dark eyes and fluffy hair. Most importantly, he made me feel comfortable, and over time, I've realized he is calm and collected, even if he can be a bit awkward. He has a lot of confidence even if he hasn't realized that himself, and I truly like being with him; he always makes me feel better.

But there is clearly more to him, and I want to know that part of him. I want to know why he's been so... off-colour tonight. I understand that there is an impending conflict, but this is something else.

I get up and walk to the mark where Mehmet was shooting from, looking around for him. It's very dark in these woods, and there is no sign of him.

Strange.

The target's only twenty feet away. The arrows can't be that far.

"MEHMET!" I shout. "Are you out there?"

No reply.

Strapping the quiver to my back and picking up the bow, I take a few steps forward and again call out his name.

I look back at Snowstorm and the light-brown Turkoman stallion and say to them, "I'll be back in a minute."

I reach the target on the tree and look around everywhere, but he just isn't here. I walk past that tree into the forest.

Okay, it's seriously dark, so I understand if he's lost.

After walking a bit, I hear a crackle a short distance in front of me.

"Mehmet?"

No reply.

I pull an arrow from my quiver and notch it on the bow. I take a few more steps, when I see a figure walking right towards me.

I raise my arms, directly aiming at the person. "Is that you, Mehmet?" I ask.

The figure continues walking straight towards me. In Turkish, I desperately say, "I'm armed, and I will shoot!"

The figure steps closer and laughs. "It's a good thing you didn't!" Mehmet says in English. "Worst-case scenario, I'd be dead. Best-case scenario, you hurt me, so I execute you for an assassination attempt. Well, best case for me."

He tosses the arrows at me.

I don't even try to catch them.

"What the hell is wrong with you?" I exclaim. "Why didn't you respond to my shouting? What is going on with you today?"

"I didn't hear you." He replies. He grabs the arrows, and we start to walk towards the horses. "I'm just tired and frustrated. I feel like I should be able to fire an arrow from twenty feet and hit my target."

"Okay," I reluctantly say, fully knowing that there is more behind that frustration. "Your stance is perfect. Your arm is just wavering as you release. You're frustrated, so just calm down and you'll be all right."

We reach the mark where he was practicing. I walk over to Snowstorm. I tenderly pet him on the neck, just behind his ears. Snowstorm softly neighs and I look over at Mehmet, who's warmly smiling at us.

"Go ahead," I say. "Take another shot, but this time be confident, steady your arm, breathe, and smoothly release."

He stands firmly at the top of the mark. He looks back me, so I nod. He stares directly at the target, raising his arms, trying to steady them. He takes a deep breath. He takes another one, yet his right arm, the one holding the front of the bow, keeps shaking. I walk up behind him. Gently, I grab hold of his arm and steady it.

"You got this," I whisper. "I know you do."

I take a step back. Mehmet looks at the target intensely, aims slightly above the bullseye. I hear him take a deep breath, then whisper "*bismillah*." He confidently releases. I hear the snap of the bowstring, the whoosh of the arrow through the air, and a thud as it hits the bullseye.

"YEAH!!" I shout as he lets out a sigh of relief.

"I knew you could do it," I say. "Really lame celly, though."

"This is practice. I don't celly during practice. It's just practice."

"Okay, Mr. Serious. Lighten up."

He shakes his head. "You're missing the joke." He slings his bow onto his shoulder and walks over to Snowstorm. He takes a metal flask out of a cloth handbag. He then walks over to the tree and sits at the base, gulping down water.

"We haven't talked about the constitution," he says, looking up at me.

"We haven't talked about anything." I go over and sit right next to him. "Why is that? I can't imagine that we exhausted all possible conversations last week, so why have you been so quiet? What is frustrating you?"

"Well... truthfully, a lot of things," he says. "But I don't wanna bore you. Honestly, I'm probably just in my own head."

"Hamdan being away probably hurts, huh?"

"Yeah, it does..." he admits.

"At least you've got Jacob and I."

"Jake's gone too..."

"WHAT? No wonder he wasn't next to you during the public address."

"Yeah... he's gone with an advance force I sent to Wallachia," Mehmet says. "Of course, I didn't mean to send *him*. That was all Yusef Agha's doing. Bastard wants revenge, I'm sure of it. Don't get me started on the public address."

"Jacob will be fine, right?"

"He should be," Mehmet states. "He's fully trained with a sword and bow, but if Vlad is smart, he'll completely avoid hand-to-hand combat."

"Who's Vlad?"

"Don't worry about it," Mehmet replies. "He shouldn't concern you."

"Okay, fine. Now tell me, what was wrong with the public address?"

"It was a total debacle. So, Zaganos never wanted me to announce that an invading army was approaching. He thought people would just get riled up, which wouldn't do anyone any good. But I did it anyways. I mean, I want my government to at least feign transparency."

"That's a good thing, right?" I ask. "Transparency?"

"I thought it so, and I still do," Mehmet says, "but all my speech did was make everyone anxious and angry. The people are scared, even more than when war was only a rumour. I've been hearing more reports of violence around town, theft and other crimes. There are brawls between Muslims and Christians. The janissaries are not doing anything to address the unrest, turning a blind eye. It's frustrating that people won't just get along. I sent out a statement today strongly condemning the inter-religious violence. The whole reason I ordered the imams to give sermons about integrity and honour in the face of adversity was to avoid this. Christianity isn't the enemy for Muslims, no matter how many Crusades try to pass through. This is all about power. Hungary and Wallachia just want more control. You know, it's just like Thomas Hobbes wrote when he talked about 'the general inclination of all mankind' as a 'perpetual and restless desire of power after power' that only ends in death. That's what's frustrating me. Well... at least one of the things."

"This isn't your fault," I say, looking around to make sure no one spots us. "Transparency gives people confidence in the government, right? Your intentions are good."

"Yes, but Sally, everything that happens under my command is *my* responsibility. The good and the bad."

"Perhaps you're overestimating your significance, Mehmet."

"Maybe," he says. "But every single matter of this sultanate is my responsibility. That's the reality I have to deal with."

"That's just piling on a lotta unneeded stress."

"This is what I'm signed up for. A great ruler walks on eggshells, making sure their people feel no harm while they try to create a better world for everybody. There's just a lot of pressure for me to lead the army against the Hungarian-Wallachian alliance. Zaganos says that since we riled up my subjects, they don't care to see peace. They want to see those that threaten to harm them dead. Honestly, I get that. But shouldn't I strive for peace?" Mehmet rubs his eyes and runs his hands through his hair.

"You should do exactly what you believe is right. But compromise could work too, right?"

"Yeah, well that's what I'm doing," Mehmet says. "I'm not personally marching out to battle, but a messenger is departing for Sofya tomorrow with a message for a force coming from Thessaly, headed by Ahmet Bey. Hamdan was supposed to take over for him and head to Silistra, but Ahmet Bey will now take that force, cross the Danube, and spread chaos in Wallachia, capturing as many towns as possible, while Hamdan and Ibn Eymen join the army at Silistra. This also means that Hamdan's threat of invading Serbia, if the Serbs join the Hungarians, will now be an empty one."

"That's, um, going to kill a lot of people. What happened to feeling responsible over the suffering of people?"

"Zaganos Pasha says I need leverage to guarantee peace, and honestly, I think he's right," Mehmet says. "Don't worry, If Ahmet Bey doesn't follow the Islamic rules of warfare, I *will* severely punish him."

"What are the Islamic rules for battle?"

"Basically, don't harm anyone or anything except for the army swinging their swords at you," Mehmet replies. "Treat everyone with respect, including prisoners."

I shake my head and mumble, "I'm not comfortable with this..."

"Neither am I, Sally, but what choice do I have?"

I fall silent for a moment. I don't know the options. I don't know the exact situation. I shake my head. "Do what you must, but get us back home without losing your soul, please."

He slowly nods. "Do you want to talk about the constitution now, or shall save that for some other time?"

"Now."

"Okay, Miss Constitutional Lawyer, what's going on with the constitution?"

"Never call me that. Ever. It's so *unbelievably* cringe."

"But I like being cringe!" Mehmet objects.

"Shut up!" I exclaim. "Now, your constitution will actually be rulebook. In fact, I don't think your ancestor even created a constitution."

"Um.... why so?"

"This is an absolute monarchy," I reply. "I can create a constitution, but there's no way for you to entrench it. Your sons can easily disregard it and strip it of its power. That's why it only makes sense to create a rulebook. I think that's what Mehmet the Conqueror did."

"You mean Bayezit and Mustafa? I'm sure if I sign it, it will be entrenched."

"Come on, Mehmet, you know that's not true," I say. "Take the Magna Carta as an example. It was signed by King John, but no one took any heed to it. Eventually, the Pope just annulled most of it."

"Okay... you're right, but I don't have angry, wealthy, and powerful barons to force me to sign anything."

"That's not true. The Magna Carta was voided after a civil war between the King and the barons. You have no one to out-and-out challenge you."

Mehmet shakes his head. "Çandarlı Halil Pasha has influence that rivals me."

"But he wouldn't confront you, right?"

"Not to my face, but he can raise easily raise opposition against me if I completely go against the interests of the influential men of this realm," Mehmet says. "Halil can gather some influential men and go to my cousin Orhan, who will have the backing of Constantinople, and they will rise up against me. If they get the janissaries to rebel, my fate is sealed. Fatih Mehmet works to erase all that during his reign, ensuring that people are extremely loyal to him, eliminating the influence of other noble families, executing anyone who stands against him and the imperial family."

"Uhhh," I say, "eliminating all rivals is an awful thing to do. A good government needs those checks and balances. That's the whole reason why democracy is so good."

"Yes and no..." Mehmet hesitantly replies.

"What do you mean?"

"If I were to say this in the twenty-first century, I'd be crucified. You can completely disagree with me if you want," Mehmet uneasily says. "The truth is that an absolute monarchy has the most potential of any governmental system. It has an exceptionally low floor, I mean, quite easily the lowest possible floor, but the highest possible ceiling."

"You're joking, right?" I laugh. "A monarchy better than a democracy?"

"It's not, but no system is perfect," Mehmet says. "The only true democracy is a direct democracy like the Athenians had, and that functioned too slowly and was littered with inequality. The one used across the twenty-first-century world is indirect. In Canada and the U.S., administrations get elected, even without a majority. In the U.S., the Senate, the House, and the presidency are always at odds with each other. In Canada, while there is a separation of governments, through convention, all power rests with the political cabinets across the country, which most Canadians don't even vote for in a majority government situation. That's basically elected oligarchies. While these indirect democracies pride themselves on freedom of speech, expression, and religion, the system just works best for the majority, and while minorities have a greater chance to fight for their rights, the system still works against them."

"Yes, but in an absolute monarchy, the monarch only works for himself," I point out. "An indirect democracy still works better than that."

"Yes, and I agree that a selfish absolute monarchy fails," Mehmet replies. "But if there was a good and just monarch who truly cares about his people, followed by successive reigns of other good and just monarchs, that empire would be amazing. Efficiency is important, and an absolute monarchy with a good line of monarchs has that. Democracy, as J. Cole says, is too effin slow. Good and just monarchs would allow the freedom of speech, expression, and religion that democracy prides itself on. At the very least, it is a utopia for the majority. In a world riddled with warfare and disease, an absolute monarchy works better than democracy. Perhaps a rulebook is what Fatih Mehmet created. You will ensure it lays down guidelines for a good and just absolute monarch."

He gets up and walks over to the mark. He cocks an arrow on the bow, I watch him breathe, raise his arms, aim slightly above the bullseye. He takes another inhale, mutters "*bismillah*," steadies his arm. I hear the snap of the bowstring, the whoosh of the arrow, and the thud. Bullseye for the second time in a row.

He proudly looks back at me.

Unbelievable.

"In the twenty-first century, would you prefer a government like the one Canada has, or an absolute monarchy like the one you envision for the Ottoman Empire?"

"For now, I prefer the absolute monarchy," he replies. "You know, it'd be jokes to see Trump and the American government, which is so heavily divided and decentralized, handle a war, plague or epidemic. In the twenty-first-century world, I'd like to see an improved democracy that actually listens to people and isn't systemically unjust. Think of it like this: in 2019, people want the government to pay for education, healthcare, employment insurance, and more stuff. These are all good things. Investing in people is the best way to grow your economy. But these things raise taxes. Taxes that I'm willing to pay, if the democratically elected government uses them correctly to assist us. In 1451, people want the government to guarantee protection and leave them alone, with minimal taxes. That is why an absolute monarchy works best here."

"So you want me to create a rulebook that will make you an absolute monarch?"

"I'm already a monarch." He lines up another arrow on his bow. "Your rulebook should make it clear that no other political family gets in the way of mine. It must assert the power of my family, making our power absolute. I want to be able to yell, 'I am the state!' just like Louis XIV."

He fires. This time, he misses by half a foot.

"Darn it!"

"Mehmet, you should know that I don't agree with this view at all," I say. "I don't think all power should reside with the monarch, even in the year 1451."

"We've already talked about this," he says. "Last week, I said the Ottoman dynasty must reign supreme. No. Matter. What."

"I didn't agree with you then either," I mumble. "I probably should have said something."

"You trust me, right?"

After what I've seen today, I don't know, I wanna say. I've seen a person who gets easily frustrated when things don't go his way.

Honestly, all of us are struggling, so I guess we're all prone to frustration and stress.

"Yes, I do. One hundred percent, I do."

He smiles ear to ear. He turns around, takes a deep breath, stares intently at the bullseye, takes another breath, raises his arms, aims slightly above the bullseye, perfects his stance, takes another breath, steadies his arm, mutters "*bismillah*," and fires.

I hear the snap of the bowstring, the whoosh of the arrow, and the thud hitting the centre of the bullseye.

Two hours later, I enter the harem.

Mehmet and I spent the last two hours talking about every single topic imaginable while he practiced his archery. However, he wouldn't talk about what's frustrating him outside of the war.

Now that I think about it like that, this situation is a lot for any man to deal with. Perhaps *I'm* the one placing him on an unrealistic pedestal. A pedestal that he will likely trip and fall from.

As I walk past a pool, I wave at a few of the female slaves who were freed by Mehmet last week. I don't know their names yet; I've been spending too much time with my nose in a book.

I tiptoe into the room I share with Gülbahar, expecting her to be asleep.

She isn't.

She's staring right at me, with the bedside medieval lamp and the hearth lighting up the room.

She looks like a mother who's caught her daughter sneaking back into the house at 4 in the morning.

"My hatun," I brightly say, "I didn't expect you to be awake. Did I disturb you?"

"Where have you been?" she demands. "I was ten minutes from sounding the alarm and waking Mehmet. None of the attendants even knew where you were."

"I-I just went for a walk, my hatun."

"Where?" she fiercely asks.

"In the woods near the palace."

"This late at night!" Gülbahar exclaims. "By yourself? Are you crazy? That isn't safe! You could have been lost! Or worse, with all the violence that has been occurring since the public announcement!"

"Walking in the woods reminds me of home," I lie. "I like to do it by myself. It's refreshing."

She studies my face, as if she thinks I'm lying.

"Next time, go with me or don't go at all," she declares.

"Of course, my hatun."

With that, she pulls up the bed covers.

Does she know that I'm lying to her?

That is truly a million-dollar question.

24. Hamdan

"May you be as eloquent as Ja'far Ibn Abi Talib."

These are the final words my best friend uttered before sending me off to die. That was nearly two weeks ago. I think today is the 12th of April. I'm not exactly sure. We've been travelling nonstop for days, going through the rough terrain of the Balkans. We *are* using all possible roads and pathways through Bulgaria and Serbia, but travel has still been tough.

After leaving Adrianople on the first of the month, we arrived in Sofya on the 5th. There, Adham Ibn Eymen and I switched horses to increase our speed, gathered food, and stayed the night. That was our first night of proper rest on this trip. All other stops were only to eat, nap, pray, and piss in the forest. On the 8th, we arrived in Niš, Serbia, and repeated the same process, but...the only problem was that Ibn Eymen fell ill, forcing us to stay in Niš until the next day. We set out on the 10th, hoping to make up speed, however, with the persistent rain, our progress has been slow. I've actually lost track of time with the consistent slow riding and Ibn Eymen constantly rambling about the surroundings, history, his family, and personal life. I do think we are close to Durad Brankovic's stronghold, though.

My body is aching, but my mind has been in overdrive, thinking about so many things. The main thought going through my head? My last words to my loved ones. The last thing my mother said to me was so simple. It was just a shout of "Go, Leafs!" as I walked out the door. I didn't even bother to reply. I wish I had said something, but it's too late now. I'll probably never see her again. The last thing my father said to me was pretty typical. He told me to clean out the shed before I left for Kingston. I didn't want to, but I did anyways. I woke up at Fajr and cleaned the shed after the dawn prayer. My father always forced me to work hard, and honestly, I'm grateful for it. I may be super-skinny, but I'm tough as nails. I think this journey has proven it. I pray he remembers me well. I can't remember what my older sister last said to me. It probably was some variation of, "Stop being so annoying, Hamdan! I'm on the phone!" My little sister...I have no idea what we last talked about. Probably something to do with me not liking her daily TikToks, as if she really is going to become an influencer. I'm not even trying to remember what I last said to my friends back home. It was probably some stupid crap about soccer or school. I had so many friends just two months ago, but I honestly don't even miss them. Maybe I'm heartless, or perhaps my longing for my family is just overwhelming.

Now, Mehmet came to visit right after Fajr on the first of April, right as we were setting out from my estate. I pretty much ignored him, so he mostly spoke with Ibn Eymen. As I finished tying up our (very light) supplies, Mehmet patted me on shoulder and whispered the words, "May you be as eloquent as Ja'far Ibn Abi Talib." He walked away without even saying goodbye.

Those words are stuck in my head.

Truly ingrained.

Does Mehmet think I can be eloquent, even in the same stratosphere as Ja'far ibn Abi Talib?

Lemme explain this the best I can... I'm not some Islamic history buff, but Mehmet's knowledge has rubbed off on me.

Ja'far ibn Abi Talib was an early Muslim convert. He's one of Mehmet's favourite Islamic figures. Ja'far fled to Abyssinia, which is modern-day Ethiopia, along with a band of other early Muslims, due to the persecution faced by Muslims in Makkah. After the Muslims were granted refuge, the idolaters from Makkah, who were trade partners with the Abyssinians, sent their most articulate men with bribes for the king, claiming that the Muslims were a group of people spreading chaos, conflict, and corruption across Makkah, and that they would do the same in Abyssinia. The idolaters demanded that the Muslims be returned to Makkah.

The king, however, being very just, refused to accept the pagans' demands without allowing the Muslims to at least speak. Ja'far Ibn Abi Talib stood up and gave a speech. Mehmet regards this as one of the top-three speeches in Islamic history.

His eloquent description of Islam moved the Christian Abyssinian king. He proclaimed that Islam and Christianity come from the same source, and that Muslims were free to live in his realm, as long as he is king.

Ja'far ibn Abi Talib, with his tongue, was able to sway a king's mind.

Perhaps Mehmet thinks I can.

But who am I kidding? I know I can't. I'm useless in this 1451 world. I'm not gifted with a "silver tongue" as Mehmet calls it. I'm not a negotiator. I only ever wanted to be an architect, but Mehmet is forcing my hand.

My anger at him has subsided in the past few days. I can see how he's kinda right. I can't just sit on my ass expecting Jake and Mehmet to do everything. I do wish he actually kept me in the loop while I was still in Adrianople, and I'm still angry at him for leaving me out, but then again, he probably thinks I'm dumb. I don't show anyone that I'm actually smart. While I know that marks are no barometer of intelligence, I've always gotten higher marks than Mehmet, who everyone thinks (rightfully so) is super smart. Even he doesn't know how smart I am.

But if Mehmet doesn't think I'm smart... why send me? I've been wrestling with this throughout this trip. Perhaps he thinks Ibn Eymen will handle the proceedings.

I look over at Ibn Eymen riding a grey stallion right next to me. He's hunched over, face pale, struggling to breathe. He's been barfing every couple of hours. Stomach flu, I think. I'm not exactly a doctor, but I don't know if he'll be able to speak to Durad Brankovic, the ruler of Serbia.

"When are we to arrive at Smederevo, Ibn Eymen?" I ask, cautiously looking at him.

"Soon, my friend..." he groans.

"Are we actually close, or are you just saying we are?" I ask. "You've been saying we're close ever since we left Niš."

"Patience, Hamdan Pasha. We will be there by sundown."

"How do you know?"

"Trust me... I know."

345

Sure enough, Ibn Eymen does know, even in his sickly state. About an hour or so later, we see peddlers heading in one direction, towards the fortress of Smederevo. Ibn Eymen and I trail behind, following them towards the city. The fortress walls come into view, so we pull aside and find a place behind some trees to change into our best clothes. I've changed into a black Ottoman *mintan* with red trimming and silver buttons. I place a white turban on my head and climb on my horse with my kilij sheathed at my waist and my dagger hidden in a pocket. I climb onto my horse and Ibn Eymen does the same. He's dressed similarly.

It's almost sundown, so we set out for the fortress to get there before nightfall. As we ride towards the gates of the city, three soldiers on the wall spot us and immediately run off.

Weird.

I look at Ibn Eymen, who doesn't look concerned in the slightest. My heart starts beating rapidly. What if they've already given their allegiance to Hungary?

Yes, Ibn Eymen has told me that the Serbs don't get along with the Hungarians, despite Durad Brankovic always playing a peace-keeping role. I, however, don't see why he'll be okay with the Ottoman Empire either, a state that was at war with them a while back. Ibn Eymen says it's because the Serbs respected Sultan Murat, who, like Durad Brankovic, was a peace-loving ruler. I don't know if that's gonna be enough to convince Brankovic to join us. I half expect someone to fire their arrows at us as we gallop towards the gates, but instead the gates to the fortress of Smederevo open. Behind the door stands a woman with a legion of soldiers.

That woman is Mara Brankovic, the daughter of Durad Brankovic. Wife of Sultan Murat. Most importantly, she's the bridge between the Ottoman Empire and the Serbian Despotate.

"Greetings, Mara Hatun!" I call out in Turkish, sounding like a snobbish dweeb.

"Hamdan Pasha... It's good to see you!" she jubilantly exclaims in her slightly accented Turkish. She looks at my companion. "Is Adham Ibn Eymen okay?"

His face seems to be going green. "He needs rest, Mara Hatun. He has taken ill during our journey."

"Of course, Hamdan." She motions to her soldiers.

Immediately, six soldiers run forward, grab hold of Eymen's horse, and lead it away along with the Nişancı.

"What's going on?"

"My men are taking him to his bed," Mara Hatun calmly says. The rest of her soldiers surround me. "I suggest you follow them to your bed as well."

The soldiers converge around me, so I say, "We came to see your father."

"He will speak to you when you are rested," Mara Hatun states. "Now, go to bed and rest."

With that, she turns and walks away with two of her soldiers as the group around me take away my sword and dagger.

What the hell is going on?

They've really thrown Ibn Eymen and me into a windowless room. The Serbs have taken away our weapons and horses to make sure we don't leave. The door to our room is locked. It's pitch dark in here, yet I can't fall asleep. Ibn Eymen keeps coughing and huffing.

"Will you be able to talk to the despot, Ibn Eymen?"

"I should be able to," he replies before going into a coughing fit.

"How on earth did you get so sick?"

"I don't do too well with travel, my friend." He breathes heavily and stretches his short arms.

"Rest easy, Nişancı Adham," I order. "I'll be the one speaking to the despot. You need to rest for our journey to Silistra."

"Do you know what to say?"

I stand up. "Of course I do, Nişancı. I may be quiet, but I'm a vizier. Don't ever forget that."

"I meant no offence, Hamdan Pasha," Ibn Eymen says. "But you weren't paying attention to what Sultan Mehmet was saying in his office."

"What did he say that I don't know about?" I ask. "We want peace, so we can't allow Serbia to join the Hungarians. I threaten them with an invading army if they refuse to accept our offer. Although there is no way Brankovic lets us leave if we threaten to invade."

"He would hold us hostage," he says. "That's when Mara Hatun will help us escape, but good, my friend. Make sure you don't reveal any details of our padishah's plans. If you do, Brankovic could lie to us and help the Hungarian-Wallachian alliance. If they find out about our plans, it will be a disaster."

"Don't worry, Ibn Eymen. I got this. Like I said... I am a vizier."

He chuckles, which leads to a harsh coughing fit.

"Go to sleep, Nişancı." I lie down on my uncomfortable cot of hay.

Ibn Eymen grunts, and a few seconds later, he's snoring loudly.

I lie down facing the wall to the left of me and sorta curl into a ball.

I'm going to be meeting an actual king tomorrow. I wonder what that will be like.

Bet Mehmet's jealous.

I'm standing in the middle of a field, right next to countless slain bodies. I look down at my hand and it's bloody, not with my blood, but with the blood of another man. Perhaps multiple men. It's sunrise, but my senses are on high alert. A fair distance away stands a small fortress. From where I'm standing, I can hardly see it. Some distance ahead of me is a river. The Danube! There are soldiers trying to cross on rowboats. Unsuccessfully. Why are they trying to cross? It's hopeless. Some reach land, but they are immediately struck down. I see a band of Hungarian soldiers reach the banks, and I am angry. The music from our side of the battlefield intensifies. Why is there music? Traditional Ottoman marching music. The leader of the band of Hungarian soldiers looks right into my face. My anger turns to rage. I raise my sword, proclaim, "YA ALLAH!" and charge. As I do that, I get knocked from the side, and everything goes black.

349

My eyes flutter open to see Mara Hatun standing over me with a jar of water in her hand.

"What are you doing?" I yell inadvertently in English.

"What are you saying, Hamdan Pasha?" she asks. "Never mind… You're finally awake. My father will see you now. Get dressed."

With that, she sets the jar by my bed and leaves. I sit up and look around. The room is now well lit, so I see it's quite spacious. I walk over to the basin in the corner, wash up, and get dressed. I finish placing the turban on my head, and there's a knock at the door. Mara Hatun walks in.

"Dressed?" she asks. "I'll lead you to the despot."

"Of course," I say. She turns and walks out the door with me trailing behind. I grab Mehmet's letter and a small chest of treasure to give to the despot.

We start walking at a brisk speed. "I'm sorry for imprisoning you and the Nişancı yesterday," she says. "I had to make a show of loyalty for my father."

"No worries, Mara Hatun."

"How is Mehmet?" she asks. "His letter had minimal detail."

"Sultan Mehmet is fine. Stressed out, perhaps a bit weary, but fine. How are you, Mara Hatun?"

"I hate not being there with him, Hamdan Pasha," she intimates. "Everyone here treats me like an outsider, despite being family. I love being reunited with my sisters, brothers, and father, but I fear I'm not completing Mehmet's task for me. I don't know what my father's planning. I only learned about the alliance against the Ottoman Empire through a servant who was in the room when my father received the envoy."

"Don't worry, that's all you really needed to do."

"In my haste to send out a letter to Mehmet, I failed to provide all the necessary information," she says. "The Hungarians have asked Skanderbeg to join their alliance as well. I know he has yet to cross my father's lands, but he's gathering his men. The numbers for the attack on Varna are likely to be higher than what I estimated."

Skanderbeg? Never heard that name before, but somehow, I instantly recognize his name as an Albanian warlord who was a former Ottoman hostage. If he rises up, he can take back Albania from the Ottoman sultanate easily. So, perhaps Mehmet's plan isn't a good one.

I guess that means my chances of survival are minimal.

I look at Mara Hatun and confidently lie. "Mehmet's battle plans are brilliant, and it accounts for everything."

"Good."

We walk in silence for a few minutes. "What is the date today, Mara Hatun?"

"The fifteenth of April," she replies. We turn into the hall leading to Durad Brankovic's Imperial Hall.

What on earth...? We are way behind schedule. Vladislav has probably left his capital by now. The plan for peace is gonna fail unless I wrap our agreement with the Serbian Despotate today.

"You must call my father by his full title, or your lordship, grace, or excellency. Do not refer to him as king. Avoid speaking with his advisors at all. Avoid speaking to my brothers. In fact, refrain from saying anything outside of Mehmet's letter or answering my father's questions."

"Uh okay..." I say. "Does your father speak Turkish?"

"No, he does not, but there is a translator in the room," she says.

Hasan Zia

"I would be the translator, but it seems he doesn't trust me. Apparently as a lady, I act blindly out of emotion, or something like that..."

Yeah, the 1451 world is super sexist...

Mara Hatun eyes an attendant, who runs into the Imperial Hall. I look to my side and see that Mara Hatun has slipped away.

Okay, shit's actually getting real.

The doors to the Imperial Hall swing open for me.

I truly hope I don't mess this up.

But what if I do...?

25. Hamdan

"My lord and prince of all Serbs, Durad Brankovic! I present to you the right honourable Hamdan Pasha! The fourth vizier from the lands of the Turks and the dynasty of Osman!"

Okay... How did I understand all of that? That was announced in Serbian. At least I think so..., but somehow, I understood it.

I look across the room to the guy sitting on the elevated throne. It ain't nearly as fancy as Mehmet's throne. It's wooden, and it actually looks uncomfortable. If I were a king/sultan/despot, I would want a seat that's either comfortable like Mehmet's, or badass like the Iron Throne. This is neither.

The despot is fairly old, maybe in his seventies. Surely, he can't be in his eighties; that would be much too old. He has thin, longish white hair, plus a fairly thick white beard covering his heavily wrinkled face. He looks like a wise man, and despite his age, he doesn't look frail at all, but rather like a man who commands respect from every person in the room.

The despot's men are surrounding him, split on both sides of the room. Most are old, although there *are* three younger men closer to him. The younger ones seem to be in their thirties and forties. The two in their forties are sitting rather than standing like everyone else. The young man in his younger thirties is handsome and stand-

353

ing closest to the despot. I suppose the three younger men are Mara Brankovic's brothers.

I step forward, perfecting the arrogant, fake-humble attitude from watching Zaganos Pasha and Halil Pasha, keeping my head down until I am close enough to the despot. I stand a fair distance from him, the same distance all the envoys visiting Mehmet do, handing my chest of treasure over to an attendant who sets it down right by the despot.

He looks down at the treasure and smiles. I stare at him for a moment unsure of what to do next. Do I bow?

You aren't meant to bow for anyone in Islam aside from the supreme Allah. I have seen some men bow to Mehmet, and he has reprimanded them for it, but some still do it.

The silence grows eerie, so I lower my head and place my hand over my chest, which is the greeting Mehmet prefers I give to him when in front of people from the 1451 world.

Despot Durad smiles. "What message do you have for me from your sultan, Hamdan Pasha?"

His translator repeats the question for me, and I pause. Am I able to speak Serbian? Should I attempt to speak it?

I can feel the impatience growing in the room due to my silence.

"I have a letter for you, my Lord Brankovic," I loudly proclaim in Turkish. The translator translates the sentence.

Probably best to keep my understanding of Serbian hidden. I might be able to find out what they all think of the letter while they believe I can't understand what they're saying.

"Very well... Hand the letter to my translator."

The Serbian translator breaks open Mehmet's seal (very violently), opens the envelope, takes out the scroll, and reads:

"To the honourable Durad Brankovic, The Lord, the Prince, and the Despot of all Serbs. From Sultan Mehmet Khan, The Second of His Name, Son of Murat, Sovereign of the Sublime House of Osman, Sultan of Sultans, Khan of Khans, Padishah of Anatolia and Rumelia."

I smile remembering that Ibn Eymen and Mehmet made sure to shorten Brankovic's title to make sure that they know who the boss is. I get the sense the room realizes Mehmet is belittling their despot too. The young man by him mutters, "Bastards and fools, the lot of them."

The translator continues.

"I send to you this letter, with my most trusted men, seeking to inform you of particular intentions. I, Sultan Mehmet, intend to maintain the peace, safety, and security, that our two realms have been blessed with for the past few years. I am working to ensure peace within all realms in the Balkans and beyond. I uphold the excellent work done by you and my father, the late great Sultan Murat. To do so, the peace agreed to by all realms just a few short years ago must be maintained. I have recently uncovered a plot by the realms of Hungary, Wallachia, Poland, Moldavia, and Transylvania. They seek to attack the port city of Varna, spreading chaos across my lands. This is an unspeakable act of cowardice by the territories involved. I, Sultan Mehmet, the second of his name, would like to make it clear that I have no intentions on any lands past the Danube bordering Wallachia and the Ottoman Sultanate, nor do I seek conflict against any state that does not seek to break the sacred peace between our realms. If it is in any way possible that the aforementioned realms have contacted you, I would like to remind you of your duty to maintain the peace. However, I end this letter with a warning: Anyone

355

who intends to harm the Ottoman people, the lands, or sultanate, will
see the ends of our swords as they pass into the afterlife."

A hush goes across the room.

The despot strokes his beard uneasily.

"We can't have the Turks as our enemies, my Lord," an older man from the far corner says in Serbian.

"We can't have the Hungarians as an enemy either, you fool," another calls out. "Hunyadi is much more proven than the son of Murat. The sultan of the Turks is just a pup, a young boy, and I say experience triumphs over youthful spirit every day."

"Yes, but the son of Murat claims that all he wants is peace," another exclaims. "Surely that alone is reason to ally with the Turks."

"You really believe the Turks want peace?" one of the seated sons of Durad Brankovic arrogantly asks. "I still haven't forgotten the day they blinded my brother Grugur and myself. I count the days till my father disposes of the slimy Turks."

"The Turks would never have blinded you or Grugur if you weren't stupid, Stefan," the youngest son of Durad Brankovic nastily asserts. "The two of you got caught red-handed trying to incite a rebellion."

"LAZAR, YOU—"

"Now, now, my sons, you are acting immature in front of our guest."

Lazar Brankovic lowers his head. "Sorry, your lordship."

"Good! Now, I don't believe we should have the Turks as our enemy. If Ibn Murat had used more resources, our realm would have been wiped out. We are lucky he did not," Durad Brankovic says in a calm voice. "And although Hunyadi is an excellent leader, the Hungarians are not nearly as organized as the Turks. Also, in my dealings with the son of Murat, during the battle of Kosovo, I found him to be an intelligent man, an ambitious man keen for battle, but also for the well-being of his realm and the world. I see no reason why he won't succeed..."

Aside from the fact that he isn't the man you spoke to! I want to scream.

"I also absolutely abhor the Hungarians. I do not like being subjugated to their rule. They have no regard for us, an act proven by the Hungarians crossing the Danube to march through our lands towards the Turkic realm. I intend to help Sultan Mehmet in hopes of securing peace for our realm and the region as a whole..." Durad concludes.

As he says that, the room goes berserk. An angry uproar.

Man... they must seriously dislike the Ottomans.

The Despot puts his hand up, demanding silence. "However, while helping the sultan of the Turks, I intend to help our realm. Ideally, this means that we pay the Turks much less and guarantee the protection of our lands. Now, Miroslav, please translate this for me: 'Hamdan Pasha, I have been invited by the Hungarians and Wallachians to join their alliance against your realm, but I have no intentions of doing so.'"

The translator, Miroslav, starts to translate Durad Brankovic's statement, but I stupidly blurt out, "Thank you, your excellency! I am sure the honourable Sultan Mehmet will love to hear these blessed words!"

I instantly regret saying this. A murmur of shock goes across the room as the realization hits them; I know Serbian and have understood every word.

I don't know if all you guys out there have gotten into an argument with someone, but after it is over, the anger subsides, and you feel regret for the things you've said.

Yeah?

Well that's how I feel right now. I feel stupid because I could not stick to my simple-ass plan.

"You speak Serbian, Hamdan Pasha?" Durad Brankovic asks.

What do I say? That I know Serbian and am in more shock than anyone in this room right now? Heck, I still feel like I don't belong here. By here I mean the 1451 world, in Eastern Europe, in the Ottoman government, being the Ottoman envoy to the Despot Durad Brankovic. I don't belong here, yet I speak the language, both Turkish and Serbian. What other languages can I possibly know? Shit's wild right now. All this is making me feel incapable. That's probably why I couldn't concentrate enough to keep to the simple plan. I can still recover this, though. Durad Brankovic wants to align with the Ottoman Empire.

"Yes, your lordship," I finally answer. "I do understand your beautiful language and am able to speak it."

The despot looks down at me and smiles. "You have a funny accent, but it will do. I am impressed."

"As I am always impressed by you, your grace."

"Now, I believe we must iron out terms of agreement," he proclaims.

I recall Mehmet and Ibn Eymen repeating that the Ottoman state mustn't give in to any demands by the Serbian despotate, and I must ensure that.

"There are no new terms of agreement, your excellency," I say. "You must keep to your word, and we'll do the same. You maintain peace and we shall as well. However, if you aid the Hungarians in any way, or do not keep your word... It will be seen as a *betrayal*. The Ottoman state and Sultan Mehmet have *NO* problem putting our swords through the guts and necks of those who betray our realm. However, if you help us, we will always help you. That is an Ottoman promise."

Durad Brankovic remains silent, contemplating what to reply.

An angry hiss goes across the room as the Serbian nobility figure out that I am threatening them with war.

Calmly, Durad Brankovic nobly replies, "Very well. The Serbian despotate will always hold firm to our oaths, as long as I am the monarch. Now, Hamdan Pasha, let's discuss the military campaign. My sources tell me that the Hungarians have yet to depart for Târgoviște. Additionally, Skanderbeg has also been asked to join. I propose that the Serbian despotate works to ensure that the Albanian force headed by Skanderbeg does not join the main army by crossing through Serbia."

Smart man. He's trying to minimize Serbian involvement, and I can abide that request, but perhaps I can take a page from Mehmet's book and find a more creative solution.

"The Ottoman sultanate appreciates the efforts of the Serbian despotate, but I have two more requests from you, your grace."

Durad Brankovic frowns. "What are your requests, Hamdan Pasha?"

"They are fairly simple, your grace. First, I would like you to break your armies into two major forces. A larger force will keep Skanderbeg out of your realm. The smaller will work as pests, slowing down the Hungarian march towards Târgoviște, allowing our soldiers to be better prepared for the attack on Ottoman lands."

Everyone contemplates what I just said.

"The men will be slaughtered!" someone yells.

"We cannot abide this request!" Stefan Brankovic exclaims.

"It is agreed upon, Hamdan Pasha," Durad Brankovic says as he strokes his beard. "What is your second request?"

"That you serve as an intermediary between all parties after this conflict is over."

"That I can do, Hamdan Pasha," Durad Brankovic pleasantly says. "Now, perhaps we can discuss this at the dinner. I hope to see you there, unless you are unable to stay."

I contemplate the offer. Ibn Eymen and I do need to get to Silistra ASAP, but Ibn Eymen needs more rest. Staying the night should do him a whole lotta good.

I place my hand over my heart and say, "Dinner would be lovely, your grace. "Your generosity is too much for me."

"Nonsense, Hamdan Pasha," Durad Brankovic proudly says. "You are excused for now. I will see you at sundown for dinner."

With that, the gates to the Imperial Hall open. I lower my head and keep my hand over my heart as I turn to walk out.

After exiting the Imperial Hall, I am exuberant. I wanna let out a loud *whoop*. Perhaps I should, cuz I did that shit. I got the lord and despot of all Serbs to bend to my will, very easily in fact. Then again, they are supposedly scared of the Ottoman Empire, but perhaps I truly am cut out to be a vizier. I don't just have to be Mehmet's lackey. I can be so much more. I can rise as a vizier. I can be creative, artful, and eloquent.

Holy crap.

I can do anything I put my mind to.

But the question is, what do I truly wanna put my mind to?

It's sunrise and I'm out in the stables at the fortress of Smedere-vo saddling the best two horses and tying up our limited supplies. Today is the 16th of April, and according to our initial calculations, Vladislav should have set out for Varna by now. However, the Hungarian force has yet to join his force, and Durad Brankovic and I believe that Vladislav has yet to set out. This is good news, giving Varna more time to prep for a siege.

Last night was a blur of excitement, joy, food, and business. While I was unable to eat the meat, as it wasn't halal, the vegetarian options were surprisingly good.

The despot and I discussed a lot of stuff, coming up with a true plan. Durad Brankovic and the Serbs are going to pretend to join the Hungarian force in limited numbers but are actually going to be working on destroying the force from within. This is through poisoning horses, setting fires, and whatever else to slow them down. And when possible, they will slip away from the attacking force and get back to the Serbian despotate. The remainder of the Serbian army will protect the land from Skanderbeg's forces.

This may sound too good to be true, but then again, they lost all leverage when they were speaking without knowing I understand Serbian.

I slept pleasantly last night. No weird dreams like the night before. That dream of the battle spooks me. I don't ever wish to enter a battle. Hopefully, I can do that by completing Mehmet's imperfect plan. I hear footsteps from behind me. I look back to see Ibn Eymen looking as assured as ever.

"Feeling better, Nişancı?" I ask.

"Better than ever, Hamdan Pasha."

"Good," I say as I climb onto my fourth horse of this trip. "We have a lot of work left, my friend."

"That we do," the Nişancı says as he climbs onto his horse. "You must tell me everything that happened yesterday.

"Of course, Ibn Eymen."

We ride towards the gates of the fortress. Smederevo looks exactly like how I would envision a medieval town. There are markets, blacksmiths, potters, and more all opening up right now. The streets are not busy with cars, but filled with people walking, on horseback, or on a cart pulled by a donkey. Soldiers walk through the streets, intimidating people with their swords, and children run through the streets away from their mothers. There are some people sketching on the sides of the fortress too. I wanna get off this horse and watch them, but I can't. I got work to do.

When we finally reach the gates of the fortress, we see Mara Hatun standing with her guard of soldiers.

"I hope you achieved your aims here!" she exclaims in Serbian.

She knows I speak Serbian? Word must've spread...

"That and more Mara Hatun," I answer respectfully.

She nods and smiles. "Give Mehmet my blessings. Long live the sublime Ottoman state and the Serbian despotate!"

"Long live the sublime Ottoman state," I repeat as the gates open.

"You be well, Mara Hatun," the Nişancı calls out.

"You as well, Ibn Eymen."

With that, the Nişancı and I set out for at least two to three weeks of long-ass travel.

Sounds... fun.

26. Mehmet

A deer stands thirtyish yards from me. Playing with a branch, just waiting to be hunted.

"Take the shot, my padishah," Zaganos whispers.

I raise my bow, perfect my stance, and steady my arm. Just as I do that, the deer looks directly at me.

Immediately I freeze, with the thought that this deer could be a father, passing through my mind.

"Take the shot, my padishah," he repeats.

A voice in my mind screams, *Why should I?*

Do I really need to eat deer? I don't think so.

"Fine, I'll do it," he murmurs as he lifts his bow. "*Bismillah, Allahu Akbar!*"

He fires the arrow thirty yards right at the deer's heart. He scurries off on his horse to make sure the gravely injured deer does not run away, bleeding itself to death.

"*Bismillah, Allahu Akbar!*" Zaganos exclaims. He cuts the jugular vein ensuring that the deer is properly slaughtered.

"Why did you hesitate, Mehmet?" Ak Shemsettin asks from his horse behind me as we ride towards Zaganos Pasha.

I ignore him and instead just look at Zaganos.

The truth is that I don't know what to say. Do I not have the stomach to kill? That can't be right. I've already killed a man, on top of nearly strangling Sally.

Do I just not have the appetite to kill a deer because I really don't need to? Beef, lamb, chicken, sheep, and goat are more than enough for me. Or is it just because of my anxiety?

The last one works as an excuse in this present situation, so I look back at Ak Shemsettin and the other scholars who have joined us on this hunt. "I failed to release the arrow because of my conflicted mind and heart, oh learned ones."

As I'm talking, we stop next to Zaganos, who's ensuring that all the blood properly flows out of the deer. The arrow pierced it right above the heart.

So much blood.

I wanna throw up.

I've only seen this much blood once before. The night of the failed attack on my life.

All of a sudden, the lifeless body of the would-be assassin flashes through my mind. I see the blood pouring out of his stomach, chest, and neck as he twitches to death. A cold feeling goes through my body as I twitch and shudder, scaring Snowstorm. He loudly neighs as he gets slightly outta control, lifting his front legs into the air, nearly throwing me off the saddle. As soon as I recover and retake control of Snowstorm, I wipe the sweat off my forehead with my sleeve, completely drenching it.

How can I feel so cold yet so hot at the same time? I actually don't know what on earth is going on with me. Is this what PTSD feels like?

Nah, it can't be. I haven't suffered real trauma.

That assassination attempt couldn't have truly been a traumatic experience. I haven't thought of it much, aside from the few days following the attack and the night a few weeks back when Sally decided to spook me.

It does not cross my mind.

I look down at Zaganos, who's cleaning off his blade and retrieving the arrow. He gets up and dusts off his clothes. Somehow this dude has no blood on his clothes.

Zaganos seriously baffles me.

He suddenly looks right at me. Angrily, he asks, "WHY ON EARTH ARE YOU HESITATING? THIS IS THE SIXTH TIME TODAY! YOU'RE LUCKY I STEPPED IN THIS TIME! A MAN WHO LEADS MUST NEVER HESITATE!"

I can hear the murmur of the scholars. One loudly whispers, "Did he really say that?"

I look at Zaganos. Man, I know he is a bold man, but I didn't know he was *this* bold. Yelling at the sultan in front of at least fifteen scholars, all of whom are respected members of the community, is not the way to go for a man who wishes to be grand vizier.

Or perhaps it is. I don't need a yes man, so I can justify raising him to that rank if the situation ever comes up. Then again, Halil, who's still in Constantinople for some reason, isn't exactly a yes man, so perhaps that's emboldening Zaganos.

Do I reprimand Zaganos?

He isn't exactly wrong.

I am hesitating.

I do hesitate.

I'm literally doing it right now.

What do I say?

Zaganos growls, "SEE WHAT I MEAN! HESTITATING AGAIN! WE'RE AT WAR, BOY!"

What is he tryna do? I don't exactly care. I need to say something.

"Who do you think you are?" I icily exclaim. "My father?"

I'm never gonna see him again...

"I AM THE ONLY MAN LOOKING OUT FOR YOU! HESITATION IS FOR COWARDS!"

"I didn't realize that failing to kill an animal was a coward's move!" I coldly utter.

"IT MAY NOT BE, BUT ALL YOU DO IS HESITATE! LOOK AT THIS WAR! YOU'VE CREATED A PLAN! A SOLID PLAN! BUT NOW? YOU DOUBT YOURSELF!"

Of course I do, but I told you that privately is what I *should* have said.

Instead, very dumbly, I whip out my kilij.

From on top of Snowstorm, I raise the blade in the air and point it right at Zaganos. "COME HERE AND LET ME SHOW YOU HOW MUCH CONFIDENCE I HAVE IN MY ABILITIES!"

He smiles and AK Shemsettin places his horse between us.

"Calm down, my padishah!" he exclaims. "You as well, Zaganos Pasha! Failing to kill an animal is far from a coward's move. It demonstrates kindness, a gentleness that resides in the sultan's heart. A gentleness I like to see in a ruler. And as for hesitation, I would hope that a leader of a large state doesn't rush into decisions. I'm a happy man if a ruler deliberates and rules confidently."

"The problem is that he's second-guessing his own decisions!" Zaganos exclaims. "That isn't a good thing!"

He's right.

I'm worried that sending Hamdan and Ibn Eymen to traverse hundreds of kilometers to talk to a ruler who is already my ally was a dumb move. I'm even more worried that they won't be able to sneak into the Hungarian-Wallachian camp and talk to the Hungarian leaders without being caught.

I'm also worried that Vlad has too much hate in his heart for this empire to truly help us. That he may do something reckless to win his birthright back. I worry that his motives will endanger Jake and my *akinji* cavalry.

"Zaganos Pasha," AK Shemsettin says. "Maybe the issue is what our *hünkar* has already stated. Perhaps his heart and mind are conflicted. He is a young man going through a major life transition. It is only natural."

A murmur of agreement comes from the rest of the scholars, but Zaganos still doesn't appear to be satisfied.

"Now, my padishah, what is conflicting your heart and mind?" AK Shemsettin asks.

Everyone goes silent, awaiting my answer.

I hate this so much.

There is so much that's going through my mind and heart, and it's no one else's concern. I also can't reveal anything in front of these men who I hardly know. Even if I wanted to reveal everything on my mind, I can't, because literally everyone will know I'm not from here.

So, what do I say? I need to bullshit my way through this.

"There is nothing I wish to say!" I exclaim. "These conflicts of my own mind and heart shall dissipate."

"MY SULTAN!" Zaganos yells before calming his tone. "How could your mind possibly be conflicted? You have the backing of the whole Ottoman state. Stop being a child, and grow up!"

"Zaganos Pasha, regardless how many people are behind a man, he can still feel despair. And while the believer always has God on their side, it is easy for the human mind to still feel despair," AK Shemsettin says. "Now, my padishah, would you like to share anything with us? You can say whatever you want, and we still have your back."

I nearly bawl out laughing.

I mean I *should* laugh out loud.

Outside of Hamdan, and perhaps Jake, Sally, and Hatice, no one here knows me at all. Even if they did, if I weren't sultan, they wouldn't give a crap about me.

"I have a lot on my mind," I say. "But I don't wish to talk about it right now."

AK Shemsettin clears his throat. "That's completely okay, my padishah. Just remember one thing. Life is but a test. That's all it is. You must be prepared to be tested with fear, failure, loss, health, as well as success, joy, fortune, and wealth. A person must learn to bear life with beautiful patience. Do you know what beautiful patience is, my padishah?"

"Um...."

"Patience is not a passive thing, my padishah. It is an active virtue that must be sought. Beautiful patience is when you actively pursue patience using proper methods of coping with the difficulties of life," he explains. "Rather than sitting around miserably all day, a person who has beautiful patience will turn to Allah for comfort. They will turn to their loved ones and talk to them. It is not a sign of weakness to disclose your troubles to trusted ones in Islam. Rather, it will help you be patient and follow the path of the righteous, the straight path towards heaven."

I nod and look the other way.

He's right about life being a test and that people should go through it with beautiful patience. I am having difficulty adjusting to this new role in my completely new life. I'd be lying to myself if I said I'm not struggling, but I'm also struggling with so much more, and who would I even talk to about this stuff?

Hamdan when he gets back? Nah, I can't bother him when he's going through the same problems.

The same goes for Jake and Sally.

Who does that leave?

No one really knows me.

Hell, even Sally and Jake don't truly know me.

The only other person who even has an inkling about who I actually am is Hatice and um... nope. She's cool, but nope.

I think the best course of action is to keep everything in.

You never know... maybe doing something like meditation will work.

Tuesday.

The 22nd of April 1451.

Time moves so freaking slowly.

Military campaigns are long.

Being from the social media generation where Vine was a thing, where Twitter, Facebook, Instagram, TikTok, and Snapchat are a thing, a twenty-day-long military campaign, where the fighting isn't even close to starting, feels like eternity.

By all reports as of this morning, the Wallachian-Hungarian alliance has yet to move from Târgoviște. Vlad the Impaler has been coordinating with Mahmut Pasha as often as possible. Although my info is possibly a couple days behind, as of now, it appears as though the Hungarian alliance has yet to reach Târgoviște.

I don't know why the Hungarians are delayed, but it is helping our cause.

Massively.

My army (gosh it's weird to say that) is marching towards Silistra, with Ömer Bey, Ali Bey, and Mahmut Pasha leading a force of 37,000. Additionally, Ahmet Bey is leading a smaller force of around 10,000 across the Danube as we speak.

I don't know exactly what Jake, Vlad, and Radu are doing with the *akinji* in Wallachia, but I hope they are prepared.

All I can really do is sit back and wait for events to occur.

The hardest part.

True: saying that sitting around is the hardest part is selfish as heck because my two best friends may die while I'm lying on my massive bed doing nothing. But the point I'm tryna make is that I wanna be out there helping my friends. Then again, I couldn't even hunt an animal properly two days ago, so how much help would I actually be?

I get up and start to stretch. It's late afternoon and I'm super sore from working out with the reserve janissary corps.

I think I like Yusef Agha's appointed stand-in deputy commander of the force. His name is Rizwan, and he's young. Older than me by at least six or seven years, but still fairly young. He's Yusef Agha's man, but he appears confident, very cordial, and completely able.

There's a knock at the door.

In walks the stand-in Deputy Commander of the janissaries, Rizwan.

"What is it?" I ask as I lie back down on my bed.

"Halil Pasha has arrived from Constantinople, my padishah," he replies. "He would like to see you."

"Send him in."

"In your room, my padishah?" he asks.

"Of course. Where else?"

Rizwan looks at me before quickly nodding his head. "He'll be here in a minute, my padishah."

I nod as he leaves.

An awkward moment later, Halil walks into the room, wearing the most extravagant clothes in the whole world.

He walks over to where I'm lying on my bed and from a respectable distance says, "*Assalamu Alaikum*, my padishah."

I look at him, get up and walk over to my desk. "What is it?" I impatiently ask as I sit down on the chair. I'm tryna sound angry at him but I don't think I sound genuine. It's hard to be angry at a dude for over twenty days.

"I'm back from Constantinople," he announces.

"What have you come back with, Halil Pasha?"

"I did what you wanted, my padishah," he replies.

"So tell me exactly what you did," I demand. "Have you officially sold your business? What exactly did you discuss with Loukas Notaras and Constantine Palaiologos?"

"My business has been sold to a rich merchant from Trebizond, my padishah," Halil replies.

A very generic answer, but I don't even care at this point. I just wanna know what he talked about with the final East Roman Emperor and Grand Duke of Constantinople.

Halil Pasha continues to answer saying, "I had long discussions with the Grand Duke, Emperor, and your cousin, Orhan."

"And what did you talk about?"

"I had to take up what Orhan is worth, my padishah," he answers. "You do realize that we *pay* to keep him locked up?"

There's a hidden scorn in his voice. Almost as though he thinks I'm a fool.

"Of course I know we pay the Eastern Romans to keep my cousin there," I say. "How much do you think he's worth?"

"All you need to know is that we pay too much to keep your cousin in Constantinople, and it's been slightly increased with your demands of renegotiating the peace."

"How much were we paying, and how much are we going to be paying?" I ask. "Also, how is Orhan? Does he resent this state and me, or is he content in Constantinople?"

"Oh, he's content in Constantinople alright. He's whoring and dining all across the city raising our bill for keeping him there," he says in disgust. "I will give him some credit. Orhan has a sharp mind, and he might just whip himself into shape. Also, we were paying 3,000 ducats. We are now giving double that."

"6,000 ducats!"

Halil nods slowly.

"Darn it..."

Now all you twenty-first-century people, who may or may not

read this, probably think 6,000 coins is not much. Especially for an empire. But ducats are pure gold coins. Just three make an exceptional daily salary for a skilled worker. If you take inflation into consideration, the East Romans are raking in *millions* from us. Now *that's* a one-sided deal if I've ever seen one.

"What else did you talk about?" I ask. "Surely you couldn't have been gone for twenty-two days just to return with this news."

"Well, there's a lot of gritty details I had to grind out. Not all the details are favourable for us, but Constantine Palaiologos is a respectable man who is willing to work with us. Your wish of peace and harmony with the Greeks, my padishah, is fulfilled for now."

"For now?"

"You still desire to take the Red Apple, my padishah, correct?" I nod. "Well, the peace definitely isn't going to last."

"But until we launch on offensive on Constantinople, there will be peace, correct?" I ask.

"That is correct, my padishah."

"And you're saying that the price for peace is 3,000 more ducats, Halil Pasha?"

"Well, there are a lot more details than that my padi—"

"Leave the details with me, Halil Pasha," I say, interrupting him.

"Of course, my padishah. I'll leave the signed agreement in your study," Halil states. "Just know that while the deal may not be favourable for us right now, it does allow you to take care of everything else you wish to complete before attempting to conquer Constantinople. That includes dealing with the Hungarians, Wallachians, as well as anyone else daring to threaten our lands."

I smile at him. "Halil Pasha, I appreciate this. Well done."

"It is nothing, my padishah."

"No, it definitely is something," I say. "Now go home and rest. You are dismissed."

He places his right hand over his heart, lowers his head, and leaves the room.

Man... can I actually rely on Halil? Maybe if I befriend him, he could be more useful to me than Zaganos. If he is a useful ally, I'll finally be able to stop worrying about Zaganos finding out my secret.

I fiddle around with the rice on my plate. I'm hungry, yet I can't bring myself to eat. The fiddling is obviously concerning Gülbahar who reaches over and grabs my hand.

"Are you okay, Mehmet? You haven't touched your food."

I gaze into her eyes. This right here is my problem.

No, not Gülbahar. She's awesome.

The problem is that she doesn't know me, and this is where it hurts. I have no identity. I mean, I have an identity, a label, but it's a false one. I try as hard as I can, and I think I do some good, but I'm no monarch, husband, or father. I'm not a man fit to represent this empire, and the truth is I don't know who I'm removed from all the labels. I don't know if I've ever known the answer, even when I was at Queen's. Perhaps I never will get the answer. Regardless, none of this will be solved right now. I've still got to keep playing my role.

"I'm completely fine, Gülbahar," I softly say. "I just had a random thought."

"Are you sure?"

"Yes."

With that, I start devouring the rice, almost to prove a point. I can tell she's disappointed. Gülbahar is a very smart women, and I can tell she knows I'm not being up-front with her. Perhaps she doesn't know what I'm hiding, but she *does* know it's something.

"You know, I got you a gift, Gülbahar," I say, hoping to distract her. "Would you like to see it?"

"Of course!"

"I guess we'll have to wait and see what it is..."

"Oh, come on! Tell me, Mehmet!"

I smile, wipe my mouth, and walk to the corner of my study. From a section of the bookshelf, I pull out a decently sized bronze chest and walk towards the table where we are eating.

"Close your eyes," I order. "Turn around as well."

"Why on earth? I already don't know what's in the box."

"To build anticipation," I reply. "Does it really matter? Just do it."

She playfully scrunches her nose and turns around. "All right, my love..."

Ugh, there it is. The thing that makes me feel like a fraud. How much longer can I keep this lie? How much is this lie actually hurting her? A lot, I'm guessing, but now is not the time to find out.

I open the chest. Inside are a couple crystal jewels, with their perfectly shaped edges glistening in the fading light of the room, but that's not really the gift I'm hyping up. The gift I'm making her close her eyes for is a dagger that I had specifically designed for her. The hilt is rose pink and beautifully crafted with a slight curve to make it easier to grip. The sheath is designed with jewels of the most beautiful matching colours. The blade is strong iron, and it looks magnificent. Her name, *Emine Gülbahar Hatun,* is engraved on the blade. I take hold of the dagger and walk over to her seat, taking a seat right next to her so close my knees are touching hers, and I can hear her heavy but calming breaths. I gently take hold of her hand and unfold her fingers one by one, so her palm is unhindered.

"Keep your eyes closed," I whisper as I place the dagger on her palm.

"What is it?"

"Keep your eyes closed and tell me," I reply.

She grips the dagger from its sheath with her right hand and starts to trace it with her fingers.

"A *Hançer...*" she whispers as she opens her eyes. "I'm in love with it. It's absolutely beautiful."

"I hope you know how to use it," I mumble. "Just in case anything happens..."

"What could possibly happen, Mehmet?" she whispers. "We live in a palace, we're surrounded by guards, attendants, and servants. Nothing is going to happen. To me or Bayezit."

"Still it would be a comfort to know that my wife and child are completely safe. Even from those who may wish to harm us from inside the palace."

She pauses to consider what I just said.

"I'm speaking in hypotheticals, Gülbahar. As a better-safe-than-sorry measure. This *hançer* is an art piece, but it is useful. Like the dagger of Aphrodite."

She nods. "Yes, of course. And to place your heart at rest, I still remember everything you taught me in the first month of our marriage."

"I taught you?" I hesitantly ask as the weight of her words are not magically popping into my head for some reason.

"You don't remember when you taught me how to fight?"

"I do," I lie. "I'm glad I did. Do you like the dagger, Gülbahar?"

"Of course I do, my husband," Gülbahar says. "I'm lucky to have such a thoughtful husband."

Again, I wanna punch a wall at that statement. I'm a perpetual liar. The worst type of person. Even now, I keep lying like a psychotic person.

"I'm incredibly lucky to have such a magnificent and gorgeous wife by my side."

She smiles as she gets up, and climbs onto me, wrapping me in a warm hug. I slowly return the hug by wrapping my arms around her. Gülbahar snuggles her arms around me, accepting the warmth of my body, and I allow her to do so. She moves her hands up, grabs the back of my head as she starts to ruffle with my hair and play with my head. She then slowly moves her head back, traces my cheekbones with the pad of her thumb and leans in for a kiss on my forehead. She slowly moves down to my right cheek, and gently plots a kiss. And then my other cheek. I try to shrug her off, but she starts to kiss my neck. Softly and slowly. My mind goes dull for a second, but the next thing I know, she's softly nibbling my left ear.

Oh gosh no. What the hell? She's not my wife. She doesn't know who I am. In fact, as far as I know, she's my ancestor. And why is she doing this today after so long?

I pull my head back and delicately whisper, "Um, we should continue eating..."

Gülbahar kisses me one more time before registering what I said. She pulls her head back and says, "What?"

"Um uh... are you not hungry?"

"Sure I am," she mutters looking deep into my eyes. Her gentle hazel eyes glisten as they peer into mine. As she leans in to kiss me again, there's a sharp knock at the door of my study. Before I can say anything, Zaganos enters with Hatice behind him.

I breathe a sigh of relief. Thank the Lord. I couldn't figure out how to decline Gülbahar without upsetting her.

Hatice looks right at me, and I stare right back at her, as her face turns red, both from embarrassment and disappointment. That's when I realize that Gülbahar is still on my lap.

"I apologize for the disruption, my padishah," Zaganos uncomfortably says while keeping his gaze low. "I had urgent business to discuss with you."

This is where I must fake outrage, to make it seem as though I'm upset that Gülbahar and I were interrupted.

"And this couldn't wait until tomorrow, Zaganos?" I ask with a false sense of irritation. "My Friday nights are meant to be spent with my wife, and they're priceless."

Hatice loudly clears her throat, as though she's reminding me of my lie. Why on earth did I tell my secret to her of all the people I've encountered at this palace? Should've told some guard or something.

"It could not wait until the morning, my padishah. Halil Pasha will be here any minute to discuss some important matters."

"And I came here to provide Gülbahar and Salmana Hatun some company," Hatice says. "If that is okay with you, Gülbahar Hatun?"

Gülbahar gathers herself, gets off my lap, and says, "Yes of course."

With that, she walks out with Hatice, firmly gripping her new dagger.

"Take a seat, Zaganos Pasha," I say as I grab my plate of food.

"I see you are again attending to your other necessary needs, my padishah," Zaganos says. "I truly am sorry for disrupting you."

Oh my lord. Why on earth is a dude with a daughter around my age commenting on the um...intimate details of my life?

"I don't want to hear you ever say something like that again, Zaganos Pasha. Is that understood?"

He uneasily nods his head. He stares down at a spot at a table. Seemingly in embarrassment.

"Don't worry, you didn't interrupt me, Zaganos Pasha," I say. "Now, I would like to know what was so urgent."

I mean, no, I really wouldn't. I desperately need a vacation, but I don't get those during a military campaign. Every day, it's meeting after meeting. Looking at financial books, maps, settling refugees streaming in from border towns, and making sure Adrianople is safe and secure. It's necessary, but it's overwhelming at times. Still, I can't complain. The ones fighting on the front lines are the ones who have that right. Not me.

Anyways, Zaganos replies. "Ishak Pasha sent a messenger to inform me of an intention by the Karamanid sultanate to besiege Ankara."

"You're joking!" I exclaim. "Another invasion?"

"Did that sound like an attempt at humour, my padishah?" Zaganos asks. "I apologize if seemed that way."

Yeah, Zaganos can really be like Captain Raymond Holt from *Brooklyn Nine-Nine*, at times.

Ignoring that apology, I ask, "Are we going to be involved in a two-front war?"

"Well, they are separate military campaigns, my padishah, but yes, we would be fighting wars on two fronts. Against all allied powers from Europe and the Karamanids."

"Can we manage that?" I ask. "Surely war on two fronts will hurt the people of this realm."

"It will hurt the people," Zaganos says. "It will also hurt our finances. Especially with the Karamanids attacking Ankara, a financial hub for your lands as well as the capital of Anatolia."

"What if we divert the attack from Ankara?" I ask. "We make sure they never get there. Making it a land battle rather than a siege."

"That will risk a lot of lives, my padishah," he replies. "However, I would advise against it."

"Why? We would win swiftly, ensuring our financial resources aren't drained."

"Human beings are a resource, my padishah," he says. "Besides, I thought you valued human life above all else. Isn't that why you want peace with the Wallachians?"

"Yes, of course I value human lives, Zaganos Pasha. Just one human life is priceless, so imagine how valuable thousands of lives are," I reply. "A siege of Ankara is just going to drag out the damage, so if we swiftly end the conflict, it will be better for everyone."

A voice from the door says, "I agree, my padishah."

I look up to see Halil at the doorway.

"Please sit, Halil," I instruct.

Zaganos angrily clears his throat. "If we are to battle them on open ground, my advice is that you lead the force, my padishah."

"I disagree, my padishah," Halil states. "There is too much uncertainty with the Hungarian-Wallachian situation, so it's probably best if you coordinate both conflicts from Adrianople."

"That makes perfect sense, Halil Pasha," I say. "I won't be leading the army. I'm sure Ishak Pasha can handle the Karamanids. Perhaps he ought to send Aslan Pasha with an army to intercept them."

"Or Gedik Pasha," Halil says. "He's an excellent adviser and military mind."

"Either one, Halil Pasha."

I don't know much about Gedik Pasha. Nor do I know much about Aslan Pasha. But I have met with Aslan Pasha, so I would prefer him. I don't know if I should mention this to Halil though.

"My padishah, how can you ask your men to risk their lives for you when *you* aren't willing to risk yours?"

"It's not our padishah's job to risk his life on the battlefield, Zaganos Pasha!" Halil exclaims.

"Of course, but--"

"Please stop arguing and let's develop our proposed strategy and pen a message for Ishak Pasha."

That shuts them up. Zaganos stalks off to the corner of the room to grab some regional maps. I stare at my unfinished food.

Zaganos is right... I'm being distant.

I don't inspire confidence, and something needs to be done to change that.

Desperately.

27. Jake

I wanna barf.

Being a soldier under Vlad the Third, or Dracula as he likes to call himself, is an absolute nightmare. It completely sucks, and the real battle hasn't even started yet.

Presently, Demir and I are digging a grave for the **seventh** group of people Vlad Dracula has killed with his Wallachian brethren. Their heads have been cut off and brought to opposing army in Târgoviște with messages attached. Vlad Dracula claims this is a scare tactic to divert the opposing army away from certain pathways fearing bandits or worse.

I hate the practice. It's a war crime on top of being super immoral. Killing is bad period, but killing people who aren't even involved in the conflict isn't just ruthless, it's plain malicious. I don't know why a Christian like Vlad can murder so indiscriminately. How can he do that while believing in a loving God?

I get the feeling that a lot of people don't like serving under Vlad. He's whipped at least two dozen *akinji* so far for not killing the *children* of the people we've already killed. Something about not leaving any witnesses for his cousin, Vladislav of Wallachia, to figure out who the enemy is. People have also lost food privileges for not being up by sunrise. Most of the punishment has been inflicted on the *akinji*. I guess Vlad is tryna prove another point to his Wallachian comrades that he has no love for the Ottomans. In fact, he's showing them he loathes us.

Sweat drips down my forehead. It's sorta hot today, even though Demir and I are shaded by the forest. I take off my shirt and use it to wipe the sweat and dust off my face. I'm glad I don't have to wear my janissary uniform anymore.

I believe that it's nearing the end of April. The group of merchants Vlad and his Wallachian brethren mercilessly slaughtered last week mentioned it was April twenty-first. It's been seven days since. If the merchants were right, then today's the twenty-eighth of April.

"Yakub!" Demir exclaims. "Help me with this rubble."

"Of course," I glumly say.

"You look sick, brother."

"That's because I hate this job," I reply. "Digging mass graves is horrific."

"Hey, at least we aren't doing the killing."

He's right about that. I grimace, grip my shovel, and start digging away at the rubble.

Due to my status, Arslan, Baver, Demir, and I have been able to secure jobs that are less gruesome, though they are critical to gaining the upper hand in this military conflict. The less gruesome work has still been fairly awful though.

As we're trying to funnel the Hungarian-Wallachians towards the Fortress of Silistra, we're doing our best to close off all possible routes of transportation that would lead the invading army to Varna instead of Silistra. Vlad and Radu's knowledge of the land is proving to be very helpful.

You're probably wondering how exactly a group of 750 light cavalry soldiers are going to pull that off, and the answer is fairly simple.

Our job is not to defeat the army, but only to slow them down and ensure they cross the Danube at Silistra rather than an easier location closer to Varna. So all we need to do is make all other routes inaccessible. That's what I've been working on with the Demir, Baver, Arslan, Radu, and the *akinji* while Vlad and his comrades spread terror.

So how do we make all other routes inaccessible?

It's complicated. Like I said, we're trying to make it impossible to move an army across certain areas. With a limited supply of men, we can't disperse them into different units to run a blockade. Instead, we're making sure other routes towards Varna are blocked off.

We've chopped down trees to block areas and pathways, started forest fires, poisoned wells on top of filling the ones that aren't poisoned with dirt, and cut off people on the road, not allowing them to get to Târgoviște or anywhere else. The ones Vlad has spared have promised to spread word of mercenary bandits belonging to a rival Wallachian nobleman along certain routes. Those who don't survive—everyone aside from the weakest—get impaled by Vlad and his comrades. The bodies sent to the Wallachian Voivode as a gift. We've also been forced to rob and pillage numerous villages, so I think I finally understand why Mehmet believes that Vlad Dracula has no honour.

I've given the men I command strict orders not to kill, despite Vlad's orders to not leave any witnesses, but I think that destroying their village serves as enough of a scare tactic. The only reason I've gotten away with this is because Vlad hopes to win Mehmet's favour, which means he isn't going to do anything to harm me.

Yeah, word has spread through camp of my friendship with the sultan. Thankfully, no one knows that Arslan, Demir, and Baver are janissary soldiers. According to Arslan, saying I'm friends with Mehmet gives them cover.

I use my discarded shirt to wipe the sweat and dirt from my face. I look at Demir, who's doing the same thing. I put down my tools and look around at our handiwork.

"Large and deep enough, ain't it, Yakub?"

I look at him and grimly nod. Now comes the hard part. Placing the bodies in the graves.

Working together, we lift them, shrouded in cloth. I whisper prayers for all the dead as we place them into the massive grave.

Demir stares at me while I pray.

"What? I never forgot the Christian prayers after I became Muslim," I lie. "These Christians deserve a proper funeral if we can give it to them."

"I wasn't objecting," Demir states as we place another body in the grave.

I still feel super-guilty.

I mean... I am truly guilty. I may not be murdering these men, women, and children, but I'm associated with men who are slaying them mercilessly. I now wonder why Mehmet would choose to associate with men such as Vlad Dracula, if he knew of his evils. Perhaps he doesn't care, as long as it serves him. Or maybe he thinks the loss of Wallachian subjects doesn't matter as much as the loss of subjects in his realm. Maybe Mehmet doesn't even care about the death and destruction at all.

I've also realized that I probably don't know him all that well. I was his roommate for only a month and a half before getting here. I've now known him about four months total. I haven't even seen him for the last month of the four.

I got no idea if he's a monster. A tyrant.

I definitely don't think Mehmet is evil. He's always polite, and he doesn't seem to be anything other than a normal kid, so the optimistic conclusion I've come to is that this was the best possible strategy he could pursue at the moment. He wouldn't have associated with Vlad if he thought there was a better option. I haven't known him for long, but I do trust him.

Somehow, he commands every person's trust and support.

There's just something about him.

Demir and I have placed the last of the smelly, scarred, and innocent bodies into the grave and have started the process of placing the dirt over them. All I can think about is how I'm burying the sons, husbands, brothers, fathers, daughters, sisters, wives, and mothers of people I've never met. Life is simply too short to be filled with hate. It's too short for the murder, violence, senseless inequality, and exploitation. Life is too short to be lived without love.

I wipe some mud off my face as I gently lay dirt over a dead Wallachian woman.

Man, it's been far too long since I've seen some of the people I wholeheartedly love.

I need to get back Priya.

Very badly.

By the time Demir and I ride back to camp, nightfall is upon us. It's fairly late at night too; most men are inside their tents.

"This is kinda strange," Demir mutters as we ride through camp. "No one ever goes to sleep this early."

"Perhaps it's late, my friend," I reply. "No one wants to wake up late in fear of Vlad."

"None of us fear Dracula," Demir states. "We just aren't stupid enough to challenge an eccentric rage-filled military commander."

"Sure, you totally don't fear him," I laugh. "Perhaps I should tell him that."

Demir chuckles. "Damn you, Yakub. It isn't funny, and you should fear the madman too."

"Eccentric rage-filled military commander? Madman?" a voice calls from behind us in perfect Turkish.

We both turn around to see Vlad Dracula, behind us. He's got a hardened expression, and he's glaring at us.

"Do I look like a madman to you, Yakub?" the Dracula asks.

He's far from a madman. He's a psychopath, but of course I can't say that.

"I'm sure Demir meant that as a compliment," I reply as calmly as I can. "Isn't that right, Demir?"

"Yes of course, Dracula," Demir asserts.

I continue. "A man who'd do anything for his goals may be a madman, but there are far worse men out there. Namely those who have goals but won't do what it takes to achieve them."

Now I don't know if I believe a word of that, but hopefully Vlad believes I think this way.

Thankfully, it looks like he does. He opens his mouth and asks, "What took the two of you so long?"

"There were a lot of bodies," I say. "Digging a mass grave and properly burying the bodies takes time."

"Well I wouldn't know, would I?" Vlad replies.

Well... he *should* know.

We've got a lot of new information today that I think you should know, so follow me," Dracula says.

I follow him to the centre of the encampment, and Demir rides away. That's where the main tent is. We're forced to camp in miserable conditions because we are essentially under cover. Vlad heads right into the tent. I get off my horse and tie him up.

I follow him inside and see Radu sitting, gulping down some broth. Vlad takes a seat next to him and spreads out a few regional maps he'd had drawn by cartographer a few years back, following the death of his father. So far, the maps have proven to be as accurate as a fifteenth-century map can get.

I fold my legs and take a seat next to Radu and Vlad. The brothers are looking more serious than ever.

It's always shocking being around historical figures—especially ones around the same age as me. Vlad is slightly older, while Radu is younger, but somehow, they both seem ancient. I guess that's just due to the fact that both were born in the first part of the 1430s, while I was born in the year 2001.

As soon as I sit on the cushion, Vlad starts to speak. "We have received some very reliable information from the man I placed within the opposing army."

Oh yeah. I forgot to mention we decided to infiltrate the Wallachian army. Vlad wants that person to kill or capture, Vladislav II of Wallachia when the time's right. Of course, Mehmet doesn't want that. Or at least I don't think he does. Regardless, a spy during a war is useful.

"What information does he have?"

"It seems as though the Hungarians have arrived in Târgoviște."

"Finally," I blurt out.

Radu weirdly stares at me. "You must have a real thirst for battle, Yakub."

I hope I don't, but I simply nod. "Of course I want this battle done and dusted."

"As do I, Yakub," Vlad says. He places his rough, battle-ridden hand on my shoulder. "Our source also tells us that the Hungarians have arrived in a battered condition alongside hundreds of Serbs."

"Battered?" I ask. "How?"

"We have no idea," Radu answers. "All we know is that many are sick, injured, and sluggish."

"Which is perfect for us," Vlad states.

"When are they to march for Varna?" I ask.

"They arrived about three days ago..." Radu starts.

"And I expect them to march at midday tomorrow," Vlad says. "Even if they don't, it's best to prepare as if they set out tomorrow. We must be prepared to swiftly attack."

"And we'll attack them just as we've planned," Radu says.

"You *do* know the plan, Yakub?" Vlad asks.

"Of course, Dracula," I reply.

"Good. Now, get some sleep," Vlad orders. "We move at dawn right after you lot pray your Fajr prayer."

I grunt and silently duck outta the tent, walking towards my grey horse with my body twitching and shuddering in fear.

Because, tomorrow morning, I am going to indulge in warfare.

I may kill someone. I may be killed. Either way, ready or not, I'm set to fight.

To live another day, to get the chance to see those I love again, to get the chance to see the *one* I love.

28. Jake

Anticipation.

Tension.

Excitement.

Fear.

That's what I feel right now.

This military skirmish against the Hungarian-Wallachian-Polish-Transylvanian-Moldavian alliance is just minutes away.

The *akinji* and I are gathered in a dense forest, split into five tight lines consisting of a hundred men each. Demir leads the first row with the archers. Baver leads the second. Arslan leads the third. Radu leads the fourth. I lead the fifth and final line. Our plan is genius. Vlad and his group will create a commotion at the head, using flaming arrows and Greek fire. When the rear is exposed, the *akinji* and I come in and flood them with fury.

We're hidden from sight. We can look out, but unless someone closely inspects or wanders into the forest, they won't be able to see us. The density of the monstrous, robust, and terrifyingly beautiful trees provides excellent cover.

I can feel the men's nervous energy. Particularly the *akinji*. They've never truly been an attacking force; they are generally used as scouts to strike fear in the enemies' hearts by playing their march-

392

ing music. They are also used to pursue retreating forces. This isn't exactly their forte.

Should I say something? Some words of encouragement? I'm not exactly a public speaker.

I look over at Radu. He's younger than me. Can't be older than sixteen. Yet he looks more determined than any of the *akinji*. He looks back at me and flashes a warm smile, his eyes set on what's to come.

Okay.

I really think I should say something, but what?

I break my line and ride towards the front on my grey stallion. In front of Demir's line, I stop and observe the men. I'm asking them to risk their lives, so what can I even say to them? I look around listlessly for a moment, when Demir and Arslan make eye contact and signals to me.

"My fellow men," I bellow, "I am not a man of many words, but I come here today asking you for one thing! Just one thing!"

I ride slowly across the front lines to make sure it feels like I am speaking to all of them.

"And what is that one thing, Yakub?" Baver calls to try to hype me up.

"We've gathered here today to fight! For the Ottoman Empire! For the Ottoman Dynasty! For Varna! The sultan is asking all of us to step out of our comfort zone. You may ask why, and it's a fair question. He will tell you it's to protect our lands, property, and people. And those are valid reasons. But I ask you to fight for more! For a chance to live another day! Fight to return to your loved ones! Fight to create a better world for all those you love!"

The *akinji* grunt and cheer in approval.

Is this garbage I just spouted actually motivating?

Regardless, I raise my karabela sword into the air and proclaim, "Now you all know what we must do! We advance! Line by line! We destroy their lines and cause as much damage as we can! If we are successful, by God's grace and mercy, we shall survive and claim victory for ourselves! For our people! And for our sultan, Mehmet the Second!"

A resounding roar of approval comes over the *akinji*.

I really do hope the enemy army does not hear us.

I raise my arm, as if I'm waiting for a high five. As my fingers close into a fist, the noise dies down. Almost magically.

That's how much obedience the Ottoman army has.

It's incredible and terrifying at once.

I ride back to my row and immediately turn towards the path outside the forest. As soon as I do, I see the military procession. Just as we planned, the army is taking the dangerous route.

Next to me, a man whispers, "They are wearing a lot more armour than they usually would for travel."

I got no idea if that is true. I know that the janissaries don't wear much medieval armour. That's all I know, but in movies, the armies are always wearing metal chain.

In response, I whisper, "That was to be expected. Remember, word has spread about the danger on all the routes. They probably want to be ready in case of an attack. Don't lose morale."

The man falls silent.

With every passing man, horse, wagon, haul, and banner, my heart pounds harder.

How much longer do we have to wait? The wait is getting on my nerves.

"That's Vladislav!" a man to my right exclaims.

I try to get a look, but it isn't a good one. Vladislav is surrounded by soldiers and his bannermen. He looks similar to his cousin, the Dracula Vlad. So kinda tall, fairly broad-shouldered, rough, angry expression with a weird mustache that sorta actually looks good.

Anyhow, this means we are looking at the centre of the army. This is where I want to attack, but Vlad stated that too many of our men would die, which surprised me, but oh well.

I look at Radu, and his face is red with fury. The brothers hate Vladislav for usurping the throne after their father's death. It makes complete sense that they want him dead.

We're supposed to wait for a commotion before advancing, so I try to listen for one. Arslan looks back at me and mouths, "This is taking so long, they might find us out."

I give him a pointed look, ordering him to focus which he immediately does.

I close my eyes and take a deep breath. My chest feels like it's going to explode. Two things are keeping me sane right now. The fact that God is always looking over me. God won't let me die—I'm sure of it. He'll see me back to my family. Back to Priya. Oh yeah, she's the second thing keeping me sane. I see her lovely smile, hear her pleasant laugh, the way she scrunches up her nose playfully, and her soft expression every single time I close my eyes. I didn't even know how much I loved her until I got here.

I open my eyes and exhale. I absolutely must be perfect here.

My mind focuses solely on the advancing army, with my ears working in overdrive, trying to hear everything. I can hear men's footsteps, the clatter of hooves, and the wheels of wagons.

No commotion... yet. I start counting the seconds. A minute passes, and another. A third minute goes by, and a fourth.

Suddenly, I hear yelps.

Shouts.

Shock.

Fear.

Commotion.

Immediately I lift my sword and loudly proclaim, *"Akinji! It is time! We attack! We march for victory! For ourselves and for a greater world!"*

Immediately, men from my line start playing the Ottoman marching band music. The beating of the drums, the blast of the trumpets are deafening, yet surprisingly rhythmic.

As soon as the music gets loud enough, Demir lifts his kilij and bellows, "ARCHERS!"

Immediately, the entire line grabs their bows.

"NOCK!"

The archers notch their arrows on the bows.

"DRAW!"

The archers oblige.

"LOOSE!"

One hundred arrows soar through the air. You can hear the woosh along with the Ottoman marching music. At least half hit a target, as men from the invading army yelp, gasp, and scream. Horses violently neigh and some throw their rider off and gallop away.

Again, Demir raises his sword and yells, "NOCK!"

"DRAW!"

The archers raise their bows.

"LOOSE!"

Arrows rain down on the soldiers, but this time they are more prepared. At least half of them get their shields up in time. Only about twenty to thirty actually hit and inflict injury, and not a single horse is struck.

Okay, two rounds of arrows have been fired on the enemy. They are now confused. Now Demir needs to—

"CHARGE!"

Immediately, Demir's row of cavalry soldiers gallop forward with a loud war cry. The drums and trumpets get louder. Many of the opposing soldiers see them approaching and start forming their lines as fast as possible. The expert Turkic *akinji* archers start firing from their horses. These nomadic men have been training to do this from the time they learned to walk.

As they get closer, Demir lifts his sword in the air and yells, "YA ALLAH!"

That's his battle cry. It means *Oh God!* That works... I guess.

The men chant, "*YA ALLAH! HAYYDIR ALLAH! HAQQDIR ALLAH!*" as they approach the allied army.

Demir is the first to reach the opposing forces, viciously slashing and stabbing at a line of infantry soldiers, striking down at least four of them. The entire section of the army that we are attacking gets fully engaged, with the rest of the *akinji* joining Demir in his assault.

The numbers of the opposing force are significantly greater than what Demir has with him, but he and the *akinji* are fighting like superhumans. Some men, including Demir, are striking down at least three to four men per minute. No one is even close to striking Demir. The infantry soldiers surrounding him can't come to close to his speed. The Hungarian-Wallachian-Moldavian-Transylvanian-Polish force seems to be recovering though.

Their lines stumble, but still hold.

My body shudders as a cavalry soldier strikes down one of the *akinji*. "Oh no!" I mutter. The man's face splits apart due the Hungarian soldier's sword.

I almost forgot that my men could die too.

My body twitches, my hands begin to shake, but I snap my head back into focus. I must lead. I can't be a spectator. The music of marching band is still going. Somehow, it still sounds rhythmic, steadily getting louder. Literally on beat, I proclaim, "SECOND LINE! ADVANCE!"

Baver looks to me and laughs. "MY MEN! LET'S CHARGE AND GIVE THESE PIGS A GLORIOUS DEATH!"

With that, the entire line charges into battle, joining the fight with Demir. The opposing force stumbles back and starts shouting at each other. I think in a bunch of different languages.

Oh gosh.

There's a language barrier in the opposing army. They don't understand each other's instructions in the chaos. They're not properly organized. They are probably wondering where we came from. They may know who we are by our war cries, but they don't know our number. If I time it perfectly, I can make it seem as though we have a much larger force, setting panic in the opposing army.

I look at Arslan, who's looking at me, waiting for his directive. I look at Baver who is fighting at a level even greater than Demir. He has twelve opposing infantry soldiers around him, but he's fighting valiantly.

The opposing army seems caught off guard, but they are too much for the force of 200 or so I have sent so far. I only have 300 more men, but I need to make sure it feels like there are way more. They are stumbling, but I don't know if their lines are going to break.

I look down to the men from my line and shout, "MAKE IT LOUDER! MAKE THE SOUND OF OUR ARMY LOUDER!"

The men oblige. The beating of the drums gets significantly louder. The sound of the trumpets multiplies, as if thousands are waiting in the forest.

Perfect.

I look back at the battle right outside the fairly dense forest. The opposing army has recovered from the burst by Baver's line.

Now the third wave must be released.

"THIRD LINE! ADVANCE!"

Arslan looks back at me and smiles, before looking towards the battle, and he charges with his line, swords raised, proudly proclaiming *"YA ALLAH! HAYYDIR ALLAH! HAQQDIR ALLAH!"*

Arslan and his line make their way through the maze of robust trees as fast as they can, joining the battle. It becomes crystal clear that Demir, Baver, and Arslan are the three greatest fighters on the battlefield. It truly is an honour to be their friend.

I know I haven't gotten involved in the fight yet, but I will say this. It is super ugly. So much bloodshed. So many limbs torn apart. Thankfully, those limbs belong to the opposing parties, but it is still ugly.

Even still, there is a hidden beauty within this struggle. There is a beautiful sense of humanity. The *akinji* have each other's backs. They are united. To protect their home and to return to their family. It just goes to show that if humans work together, we can achieve anything. One day, hopefully, it will be towards something good rather than senseless warfare.

Now, back to the battle at hand. The opposing force seems to be in shock, yet they are still resisting. The best part is that we are just attacking the last quarter of the army, which is still a significant number, but the rest seem to have moved on. Dozens of (smart) Serbian soldiers are also riding away after the larger army. The rest will be dealt with.

Very soon.

For now, we need to take care of this lot.

"FOURTH LINE! ADVANCE!"

Radu looks at me, then with a boyish smirk, he looks towards the battleground and shouts, "LET'S DESTROY THESE SCUM!"

His entire line gallops in and joins the battle. The music from my line gets louder. The enemy is stumbling, struggling to hold their thin lines. The cavalry is going to break through. No, Baver has just broken through the enemy lines. Oh my gosh, we are going to win! I look around for Vlad. My line is supposed to attack after he comes into sight.

Literally on schedule, a man approaches on horseback. He waves his arms, motioning to the battleground.

I look closer. It's Vlad. The Dracula.

I nod, take my sword out, charge forward on my stallion, and loudly say, "FINAL LINE! ADVANCE! YA ALLAH! LET US GAIN VICTORY!"

Yes, God will see us to victory. I firmly believe it. Even if I am fighting against Christian men, I think we're in the right. We are defending our lands. God will see us to victory. He will see me back home. I know He will.

We charge forward and straight into battle, as the enemy lines have crumbled and fallen into disarray. Every man on the opposing side is fighting for himself. I look next to me to see that Vlad has also entered the battle.

Okay, so where do I even attack? I've got no idea. I sorta freeze and look around for my friends. Demir, Arslan, and Baver are on the front lines. All of them have abandoned their horses and are chasing some men away. Suddenly, I notice three men approaching me. I grip my sword, but instead of galloping towards them on my stallion, I ride away towards a less congested part of the battleground.

What am I doing? Am I a coward? Why am I avoiding the fight? It isn't noble of me. The men looking up to me are valiantly fighting and are moments away from a glorious victory. Yet I'm standing at the side. This might be dumb, but if I'm afraid of killing someone, I should just jump into the middle of the battle. That will force me to fight, to face my fears, making me properly earn the trust of all the men I serve.

I shake my head. I'm being stupid, but let's go fight some people with swords.

I ride straight towards the heat of the battle. Immediately, I hear some Wallachian men from the opposing army bellow out orders. Then, Radu and Vlad loudly proclaim, "THE ENEMIES ARE RE-TREATING! THE COWARDS ARE RETREATING!

Immediately, the *akinji* chant, "*ALLAHU AKBAR! ALLAHU AKBAR! ALLAHU AKBAR!*"

The section of the opposing army starts to dash away with Baver, Demir, Arslan, Radu, and about a hundred *akinji*, giving them chase. I look to see if Vlad is also going to pursue the soldiers. Instead, I see there are about sixteen enemy Wallachian soldiers headed right for him. How those men got through the *akinji*, I don't know. But they *are* headed right for him.

I'll be honest, a small thought going through my head is to forget Vlad. He's a monster who doesn't deserve salvation.

But I can't. No matter how monstrous he is, Vlad is still a Christian. He is still a human being. He deserves to live and seek penance for some of his actions.

I shake my head and ride straight for him, twirling my Karabela sword in my hand.

Vlad notices the men approaching and starts fighting back.

Masterfully.

Vlad sidesteps the first soldier, ducks under the second, slashes and stabs the third. He then pushes back the first two and kills the fourth and fifth. The next two soldiers shriek in fear and turn to run away, but Vlad's speed is insane. He chases them down within six steps. That's seven soldiers down in a minute.

He's the greatest fighter I've ever seen. Even better than Baver and Mehmet.

I get to him and jump off my horse, hopefully looking like that super-cool dude from that Turkish show, *Resurrection Ertuğrul*, that Mehmet was obsessed with back at Queen's.

Straight away, I engage with three soldiers. I slash at one, sidestep the other, and thrust at the chest of the third. All that did was get me out of position, so I jump back and retreat. The three soldiers start to chase me. I charge towards them. I grip my sword with both hands and directly go for the first soldier's neck, lobbing off his head. Next, I feint at the second soldier's hip and stab the third in his family jewels.

"OW!" the man yelps.

That's gotta hurt.

I truly am sorry.

I use that moment of shock to slash the second soldier's stomach and his insides pour out.

Disgusting.

I take a look at the third guy. Is he going to die? If he is, I may as well complete the task. I lift my sword but hesitate. Somehow, I can't bring myself to do it. I bring down my sword and use the hilt to knock him out.

I look at Vlad who's fighting off four soldiers. I walk towards him. Hopefully, I can creep up and wipe out a couple guys. Suddenly I notice that one of the Wallachian soldiers has found a weak spot. Vlad strikes at the three soldiers in front of him.

"NO!" I yell as I charge and strike the soldier attacking the Dracula from the blind side. I stab his back and he immediately goes down. I take a look and find his lifeless eyes.

I am now a killer.

Three times over. Four if you count the guy I stabbed in the nuts. There is no way he survives for long. There is no going back. I feel different. I feel worse.

I shake my head and take a look at Vlad who has dusted off the three other soldiers. He has literally killed twelve of the sixteen guys attacking him. An incredible and gory battle feat. The Dracula looks at me and bawls out laughing like an evil villain. Think of Voldemort, but worse. This ain't fiction.

"You saved my life, Yakub," he exclaims. Somehow the fighting has died down. All the opposing soldiers are injured, killed, or being chased into retreat.

I shake my head, but Vlad loudly laughs. "I know you did, friend of Sultan Mehmet. I know you did. I don't know why you did, but you now have my respect. For life. Now, it is time for the final act of this glorious battle."

"What do you mean?" I ask. "We have done what we planned. We have the decisive victory. It is now time to recuperate our injuries and chase them to Silistra, inflicting as many injuries as possible."

"Vladislav knows I'm behind this. Those soldiers were specifically meant for me. I don't know if you noticed, but they were chasing me from the very second the first arrow was released by the Wallachian soldiers on my side. While he wants Varna, he wants my head as well. He wants the throne for himself, and I'm his last obstacle. So this us why we must put the fear of God in them, Yakub. Surely you understand. This is my chance to send a message."

With that, he gets on his horse and rides to the centre of the battleground.

What does he mean sending a message? Surely not killing more civilians.

From on top of the horse, in his harsh voice, he announces, "We have earned a marvelous victory! We have earned this victory for Wallachia and the Ottoman Sultanate!"

The *akinji* break out into cheers, chanting, "*ALLAHU AKBAR! ALLAHU AKBAR! ALLAHU AKBAR! ALLAHU AKBAR!*"

Vlad lifts his sword, and the chants die down. "We have sent a message to these bastards. The Hungarian, Polish, Transylvanian, Moldavian, and Wallachian pigs have received a message! But it isn't enough! A simple victory isn't ENOUGH! We need to make them FEAR US!"

Dracula jumps off his horse and grabs a pike, the same ones he's been using to impale the civilians. He stomps over to an injured opposing soldier, standing over him then spitting a giant wad right on him. He then steps on his chest wound and laughs freakishly while the soldier screams.

I wanna step in, but after that show Vlad put on with a sword, what can I honestly do?

He pushes his foot deeper into the wound and snickers while the soldier pleads in a language I don't understand.

Vlad again laughs, lifts his sword, and presses it into the soldier's body. He picks up the man as blood spurts out and patiently waits for his body to stop twitching. As soon as the soldier goes lifeless, Vlad lobs his head off and impales it on the pike.

Jesus Christ.

I've spared the life of a savage.

"This is how we continue to send a message!" Vlad shrieks. "Do this for all the enemy men left on the battleground and burn their bodies."

What have I done?

I knew he was bad, but I didn't know it went this far.

He grounds the pike with the impaled head and yells, "Now we make the bastards cower in fear as we force them to the fortress at Silistra! With numerous victories along the way! We can celebrate later! Time to get to work!"

Yes, we've gained a victory, but with the warpath that the Dracula is on, we will never secure the peace Mehmet wants. There will be more suffering and bloodshed. And now I think all falls on my shoulders. I bear the burden of death and destruction.

How can I get back to the ones I love after all this?

They will never accept me...

I'm not the same man anymore.

I'm a thousand times worse.

29. Mehmet

For some reason, I'm sitting in an unrecognizable room. I look down, and I'm dressed in normal clothes, a tie-dye LA Lakers hoodie and black jeans. I'm holding my phone. The TV is on, and it's a local newscast. The reporter is at Queen's, right by the football field near Victoria Hall.

"You know, Jamie, the whole Kingston community is baffled by the disappearance of four students last year. Today marks exactly eight months since three Queen's University students and one Ryerson student went missing. Their names are Jacob Brannan, Sally MacLeod, and Mehmet Osman. The student from Ryerson is Hamdan Naeem."

The news cuts to pictures of us: one of Jake with his family, looking as happy as ever. A picture of Sally winning a medal for her equestrian stuff. The pictures used for Hamdan and me, on the other hand, are awful. Mine is the student ID photo that looks like a mugshot — same for Hamdan.

The reporter continues. "The reason this case is baffling is because there are no apparent leads. All we know is that Hamdan Naeem drove up to Kingston from Mississauga to meet up with Osman and Brannan. Their plan was to drive down to Toronto to watch a Leafs game and check into a hotel for a night. That never happened. Their game tickets were left unused. The hotel room was never checked into. Naeem's car did not leave Victoria Hall until it was towed later that day. Sally Ma-

cLeod was supposed to head home for reading week but after reportedly seeing Osman, Brannan, and Naeem in their room, she was not seen again. Witnesses say that all they heard was a loud ruckus in the room. No one saw them leave the room. There is no evidence of them leaving the room. All their clothes, books, devices, toothbrushes, keys, and suitcases remain in the room. It's as though the four have been wiped off the face of the planet. Authorities have ruled nothing out yet, and that means they have yet to rule out foul play. Images from dorm room where the four teens were last seen, are startling."

The camera pans across my dorm room. Whatever commotion happened really did a number on it. The beds are torn apart with the mattresses on the ground, the desks are cracked and broken, the closets are in disarray with our clothes all over the floor.

"Our camera crews were allowed inside the dorm room for the first time today, following months of investigation by law enforcement and scientists. As of now, there are no signs of foul play, but nothing has been ruled out yet after eight months of investigation."

The camera cuts to the entrance of Victoria Hall, where a vigil is being held. Why after eight months, rather than six or one? I don't get it, but sure.

My parents and grandmother are standing there. Hamdan's family is there, as are Jake's and Sally's, and a few friends of Hamdan and mine. Standing next to Jake's parents is Priya, a decently tall and unbelievably good-looking girl of Indian heritage, with long, wavy hair. Tre and Hussein are there. A bunch of Sally's friends who I hardly know are there. Plenty of students from Victoria Hall have gathered as well. A man approaches my family. It is none other than Dr. Abbas Rizvi, my history professor. Wonder if he ever recovered the bloody diary of Mehmet the Conqueror?

I don't know if I can describe how painful this is. Imagine you're dead, no, alive... ugh, how do I describe it? Well, I hope you all get this...

You see, I'm safe. I'm guessing that I'm in a strange dream right now, but I'm chilling in a massive bed, sleeping in the Adrianople palace, while my parents, grandmother, and friends all worry I'm in danger, or worse. I don't even know if I'll ever be able to get back to them.

Watching this... sucks.

I stand up. I try to look down at the phone or grab the remote, but I just can't. I guess a man is never in control of his dreams. My body goes over to the TV, raises my arms, and strikes a massive punch right down the middle.

As soon as my fist connects with the TV, the room shimmers. Next thing I know, I'm sitting in a well-lit tent. Maps and records are laid out on an easily movable desk. There is a man to my right wearing medieval Hungarian battle armour with the chest, back, shoulders, and thighs covered with thick metal chains. Underneath the chain, he wears black and dark red. Two other men sit there. There isn't a single young man sitting in this room; they're all at least forty. The two guards by the entrance of the tent are younger in comparison, though they still look old compared to the nineteen-year-old me.

So, what's going on? This is what I want to ask, but I can't. I'm in zero control. I can't even look down when I want. The men are talking in a language—Hungarian—which I surprisingly understand.

"Those blasted buggers," one dude says. "Not one day of relief since the Serbs joined our group. Then, after leaving Târgoviște, we've been getting picked off by Wallachian men opposing Vladislav. This campaign is useless. I doubt we get to Varna alive."

"I say we pick up and leave now," another says. "This has been futile from the start. The men are injured, sick, and beaten."

"But if we cross the Danube from here, we lose the Wallachian fools,"
a third man says.

"There's a fortress across the river though," the first says. "What if it
is flooded with Turks?"

"Well, we won't know unless we cross the Danube," I say in a strange
voice. What the hell? I wasn't tryna say anything. That voice I spoke
with was so weird and harsh. Am I in another man's body? Am I view-
ing this dream from the perspective of a Hungarian general?

A soldier walks in.

"Commander, some Wallachian men are here to see you," he says to
the man sitting to my right. I should mention that this so-called com-
mander is massive.

Unbelievably so.

"Wallachians?" the commander asks. "Why do they wish to speak to
me and not their ruler?"

"Beats me, to be honest," the soldier says. "I haven't seen them in
camp at all. They are somewhat different, my commander."

"Different how?"

"I think they are from the opposing Wallachian camp, commander."

"Really?" He strokes his chin. "I'd like to see the Wallachians then."

Who could this be? Vlad the Impaler? Is this cunt going to betray
us?

The soldier nods to the commander and stalks off. One moment lat-
er, he returns with Radu, Ibn Eymen, Hamdan, and three Wallachians.

Oh, God... Hamdan and Ibn Eymen are about to accomplish my
plan for peace! I knew they could do it!

Hamdan and Ibn Eymen step forward, with one of the Wallachi-
ans. They are all dressed in similar clothing and armour, which I guess
is what the Wallachians wear to battle. It's similar to the Hungarians,

but the shade of red is darker. There are hints of yellow and the armour does look fiercer than the Hungarian armour in a way that I can't really describe.

"Introduce yourselves for me, please," the Hungarian commander orders.

Hamdan answers. For some reason, I can't understand him. Like, it's crazy. He's clearly speaking Turkish, but it sounds foreign to me. Like I don't know the language. When Hamdan finishes, the Wallachian translates.

"András, Commander of the Hungarian forces. We are not actually Wallachian soldiers. Well, three of us are, but we are not aligned with Vladislav. Now, before you kill us, please respectfully listen to what we have to say."

"Of course," the commander named András says. "You have every opportunity to speak. Are you men the people who have been attacking us since Târgoviște?"

Hamdan replies, and I wait for the translation by the Wallachian man.

"Commander András, we are indeed the men who have been pestering your soldiers..."

András angrily stands up and shouts, "WHY SHOULD I SPARE YOUR LIVES THEN?"

Without missing a beat, the Wallachian man continues translating, "We are here to offer peace. Peace with the Turks and Wallachians on top of a safe passage home for your men."

"Now? After all the killing you've done? Why should I accept?"

All valid questions. I would ask that too. Any sane commander would. This is where Hamdan must be perfect. He has to bring this home. I'd prefer Ibn Eymen to handle this with his experience, but it seems as though they've decided Hamdan is the man for the job. That's okay. Hamdan is smart, even if lacking experience.

After the Wallachian finishes translating Commander András's question, Hamdan pauses to consider an answer. Through the Wallachian soldier, he says, "First, I ought to introduce myself. I am Hamdan Pasha, the fourth vizier of the Ottoman state. I am present with the official seal of the Ottoman state, Nişancı Adham Ibn Eymen. Also present in this tent is the younger son of Vlad Dracul, Radu."

"Of course the bloody Turks are behind this..." the Hungarian Commander András mutters.

Not missing a beat, the Wallachian translator continues to translate Hamdan's answer. "Now the answer to the questions you have posed is very simple. You must accept our offer. You have no other choice, Commander András."

"Or what, Hamdan Pasha?" Commander András interrupts the Wallachian. "What are you threatening me with, exactly?"

Hamdan's translated answer is: "Death. I am threatening you with death and destruction. You cross the Danube; your army will be destroyed."

"Why would you be here with your empty hands offering peace then, Hamdan Pasha?" Commander András aggressively asks. "No one offers peace from a position of strength. The likeliest possibility is that your state is far from ready for our strike on Varna, so you are trying to stop it from ever occurring."

Hamdan arrogantly laughs in a way I've never seen. "There is an army of over fifty thousand men waiting for you to cross the river. Oh, by the way, I know about the injuries your men suffer. Their lack of food. The sickness that has come across the camp. You may not even be aware that the Serbs have been working against you the whole time, helping

411

the cause of the Ottoman state, by inflicting wounds to your soldiers through various means. Also, we have a separate force marching straight for Târgovişte, capturing as much land as possible. There is no one stopping that force. You will be cut off from Hungarian reinforcements. You can't hold a siege, you can't directly attack us, and soon, you won't be able to return home. This campaign has been doomed from the start. Now, Sultan Mehmet the Second does not wish to take advantage of your weak state. He desires a better world. As such, he offers you a chance to cut your losses and head home unharmed."

That was perfect by Hamdan, I think. Dude's probably more qualified to be sultan than I am, to be perfectly honest.

The Hungarian commander glowers then mutters, "What exactly are the terms of peace?"

The Wallachian soldier hands over the two letters I had penned at the end of March. One for the Hungarian commander, and one for János Hunyadi.

The commander rips open the letter. Pretty angrily, I should probably mention. I should also probably mention that I had this letter written in Hungarian. Why? Because I was bored, and I wanted to do this. So I had a slave of Hungarian origin pen the letter, and I freed him in return.

Anyway, the commander opens the letter and starts to read it to himself. With each passing line, he gets more furious, and I get why. My demands are harsh. I mean, they ought to be unforgiving. The Hungarian empire is trying to invade our lands with Wallachia and a bunch of other states. They threaten our social and economic prosperity with the potential of mass death and destruction. The penalty for doing so must be harsh. The Hungarian Empire should pay for their actions in both coin and political control.

412

"8,000 ducats per year..." Commander András mutters. *"That is an asinine number. There is no way Hunyadi accepts this for Ladislaus."*

I should add that Ladislaus is the official ruler of Wallachia. I don't know how to describe his rule. He doesn't actually wield much power. Hunyadi, Ladislaus's regent, holds the true power.

Regardless, this info isn't that important at the moment. What is important is that Hungarians are pissed. I guess they shouldn't have dared to enter our lands with minds of destruction. Oh, by the way, on top of asking for 8,000 ducats, I'm also asking for the eldest male child of every Hungarian nobleman as hostage. Not tryna be sexist, but that's all those fools care about. Male children. Oh, I also state in the letter that Vladislav II ought to be deposed as Voivode of Wallachia and be replaced by Radu.

Yes, Radu. Not Vlad the Impaler.

You may believe these aren't terms of peace but of surrender, and you'd be somewhat right. Like I said, these are harsh terms. The Hungarians are the aggressors of this conflict, but they are acceptable in my opinion because they truly have no other choice. They take our offer, and we promise no economic and military conflict for years. They survive and return home. They reject our offer, and they'll surely die.

That is why the Hungarians are seriously discussing the terms presented by Hamdan.

"Surely we can't agree to this," one dude states in a hushed tone.

"Hunyadi would never agree to these terms, Commander András," the other guy whispers.

"I know that Hunyadi would reject these terms men, but we were just discussing plans to return home," Commander András says in a louder tone. *"Fifty thousand men who are much healthier and rested,*

413

await us if we march towards Varna. We can't hope to defeat them. So I'll be accepting the offer."

He looks towards Hamdan and says, "We graciously accept this offer by you, Hamdan Pasha, the fourth vizier of the Ottoman state. As soon as possible, our men will march back to Hungary and present these terms to the regent of our lands, Jànos Hunyadi, as well as to King Ladislaus."

The Wallachian translates it and Hamdan smiles, walks forward, and shakes the hand of Commander András.

The Wallachian steps forward with a quill, ink, and parchment. The men gather around the Wallachian as he draws up the terms on two separate documents. There is a fair amount of debate over the words as the Wallachian, whose name I've come to know as Florin, writes everything down in Turkish and in Hungarian.

Ibn Eymen signs both documents with my Tughra and Commander András signs them as well.

Uneasily, Hamdan and Florin lead their groups out of the tent.

How can this be so straightforward? How is everything going according to plan? This could just be a normal stupid dream, but it feels so real.

Did I make a smart plan or are we just lucky if all this is true?

"Why would you accept such an offer without proper deliberation?" one Hungarian dude asks. "We are the clear losers here."

"We're returning to our lands with a beating. Not by sword, but by intellect and the pen!"

Commander András walks to the other side of the table looking angry. I do not want to be in front of this man right now. Why am I still in this dream?

He looks angry.

Fierce.

Enraged.

Commander András takes a deep look at us before shouting, "WE CAN'T BE BESTED BY THOSE HALFWITS AGAIN!"

This dude grabs the table, yells, and flips it over.

Hamdan and I really did this to some Hungarian commander the size of Hagrid. We really got some blasted fool from the mid 1400s pissed at us.

If I could laugh in this dream, I sure as hell would.

All of a sudden, Commander András picks up the signed document and stabs it with his dagger right in the middle. He proceeds to rip apart the parchment with his hands.

"THERE IS NO AGREEMENT! WE EXECUTE THE TRAITOROUS SERBS AND MARCH ON THE TURKMEN TOMORROW!"

As he says that, the dream shimmers and my eyes flutter open.

I'm lying in bed with Gülbahar sleeping next to me.

Was this dream real? I truly think so.

Apparently, we've been missing for eight months. (It's the eighth of May 1451.)

My parents probably think I'm dead, and my best friend is about to unknowingly fight in a war with no experience or training.

I could lose Hamdan, my best friend, my day one, and we argued the last time we saw each other. He is my last connection to my previous life. Jake is cool, but he doesn't remind me of home. Sally? She mostly fills me with hope. Hope that makes me feel like I'll succeed here and return home, but I can't lose Hamdan.

I get out of bed and go over to the large window. As I look out, I hear Gülbahar stir from bed. I must not have been quiet. She looks at me and gets up, wrapping her arms around me from behind, providing comfort.

"Are you alright? You were tossing and turning in bed."

"Just a weird dream, Gülbahar," I say. "You can go back to sleep. I am perfectly fine."

"Are you?" she presses. "You've been distant since you ascended the throne..."

"It's just pressure and worries, I guess," I say. "Nothing I can't handle."

"Fill me in on the pressures and concerns," Gülbahar says. "Allow me to ease your burden." I grab her hand and slip myself from her grip and walk to my bed. "What is worrying you?"

"Right now, the thought of losing my best friend. The thought of losing Hamdan."

"Of course..." she whispers as she wraps her arm around me in a genuine embrace.

And for a sliver of a second, I feel comfort.

30. Hamdan

"The emergency divan is now in session," Halil Pasha proclaims. "It is after Isha on Monday, the 26th of May 1451. It is late, but we have urgent business."

Mehmet looks down from the throne. He looks angry—I'm not too sure. I've never actually seen this look from him. He looks across the room at Saruca Pasha, Radu, Ali Bey, Ömer Bey, Ibn Eymen, and Jacob before setting his eyes on Mahmut Pasha, who's standing at the head of our group.

Mehmet has yet to look at me once.

As you have probably guessed, we're back from Silistra. Back from the Battle of Silistra. The leaders of the Ottoman army present at battle, me included, are standing in front of Mehmet.

This Mehmet does not look like my nerdy and unironically funny friend who loves hockey and history. He looks distant. He looks like Sultan Mehmet, not Mehmet Osman, if y'all get what I'm tryna say.

"Mahmut Pasha, tell me about the battle," he demands. "No details spared."

"Of course, my padishah," Mahmut Pasha replies. "My padishah, on the 9th of May, our army was situated by the fortress of Silistra, preparing for battle. Following the Maghrib prayer, the military leadership present, met with me to discuss plans. Following this meeting, Hamdan Pasha told me of his instruction from you to meet the Hungarian commander, with hopes of securing peace with Hungary. Of course, if Hamdan Pasha was able to talk the Hungarians into leaving, it would effectively end the military campaign. No other state aside from Wallachia would remain. Even Wallachia would have been forced to sue for peace. Because of this, we started discussing ways to sneak Hamdan Pasha into the Hungarian camp."

Ya Allah... why is Mahmut Pasha explaining Mehmet's own plan to him? If I could facepalm right now...

Mahmut Pasha starts detailing the plan of how we were to sneak into the Hungarian encampment and as soon as he starts retelling the story, my mind drifts to the night in question. Particularly the moment when we snuck into Vlad's camp and met Radu. It took us well over an hour to convince him he would be a better ruler for Wallachia than his brother. He didn't want to be disloyal to his brother.

As soon as Radu accepted our support for his claim on ruling Wallachia, we rounded up a few loyal Wallachian soldiers to help. We got lucky that one of them, Florin, knew how to speak the language of the Hungarians.

So with Radu, his three Wallachian companions, Ibn Eymen, and I left for the Hungarian encampment, dressed as Wallachian soldiers, high-ranking Wallachian soldiers.

After sneaking into a sleepy Hungarian encampment, we cornered a Hungarian soldier and forced him to get us an audience with Commander András.

"Well, I'm glad to hear that you perfectly executed out a plan that I created, Mahmut Pasha, but tell me the details of the conversation with the Hungarian military commander," Mehmet says.

"Perhaps Hamdan Pasha, Nişancı Adham Ibn Eymen, or the son of Dracul can enlighten me on the details."

Ibn Eymen gives me a look that tells me that he's got this. My appreciation for him has grown vastly in the last couple of months. Being with him every day has certainly brought us closer.

I glance over at Zaganos, who's standing close to Mehmet's throne, looking as sullen as ever.

Ibn Eymen starts to speak, and I recall that evening.

After walking into the Hungarian Commander András's tent, I was worried.

I thought speaking to him would be like speaking with Durad Brankovic, but I was totally wrong.

It was stratospheres from that.

Commander András is menacing, to say the least. He makes *The Rock* look like a pebble. He kept a hard expression on his face the entire time, one that would put any middle-school principal to shame. Except András also looks like the Hulk.

Truly intimidating.

I was hoping that I'd be able to understand their language like I did with the Serbs, but unfortunately, I couldn't. Why I know Serbian and not Hungarian, I don't know, but that's how things worked out. Fortunately, we had our own translator to converse with Commander András.

The conversation was fairly brief. I handled most of the conversation through Florin, the Wallachian who speaks the language. I genuinely thought it went well. I got them to agree to the exact amount for war reparations, length of the agreement, withdrawal of troops from Wallachian lands, and certain trade agreements. We also got them to agree to support Radu's claim to the title of Voivode of Wallachia.

After it was signed, I felt a sense of accomplishment. I mean... Why would I not? With no real training as a negotiator/diplomat or whatever-the-hell they call the thing I was doing, I negotiated our way out of a military conflict.

Except... "_They_ broke the signed agreement between our states!" Mehmet exclaims in a way that denotes shock, but feels fake, almost as though he expected it.

"We apologize, my padishah," Ibn Eymen says.

"No need, this wasn't the fault of anyone from our camp," Mehmet warmly says to Ibn Eymen before giving me a cold-ass look.

The hell? What did I do to deserve that?

"So, tell me, when did you find out about the Hungarian betrayal?" Mehmet asks. "How did you find out and what happened exactly after you found out? I would like Mahmut Pasha to answer this."

Mahmut Pasha steps to the front of the group. "We were up early that morning before the start of Fajr. Hamdan Pasha had returned to our camp about an hour or so before. With his excellent news, we were rejoicing and preparing for our departure. With the abrupt end to the campaign, the men would get restless without the spoils of war, making it difficult to maintain order. Then, seemingly out of thin air, we saw their ships approach in the dark pre-dawn sky. While it may have been a grave shock to everyone, I had kept our preparations intact, after all, there was no guarantee that the Hungarians would keep their word without a hostage exchange."

This dude really just threw Ibn Eymen and me under the bus.

"A hostage exchange?" Mehmet frowns.

"Yes, my padishah," Mahmut Pasha says. "There was no exchange of hostages. Such an exchange could have ensured that the Hungarians stuck to their words."

Mehmet's expression turns hard out of contempt.

Self-contempt?

He looks over at Ibn Eymen and me, face glowering with rage, closes his eyes, slowly breathes, then says, "Please continue, Mahmut Pasha."

"Of course, my padishah. Well, as you may already know, we had been camped at Silistra for about two weeks. Your instructions were clear that if a fight took place, it would be at Silistra. As such, we ensured that the surrounding areas were cleared of civilians. After that, we started to prepare the land for battle. Because the Danube runs through our border with Wallachia, I presumed that the Wallachians would use the river to maneuver away from us. We could not let them do that, so we did our best to manipulate them in the direction we wanted, between the island and the land we stood on."

Okay, I should probably give y'all a lay of land so this conversation can make sense. The Fortress of Silistra is on the southern bank of the lower Danube River. However, the actual fortress isn't adjacent to the river. It is some distance away. In fact, the distance between the fortress and the river can hold a small city with a modern-day population of around 40-50,000. That distance is mainly made up of fields, but there are very small communities living by the banks of the Danube. These fields are where the Ottoman soldiers made camp. The civilians were placed within the actual fortress.

The north of this land is draped by the Danube. Directly crossing into Wallachia would require some time on a boat because it isn't exactly a stone's throw from the shores of the Ottoman state. But to the northeast, there are a few small islands that split the Danube, making it significantly narrower. The closest island is where Mahmut Pasha wanted to manipulate them into going so we could attack them from both banks and force them to dock.

"So, how exactly did you *manipulate* them towards the waters you wished for them to travel?" Mehmet asks.

"We set out boats, but it's far too large to divert them without a chain preventing them from a certain route. Our boats were pathetic ones owned by the locals, so we could not really stop them. We did, however, have about three hundred or so archers on the nearest island. This was done in hopes of the opposing army choosing to reach land where we wanted them to because of the persistent danger of being struck down by arrows. However, none of what we did actually mattered. It seems as though they wanted the direct strike. The opposing bastards had clearly grown impatient."

Mehmet smirks. To Zaganos, he whispers, "What did I tell you? If they rejected peace, they were always gonna directly attack us and try to take hold of Silistra. That would be their only hope of survival."

"Yes, I know, my padishah," he replies.

"Continue with your tale of the battle, Mahmut Pasha."

"Despite all our preparations, my padishah, we were caught off-guard by their initial assault..."

My mind immediately drifts back to that morning. Honestly, it feels as though I'm still there. The events on the grounds by Silistra will live with me forever. No one will ever get what that day was like. You just had to be there.

I was one of the last ones to find out we were going to be fighting an opposing army after all. After we got back from negotiating peace terms with the Hungarians, Ibn Eymen and I retired to rest, which we desperately needed, while everyone prepared for departure from Silistra. Our rest was cut short when Mahmut Pasha woke me up dressed in full armour.

With that, I went into shock, with pure anger, fury, and resentment taking hold in a way I haven't felt before.

That's when it hit me that I've changed.

Never have I been so consistently angry as I have ever since I arrived in the Ottoman Empire. It's just so much.

First, I'm away from my family and homesick. I can't even Facetime them, or as we do in the fifteenth century, send them a letter.

Second, I've lost an identity. I have a totally different identity, but I didn't build it. It was created for me.

Third, the totally different dynamic between Mehmet and myself. I've always lived in his shadow, but this is different. He's not only my best friend, but he's my boss, my emperor, my sultan. He holds the power. What kinda friendship is that? I have incredible love for him, but the dynamic sucks.

Lastly, I want to be good—more than good. I want to be great. I think everyone on this planet does, and anything less than great pisses me off.

The anger I felt when I heard about the broken promise by András was a culmination of all that frustration. I tried to take a bit of it out on Mehmet, by foolishly releasing the pent-up frustration residing within me before leaving for Smederevo and Silistra, but that didn't make a dent in all the anger I had. That anger kept growing as I got into my armour and rode out towards the ongoing battle east of the fortress on a slight curve in the Danube, which is the narrowest point between the fields by Silistra and the closest island.

The allied invading army chose to attack us in the dark. Their initial attack was ferocious. We barely got our lines together in time and were severely pushed back. I observed all of this from the saddle of my horse. I witnessed men being killed from both sides. Every time I'd see or hear a person slain; a pang of guilt would strike my heart. Yes, I shouldn't be accountable for the actions of other men, but what if I did something differently? What if I actually knew what I was doing? Although, the fact that such an untrained and inexperienced person, like myself, was negotiating such a tenuous peace agreement with Hungary is solely on Mehmet.

My best friend and I are partly responsible for the deaths of hundreds. You'd think that I would feel remorse, but I didn't. All I felt was anger.

Wrath.

Indignation.

Blood-boiling rage in a way that I've never felt.

The allied opposing army did not use a single horse. They moved swiftly within small units after reaching shore, attacking the vulnerable portions of our lines. Their attack was smart. Something none of the Ottoman army's leadership could have imagined coming from an army led by Vladislav the Second, which is why I believe the real mastermind behind the battle plan was Commander András.

The only problem for the allied force was that our numbers were simply too large. After their initial assault, our infantry forces were able to recover, even in the darkness of the twilight sky. Our numbers and position were simply superior. Our army struck back ferociously, with Ali Bey and Ömer Bey directing coordinated attacks against the flanks of the enemy. However, there seemed to be an endless supply of enemy soldiers. Behind the battleground, from the island across the narrow section of the Danube, archers were firing arrows at the waves of enemy soldiers but had minimal success due to the darkness. With twilight breaking into dawn, it became much easier for them.

The enemy army scattered after our counterattack, retreating to their own state's banner and friends, not standing together as a proper unit. Slowly but surely, our side started to dominate. As the tide of the battle started to turn around sunrise, the first group of Hungarians joined the fight.

At this point, my anger grasped complete hold of my mind, heart, and soul. Nonsensically, I jumped off my stallion and sprinted into battle.

Sluggishly.

Very sluggishly.

Yeah, it had been *some time* since I'd gone on a run. I wasn't as athletic as I should have been.

I ran straight towards the oath breakers... that's a nerdy and awful term for the Hungarians, but I've been using it, so bear with me.

So I ran straight towards them, striking down anyone in my way.

Most of the oath-breaking Hungarians were killed by the time I arrived. But with the help of a couple other Ottoman soldiers, we brought down the rest of the force.

This happened again and again. Wave after wave of Hungarians came in small regiments, but we struck them down.

Even I killed some men.

There is blood on my hands, but it doesn't make me feel remorseful.

It makes me angry.

Angry at Mehmet.

Angry at the world.

But mostly, I'm angry at myself.

I'm a killer.

A goddamn motherfucking killer.

At sunrise, the final groups of Hungarians were crossing the Danube. The final group was led by none other than the one and only Commander András, the chosen commander of the Hungarians. A man who could put the Hulk to shame in stature. At that point, I had just slain a man, still completely in shock that I actually could fight properly. At that sight, my anger reached a level beyond boiling.

I went Super Saiyan.

Well... in my head at least. I dashed like a madman towards the commander, but suddenly, out of nowhere, I blacked out.

Next thing I know, I'm lying in a cart, head wrapped and Ibn Eymen looking over me. He whispered, "I saved you from your own foolishness. You are young. Live to fight another day. Live to fight greater battles. The physical, mental, and emotional ones."

"What happened with the battle? Did we win?" I asked.

"For every man lost to the Ottoman sultanate, *eleven* were lost by the opposition. Right now, Yusef Agha, the janissaries, Vlad, and his Wallachian comrades are pursuing the retreating forces. They should arrive a few days after us in Adrianople."

The final death toll was... "1,000 of our men dead! 11,000 thousand of the opposition! 12,000 deaths due to this military campaign!" Mehmet angrily exclaims.

"That is an approximation, my padishah," Mahmut Pasha says. "Of course this estimate excludes the men lost during Vlad's quest to slow down the enemy allied army, the five hundred Serbs executed by Commander András, the lives lost in the skirmish between

Skanderbeg, the lives lost with Ahmet Bey's excursion into Wallachia where he still remains, and in Baltoghlu Süleyman's defence of the port city Varna against the failed siege by the Moldavian Navy."

"I thank you for correcting my misstep, Mahmut Pasha," Mehmet says. "Regardless, the loss of life deeply hurts."

"That, my padishah, is the price one has to pay for attacking the Ottoman people, lands, and the sultanate," Halil states. "The loss of life for the other states should be of no concern. We are not at fault for those lives."

"That is true, my padishah," Zaganos says. "You can't hold yourself to account."

"The loss of every life from this senseless conflict falls on the shoulders of all political leaders involved, Halil Pasha," Mehmet says as he looks at me grimly. "We missed our opportunity for peace. The responsibility falls on all our shoulders."

Why does it feel like he is speaking strictly to me? There is absolutely no way that Mehmet is going to place the blame on me, right?

I mean it isn't just my fault. I don't know what else I could have done, to be honest.

Mehmet stands up and orders, "Bring in the prisoners!"

The doors to the Imperial Hall open up, and in rough chains that completely shackle and immobilize, two men are dragged in. They are none other than Vladislav II of Wallachia and András of Hungary.

They are dragged to the middle of the room on their knees, then they are abruptly dropped down to their forearms. Each man sluggishly gets up to face the imposing Ottoman court, with his feet and hands shackled to chains and bare navel exposed.

"Is there anything you'd like to say to your cousin, Radu?" Mehmet asks.

Radu shakes his head. "Nothing's to be said, your excellency."

"I would like for you to translate what I wish to say," Mehmet commands. "Vladislav of Wallachia, this is the price you pay for breaking the sacred peace of our lands. You are our prisoner until our states reach an agreement. In the meantime, you will be sequestered to your quarters, I now ask someone to translate the same for Commander András."

We wait for the statement to get translated. Mehmet abruptly gets up and announces, "I'm done for the day. I would like to see Yakub and Hamdan Pasha in my study at their earliest convenience tomorrow morning. I need rest and time to think."

With that, he speed-walks out of the Imperial Hall, with at least seven or eight men scurrying behind his flailing red robes as the prisoners are slowly led out of the room.

Jake walks over to me and says, "He couldn't even talk to us tonight? He must really be angry."

"He has no goddamn right to be…"

31. Jake

I've always been a morning person. My parents stress time management, and the small-town life, made it so I just had to be. I had a strict schedule of waking up at 5:30 a.m. and getting all my chores done, so I could spend the rest of the day on school/work, sports, friends, family, and with Priya. It was a good schedule: I had time for everything, and I did everything I put my mind to. My life was ordered and uncomplicated. Then came university, and it truly was an adjustment. Yet I kept my order, at least for the month and half I was there, and my life remained uncomplicated. Then, Mehmet's ancestor's diary magically brought us here, and the strict order has remained. There is a reason why the janissaries are the greatest infantry soldiers in the fifteenth century. It is due to their discipline. However, my life is now far removed from being uncomplicated. I am unable to see my parents, sister, a lot of friends, and my girl. I fight in medieval military battles and have killed other men. All to try to get back to my uncomplicated life. But now I worry, is my life going to be uncomplicated when I get back? Will I be able to look at my parents, my sister, or Priya the same way after everything I've done? Being the deputy commander of the janissaries has changed me.

I don't know how yet—if it's in a good way or a bad way.

I'm a morning person, and yet I don't wanna get out of bed. If I could, I'd stay here all day.

But I can't.

I'm to meet Mehmet in a bit. Probably to catch up on everything. We haven't spoken since the 31st of March. Today is the 27th of May.

It's been *some time*.

I hear a knock on the door. "Come in," I say in a dreary tone meant to denote exhaustion.

In walks Baver, sweating furiously from his early-morning run. He grabs a cloth from my messy desk and wipes his face. Then he sits at the foot of my bed.

"Are you done moping around, or are you going to face what awaits you?" Baver asks. "The longer you lie in bed, the more respect I lose for you."

"I'm losing your respect by being lazy?" I ask rhetorically. "It's the day after an eight-week military campaign that still isn't officially over, Baver. I think I've earned my rest."

"I was far more involved in the actual hand-to-hand combat than you, Yakub," Baver boastfully asserts. "If anyone has earned rest, it is me."

"That's debatable."

"Damn you, Yakub," Baver says. "I'm the one who first penetrated the enemy lines."

"Who planned the surprise attack with the sons of Dracul?" I ask. "It was yours truly."

"You're missing my point, boy! I know the padishah is upset with the military leadership. I also know that he wishes to meet with you and Hamdan Pasha today. That can't be good. Am I right?"

"I can't possibly see how he could be angry with me, Baver. We completed our task with near perfection. I don't know what to expect when I see our padishah, and that concerns me."

"Then go to the padishah and talk to him without delay," Baver says. "Men should not lie in bed all day contemplating the what ifs. They jump into action. That's the only way to win at life."

"Life is not war, Baver," I complains.

He chuckles. "What is life but a series of battles? You win some, you lose some. At the end of the day, you ought to give it your all, so when you reach your deathbed, you can truly be satisfied with what you've accomplished before meeting with your lord."

I stare at him in bewilderment. "You know, Baver," I say. "That may just be the smartest thing you've ever said. Perhaps there's some intellect in that big head of yours. A teensy bit, but some."

"Are you calling me dumb, Yakub? It would take me about half a minute to defeat you in battle. A dunce could never do that."

"I'll keep that in mind," I mutter as I get out of bed. "Now, leave so I can get dressed and meet the Sultan."

Baver nods and leaves the room.

He's right. I can't be worrying about what my friend might say to me. Even if Mehmet is angry at both of us, like Hamdan seems to believe, what's the worst he can do?

Yell?

He needs us just as much as we need him.

"So…" Hamdan says as we walk towards Mehmet's study. "How do you think Mehmet will receive us after two months apart?"

"He hardly gave us a look last night," I reply. "I hope that was all to keep this act of ours, rather than how he actually feels."

"There's no way he can be angry at you, fam," Hamdan says. "It's me he's angry at, and I'm ready for it. If anyone has a right to be angry, it's me."

As he says this, the door to Mehmet's study comes into view.

Some fireworks are about to go down.

That's for sure.

Two angry best friends.

Whatever happens, it's not gonna be pretty.

Saad opens the door to the study, and Mehmet is sitting at his desk, next to the kadi'asker, Mawiz Ibn Hasan. Mehmet says a couple words to Mawiz then he gets up, grabs his papers, and leaves, muttering to himself about the multiple trials he has to oversee before nightfall.

We take a seat across from Mehmet, who leans back in his overly large chair, making it feel as though we're in the principal's office, but this is no principal, this is the sultan of the Ottoman Empire.

"Glad to see you are well, Hamdan," Mehmet says and grabs a piece of fruit on his desk. "No apparent injuries. You're safe and that's what's important first and foremost. Everything else I want to talk about comes second to that. And you, Jake. I spoke to Radu early this morning. He had the greatest things to say about you. The way you handled yourself. Your military genius, your ability to lead in battle were all beyond excellent."

"Okay, that's well and all, Mehmet, but why on earth would you align yourself with Vlad?" I ask with a smile to acknowledge his compliment. "Do you know how much of a monster he is?"

He looks down at the fruit tray with a painful smirk, then somberly looks right at me.

Hamdan shakes his head and turns away in anger.

"Jake, I should have told you everything I knew about Vlad from the jump. But certainly everything I know about him has to be exaggerated to some extent."

"Trust me. Whatever you know about him is understated," I reply. "He truly is the devil."

"So he actually acts like a bloody vampire?" Mehmet asks. "Like he drinks the blood of the men he's killed after impaling them?"

Perhaps I should have let him continue. "Well no," I say. "But he did—"

"Impale the ones he killed?"

"Well, yeah, but—"

"Of course he did." Mehmet grimaces. "He is Vlad *the Impaler* after all.

"What?" Hamdan exclaims. "Why is he called that?"

"He impales his victims," Mehmet replies. "In 1462, he's gonna impale thousands of Ottoman soldiers to deter my ancestor's forces from pursuing him."

A monster.

How can Mehmet stomach working with him?

Hamdan stands up and rubs his fingers against his forehead. "Impale? What is that?"

"It's basically taking a sharp object, like a stake, and using it to pierce through the body," I reply. "So, like, it goes through like a spear does, and then they set the stake into the ground. It can be used for torture and execution. Vlad does it to send a message, through torture, humiliation, and execution."

"How the hell could you align yourself with someone like that?" Hamdan asks. "And how could you ask YOUR FRIEND Jake to work with him? He's your friend, for God's sake!"

"The enemy of my enemy is my friend," Mehmet says calmly. "Even if he is to later be my enemy. I suspect he'll be a thorn in my side as soon as he finds out I'm supporting his younger brother's claim to the throne. Also, I didn't want Jake to join Vlad's campaign into Wallachia. That was all Yusef Agha's doing, as I'm sure Jake can attest."

"Yeah, Hamdan," I add. "It was Yusef Agha who ordered me to join Vlad and Radu. I doubt Mehmet even knew I was gone until we had long since left the gates of Adrianople."

"Okay, but Mehmet still needs to be straight with us," Hamdan says.

"I told you guys everything you need to know," Mehmet insists. "Jake, if you had known Vlad was a psychopath, would you have gone along with any of his commands from the start?"

I shake my head no, and Mehmet continues. "And Hamdan, I gave you all the ammo you needed to secure a peace agreement, so it really is a damn shame that you couldn't."

Uh oh.

Hamdan shakes his head. "You really thought a completely inexperienced guy could sign a compact peace agreement with the clock ticking? THAT IS JOKES!"

"I had total faith in you, Hamdan," Mehmet replies. "The fact that you were unable to complete this task doesn't change the belief I had in you."

434

"HAD?" Hamdan asks. "Past tense? Has your confidence in me dropped? Do you think you would have done any better than me with your pea-sized brain?"

Mehmet picks up a goblet and sips his water, deliberating as if he's trying to be as diplomatic as possible. By the look on his face, he genuinely believes he could have done better.

"Hamdan, I won't ever lose the faith I have in you," Mehmet starts, "but the failed agreement falls on your shoulders. You had Ibn Eymen with you the entire time, yet you were the only one to speak. While you did an *adequate* job negotiating with Commander András, and I was certainly impressed by the way you carried yourself in the conversation, it wasn't enough, and that partially falls on your shoulders. You didn't use all your resources."

"And you would know this how?" he asks. "You weren't there."

"Except I was. You used a Wallachian translator by the name of Florin. You spoke with four Hungarian leaders, but the convo was entirely between Commander András and you, through Florin. I saw all this in a dream. I was looking at the proceedings through one of the Hungarians. I saw Commander András go into a fury of rage after you left his tent and in that fit of anger, he decided to execute the Serbs and attack my army in the morning."

"Why would you have a dream about a conversation happening leagues away from where you were sleeping?" I ask.

"I don't know, man," Mehmet replies. "I've been getting weird dreams since the moment I touched my ancestor's cursed diary."

"That's strange..." I mutter as I study his face. "Maybe it's connected to how we return home?"

"Let's leave that for later, Jacob," Hamdan orders. "Right now, I

435

want Mehmet to tell me how it's MY fault that a battle took place. If anything, it's *your* fault. Your plan was flawed from the start."

"There is nothing I can do about that, can I?" he asks. "I had to be quick to come up with a plan weeks in advance. You went into that tent only to deliver the knockout blow, which you were unable to do, so our army had to do it. Unfortunately, that knockout blow was packaged with thousands of deaths."

"And all of that is MY FAULT?"

"Did I say that, Hamdan?" Mehmet asks. "I didn't. The blame lies with everyone, but surely even *you* feel you could have done some things better? Am I wrong?"

"You aren't wrong there, but you make it seem like I had a simple task, when it was far from that."

"I never called your task simple, Hamdan," Mehmet says in a dismissive manner. "The truth is that my plan made it easier for you. You just got stopped a yard short of the end zone. No shame in your work, bud. Even an experienced person like Zaganos or Halil may not have done as well."

"Of course, I would never have been able to do anything without you, right?" Hamdan sarcastically asks. "Obviously, I can't do anything without the help of Mehmet Osman. No one truly can."

"WHAT IS THAT SUPPOSED TO MEAN?" Mehmet yells as he stands up from his oversized chair.

"Exactly what you think," Hamdan calmly replies. "Your life ain't a movie, Mehmet. Nobody wants to walk in your shadow like I have my whole life."

Oof, I can feel that dagger being thrust into Mehmet's soul.

Cooler heads need to prevail.

436

"Guys, guys," I say. "Let's calm down. No reason to get heated. We're all working towards the same things."

Mehmet sits down. "I really must be the worst friend ever, but there has never been a time where you have had to live in my shadow. I don't know where you're getting this load of crap from."

"Really?" Hamdan asks. "The constant comparisons, the competitions, being defensive partners in hockey, the way everyone thought of you before they ever thought of me. To everyone, I was just Mehmet's friend, not Hamdan. Here, it's just an exaggerated version of that."

"Don't be so dramatic," Mehmet exclaims. "It was never like that. You have always been your own person. Don't give me this shit."

"How blind are you, fam?" Hamdan sounds angry. "How bad is your memory? Or how filtered is your memory? There are other people in this world to consider!"

"You're speaking as though I don't think about you."

"You know, it feels like that sometimes," Hamdan counters. "Sometimes you can really feel selfish. You have such a 'woe is me' attitude that is just so fucking dumb. Like, maybe you ain't as important as you think you are."

Oh no.

"You're saying I'm not important *now*?"

"I didn't say tha—"

"YOU KNOW WHAT?" Mehmet yells. "You are your own person. I have never forced you to be friends with me. If being my friend is so difficult, the door is right there. Just walk away, and you'll never have to see me again."

"Fine by me." Hamdan gets up and walks straight for the door with anger steaming from his ears.

"You don't mean that, Hamdan!" I exclaim.

"You need to shut your damn mouth, Jacob," Hamdan growls with his back to us. He walks out.

"Mehmet!" I yell. "Is that really all you have to say to your BEST friend?"

"I said my piece, Jake," he mumbles. "I don't know what Hamdan was going on about, but I don't need that negativity. Now, sit down, so I can tell you about our eastern border with the Karamanids."

I sit and Mehmet gulps down the rest of his water.

What do I say? He and his best friend just had a major argument. It was very confusing, and it felt like they were just spouting by the end. What I do know, however, is that we are never going to get back home this way. We can't be four separate and fragmented individuals. We need to be united. We need to come together as one to get back home.

It is the only way.

32. Mehmet

A loud knock on the door makes my eyes flutter open. I had yet another late night just chilling in my own room, doing nothing in particular. My body was unable to sleep, but I probably should have tried harder. I'm ruining my life more than I already have by not sleeping properly. All I'm doing is adding unneeded stress on top of all the stress I already have. Perhaps running an empire, feeling the need to be perfect, and regretting my missteps has started to get to me.

The knocking on the door persists, so I grimly yell, "Come in, you annoying bastard!"

In walks Jake, with a recently trimmed haircut, a freshly shaven face, and new clothes. He doesn't look like he just went through a military campaign.

He walks straight to my bed and violently pulls off the sheets and covers.

"What are you doing?" I exclaim. "If you want something, just ask."

"You need to get up," he demands. "You've been working from your room for nearly four straight days. You haven't left this room once. You look a mess, and the whole palace has been whispering about what's going on."

"What are the palace dwellers saying?" I ask. "Surely they all believe that I have a fever or something."

"Well, that's not what they're saying, Mehmet. Everyone knows about your fight with Hamdan."

"How's that possible?" I ask. "No one except you was in the room during the spat, and I'm sure you wouldn't have told anyone."

He sits down on my bed. "The rumour is that you had a serious disagreement with Hamdan, perhaps on a personal matter. The slave named Saad probably told his friends, which is how it got started. People think that your deep anger is why you haven't left your room. Hamdan has been instructed by Zaganos, Halil, and Ibn Eymen to not leave his estate. Mahmut Pasha has remained in the capital just in case there's a shakeup in the administrative structure. No one knows what your mood is right now, which explains the uneasiness. You must come out and show your face. Attend the divan, go to your meetings, work out in the evening with the janissaries. Be yourself, and show everyone you are fine."

"The second I leave this room, I'll be surrounded by people. Everyone's eyes will still be on me. I always hate it, but I can't do that right now, dude," I say. "I'm pissed off at Hamdan. I don't want everyone to see. I don't get why he's being so darn annoying. He's never this way."

"Perhaps if you listened to what he has to say, he wouldn't be so annoying?"

Who on earth does this Jacob Brannan fella think he is? "You don't have any right to comment on my friendship with Hamdan," I say. "You've been my friend for less than a year. You hardly know me. You have to work your way to the top of the pecking order. If you're trying to rile me up, it worked, so I'll attend the divan, but only because I don't wanna have this pathetic conversation with you again."

"I'd recommend a bath, my padishah," Jake says. "You reek and that is me putting it lightly."

"Just get out, you prat!"

"I'll see you at the divan then." Jake exits the room.

I lie on the bed again and bury my face under a cushion. What is wrong with me? I just beefed with my two closest (only?) friends at the same time. I'm the shittiest friend in the world.

No.

I'm the shittiest person in the world.

I open the door and leave my quarters for the first time in what feels like weeks, but in reality, it's only been around four or so days.

Immediately, the janissary guards, who were fooling around, stiffen up. The two slaves cleaning up outside immediately step to the side and lower their heads. The light atmosphere gets tense.

Cold.

That's not to say palace life is cold, or gloomy. The palace can be very cheery.

I just haven't witnessed it.

People feel the need to be perfect around me.

That's why I want my friends to be normal around me. No, I *need* them to be normal.

Jake was just tryna be a good friend earlier today, I shouldn't have mouthed off at him. I haven't known him for long, but he's still my broski.

My nights with Sally on Sundays are so relaxing. I listen to her talk about whatever she wants to. I know so much more about her. She tells me important details, like the fact that she is agnostic, to smaller details like she is a dog person, but she also has two cats named Milo and Lily. We talk a bit about our present lives, but mostly we desire our lives 550ish years into the future. I look forward to Sundays solely because of her.

Hamdan, on the other hand... fucking Hamdan, man. This dude has been acting very different, as though he's angry all the time.

Sullen.

Annoying.

I'm generally the annoying one. The grim one. The friend who is frustrated with the world.

But this new attitude of Hamdan's can't fly. It pisses the hell outta me because I don't get it. Where's all that anger coming from? The talk of living in my shadow makes no sense. I always felt as though I lived in *his* shadow.

Man, I can't be doing everything wrong... but what if I am?

It feels like I am messing everything up, which is infuriating. I feel like I fail at everything, and the one thing I shouldn't fail at, I'm in the process of failing.

I don't know.

My mind is a minefield right now.

I don't know if I'm angry at Hamdan or myself or even the whole world for just being plain awful.

I'm just angry.

Pretty sure a good sultan should not be in the mindset I'm in right now.

Then again, I'm an awful sultan.

I forcefully smile at the guards and slaves as I start for the Imperial Hall. They all brightly smile as soon as they realize that my gaze is on them. I turn out of the corridor and walk by the front entrance of the palace.

There I see the jubilant Hatice out of the corner of my eye.

"How are you on this lovely day, my padishah?" she asks.

"Feeling great!" I lie. "How are you doing? What has you in such exuberant spirits?"

"Oh, nothing, Mehmet!" she playfully replies. "Just thankful that Allah has blessed me with life for yet another year."

"Oh, happy birthday!" I exclaim. "I hope you have an excellent day! I apologize for forgetting about your special day. You had mentioned it to me once."

"It is quite alright, my padishah. An eighteenth birthday isn't that special."

"You know, Hatice," I whisper as we stroll back toward the Imperial Hall. "An eighteenth birthday is especially special in the timeframe and land I'm from."

"Why is that?"

I look around, hoping no one is listening to our conversation. "It's the age of when one is finally considered to be an adult. At that age, people are able to do everything an adult is allowed to do, like pay taxes, vote in federal, provincial, and municipal elections, as well as—"

"What do you mean by voting in the... elections?"

"Oh, in my country, Canada, and many parts of the world, we

hold elections to determine who our leaders should be. So, it would be akin to subjects deciding who the leader of Adrianople should be, who the Governor of Rumelia should be, and who the sultan should be."

"But why?"

"It's what we've determined to be the best way to govern ourselves."

"I really would like to learn more about this future world, Mehmet," she says. "I have so many questions, but for now, I have one burning question."

"Ask away."

"Why is eighteen the chosen year for children to be considered adults?"

I laugh at the question. I mean it is a weird question to me. It's never been something I questioned to be honest.

"I don't know, to be perfectly honest. I guess because in Western culture, eighteen-year-olds are expected to live by themselves. Perhaps there is a scientific answer, but I really couldn't tell ya."

"It's just weird to me, Mehmet. Think about it, you married Gülbahar Hatun when you were fourteen, Gülshah Hatun when you were seventeen, and ascended the throne at age twelve and eighteen. While you were *still* fairly young when you married and ascended the throne, it isn't out of the ordinary. My father has been looking for a suitable husband for me since I turned sixteen."

"That is too early," I declare. "Also, I find it shocking that you haven't found someone if you have been genuinely looking for two years."

"Well, I've rejected a few suitors who weren't right for me," she replies. "Also, sixteen is not much younger than eighteen, which I assume is when people in your time start looking for marriage."

"Well... people generally get married much later in the year 2019. Many don't get married at all in fact. They do not want to."

"How is that possible?" she exclaims. "Why would people delay their marriage? Why would people deny themselves the joys of marriage?"

"The world in 2019 is very different from the world in 1451, Hatice," I say as the Imperial Hall comes into view. "It's difficult to describe."

"I want to see it," she retorts. "While I think I may enjoy my life here better, I do like to explore."

I smile as we approach the gates.

"I wish you luck in your pursuit of marriage, Hatice," I say. "I really hope we get the chance to talk again soon."

"Inshallah, my padishah," she murmurs. Jake comes over. I don't think she's figured out who my friends are, which is why she's starting to slip away. "Have an excellent divan."

"Salaam alaikum, Hatice," I say as she gracefully walks away. "Have a wonderous eighteenth birthday."

Hatice turns ever so slightly to gaze into my eyes and give a shy but bright smile, as she slowly twirls her hair to move it behind her ear.

I look at her as she walks away until Jake extends his fist right in front of me. I give him a solid fist bump. "Sorry for getting angry this morning. It should never have happened."

"Don't worry, Mehmet. I get what you're dealing with. Now, let's put everyone at rest during this divan."

"Let's get this, fam."

With that, we walk into the hall, ready for whatever is on the docket for today.

I take a seat on my throne as I observe the near full room. Present are my viziers, Halil, Zaganos, and Mahmut Pasha. I'm guessing Hamdan is still holed up in his estate. Ibn Eymen is present. So are the defterdar and the kadi'asker. Jake, of course, is in the room as well as Saruca Pasha, Ömer Bey, and Ak Shemsettin.

There is also a young man in the room who I do not recognize. He stands further away from the others, almost at the door.

I stare at him. Is he a foreign ambassador?

I can't tell, and it's yet another thing that pisses me off. Why can't I control this subconscious knowledge I have?

The strange man's eyes have been on my top two viziers.

The atmosphere is quite serious, and the room is eerily hushed, when it is usually boisterous. It's almost like everyone is nervous.

Halil steps up, unrolls a scroll, and dimly announces, "It is Saturday after Dhuhr on May 31, 1451. Welcome to today's divan. Twenty minutes ago, I received some vital news, which will be the topic of discussion today. We can table the conversation about exchange of the Hungarian and Wallachian hostages later."

Halil looks towards the strange man furthest from me, standing near the door. He raises his voice. "Gedik Pasha, the floor is yours. Please convey the message you bring from Ishak Pasha."

The man approaches the throne. I recognize his name as the one Halil suggested I send to negate the Karamanid threat. I disagreed because I knew nothing of him, despite the name's familiarity, which is why I sent Aslan Pasha instead.

The latest I've heard is that Aslan Pasha awaits the Karamanids at an advantageous position a hundred or so kilometres from Akşehir, which is a short distance from Konya, the capital of the Karamanid Sultanate. I received that news on the day of the Battle of Silistra, which was the 10th of May. Of course, the news was delayed by about a week, so he was there on the 3rd.

Aslan Pasha's instructions from me are clear. He must stop the Karamanid attack in its tracks. They mustn't get anywhere near Ankara. That city is too important to be besieged. If he can inflict a decisive wound to the Karamanid army, that would ensure no siege takes place. Of course, after that, a retaliatory battle would have to take place and then probably a conquest of the Karamanid territories, but Aslan Pasha needs to win this.

I pray that he does.

But now Gedik Pasha stands right in front of me. My hope is that he comes bearing good news, but it doesn't look that way.

As I've stated, the attitude in this room is tense. Men are filled with anticipation.

Gedik Pasha stops about two metres from my throne. Out of respect, his head is lowered, but as soon as he stops, he lowers his upper body into a proper bow—the type of thing I hate. I am not God.

"Stand up straight and look me in the eye, Gedik Pasha," I snarl. He does what I ask, and I continue, "Now, tell me, what news do you bring?"

447

Gedik Pasha takes a letter from the pocket of his navy-blue robe. He breaks the seal and unfolds the parchment.

"My padishah, I have come to you as expeditiously as I possibly could with this letter. Do I have your permission to read it aloud for the room?"

"Go ahead," I say. "Everyone in this room has the right to hear the message."

Gedik Pasha looks down and reads. "*To Sultan Mehmet Khan, The Second of His Name, Son of Murat, Sovereign of the Sublime House of Osman, Sultan of Sultans, Khan of Khans, Padishah of Anatolia and Rumelia. From the Provincial Governor of Anatolia, the right honourable Ishak Pasha, delivered by his trusted advisor, Gedik Pasha.*"

Surprising that Ishak Pasha has shortened his titles.

I wouldn't've.

Titles are bragging rights.

You need bragging rights to advance in life.

That's what I've learned in my months here.

"*My padishah, I send you this letter in haste, relating urgent information. On the eleventh of May, Aslan Pasha engaged with the Karamanid forces at the plains of Akşehir. The battle raged on for the whole day and Aslan Pasha's forces were devastatingly defeated, with approximately half the men perishing in battle.*"

"Half the men have perished?" Çelebi exclaims in shock.

Gedik Pasha uneasily nods. "Thirteen thousand men have been lost in service to this sultanate."

THIRTEEN THOUSAND MEN. How?

My body stiffens and shivers at the same time. That is thirteen thousand men dead on my head. I'm responsible for these lives lost. What the hell is wrong with me?

I hear Zaganos say under his breath, "Perhaps he should have sent Gedik Pasha or any other commander with balls…"

Huh?

How the hell am I to know who to send? Then again, it's my job to know. Hearing that from Zaganos just infuriates the heck outta me.

Bloody hell, my mind ain't working at all.

I take a deep breath. "Is that all the letter states, Gedik Pasha?"

"No, there is more," he replies as he looks at the parchment. He reads, *"Aslan Pasha has managed to slip away with the remaining thirteen thousand or so men to the outskirts of Isparta. I pen this letter on the sixteenth of May, while marching towards Isparta with 35,000 of my men to join Aslan Pasha's forces. I should reach Isparta by the 22nd of May. I do not anticipate a battle for many weeks. It looks as though the Karamanids, led by their bey, Ibrahim II, are awaiting reinforcements. This letter has two purposes: to inform you of the latest news on this warfront, and to plea for further reinforcements. I anticipate the Karamanids will march towards us with an army upwards of 40,000 men. I need more men to win a decisive victory."*

With that, Gedik Pasha folds the letter and hands it to the Kadi'asker Mawiz Ibn Hasan.

The room looks at me for a response.

The only problem? I don't know what to say, I'm so goddamn angry.

At the Hungarians for invading Rumelia by using Wallachia and a whole host of other states.

At the Karamanids for invading Anatolia.

At the fact that I have been placed in this uncomfortable position.

I feel like the blame rests somewhere, but I can't figure out exactly where, which is why I blame myself.

How do I stop blaming myself?

When will I stop feeling empty and actually do what's needed?

I look at the faces across the room. Faces that are uneasily waiting to hear what I have to say. But what do I say?

So far, I've sent people to complete campaigns for me. I've given them missions, and they have failed to fulfill my expectations. Maybe that's my fault. Perhaps I don't know what is realistic and what isn't. That's probably why the campaigns haven't gone according to plan.

I stroke my bearded chin as the tension of the room grows in silence. Out of the corner of my eye, I see Zaganos shake his head out of frustration and step up to distinguish himself in the Imperial Hall.

He looks at me, softy clears his throat, and says, "My suggestion is that you, my padishah, head the reinforcements towards Isparta. From there, *you* take control of the Ottoman forces and lead the assault on the Karamanid army, to defeat the weakling by the name of Ibrahim Bey."

The room immediately bursts into a series of hushed comments.

Without delay, however, Halil steps forward. "There is still an uncertain situation at Rumelia's border. We must ease relations with the empires neighbouring that particular border while defending ourselves from the Karamanids. Send Zaganos Pasha, or Gedik Pasha, with the janissaries after Yusef Agha arrives. With that, you will have trustworthy leadership on that front, protecting our lands and the people in Anatolia. Then you can work to repair relations with the European empires."

"You're just trying to contradict me, as always!" Zaganos exclaims.

"No, I'm being reasonable," Halil states. "Giving reasonable and sound advice is the job of a vizier, particularly the grand vizier. It isn't to give rash, emotional advice like you've just done."

"There's no point in being conservative and reserved!" Zaganos declares. "The Karamanids were dominant in Anatolia for so long. We have been stronger for the last couple decades, but because of conservative strategy, they have persisted, and we have missed our opportunities. If Sultan Mehmet marches, it signals to the world that he is all in on conquering lands and making the Ottoman Sultanate greater. It shows that he is willing to do the work himself to elevate the empire."

A few nods go across the room in agreement. One of the heads that nods in earnest is Ibn Eymen's. He's the man I respect the most after Jake in this room.

Halil looks around with a deep sense of frustration. "We should not make it seem that we are all in on a singular conquest. We are not a small territory, as we were over a century ago. We are an established and growing sultanate. We must move rationally, not rashly. As such, we—"

"Why can't we go all in?" I ask.

"Because if our opponents believe that we are in an all or nothing situation, they will use it to their advantage."

"I fail to see how that's problematic, Halil Pasha," I retort. "I am all in. I am all in when it comes to the growth and prosperity of this empire. Defeating the Karamanids will help with that, so I am all in."

"My padishah—"

"SHUT YOUR CURSED MOUTH, HALIL PASHA!" I yell, letting all my anger stupidly consume me. I stand up to look intimidating. "I AM ALL IN. THAT MEANS I WILL BE LEADING

THE ATTACK AGAINST THE KARAMANIDS PERSON-
ALLY. YOU AND ZAGANOS PASHA WILL ACCOMPANY
ME. MAHMUT PASHA WILL ENSURE NOTHING BOILS
OVER WITH THE CONFLICT AGAINST THE HUNGAR-
IAN-WALLACHIAN ALLIANCE, AND HAMDAN PASHA
WILL REMAIN HERE TO, UM, LOOK OVER ALL AFFAIRS."

An instant murmur goes across the room following my sudden
and angry declaration.

I immediately look at Jake as I sit back down on my throne. He
shakes his head but gives me a sheepish smile and a weak thumbs up.

"Now," I declare, "let's discuss strategy."

Immediately, Ali Bey, Gedik Pasha, Ömer Bey, Saruca, and Zaganos start talking military strategy. I try to listen. I really do. I must
if I want to survive, let alone win.

But there is only one thought circulating my head.

One question flowing through my brain.

What on earth have I gotten myself mixed up in?

33. SALLY

"SO YOU'RE GOING TO FIGHT IN A WAR?"

"Yes," Mehmet whispers, "I'm going to lead an army into battle."

I take a deep breath and look around. The two of us are sitting right outside the palace grounds, a few metres from the still half-broken fence, the same place we sat over two months ago on Mehmet's birthday.

Both of us are resting on the ground, gazing into the gorgeous starlit sky, finding comfort in each other's presence. That is, we *were*, until Mehmet dropped the bomb that HE will be leading the Ottoman army against the Karamanids.

"Why are would you do that?" I repeat. "Is there no one else you can send in your place? You are the sultan, after all."

"Sally, would you send someone you hardly know to battle?" Mehmet asks. "Or someone you don't trust at all?"

I look at him closely, trying to find an answer different from the one he clearly has in mind. The problem is that there just isn't another answer, so I whisper, "Yes."

"And what justification is there for that?" He turns his face to place all his attention on me.

I peer into his eyes. "The truth is I would never send anyone I don't know or trust to lead people. I'm just worried for you Mehmet, that is my job. You have never been in a battle before. Are you sure you can handle yourself?"

Mehmet looks away from me sighing. "I'm going to have to be able to. Can't walk away from this now, can I? Everyone knows that I am to march. An announcement was sent out this morning. Preparations have been taking place all day."

"When do you march?"

"Very soon," Mehmet replies. "In four days at the latest. We've selected the troops that will march with me to Isparta, while the remainder of the men will march with Mahmut Pasha back towards the Rumelian-Wallachian border, where Mahmut Pasha will have full reign to do as he pleases. We are pretty much just waiting for Yusef Agha to return so we can leave, but if he isn't back after four days, we leave regardless. Jake will end up leading the janissary corps if Yusef Agha doesn't return in time."

"So will Jake and Hamdan be with you?"

"Hamdan is to remain in Adrianople, taking care of all non-war related matters. Titrek Sinan will remain with him, and he's going to have to rely on Gülbahar's smarts. For Jake, it depends on what I've already said. If Yusef Agha returns within the next four days, Jake remains here. If Yusef Agha fails to return in time, Jake will march with me to Isparta. He will lead the janissaries until Yusef Agha joins us."

"So it's likely that neither of them will travel with you?"

"Uh-huh." He stretches his long, muscular arms, pulls his curly hair back and shuts his eyes.

I look at him with a hint of concern. He looks both better and worse than he did when I first met him. The slightly longer hair, slightly thicker beard, sharper jaw, and lean body looks good on him, but he looks much more tired. Both physically and mentally. If he could just get ample rest, if he could put his mind at ease, I don't think anything in the world could stop him.

But how is he supposed to get rest and clarity while leading an army into battle, surrounded by people he doesn't trust?

"Hey Mehmet," I say.

"Yeah what?"

I take a deep breath and lightly say, "I believe I should go with you for this war."

He opens his eyes and looks directly at me. "There is no way you accompany me on this campaign."

"Why?" I ask. "I want to, and no one will even find out that we are close to each other."

"Disregard the fact that we can't let anyone know about our true identities," Mehmet says. "How are we to keep you safe?"

"Shouldn't you be worried about how to keep yourself safe?" I ask. "You're the other army's top target!"

"But I'm surrounded by guards at all times," Mehmet objects. "There is no way they get to me."

"You were nearly assassinated," I say with a hint of amusement. "You have no ground to stand on."

"I will never forget that night," Mehmet hoarsely whispers. "But please tell me, how do you plan on staying safe?"

"Well, I presume y'all will be taking some servants and attendants," I say. "I could join them, you, whenever I can."

"You don't think that will draw attention?" Mehmet asks. "This is pointless, you can't go."

"Oh? Who are you to force me to stay?"

He turns onto his side and hesitates. Then he firmly places his hand on my shoulder and with a serious look, he says, "Sally, I genuinely care about you. I care about you a lot."

"And I care about you lots, too. Mehmet," I murmur. "But what are you getting at?"

"That I need you to stay."

"So you want to stay apart from me for over a month because you care about me? Is that why Hamdan is also staying back? And Jacob?"

Mehmet's face sours for a second. "As much as I'd like to have you at my side, staying in Adrianople is for your own safety and security. On the warpath, men are not the best people to be around."

"Well, men are never the best people to be around," I tease.

"Ignoring that," he says, "it just isn't safe for you. That's my final word on this matter."

With that, he lies on his back and closes his eyes.

I keep my gaze on him for a while.

I want to say something.

I know I'm right.

He needs me there with him on the military campaign.

I don't want to go for the fun of it.

Mehmet, however, can be stubborn. I think it's for the sake of others, but it can be selfish. So while I want to accompany him, I don't want to potentially upset him by pushing this conversation any further.

I don't know why, though. I'm not a pushover. While I'd like to think of myself as warm, polite, and friendly, I don't let people shut me up. I don't know why I'm letting Mehmet shut me up.

Maybe I want him to truly like me.

Maybe I need him to like me.

Or maybe I like him and that is why I want him to like me back the way I like him.

I don't know the answers to any of that.

But for now, I move as close to Mehmet as I can, embracing his warmth, staring into the magnificent night sky, simply enjoying his presence.

34. HAMDAN

I see myself opening a locker. A high school locker. My high school locker from my senior year. How am I seeing this? Is this a dream? It feels so real. Then again, this isn't the first ultrarealistic dream I've had since I've arrived in the 1451 universe. Mehmet said he's having these dreams too.

Why am I dreaming of high school?

I look up and down the locker. Inside, I see my winter jacket, an extra pair of shoes, gym clothes, and my calc and physics textbooks.

This must be February of senior year. That means it's right around the time of—

"YO!" a recognizable voice calls. "HAMDAN NAEEM!"

I see my friends, Marcus, Carl, and Jaden, walking towards me. Marcus, the one who called my name, reaches me first and punches my shoulder while I place my bag in my locker, without any control over what I'm doing.

As I turn around to dap up Marcus, Carl, and Jaden, I see Mehmet out of the corner of my eye, looking utterly exhausted. He's with a couple guys on the hockey team, coming back from seeing Coach Parker, pretending like he's energetic when he's clearly not.

Is this dream going to be about something that actually happened? Am I seeing the past?

Mehmet smiles at the two hockey guys as they walk into the cafete-

458

ria, then he turns to come straight to us. He stretches his arms to shake off some tiredness and in a low voice says, "Hey, y'all. How are we doing today?"

"The real question is how are YOU doing, man?" Marcus asks.

"I'm doing great, fam," he replies while stifling a yawn. "Think I aced both history and philosophy tests this morning. Now all I got left is my spare period and an English presentation. Had hockey practice in the morning and a team meeting just now, so the rest of the day is chill."

"DUDE!" Jaden exclaims. "Do you not know what everyone's been saying about you all day?"

"What are you guys talking about?" I say without being able to control my words.

This conversation feels like déjà vu.

"Come on!" Carl interjects. "There is no way you don't know what everyone's been saying about you?"

"Yeah, I got no idea what you lot are talking about," Mehmet irritably says. "It's a goddamn Monday. I've been busy with hockey and tests. My phone's been off, and I've talked nothing but hockey with people so far."

"Okay, before you turn it on," Marcus says, "tell us what happened at Luisa's party. All we know for sure is that you left early with Matthew, Sabraj, Alex, and Hamdan, leaving Harris behind, when you and Hamdan were meant to be his ride home, considering the two of you do not drink."

Oh my lord.

I remember this exact conversation.

Why am I reliving it?

I do not want to.

How do I snap outta this dream? I try to move, but I'm stuck. I can't do anything I want to do.

I'm going to have to watch this ugly scene play out.

I see Mehmet take a deep breath. "I was mugged outside Luisa's place by five or six jerks from Riverwood High. Something to do with a hip check I threw in our game last week that knocked their friend outta the upcoming tourney. Lunatics to be honest. Took nothing but my broken watch and creased-up Jordans," he says.

"Yeah, but what else happened?" Carl says. "That can't be all?"

Mehmet lowers his voice. "I've already told Hamdan, but Carl, Marcus, and Jaden... please don't tell anyone this just yet."

"Of course we won't," Jaden eagerly says. "Did you hook up with that shordy?"

"What on earth are you talking about, fam?" Mehmet asks. "All I was about to say is that when I went back in, I wanted to go home and just chill. So I rounded up the guys I went to the party with... Matthew, Sabraj, Alex, and Hamdan. I looked around a bit for Harris and I found him upstairs hooking up with Luisa. Of course I stopped that—"

"Bro, what?" Carl exclaims. "I thought he was dating Hana?"

"He is," Mehmet states. "That's what I told Luisa, which is how it stopped. I ain't letting my friends Luisa and Hana get played by Harris, even if he and I were boys. Though Harris has been acting like an asshole all year."

"The rumours make sense now, Carl," Marcus says. "Harris must have made out with Luisa after catching Mehmet with Hana earlier that night."

"What on earth are you talking about?" Mehmet whispers. "First of all, Hana is just a friend. Harris met her through me since she goes to another school. Second, Hana was tipsy, so she went to bed in Luisa's sister's room. All I did was get her a water bottle. Where on earth could this rumour have come from?"

"From Harris," Carl replies. "He told Luisa that this morning. Oh, he also told her that you're only friends with her cause you like her."

"That's not remotely true!" Mehmet exclaims. "Luisa has always been a friend. Oh, gosh, she's gonna think me a liar now."

"Guys, Mehmet's telling the truth," I say. "I know we've joked around about him liking Luisa, but I don't think he's ever had feelings for her."

"MEHMET, YOU FUCKING ASSHOLE!" a voice shouts. That irritating voice belongs to the one and only Harris Richards. He is approaching us with his boys, Matthew, Alex, and Sabraj. All guys from the basketball team. That very basketball team that just made the provincial playoffs.

Mehmet has hung out with these guys since grade 9. He doesn't like them much anymore for good reasons, like the fact that they'd always belittle him because he wasn't as popular, and because he's religious. I should also add that they can be quite racist.

Mehmet turns to face them.

Marcus, Carl, Jaden, and I all move away from Mehmet as Harris and his friends approach.

"Hi..." Mehmet says.

Harris has a lanky 6'5" frame, Sabraj is a hard-built 6'4", and Matthew is a hunched 6'1". They slowly circle Mehmet, basically forcing a confrontation.

"YOU REALLY THINK YOU'RE ABOVE EVERYONE ELSE!" Harris shouts at the top of his lungs. "WELL, YOU'RE NOT!"

"Harris, you could just tell Hana you were cheating on her," Mehmet calmly replies. He's backed into a corner that is a blind spot for our crappy school cameras.

A small crowd gathers. I can see Luisa out of the corner of my eye. A few of the guys on the hockey team are here as well, as is the entire basketball team.

Harris haughtily laughs. "Come on, man. You really think Hana didn't tell me about the tiny pecker you're packing before I dumped her ass and went to Luisa?"

I see Mehmet flex his fingers and wrists to loosen them up. "I would never ruin my friendship with Hana by sleeping with her. I'm not a fucking idiot like you. I know that you haven't broken up with her yet. I give you till the end of the day to do so before I tell her." Then he looks at Luisa and says to Harris with a smirk, "then you'll lose both Luisa and Hana in the span of twenty-four hours."

"You filthy Arab terrorist," Harris says in a hushed tone. He then raises his voice. "Not a single person in this school gives a damn about you! The only reason anyone even talks to you is because you were my friend!"

"Say that again!" I hear Mehmet mutter as he looks around the hall and then directly at Carl, Jaden, and Marcus, with a realization hitting his face. A look that tells me that he believes every word uttered by Harris. "Call me a filthy Arab terrorist again! I'm sick and tired of you acting like a racist and a bigot around me! Say that ONE MORE TIME, and I'll tell Hana everything awful about you!"

"You're just a jealous ugly Arab terrorist," Harris states. "YOU COULDN'T GET WITH A GIRL IF YOUR LIFE DEPENDED ON IT. OH, ALSO, NOT A SINGLE PERSON HERE GIVES A DA—oofff!"

Harris's voice trails off as Mehmet lands a punch square at his stomach. Mehmet then quickly pulls up the hood on his black Adidas hoodie before pushing Harris against the rough brick wall. Mehmet glares at

Sabraj, Matthew, and Luisa, then throws two jabs at Harris's chest and then an undercut with his right that was half-stopped by Harris's hand.

Harris then yells a slur so dirty that I refuse to repeat.

At that very moment, Sabraj and Matthew jump in.

And I can't.

Because I never did on that fateful day.

Everything I've ever said about having my best friend's back has been a lie.

This may have been a petty and useless high school fight, but the point still stands.

I helplessly watch Mehmet take an elbow to the back of his neck from Sabraj before getting slammed to the ground by Matthew. I see the rest of the basketball guys jump in, followed by the hockey guys. I see Mehmet slip outta the pile, take a look at Luisa and then me, as though he wants to escape into a hole. Instead, he looks back at the beat-up Harris (hockey guys can absolutely brawl) and runs away about 30 seconds before the teachers arrive.

At that moment everything goes black. Next thing I know, I feel a soft touch on my shoulder. A sweet voice says, "Wake up, Hamdan Pasha, wake up."

My eyes shuffle open. My hands are sprawled over the papers on my desk. I was dreaming with my head face-down with the beautiful slave woman, Hafsah, at my side. She basically runs my estate, while Mazhar runs the business.

"I am here with your tea," Hafsah murmurs as she pours the tea into a cup. "Oh, here's a letter that arrived from the palace a short while ago."

As she starts to walk away, I nervously say, "Hafsah... would you like to sit for a bit? At least while I drink my tea and read the letter?"

463

"Of course, Hamdan Pasha."

Hafsah grabs a seat across from me and places the tea set on the desk. I break open Mehmet's *tughra* to find a letter clearly penned by him.

His writing's so messy that it's a nightmare to read. The letter, written in English, says,

Hey Hamdan,

Or is it dear Hamdan? Does every handwritten letter have to be formal? Or can they be like a text? Oh I also wonder what the equivalent of sliding into DMs in this time period would be. I mean how would guys do that through a letter? Anyway that's all beside the point. I've got to update you. Tomorrow, at noon, I'll be departing for the plains of Isparta. I will be leading a military campaign against the Karamanid sultanate. Most of the senior ministers will accompany me, including Halil and Zaganos. You will remain behind with Titrek Sinan Çelebi and oversee the affairs of the government in our absence. Titrek Sinan has more details on what you need to be doing, but basically, we are hopefully going to be signing multiple treaties by the end of this year so we can focus on Constantinople. Please don't get angry that I'm leaving you behind. I do this because I trust you with my life, and not because I was angry. I also believe we may need some space to cool off, but know that you are my brother and I love you as such. Inshallah, we will see each other soon.

Mehmet

I slowly fold up the letter and look down at the tea sitting in a beautiful and colourful cup, my mind immersed in thought. I'm surprised that his tone isn't angry. That's probably because it's been nine days since we argued senselessly like children.

But he also used the words, "I trust you with my life," and "Know that you are my brother."

After viewing that dream, I don't deserve to read or hear those words from Mehmet.

I was neither of those things.

During high school, I watched all that shit build up till it reached a boiling point, and even then, I never stepped in. Over here, I've been selfish when I should've been doing my job and supporting my friend. Mehmet has to make difficult decisions. He may not like some of them, yet *he* is the one who must make them.

If we don't band together, there's no way we succeed in getting back home. That much is clear to me now. It should have been obvious before, but let's move past that.

This might just be a selfish thought, but if I'm busy supporting him, being there for him, who is there to support me?

Yes, I know that Mehmet is there for me.

He always is.

However, he has Sally and Jacob too. Maybe I could add Zaganos to that list as well. I only got *one* person in my corner here, and he's almost always preoccupied.

I run my hands through the annoying long hair on my head, setting my eyes on Hafsah who patiently waits for me to say something. I then sip down the now lukewarm tea.

"Hafsah," I say. "How is everything with you?"

"Everything is well, Hamdan Pasha," she replies. "Everything is the way it usually is. I'm busy coordinating the household, through cleaning, cooking, and yard work, and more. It's a lovely day when all goes smoothly, which it usually does. So every day is magnificent if you think about it."

Surprisingly cheerful.

She's clearly an optimist.

Wouldn't have thought that, to be honest, but it's clearly a breath of fresh air.

"That's wonderful to hear," I say. I open my mouth to say more, but words fail me.

What do I say to her? What was the point of me even asking her to sit with me?

I awkwardly sit, pouring more tea into my cup, while just staring at Hafsah.

Thankfully, she breaks the awkward silence. "It seems as though you have a lot on your mind, Hamdan Pasha. I can listen to whatever you'd like to say to lighten the burden on your shoulders."

I take a good look at her, trying to assess how genuine she is.

Why would she want to hear me drone on about my problems?

She would never get anything unless she understood the context. But what if she did understand the whole picture? How much help would she be?

I deeply exhale as I look into her eyes.

"Whatever I say can't leave this room," I order. "Is that understood?"

"Of course, Hamdan Pasha," Hafsah replies with nervous excitement.

Am I really about to tell her everything?

Damn right I am.

"The padishah is going on an expedition to the east to fight against the Karamanids. I am to remain behind to manage the affairs of the state," I say. "To many, this will be seen as me being snubbed by the padishah, but he and I see it as a blessing because of our history together. We see it as a chance to refresh and be able to work together smoothly once again."

"I can't see why he would snub you, Hamdan Pasha. You've been by his side for everything since the two of you were fourteen."

"No. I've been best friends with Mehmet since the day we were born," I say firmly.

"How is that possible Hamdan Pasha?" she asks. "You were born in the city of Amasya, far from Adrianople, and lived there for a few years before moving to this estate. You couldn't have possibly known the padishah from birth."

Why does she know so much about my ancestor's life?

"You probably won't believe me when I say this," I start, "but I'm not the Hamdan Pasha you've come to know in the many years that have passed. I come from a different time, a period that is centuries into the future."

Hafsah sits there, I'm guessing confused, while trying to assess if I'm serious. She doesn't say anything though, so I continue. "I come from a land called Canada, a land far west, seas and oceans away from Adrianople. My parents were born in a place that will be called Pakistan. The place would be called Sindh right now, I believe."

I stop for a moment, in hopes of gauging what she believes. I'm finding it extremely hard to read her. I think she's confused, but that's just an honest guess on my part.

"Hafsah, do you have nothing to say? I understand that this news might be difficult to grasp."

"It isn't my job to figure out if you are telling the truth, Hamdan," Hafsah replies. "That is your name, correct?"

"Yes, believe it or not, Hamdan actually is my name."

"Well, Hamdan, I don't understand what's going on, but I will follow whatever you say," she firmly says.

"Why?"

"Because as far as I can tell, you look just like the person I've been serving since the death of Hamdan Pasha's father."

"Surely, it can't be that simple for you," I say. "Do you not have any questions?"

"Oh, I have a lot of questions."

"Ask away, then," I say. "Anything you want to ask, you can."

She sits still for a moment. After what feels like an hour of consideration, but in reality, takes about two minutes, she says, "Okay. I want to know your life story. How different was it from Hamdan Pasha's?"

I smile at her, immediately grateful that Hafsah is the one I've told this secret to.

"Hafsah... my life could not be more different than Hamdan Pasha's. In fact, you could even say that our lives are *worlds* apart."

35. Sally

Light hands softly graze my shoulder and hip, stirring me awake. I see Gülbahar uneasily twisting and turning in on her side of the bed.

The reason she's shuffling uneasily is also the reason I've hardly slept all night.

Today is the 5th of June. Today is the day Mehmet embarks on his first military campaign. Not only is it his first *ever* campaign, but it is also his first time leading an army into battle.

When Mehmet leaves, he won't be back until at least late July or early August. That would mean the two of us wouldn't see each other for nearly two months.

That is some rough shit.

I'm trying to ignore my personal feelings. These feelings are hard to ignore because I may have felt the teensiest spark between us the night he told me he'd be leading an upcoming military campaign.

When Mehmet said he genuinely cared about me, it felt as though there was something more than friendship. It felt like he wanted something more.

It's either that, or I'm envisioning something I want.

Something I want.

Feels weird as hell to think that.

Do I want to be more than friends with him? This question has

469

been festering in my mind for the past four days. The conclusion I'm reaching? It's complicated. I might just be down bad, or perhaps there's just something special about Mehmet, and I don't want to miss out on that. I've been trying to avoid this question, instead placing my focus on what actually matters. Mehmet needs people he trusts around him. He's leading a whole military campaign and has no one to trust.

Okay, Jake might be accompanying him, but even that probably won't be enough. Jake will have his hands full leading the janissary corps for what's *officially* going to be the first time ever. That is, of course, until Yusef Agha arrives and then Jacob will have to go back the capital to oversee the reserves and protect the city, which is his duty as the deputy commander.

When that happens, Mehmet will have absolutely no one.

No one he trusts.

That's why I've been secretly preparing to depart with him and the Ottoman army.

The truth is that I've hardly got a plan.

I've packed some dark and rough clothes for the journey. I know which horses aren't being taken by Mehmet, so I've picked out the best horse from the remainder and gained some familiarity with the stallion. He's a champagne-gold-coloured Turkoman horse. I named him Vegas, because of the gold.

Beyond that, I haven't done much. I did nick about 40 or so arrows and a bow from the palace armoury, but nothing has been planned for my actual escape from this palace.

Y'all probably think I'm delusional, but I'm not, or at least, I don't think I am. I think my reasons are genuine and proper.

Totally not out of emotion. At all.

But how do I get out of this place undetected? How do I catch up with Mehmet's forces? How do I even get in contact with him once I do locate the army?

I don't have the answers.

But the day is just getting started, so I slip outta bed, wash up, and change into my dress for the day. It's a dark-blue dress that is rough enough for fifteenth-century travel. I have to be ready to seize any sliver of opportunity to leave.

Judging from the sky, it looks to be the start of Fajr. Gülbahar is still asleep, so I don't have to pretend to pray. Instead, I stand patiently at the large window and gaze into the dawn sky.

The army marches out of the walled portion of Adrianople at noon if I'm remembering Mehmet's words correctly.

I've got a few hours before then. I am 100 percent sure of one thing. I am going to have to depart today. It's the only way I'll be able to catch up with Mehmet without overextending myself. Perhaps the best chance of leaving would be around Maghrib. The sun will be setting, and people will be praying.

Wait.

Oh gosh.

Right now would be the perfect time! Hardly anyone's awake. The streets should be empty. I can escape the palace walls, travel a fair distance, and wait for the army. Gosh, I've got little time on my hands.

Am I really going to do this? I can't chicken out now.

Or actually, this would be the only time I could possibly chicken out.

I'm not going to. My mind is set. I have to do it. I have to look out for Mehmet. Who cares what may go wrong? There are a lot of things that can, but I don't really care.

I'm going for Mehmet.

My heart is telling me to go.

I glance at Gülbahar, who's still uncomfortably sleeping on the bed. I tiptoe over to a cabinet in the far corner of the large room where I stored the bow, quiver, arrows, and clothes.

Grabbing them, I peek at Gülbahar then dash to the door. I peer out, checking if the coast is clear. The second Rabiyah Hatun starts her Fajr prayer, I sprint as fast as I possibly can to the gates of the harem. I open the gigantic doors and glance back at the beautiful harem. I look at the water fountain, the hall, and the cozy and lovely sitting area.

I might never be back.

I jog out the gates, hearing them slowly close behind me. Without looking back, I sprint towards the palace exit. I pass Mehmet's room and see that the guards at the door are asleep. I run past a few offices until I reach a back stairwell leading out to the stables. I nearly trip down the staircase in my haste. At last, I open a back door. The crisp fresh air of the early June morning strikes my body passionately.

Refreshing.

I take another look around and scurry towards the stables. Again, I glance inside, then dart towards Vegas. I hasten to saddle the graceful stallion and attach my belongings. With the quiver on my back and the magnificent Ottoman bow on my shoulder, I climb up onto Vegas and lead him out of the stables.

As I'm about to exit, from behind, I hear a sweet voice urgently say, "Salmana Hatun! Please wait!"

I turn around to see the exceptionally pretty Hatice.

Yes, I am jealous of her extraordinary beauty, but what on earth is she doing here? I take a deep breath, trying to think of what to do. "Hatice! What a pleasant surprise!"

"Where are you going?" she asks in a polite manner. "It is very early in the morning."

"I could ask the same of you," I say to throw the ball back in her court. "What are you doing in the stables so early?"

"Are we just not going to answer each other's questions?" she asks.

"I guess not."

"Very well, Salmana Hatun."

I smile at her, turn from her gaze, and grasp the reins on Vegas.

As I'm about get going, she loudly exclaims, "Have a great day, friend of Mehmet Osman."

I immediately freeze.

What the... how?

How on earth does she know Mehmet's last name?

How on earth does she know I know him?

I quickly turn Vegas around to face her. She looks up at me with a tiny smirk on her face, as if she's done something wild, which she most definitely has.

"Who is Mehmet Osman?" I ask trying to feign confusion.

"The descendent of Mehmet the Second," Hatice calmly replies. "He's from the twenty-first century, where he lived in a country called Canada. He accidently came here with three of his friends and was mistaken for Mehmet the Second. He now reigns as sultan until he can return home. If I am correct, you are one of his friends, Salmana Hatun."

How does she know so much?

473

Like, how is this possible? Clearly someone must have told her.

The only person who could have been in the position to tell her is Mehmet. Damn that bastard.

I have no idea how much he's told her, so I've got to proceed with caution.

I look down at her with a warm smile. "That's correct. I did travel back in time with Mehmet Osman. My name is Sally MacLeod."

"Sally MacLeod..." she whispers in a Turkish accent. "Is it alright if I keep calling you Salmana Hatun though?"

"Of course."

"Very well, Salmana Hatun," she excitedly says. "Where are you off to in such a rush this early morning?"

"I'm going to accompany Mehmet out to battle," I say. "That's why I'm leaving right now, to escape detection."

"That plan has certainly failed, Salmana Hatun," she replies. "My father and I both saw you as we entered the palace a few minutes ago. There's no way I'm letting you go to war, and I'm sure Mehmet would rather you stay behind."

"You have no right to tell me what to do!" I object. "I must go! For his sake!"

"Gülbahar may hold you in high regard and you may be friends with Mehmet, but in this era you are a servant, while I am the daughter of the second vizier," Hatice says arrogantly. "I can certainly tell you what to do."

What an asshole.

"But I just wish to understand why you believe you must go, Salmana," she insists. "Why would you want to go off to battle?"

"Mehmet needs me even if he doesn't know it," I reply. "He needs people he trusts around him."

"Mehmet is a grown man," Hatice objects. "Surely, as a friend of his, you ought to know he can take care of himself. He is mature, smart, passionate, and objective. He will do fine on this campaign. My father is by his side, and he is completely loyal to Mehmet the Second. Since he believes Mehmet Osman to be Mehmet the Second, Mehmet should be able to completely trust him."

"He doesn't have anyone who truly cares for him as Mehmet Osman by his side, Hatice Hatun. He needs that. He needs someone who loves him by his side."

Hatice studies my face for a second. "You're unfathomably love with him, Salmana."

"No, I'm not!" I cry out. "I care for Mehmet as a friend."

"Would anyone do what you are doing just for a friend?" Hatice asks. "Salmana, you are secretly attempting to accompany a sultan off to war. If the battles go poorly, you risk getting captured by the enemy forces, whereafter you could be sold into slavery, beaten, raped, or killed. Even if the war does go well, you're surrounded by men who haven't been around women in months. While it's absurd that one would do this, the reality is that a solider may force himself on you. You may even be taken captive before you even find Mehmet's forces today."

"I'm willing to risk that for Mehmet. Maybe this is an emotional decision, but what will happen if he loses it on the battlefield? How will my friends and I return home?"

"Perhaps you should place more trust in someone you love," Hatice retorts. "I genuinely wish you tell him the true affection you have for him while on this military campaign."

"There is nothing I need to say to him."

Hatice sarcastically chuckles. "I had an inkling when I saw you darting towards the stables at full speed that you were going to do something like this..."

She reaches inside her fancy cloak and pulls out a carefully folded map. "So, I nicked this from my father. I've sorta become skilled at stealing documents from my father. This map should tell you exactly where to go. I wish you luck, Salmana. Mehmet's a good man, so tell him how you feel."

I smile at her as I reach down from Vegas and grab the map.

"Thank you, Hatice," I say as I urge Vegas forward.

"Good luck!" she cheerfully calls. "May Allah be with you on this journey!"

I don't back. I urge Vegas to go faster, heading straight towards the half-broken fence behind the palace grounds.

You know, maybe my reason for doing this is grounded in emotion. Perhaps I do like Mehmet as more than a friend. Maybe my mind is just a tad erratic right now, but I feel as though I'm doing the right thing. I'm doing what I want to, rather than following someone else's orders. As I get Vegas to leap over the fence, I have never felt freer,

Godspeed, I guess.

36. JAKE

"You ready?" Arslan asks as I stand in front of a looking glass, carefully ensuring that I look perfect in the freshly-sewn janissary uniform. The baby-blue robes under the red overcoat look immaculate. I place the tubular pure-white headdress on my head, and stand there looking at my reflection.

"Looking sharp, you stupid bastard," Baver says. "Now wipe that arrogant look off your face. We are minutes from marching off to battle. You are to lead the entirety of the janissaries out to battle. This is a proud moment, but you mustn't look proud. You must look like you've done this countless times."

"Baver is absolutely correct, Yakub," Arslan mutters. "I guess there's a first time for everything."

"Piss off, oaf," Baver grumbles. He places his hand on my shoulder. "Let's go, Yakub. The janissaries and the sultan await you outside the garrisons."

I turn around to see Demir and Arslan smiling at me while Baver looks extremely irritated. I smile at Baver in an attempt to lighten his mood. Of course, I will never succeed at that, so I calmly say, "Let's go, fellas."

This whole calm exterior is a mirage. The butterflies in my stomach are not only fluttering, but they're doing jumping jacks.

My mind is buzzing with millions of possibilities, none of them positive. You'd think this would be easier, considering this is my second military campaign.

But it isn't. All I can think about is the multiple men I've already killed and the many more I'll have to kill in hopes of getting back to Priya.

How am I doing this? I guess I'll never figure that out.

As I'm walking through the garrisons towards the exit, my body feels tense, but my mind feels capable. I think that's the best way to describe it.

I'm in a nervous, yet positive mindset.

Why?

It's because I'm confident that we will succeed. There's no doubt in my mind. However, I'm worried about the violence needed to succeed. I'm a firm believer in the mantra, kill 'em with kindness. Bloodshed, wars, and death aren't for me.

But I'm forced to make it part of me.

I'm now leading the greatest infantry troops in Europe. Perhaps in the whole world.

Bloodshed, violence, warfare, death, and destruction are now becoming part of me.

I don't know how I feel about that.

I wipe out all thoughts from my mind as Baver, Arslan, Demir, and I exit the garrisons to breathe the cool fresh air.

Most of the forces have been marching for the past hour or so. The palace is situated on a former hunting ground, so the higher-ranking officers and the more celebrated troops are situated in the garrisons on the palace grounds, while the rest wait for us outside the city. Other troops will also join us on the journey to Isparta.

As the stand-in leader of the janissaries, I march alongside Mehmet, like his personal bodyguard. In fact, all the janissary troops will marching closest to the sultan.

As Baver, Arslan, Demir and I walk to the front entrance of the palace, we find Zaganos, Halil, Nişancı Adham, Kadi'asker Mawiz, Gedik Pasha, and Ak Shemsettin awaiting us. Mehmet's white Arabian stallion is saddled. Next to the white stallion is a shiny black one, also saddled and ready for whoever chooses to sit on it.

In front of the ministers, the janissaries are in organized lines in the hundreds. 1,200 janissaries are marching on this military campaign, with 200, whom I've placed under the command of a soldier by the name of Burak, remaining behind. The remaining 1,300 are with Yusef Agha and still haven't gotten back to Adrianople. From my conversation with Mehmet last night, I think it's concerning him, but it's hard to get a proper read on him.

We walk closer to the men. Adham looks at us and waves. At that moment, Baver, Arslan, and Demir break from me and walk straight towards a janissary by the name of Rizwan, a snobbish soldier fiercely loyal to Yusef Agha, who served as deputy commander during my first absence.

I walk straight to the senior ministers as Kadi'asker Mawiz yells out, "Yakub Agha, take your place next to the padishah's horse."

Yakub Agha.

Who would have thought I'd be called that just a few short months ago?

I nod and scurry right over to Mehmet's horse and stand next to it. All the men stare at me with a hint of amusement before Adham takes pity on me. "Yakub Agha, as the leader of the janissaries, you are meant to ride next to the padishah."

"Oh, of course," I mumble as I feel my face redden. I climb onto the shiny black stallion. Baver and Demir snicker while Arslan scolds them.

Those three stooges, man.

I shake my head at my three friends, and I hear Halil Pasha, who's only a metre or so away, mutter, "Oh look, the pompous arse is here."

I turn to see Mehmet walking out of the palace doors, dressed in his finest travelling clothes in red. On his shoulders sits the young prince Bayezit. Clinging onto his right arm is Gülbahar Hatun, looking benevolent in her matching outfit. They walk slowly but surely towards the white stallion, with the wind blowing heavily, almost telling Mehmet to stay behind

I watch him wrestle Bayezit off his shoulders and place him on the ground next to Gülbahar. At the same moment, the janissaries start filing out. I look back at Mehmet. He's engulfed in a bear hug from Gülbahar, which instantly reminds me of Priya. He awkwardly hugs her back and whispers something to her. Their embrace goes on for a hot minute before he wrestles himself away and climbs onto his stallion.

"May Allah bless you and return you home safely, my love," Gülbahar says.

Mehmet softly mumbles *ameen* and warmly smiles at his wife and son as they walk back to the palace doors.

He nervously smiles at me.

"You ready for this?" I ask.

"I am."

I look up ahead to see the last of the janissaries exit the palace gates.

Adham loudly clears his throat. "My padishah, it's time we set off and join the rest of the army."

Mehmet looks around at every single section of the palace grounds and closely examines the palace one last time, as if he's looking for someone. He looks back at me with a hint of disappointment. "Very well, lead the way, Ibn Eymen. May Allah be with us on this campaign."

With that, we rush out of the gates and head to the streets of Adrianople. It is weird being at the centre of this. The streets are packed with people trying to get a glimpse of the sultan. I feel as though a bunch of eyes are on me, but they're actually looking past me at my friend.

Mehmet Osman. The Sultan of the Ottoman Empire.

Mehmet doesn't acknowledge the crowd once. He keeps his head straight and his face neutral as the adoring crowds revere him.

I don't get him sometimes.

As we leave the city of Adrianople, I ask him, "Why are you so quiet?"

He shrugs. "I hoped to see someone before we left, but I didn't. Not a big deal."

With that, he shuts up and speeds up to talk to Adham. I follow, trying to discern what he meant. Was he hoping to see Hamdan? Or Sally? I'm not too sure. One thing is clear to me though.

Mehmet's going to be a closed book for the entirety of this campaign.

37. Mehmet

The setting sun lays beautifully on the canvas of the magnificent evening sky. I rest against a robust tree, deep in thought, as the forces hitch up the tents for the night. Tomorrow, my 14,450-strong relief force cross the Sea of Marmara and enter Anatolia as we march towards the plains of Isparta. This evening is the end of the fourth day of travel. We have many long days ahead, but for the past four days, only two people have been on my mind. I haven't been able to think of much else. I try to think of battle, but my mind returns right back to them.

Hamdan and Sally of course.

I am worried about Hamden. He's been angrier than ever. I don't know if y'all understand this, but Hamdan and I have never truly fought. We just got along perfectly our whole lives. Then all of a sudden, the lost diary of Mehmet the Conqueror magically brought us here, throwing a wrench into our relationship by changing the power dynamic of our friendship. Now, I don't know if he'll ever speak to me again.

That would be...What's the word? Sad? Depressing? Catastrophic?

I feel like the weight of those three words wouldn't describe the angst I'll feel if I never get to talk to Hamden.

On the other hand, I'm not worried about Sally at all. I just know that I miss her. Yes, it's only been four days since we've spoken and typically we only speak once a week, but it just feels so different.

She feels so close yet so far.

By close, I mean she hasn't left my thoughts. I see her brown eyes and beautiful face every time I close my eyes. I've always sorta known that I've got a crush on her. If anyone ever said that aloud, I'd deny it with my life though.

Until recently, I'd hardly ever given my slight crush a second thought. It's simply because I needed friends, and she became one. A real darn good friend at that.

Also, I'm Muslim and the whole "don't go anywhere near fornication until you're in the bonds of marriage" sorta puts a damper on having a romantic relationship prior to marriage.

The third reason is that I've never felt that she's had a remote interest in me as anything more than a friend. Which is why I've tried to make it seem like there are absolutely no feelings from my end. But in our last talk, I may have had the smallest inkling tell me that, maybe, just maybe, Sally might like me. She literally snuggled right next to me the other night. Now, I did let her, but I usually make sure to keep my distance, ensuring I don't touch her at all. This time, Sally initiated contact through snuggling against me.

Perhaps I'm reading too much into it, but all her good qualities are just flying into my brain. She is warm, cordial, caring, compassionate, down-to-earth, easy to talk to...

I'm simping, but I ain't wrong. She a 20 out of 10. Any man would be incredibly lucky to be with her. I just can't get her outta my head. She's the object of all my thoughts. The heartbeat behind my desires. The subject of my dreams, and the apple of my eye.

Astaghfirullah, I gotta stop. I shouldn't think about Sally like that. It ain't ever gonna happen. It's too complicated to ever happen. I can't even explain why; I just know it is.

I sigh loudly, get up, and walk away from the encampment. My guards, Jake and Rizwan, don't notice because they are busy coordinating shit with the rest of the janissaries. I walk further away, at least 100 metres from the encampment.

Where I stand right now represents everything I'm feeling. I'm on the outside looking in. That's how my whole life has been, but never more than now. I've always felt like an outsider.

Someone who's never fit in. At the masjid, I wasn't religious enough for some people. On my sports teams, I was too different for some people. My awkwardness and silence stood out amongst the boys. At school, I was always just there with a few friends, but not someone memorable.

The only place I ever felt comfortable was at home.

I enjoyed playing hockey, hanging out with friends, going to the masjid, but true comfort and peace of mind came at home—the only place I could ever truly be myself, the only place I ever felt normal. And there is only one reason for that: my family.

Baba.

Anne.

Babaanne.

Hamdan.

With them, I was always at peace. They all got my back. No matter what. That's what family is at the end of the day. No matter how difficult times get, no matter how tense things get, no matter how much you irritate each other, they are always there for you.

The familial bond is inseparable. It helped me balance all my identities.

But now I'm here, separated from my family. The guy who's basically my brother is beefing with me. I feel like I'm on the outside looking in. No matter what I do, I don't feel at home. I'm in my family's homeland, sitting on the throne of my ancestor, donning his clothes and weapons, but I don't feel at home. In fact, I've never felt more alone. I feel lost. I worry I'll never get back. I'm running around helpless.

I wanna scream. Bellow. Let the earth know how I'm feeling.

So, I stretch my arms and yell out the roughest scream at the top of my lungs, unbothered by anything else. As my lungs give out, the soft neigh of a horse startles me, causing me to fall over.

I push myself back up. A horse? I swear I walked well over 100 metres from anyone. How can anyone be nearby?

I pretend as though I don't hear the neighing as I scurry forward, only to be stopped by a pleasant voice. "Mehmet Osman, wait up!"

I stop suddenly. My shoulders and back tense up. I recognize the voice immediately. There is no way. I must be dreaming. It's the soft and lovely voice I want to hear every day. It can't be. My ears deceive me.

I pull out my kilij, turn a full 180 and point it directly at the figure on the saddle of a horse that sorta looks gold.

My eyes deceive me. It isn't possible. Surely. The figure is... Sally MacLeod? Dressed in nice travelling clothes, carrying a bow and quiver.

"Sally...?"

"Yes," she replies as she climbs off the stallion and walks towards me. "Who else would I be, nimrod?"

"Um... how are you here? Am I dreaming?" She slaps me. Like,

485

absolutely smacks me. In complete shock, I ask, "What on earth did I do to deserve that?"

She raises her hand again and slaps me on the other cheek. "Does this feel like a dream?"

"No."

"Then why say that?"

"I-I just don't get how you're here," I reply.

"Let's take a walk and I'll explain."

She leads her stallion forward and I stride to keep up.

I'm so confused. Why is she here? I had specifically told her to stay behind. But she didn't.

"I'm not going to bore you with the details, Mehmet," she starts. "I just snuck out of the palace hours before the army departed and, uh, Hatice actually helped me escape. By the way sir, she *knows* about our identity. In fact, she claimed that *you* told her."

"Yeah, I told her," I reply, "about my identity."

"Why on earth would you ever tell her?" Sally exclaims. "Also how did she figure out who I am?"

"I had my reasons for telling Hatice my secret," I answer. "I have no regrets. I believe it was an excellent decision. How was I to know she'd figure out yours?"

"It wasn't your secret to tell!" she exclaims. She takes a deep breath to calm down. "You should have talked to us first."

"I'm sorry. It was a spur-of-the-moment thing," I say. "I should have known she was smart enough to figure out the identity of at least one more of us. It's my mistake."

Sally looks at me and her expression turns soft. "Don't worry, Mehmet. Hatice seems to be a lovely and trustworthy lady. Her knowing our secret isn't the end of the world."

I raise my eyebrows. Surely, she's not letting me off that easy. Telling someone about us is a big deal. If she had done so, and I hadn't known the circumstances, I'd be cheesed.

"Are you seriously okay with this, Sally?"

She gulps down a deep breath. "Not entirely. I don't understand why you'd withhold such a big thing from me. I do trust your judgment, but honestly, just don't keep anything from me. I'm only tryna help you."

I intently look at her trying to figure out how to counter her statement, but I sigh and relent. "You deserve my honesty. You have a right to know what I decide. I'm wrong for keeping things from you. I'm truly sorry for that."

Sally looks up at me. Her face softens a warm smile. "I'm glad we've sorted that out."

"Yes." I smile back. "Now, are you gonna tell me how you found the army?"

"Okay, so, Hatice gave me maps that detailed exactly what direction you guys would be heading. She nicked them off her father when she saw me running away from the palace."

"So, that's where the maps went!" I exclaim. "Zaganos couldn't find them as we set off, but luckily Halil was prepared. The whole time Zaganos thought Halil did something to sabotage him."

Sally bursts out laughing, but I get serious. "How was your journey up to this point? Are you alright? You're not hurt or anything? You must be hungry and exhausted."

"Not really," Sally replies as she stifles a yawn. "The journey was easy enough. I kept a few hours ahead of your forces and sustained myself through foraging. I will admit to being tired."

We walk over to a tree, and she collapses onto the ground to rest. I sit down next to her trying to think of something to say.

Seeing her makes me happy. I can feel a rush. I enjoy her company, but I asked her to remain at the palace for a reason.

"You have to go back," I start to say.

"DON'T!" she loudly interjects. "I didn't come all the way here to be forced back!"

"But you have to," I say. "How are we gonna explain your presence here?"

"You won't have to," she calmly replies. "I'll just blend in with the slaves. We'll figure out a way to see each other."

Something about the way she says this makes me feel like it's not a solid plan. How can she be so calm? There's way too much of a risk of someone, anyone, finding out we aren't exactly who we say we are.

So, I counter, "How exactly are you gonna blend in with slaves with those clothes on?

"Can't be that hard, really," she replies.

Oh gosh, she really hasn't thought this through. How does she seem so calm then? I guess that's just her self-confidence, trusting her own instincts. Perhaps I should trust her instincts as well, but *my* instincts say she's wrong, and my brain can't wrap around that.

"You'd be near battle, in harms way," I counter. "I can't have you near that."

"You can't decide that for me," she says. Her tone makes it seem as if she's trying not to get angry.

"You're right," I say. "I can't decide anything for you right now. I can suggest and tell you what I prefer though."

I pause, waiting for her to say something but she doesn't, so I continue, "Returning home would be a preferable idea in my opinion. No one will ask any questions, and you're smart enough to navigate through any questions Gülbahar might have."

"No!" she exclaims. "I will not go back unless it's with your returning army."

"I'm not gonna turn this army around for you, Sally," I say. "Please, just explain why you felt like you had to do this?"

"You really think I'd leave you alone on a campaign like this?"

"I'm not alone!"

A blatant lie. The pang of loneliness hits me many times throughout the day. The fact I can't ever be myself, even around Jake these days, deeply hurts me.

Sally being here, traversing the land for a few days, just to be with me does feel comforting.

I want her to stay, but I know she shouldn't.

"If you stay with me, it's a risk to your safety, and our secret, which means it's a risk to your life and Jake's, even if you survive the violence," I explain. "It's also a risk to the state through—"

"That's just lies! There is no way my presence can attract so much danger. I am just the attendant of the sultan's wife."

"The attendant hanging out with the sultan?" I ask. "Showing up all of a sudden? It's gonna raise questions. If the wrong people find out about our secret, they'll try to turn me into a puppet—a puppet sultan, where they control the government, and I'm forced to do whatever they say."

"That's why I'll blend in with the slaves."

"You are not gonna do that," I demand.

"Why are you being so...ugh! You can't order me around!"

"You say you're here for me, but how am I even supposed to focus with you acting like a slave, nursing the wounds of my men? That would divert my attention."

"Are you calling me a distraction?" she asks. "I am absolutely NOT that."

"That is not what I meant at all," I plead, trying to catch her eye. "I meant that I don't want you to do that. There isn't any need."

"Why not? Why can't I be useful? Oh, that's much too distracting for you, right?"

Oh God, she's being sarcastic. Clearly, I've pissed her off. This is the first time we've ever had something even close to an argument.

I take a deep breath and carefully craft my words. "Sally, you could never be a distraction to me. I'd just prefer you by my side or somewhere safe. That isn't because I don't trust you. I simply care for you far too much to be away from you with no assurance of your safety."

She looks at me then immediately averts her gaze. "You know, I expected a better reaction from you." She sounds sad. "I literally rode a horse for days to stay with the Ottoman army. I left the comforts of the palace to endure this journey and campaign with you. I don't want you to feel like no one is there for you. You need people who have your back as Mehmet Osman and not just as Sultan Mehmet. I don't want you to feel alone. I don't wish to be separated from you."

The hairs on the back of my neck rise as I look into her beautiful eyes.

"Y-you don't?"

"I care too much about you to not be by you on this campaign." She softens. "That's why I'm staying, no matter what you say. I know the dangers, but you, Mehmet, are my reason to stay."

I smile at those words. "I'll figure out something to keep you by me for the rest of the campaign. Wait here, I'll be back."

"Where are you going?" She grabs my hand as I head back to the encampment.

"To find Jake," I say. "We'll figure this out and come here to consult with you."

"Okay..." she murmurs as she lets go.

I smile at her and scurry off, rushing towards camp, on the lookout for Jake. To my luck, as soon as I get near to camp, I spot Rizwan.

"Rizwan!" I exclaim as I catch my breath. "Find Yakub for me quickly."

"My padishah, why aren't you guarded by anyone?" Rizwan motions for five soldiers to stand near me.

"That's because I asked my guards to leave me alone," I say. "Now quickly, go find Yakub please."

Rizwan runs off. I smile at the unknown janissaries guarding me and awkwardly say, "Salaam brothers." They politely lower their heads and mutter their replies.

Now... how do I ensure Sally stays without detection? How much control do Jake and I have over the janissaries? Will a select group of them be discreet and shield her from view?

I don't know.

Perhaps I should trust Zaganos and tell him our huge secret to protect us. Maybe if I promise him the position of grand vizier, it'll be able to convince him to help. To be honest, even if he tells anyone, will they believe him? They'll just call him a madman. He'll never have proof. But no, I can't tell him. I can't enflame those sparks. I can tell him Sally is here, but I'll lie and say Gülbahar sent her.

Okay, but what would my wife send Sally for? To keep an eye on me? No, that would be absurd, plus Zaganos would shield her far away from me.

Ugh, what on earth do I say if I wanna get him involved? I look up to see Jake approaching with Rizwan, so I stand straight and say to the others, "You may disperse now."

With that, the soldiers head back towards camp. Jake looks confused. He directs Rizwan back to camp.

"Sup Mehmet," he says. "Do you need anything?"

"Walk with me." I start walking back towards Sally.

"What's wrong?"

"Sally is here."

"WHAT?" he yelps. "YOU MEAN *YOUR* FRIEND SALLY MACLEOD?"

"Quiet down," I say. "Do you want the entire army to hear you?"

"Sorry," Jake whispers. "But you're joking, right? How is Sally here? Why is she here?"

"Does it look like I'm joking?" Jake shakes his head, so I continue. "She says she's here for me. That I need people who truly have my back as Mehmet Osman by my side."

"But you have me..."

"I know," I say. "That's what I don't get, but it's still cool she's here. I want her to return, but she insists on staying. We gotta fi—"

"She wants you, my man," he says, "She's in love with you."

I scoff. "You've gone mad, my friend. She's just an overly friendly person."

"Yeah, no girl is doing that for just a friend. She likes you and I think you lowkey like her. You just aren't sure how to express it."

"Just stop, Brannan," I say. "I don't need you to tell me how I feel. Sally is just really friendly."

"You're missing the obvious, Mehmet."

"Brannan, just stop. We gotta figure out how to keep her presence a secret."

"From everyone?"

"Yup."

"Even Zaganos?"

"No," I say. "I think it's best to keep him as informed as possible without disclosing our secret."

"Do you know what you're gonna say to him?"

"Not yet." Sally comes into view. "I'll figure it out."

She sees us, gets up, and exclaims, "Jacob!" She runs over.

"She sounds like my granny, saying my name like that," Jake mutters under his breath as he smiles and hugs her. "I hope you are well."

"I am," she calmly replies.

"I probably should have said this while we were near camp," I say as I stifle a nervous laugh. "Go back to camp and return your seven most trusted soldiers."

"Um, okay..." Jake says with his eyebrows raised.

"Come on!" I urge. "Go now!"

"Alright, alright." He scurries off.

I watch him stride away as I awkwardly turn to Sally and the gold stallion.

I walk next to her and murmur, "What's his name?"

"Vegas," Sally replies. "For the gold-."

I reach out to pet the horse while Sally rambles about how amazing Vegas is. She looks at me and brightly smiles while I focus on every word she utters. I cant stop smiling seeing her face twinkle with happiness.

For the first time on this military campaign...I'm relaxed.

"Go get Zaganos," I order Jake as we place Sally's belongings in my tent, secretly with the help of the seven janissaries—Arslan, Demir, Baver, Rizwan, Altan, Barış, and Çetin.

Jake believes that Arslan, Demir, and Baver will do just as he asks. He isn't as assured about Rizwan, Altan, Barış, or Çetin, but he believes that their loyalty to Yusef Agha will ensure they are loyal to me. I'm not too sure about that, as I'm pretty sure Yusef Agha hates me, but I can't be choosy at a time like this.

I get what I get.

Right now, they're all standing guard by my tent. Making sure that no one enters without my consent until Jake gets back with Zaganos. Sally collapses onto the bed. I walk around the tent, anxiously awaiting Jake and Zaganos.

I still haven't figured out what to say, so I will have to wing it on the spot. I think I should make it clear that Sally is important to um... the state (?), but how do I convince him that someone that's basically a servant is that significant?

I start pacing around the room faster. And faster.

And faster.

And faster.

"Stop that!" Sally orders, right as Jake and Zaganos duck into the tent.

Zaganos awkwardly looks at Sally then turns his attention to me.

"My padishah," he says with deep concern that somehow feels fake. "Is everything alright? Why did you ask for me?"

"Perhaps we should take a walk, Zaganos Pasha," I say to buy time. "Away from any listening ears."

"Of course, my padishah," he replies as we step out of the tent.

Okay. I gotta make it seem like Sally is important, not just to me, but to Zaganos and the Ottoman empire as well.

After a short stroll, Zaganos Pasha softly places his arm on my shoulder. "What has you so concerned? Surely it can't be the battle plans. Those are well planned out."

"Did you not see the girl?" I ask. "Salmana Hatun."

"Yes, what is she doing here?" he asks.

"I asked her here," I lie.

Why did I just say that? That isn't what I wanted to say.

Zaganos Pasha looks taken aback. "Why did you ask her to come along with you, my padishah? I know it isn't my place to ask, but have you bed her?"

"It definitely isn't your place to ask, Zaganos Pasha," I say. "But no, I have not, and I do not plan on it."

"Then why did you ask her to be here by your side? Why did she come in such secrecy?"

"Zaganos Pasha," I say, "Salmana Hatun is of great importance, not just to me, but to you and the whole of the Ottoman empire."

"My padishah, how is a servant to your wife, originally from an irrelevant land you call Scotland, of any use to me, the state, or you?"

"You'd think that," I chuckle as I freak out over what to say, "but trust me, there is something peculiar about her. There's a reason I'm keeping her around."

"What is that?"

Ugh. I've got nothing.

"Do you not have any in trust in me, Zaganos Pasha? Is there no belief in your heart for your sultan?" I ask.

"N-no, my padishah," he stutters. "What is it you need from me?"

"Discretion," I demand. "No one is to know about Salmana Hatun aside from us and the soldiers assigned to protect her."

"Why is that?"

"If anyone opposing me discovered her presence, there would be danger to her life and the empire," I reply. "No one can discover her."

"My padishah, may you please explain her importance, so I know what exactly I'm dealing with?" Zaganos requests. "How am I to do what you ask without any knowledge?"

"My word should be enough," I answer. "I didn't have to say anything to you. I *chose* to because of the high regard I hold in you. You don't have to take care of any logistics; that will be handled by Yakub. All I need is your discretion. You must cover for me, when required."

"Of course, my padishah."

"Now, return to your tent, and we'll pretend this conversation never happened."

"Yes, my padishah."

With that, he strides off to his tent and I go towards mine. *Wallahi*, I just want this campaign to be over sooner rather than later.

38. HAMDAN

The most powerful man in the city. That's me.

Unbelievable, isn't it?

With Mehmet gone, I have unquestioned power in the city of Adrianople right now. Everyone does exactly as I say. They treat me with proper respect. Like a king, or a sultan, to be more accurate.

But it feels fake.

They do what I want because they have to, but they don't have any respect for me. That gives a man a chip on his shoulder, makes a man look over his shoulder. Envious eyes are always lurking. Eyes of people who are searching for ways to advance in the Ottoman court, hunting for a fall from grace, which may happen as quickly as the snap of your fingers.

It's nerve-wracking. Tenses you up. Stresses you out. Leads to only trusting one person.

Yourself.

Presently, I stand on top of the fortress walls of the capital, watching the beautiful sunrise, anxiously awaiting the janissary forces, headed by Yusef Agha. About half the forces are returning, while the rest stay back to patrol the border with Wallachia. Not even gonna lie, I don't know too many details. Mehmet handled all those plans with Mahmut Pasha before he left for Isparta with the army.

That was over a week ago. Today is Friday the 13th.

In Mehmet's absence, I've been settling the affairs of the government, by handling the different foundations, looking at legal matters, commerce, etc.

This is all done with the aid of Titrek Sinan. His help has made everything much easier for me.

I stand on these walls today with a bit more understanding. I finally get why Mehmet has been more closed off than ever.

Having so much power is terrifying. I should've been more understanding. That's not to say I should've backed off, but I didn't communicate my thoughts at all. I need to do a better job of that. That's what I'm gonna tell Mehmet in this letter. I'll get Yusef Agha to deliver my message to him.

I stand on these walls, feeling like the most powerful man in the city. Alongside me are the city guards, Titrek Sinan, a religious leader called Mullah Rashid, and the son of the infamous grand vizier, Ibrahim Pasha (known as the younger).

I'm standing with the elite of the city, the type of thing any guy dreams of, but I know that I ain't elite. I'm just a kid from Sauga, who, through good or bad luck, has gotten this position. I gotta stay humble because this is only temporary.

I gotta truly earn this position.

That's what I'm tryna do here in Mehmet's absence. The fact that someone (Hafsah) now knows my secret makes everything easier for me. The burden has been slightly lessened.

"Hamdan Pasha," Mullah Rashid says. "Look."

I look at the horizon to see men approaching. Soldiers. The janissaries.

I glance at Ibrahim Pasha who motions towards the city guards. I descend the walls with Titrek Sinan, Mullah Rashid, and Ibrahim

Pasha. Once I step in front of the fortress gates, I take a deep breath and look around. A decent-sized crowd has pulled up and surrounded the road. I look towards a few city guards, raise my hand, and flick two fingers, motioning for the gates to be opened.

The guards to the city slowly start the process of opening the gates. I intently look down at a stone by my feet and close my eyes.

I am smart.

I am calm.

I can do anything I put my mind to.

I will be confident and deliver Mehmet's message to Yusef Agha.

There will be no complications.

Everything will go smoothly.

I just know it.

I look back up to see that the gates to the fortress city of Adrianople are open. The janissaries march inside in an organized manner, almost like the unsullied warriors *from Game of Thrones*, but there is a different fanatic energy from this group. They don't have that depressed and submissive energy. They passionately support this empire, displaying their valour, might, spirit, and love through their fierce but beautiful marching music.

They march as a ferocious unit through the gates of the fortress. The people of Adrianople stare in awe at the unparalleled form on display. I scan through the men, looking for Yusef Agha, without any luck. I just can't seem to locate him.

"Do you see Yusef Agha?" I ask Titrek Sinan.

"I do not, Hamdan Pasha," he replies. "He will approach you though, don't worry."

I smile at him and continue to look through the crowd. To no avail.

I look back at the group of men accompanying me and say, "Let's just go back to the palace; we'll see him there."

With that, I start back to the palace with disgust, but at that moment, a man calls out, "Hamdan Pasha!"

I turn to see the old-ass Agha of the janissaries approaching.

"Is the fool too busy to greet his hardworking troops?" Yusef Agha asks.

"Who is this fool you're referring to?"

"Our foolish Sultan Mehmet," Yusef Agha replies. "Is he too busy to greet his elite forces? Or does he find it beneath him?"

Why does this prick hate Mehmet so much?

"Mehmet is far from a fool," I say. "It is *his* plan that's leading us towards a resounding victory against the allied Balkan forces. Mehmet will lead the Ottoman army to victory against the Karamanids."

"The fool's gone to fight them at Ankara?" Yusef Agha asks. "Truly ludicrous behaviour."

"No battle is going to occur at Ankara," I say. "They were diverted to Isparta after a battle at Akşehir fought by Aslan Pasha."

The Karamanids' original plan was to besiege Ankara, though. There is no way he knows about that. I mean, there is no way he *should* know about that.

But somehow he does. Could just be an educated guess... He has been a military leader for years. But then what if he's been in cahoots with the Karamanids? Nah, that ain't possible.

"So I take it that Yakub is leading the janissaries in my absence?" Yusef Agha asks.

"Yes, he is."

"Has the padishah requested that I join him on this military campaign?" Yusef Agha asks. "If that is the case, I should leave the city by nightfall."

Yusef Agha is meant to go. Go meet Mehmet and help him gain his victories on the battlefield. Help him demolish the Karamanids forever.

But the way he immediately said that Mehmet's gone to Ankara to battle the Karamanids feels a bit sus to me. Like how does he know that the Karamanids were initially intent on besieging Ankara?

I'm overthinking, aren't I? Mehmet would have thought of everything before he left. Zaganos would've advised him to leave Yusef Agha behind if there was anything sus with him.

Yeah, ima leave it.

"Hamdan Pasha," Yusef Agha authoritatively says. "Does the padishah require me to join him at Isparta?"

"Yes, our padishah requires your presence," I reply. "Please rest and depart for Isparta by Fajr at the very latest."

Yusef Agha smiles at me. "I'll be out of the city by Maghrib." He turns to walk towards the garrisons.

I watch the old prat walk away with a pang in my stomach that I don't think will leave till Mehmet and Jacob get back. I know Mehmet ordered that Yusef Agha join him on this campaign, but I can't shake this feeling telling me that there is something very off with this whole military campaign.

I might be overthinking.

I might not be.

Time will tell.

39. Mehmet

Monday, the 16th of June 1451.

My army's been travelling for eleven days.

Gosh, I've really been the commander of an unbelievably powerful army for eleven days! This would be beyond my wildest dreams if I already weren't the sultan of the Ottoman Empire for nearly four months now.

Literally everything feels like a dream. Or a nightmare. Depends how you look at it. Okay, let's not get sidetracked with my boring thoughts.

We are minutes from joining Aslan Pasha's retreated forces at Isparta. This is starting to feel real. Now that Isparta has come into my sights, I get why Aslan Pasha retreated here. It's a city surrounded by mountains, while the actual land is flat. The mountains don't trap the city; they shield it. A perfect place for a retreating force as it awaits reinforcements.

Reinforcements are definitely needed to win this war, particularly if it's fought in an open field. Manpower is needed.

And boy, there is a lot of just that.

Of Aslan Pasha's initial 26,000-strong force, about half perished at the hands of the Karamanids, so only around 13,000 remain. Then you add the 25,000 who have arrived with Ishak Pasha as well as the

14,450 men accompanying me. That's 52,450 men. If Yusef Agha joins us at a reasonable time, it will take us to 53,000.

53,000 men. 53,000 warriors.

I'm leading them into battle. ME!

Bloody hell. Shit's blowing my mind.

Will I be remotely successful? Will I screw it up? Time will tell.

For now, I look forward to settling in, meeting with my commanders, and assessing the information to develop a concrete strategy.

The already large encampment comes into my view. I look around at Jake, Gedik Pasha, Ibn Eymen, and Zaganos and smile. "*Alhamdulilah*, we're blessed by Allah to have arrived quickly, comfortably, safely, and to find our fellow comrades safe."

"*Alhamdulilah*," they murmur in response as we enter the camp. The soldiers accompanying me scurry to pitch up their tents, as I make my way to the centre of the camp along with Zaganos, Halil, Gedik Pasha, Ibn Eymen, Kadi'asker Mawiz, Ak Shemsettin, and Jake.

"I would have expected an entourage to welcome us," Zaganos Pasha says under his breath. "Not a single person..."

I look over at Jake, who looks concerned. I smile to keep him (and myself) in good spirits.

We find the gigantic war tent at the centre of the encampment, and boy, it really does look like the ones from the movies. I jump off Snowstorm and duck into the tent, followed by my men.

The inside looks like it's straight outta *Game of Thrones* or *The Tudors*, except it's the Ottoman version. This is even better than anything in those shows. War may be brutal and sluggish, but witnessing all this is dope. There are men at the war table, and I only recognize two people, Aslan and Ishak Pasha.

"*Assalamu alaikum*!" I say. "How are we doing today?"

The men stiffen and stand in unison. "*Walaikum Assalam*, my padishah!" They get up from their seats and leave room for us to sit down.

Ugh, I feel like a tyrant with the way these men act around me, but I guess they are nervous for a good reason. The lost battle at Akşehir is why we're gathered here today. That lost battle was led by Aslan Pasha, who's going to answer for his failure.

I move towards the head of the table and take my seat. My viziers and advisors take their seats as well.

"Let's get started," I say. "Before I hear anything about what's to come, I'd like to know what has already happened. Aslan Pasha, will you fill me in on the battle at Akşehir?"

Aslan Pasha stands up and nervously gulps.

I should put him at ease with calming words, but I don't want to seem weak in front of all these men with a fifteenth-century mentality.

"Spit it out please," I say. "We don't got all day."

"Of course, my padishah," Aslan Pasha nervously states. "A bit over a month ago, after the zuhr prayer, our two sides met for battle outside of Akşehir. The battle was fought in an open field, and the decisions I made leading up to it, didn't allow me my choice of battleground nor vantage point. Those were chosen by Ibrahim Bey of Karaman. Once that happened, I decided that the best course of action was a direct assault. Unfortunately, Ibrahim Bey and the Karamanids maneuvered to outflank us. Once that happened, my men started falling as though they were insects battling elephants. I was forced to retreat to protect the remaining men."

"And... half of your men perished in this battle," I say. "Is that correct?"

"Yes," he replies. He looks straight down at his hands. "Half the men perished at the hands of the Karamanids, my padishah."

"And how many of their men were lost?" Zaganos asks.

"We can't say for sure, Zaganos Pasha," Aslan Pasha replies. "But enough to keep them encamped at Akşehir till now."

"What was their estimated number in your clash against them?" I ask. "Perhaps you dealt a significant enough blow to cause their whole campaign to falter from the start."

Aslan Pasha nervously clears his throat and hoarsely whispers, "They were numbered at around 15,000..."

Halil and Zaganos both angrily stand up. "Bastard!" Zaganos exclaims.

"You got outflanked in our *own* lands by a force with 11,000 fewer men?" Halil asks.

Aslan Pasha scarcely murmurs, "Yes."

"How?" I ask. "How did he manage to outflank you with his fewer troops?"

"Deceit."

I study Aslan Pasha's frazzled face, then I ask, "What do you mean by deceit? How did Ibrahim Bey deceive you?"

"We captured a Karamanid scout, who told us the Karamanids marched north with 7,000 men. As we had the numbers advantage, we engaged in battle. The visible Karamanid force south of the battlefield did indeed look to be that number. So we attacked them head on, in our organized lines. To their credit, the smaller Karamanid force held their lines for nearly three hours of battle," Aslan Pasha says. "After another failed surge, Karamanid warriors emerged from the north of the battlefield and suddenly we were fighting the enemy on two fronts."

Zaganos angrily clears his throat. "You still had the numbers advantage. If you had split the lines and fought together in a compact manner, victory would have been yours. The best defence to a flanking maneuver is to hold a tight line."

"Yes, Zaganos Pasha," Aslan Pasha agrees. "That's the best way to defend against the flanking maneuver, but the men were never able to get properly formed. Within half an hour, it became every man for himself. The 13,000 of us able to escape are lucky."

"The blame belongs to you," Zaganos mutters. "You should have gotten them in proper order."

Aslan Pasha starts to counter, but I quickly interrupt. "How did you not notice the other Karamanid force? Even a blind man could spot 8,000 warriors."

"They were hidden in the mountains by Akşehir."

"Ibrahim Bey of Karaman is a clever man," I say. "He simply outthought you."

"As much as I respect Aslan Pasha, he deserves a severe reprimand," Halil quietly says.

My face turns cold as I look at Halil. At that moment, Zaganos whispers, "Execution."

As the words escape the second vizier's mouth, my heart stops. Execution. What. The. Fuck.

He took an L. That happens to the best of us. To die for that L seems extreme. Not just extreme, inhumane. Looking around the room though, no one looks surprised.

506

Out of the corner of the tent, a man taller than Jacob with a dark complexion steps up. Someone who's always been around, but has never. I know this lad's name to be Kazir, the sultan's justice, the state executioner.

I sit and watch the events unfold, not saying yes or no. The room goes quiet as Aslan Pasha stands and wipes the nervous sweat off his face with the sleeve of his robe.

The whispers around the room are remorseful. I don't think anyone wants the man dead. Why did Zaganos even suggest it? I know that failure is deemed unacceptable, but I didn't know it always resulted in death.

I stare at Kazir for a moment and then realize that everyone's waiting for me to say something.

I don't know what to say. I don't know what to do. I need to keep my identity, but I'm also looking for a lifeline, to save his life.

Doesn't look like I will get one.

I look up at Kazir and order, "Go ahead. Complete the act in full public view, so that people know that failure is unacceptable."

Subdued voices flutter around the room, clearly talking about what I just said. Kazir walks up to Aslan Pasha and without looking like he's even trying, grabs him and starts dragging him outta the tent. Zaganos stands to follow him as do the rest of the men, so I follow.

As I duck out of the tent, I see a small crowd gathering. They watch Kazir drag Aslan Pasha across the camp. I gulp. Aslan Pasha yells, "OH ALLAH! OH ALLAH! THE MOST BENEVOLANT! THE MOST MERCIFUL! SAVE ME, OH LORD! SAVE ME FROM THIS INJUSTICE! FORGIVE ME FOR MY SINS!"

Yikes. Man. I'm why he's yelling that.

I watch as his head is placed on a rocky surface.

The crowd's builds up in size. Kazir finishes tying Aslan Pasha. He looks at me for the final order.

With one word, I can kill a man. This is freakish power. A power I don't want. A power no one should have. I am not a God. I am a mere mortal. I can't take a life away.

I'm no longer the hero of this tale. I'm slowly becoming the villain. I don't even know who I am anymore. I take a deep breath. Just as I'm about to give *the* order, I hear the words I want to hear.

"My padishah," Halil softly says, "you don't have to go through with this." I internally sigh with relief as I listen. "Aslan Pasha has served this realm valiantly since the day he was born. He was trusted by your father and many more. He's a loyal man who did his best. While his best wasn't nearly enough, and it led to a disastrous defeat, he still got many thousands of men out of that disaster and led them to safety. And remember, Allah is the most merciful and forgiving. It is only proper that his worshippers reflect that."

I feign being stern. "Still, there must be a severe punishment for that failure. It must be understood that failure is not an option in any government run by me."

"I understand, my padishah," Halil says. "All I ask is that you lessen the punishment. Wasn't it you who said a human life is priceless?"

I look at him with a fake look of anger. "Aslan Pasha is banished! Boycotted! No business in this entire sultanate is allowed to sell to him and his family. No one is to marry his sons or daughters. They are to leave here and live in exile."

"Yes, my padishah," Halil states. He runs off to stop Kazir.

"The people will not forget this," Ibn Eymen whispers.

"What do you mean?"

Ak Shemsettin answers instead. "The people will not forget the severity of this punishment, but they will also not forget that you spared him from execution."

"What does that say about me?"

"It reveals that failure severely angers you, but there is a hint of mercy in your heart as long as they serve the realm courageously," Zaganos chimes in. "Or they'll think you're a soft ruler."

Jake gets the final word in. "Let's just pray that it's the former and not the latter."

An hour or so after sending Aslan Pasha packing, we gather around the table in the strategic tent again with a small group of warriors specifically chosen by Zaganos. The exact order for Aslan's exile is that they are to escort him to his family and out of the sultanate within one month. If he remains on Ottoman lands after a month, he is to be killed.

Brutal.

This is one of the scarier moments of my life as sultan so far, but something tells me that there are scarier times ahead. The battles ahead will be frightening. However, I'll need to endure to be victorious.

Right now, there's a tense silence in the tent. Aslan Pasha's punishment has shaken the room. It's shaken me, and I don't even know the man. It's just now hitting me that I can change lives just like that. With just a couple of words.

I look at Halil and nod. He stands and begins to speak. "I know that today's events are deeply imbedded in your minds, but we have a lot of work left to do."

I stand and interrupt. "We need a strategy that will level the Karamanids in one strike."

Halil staggers and says, "Ishak Pasha has briefed me on the situation. The Karamanids remain in Akşehir awaiting serious reinforcements."

Ishak Pasha steps up. "The Karamanids have been ransacking the lands surrounding Akşehir for a month now. The reinforcements are nearly there for them. They will have a force of over 40,000 when those reinforcements arrive."

"And that's why we march by tomorrow at the latest," I say. "We march to prevent further growth of their forces. Our scouts and spies inform us that the Karamanids presently number 30,000 with one final force joining them. We've also learned that they plan to march towards Ankara before reinforcements arrive."

"And Ankara is nearly defenceless," Zaganos chimes in. "Ishak Pasha marched out to provide reinforcements to Aslan Pasha, believing that the Karamanids would pursue that force, but they seem to have been one step ahead of us. Now, we need to stop them from getting to Ankara."

I open my mouth to say something, but immediately stop, fearing that I may sound dumb. The truth is that I don't really get why Ishak Pasha marched outta Ankara in the first place. That city houses more people than what remained of Aslan Pasha's force. It is also *the* major commercial centre of Anatolia. Why leave that city to protect a smaller force? I don't have an answer. I don't get it, and I think he's in the wrong for leaving, but then again, hindsight is 20/20.

So I keep my mouth shut and listen to the men suggesting battle plans.

"The battle should happen as close to Ankara as possible," Halil suggests. "That way the Karamanids would be a tired bunch but also, we'll be able to get the necessary reinforcements from the city."

That's a horrendously shit plan… is what I should say, but I don't.

Zaganos counters Halil's plan (of course). "We should launch a direct assault on Karamanid lands. As we march towards Konya and Karaman, we send a letter to Hamdan Pasha ordering reinforcements to Ankara so that the city is adequately defended. The Karamanids will be stuck in the middle, with no move to maneuver.

"That is a very bold plan, Zaganos Pasha," I say. "Very bold."

What I don't say is that it's far too bold. I'm a firm believer in offence being the best defence, but this seems reckless. Ankara is far too important to leave behind to attack Konya. I can't risk it being captured.

The point I'm tryna make is that Zaganos' plan seems much too complex for me.

Ideas keep coming in, but none are worthy.

It might just be time to speak up.

I pick up my cup and harshly knock it on the table. Immediately, silence befalls the room. I stand up with my chest out. "I don't believe in any of your suggestions."

Halil Pasha interrupts. "None of them? How is that possible?"

I ignore him and continue, "What we will do is march at midnight. We will catch up to the Karamanids before they reach the ancient city of Gordion. We will attack them while they are sleeping in the darkness of the night sky. We will crush them and defeat them mercilessly."

"An attack in the death of the night is classless!" Halil exclaims.

"Attacking our lands and hurting the lives of innocent people is true classlessness," I counter with finality. "Now does anyone have a problem with my suggestion?"

Silence. Not a whimper or a whisper.

"Good," I say. "Now let's send the Karamanids back home to their women with swords in their guts as defeated men who won't dare to ever dream again."

40. Mehmet

The day is July 1st. And tonight is that cursed night. The night where it all goes down. The night I'm betting on to make my first true mark as sultan. The night where I show the whole world that I'm truly capable.

July 1st is ordinarily one of the happiest days of the year for me. It's Canada Day, the holiday that basically kicks off summer vacation. I'm done with the school year, my parents have the day off, and to celebrate, my grandma makes *lokum* (Turkish Delights) and shares it with the entire neighbourhood. Hamdan would come over, we'd hang with friends, and boy, it was like a third Eid.

Today, however, is the complete opposite.

Tonight, we're launching an attack against the Karamanids.

We are encamped far enough from the Karamanids to remain undetected.

One thing has been stuck in my mind all day. I've only ever known Gordion as the capital of ancient Phrygia. I don't know of any Ottoman war that happened here. This is the first battle I'm fighting in place of Fatih Mehmet. If his first battle was a night battle against the Karamanids, it would have been recorded in history.

But it's not.

To my knowledge, what's about to occur has never happened in history. That's scary.

It's either that history is changing, or it's that I'm taking different steps towards the same outcomes. If it's the former, then there's trouble, but if it's the latter, I think it means that I might have more control of my destiny.

But... there's no way of knowing the answer for some time. I can't remember what sparks the conquest of Constantinople, but I guess I won't find out the answer till then.

For now, I can only control what's in my own hands, and this is the outlook I gotta have. I try my best in the present and leave the future up to Allah. Unfortunately, I haven't always kept this mentality, and that's gotta change.

Presently, I'm in Jake's tent getting my armour adjusted by Armin, who is also in charge of the Sultan's armour. We aren't in my tent because we're still hiding Sally there. I don't feel comfortable leaving her alone with Rizwan and co, but oh well.

"Yo, Jake," I say, talking in English so Armin can't understand. "How are you feeling?"

"A tad nervous, to be perfectly honest. But that's how everyone feels, I think. Remember, this isn't my first rodeo, so I'll be fine. How are you feeling though?"

"I feel fine right now, I think," I say. "Just worried about a couple things."

"And what's that?" Jake asks. "You gotta tell me, man."

I ain't gonna tell him what I'm actually thinking, but I will say... "Yusef Agha's absence is really starting to concern me. We left behind someone at Isparta for him. We've delayed so that he may catch up, but he hasn't."

"Don't worry, everything will work out," he assures me. "Besides, I'm ready for the job."

I smile at him and fall silent while Armin continues to adjust my armour. It looks a lot like my regular robes, except for the thick metal chain all over the jet-black robes.

It's really darn heavy.

"Were you speaking English again, my padishah?" Armin asks in Farsi.

"Yes, I was." I angrily shrug off Armin's nosy ass. "That's enough, Armin. The armour fits perfectly."

I grip my kilij sitting on the other side of the tent. "I'm sorry my padishah, I just can't contain my excitement. To be tutored in a language by the sultan of the Ottoman empire is incredibly exciting. Even Zaganos Pasha failed to believe my words when I told him you offered to teach me English."

"You told him WHAT?"

"That you offered to teach me English. Then he asked where you learned the language," Armin says.

Bloody hell. I can't even remember the story I fed Armin.

I hardly remember offering to teach the Persian barber/armour guy English, and now he's told Zaganos, the man who knows Fatih Mehmet better than any other man, the exact fake story of how I know it.

I hate it out here. No, I got to be positive. *Inshallah*, nothing bad will come of this.

"Armin," I say, "what did you tell Zaganos Pasha exactly?"

"That you offered to teach me English," Armin says again. "He then asked where you learned it, so I relayed what you told me."

"And what did I tell you?"

"That you learned it off an English sailor," Armin replies. "That is correct, yes?"

I nod slowly and whisper, "You are dismissed, Armin. Find a safe place to stay during the battle."

"My padishah, I will be fighting alongside you," he replies.

I smile at him. "May Allah provide you the strength and fortitude to come out of this as either a victor or a martyr."

"*Ameen*," Armin whispers as he makes his way out.

As soon as he does that, I lift my beautiful and unscarred kilij, look in all directions, and absolutely smash a looking glass into a million pieces, in a furious fit of rage.

"What on earth, Mehmet?" Jake whispers. "Why?"

"Never mind it," I say. "Just knocking out some nerves."

"Oh, okay." He returns to his stretches.

I lied to him of course. My nerves have been completely replaced with anger. Fury. Resentment of my own actions.

My indecisions, my actions, and my words are hurting not only myself, but my friends and the people around me. I'm tryna be positive today, but my faults seem to be catching up to me. I hate this, but there's nothing I can do about it. I just got to go out and win a bloody battle.

And win it I will.

41. MEHMET

Ya Allah. It's really about to happen.

At this moment, we're approaching the ancient city of Gordion, encircling it like bullies around a scrawny kid, with four forces equally divided.

The *akinji* are evenly divided across the forces as the first line of attack. They will shoot arrows laced with flames directly at the Karamanid tents. They will be followed by infantry troops. First, the cannon fodder, the poor who are scarcely armoured but hold a whole lotta courage and honour. They will be followed by infantry troops with more armour and skill. Next the *Sipahi*, the janissary equivalent of the cavalry, the elite cavalry of the Ottoman Empire, will file in. Finally, the janissaries will come in alongside the military leaders and pick off the rest of the Karamanids. One by one.

Inshallah, the plan will go off without a hitch.

Any minute now, we'll be surrounding the Karamanid camp.

It's so dark that I can hardly see any further than the men next to and ahead of me. We're being careful not to be detected before we start the attack, so no torches have been lit. The hope is that the Karamanids never even realize that we have been tracking behind them.

I close my eyes and whisper, "Deep breaths Mehmet, deep breaths. My nerves have crept back in, extracting even more wrath towards my own soul. I hear Jake's voice softly muttering something about Priya while making some Christian prayer and realize that I should do the same.

Under my breath, I whisper, "Oh lord of all lands, oceans, skies, stars, and worlds. Do not impose upon us a burden which we would fail to overcome. Shine upon us your light of mercy and pardon us for our sins. Grant us strength to overcome this conflict and emerge as victors or martyrs fighting for the cause of making this world greater for all persons and not just ourselves. Oh king of kings, oh lord of lords, grant us victory, not only in this life but in the next. *Ya Allah*, let us be the victors."

I open my eyes to find Jake smiling at me. His smile captures my nerves and starts to beat it. Such a small sign of warmth in a tense, bitter, and cold hour feels satisfying.

Yet it doesn't last.

"AAAAAAAAAAAAGH!" a collection of voices shriek as flames erupt and horses violently neigh from afar.

What on earth?

No arrows were to be fired until I ordered it. I look at Jake and he's confused as well. I look to Halil who doesn't seem fazed and simply looks ahead, so I follow his lead. That's when I notice the rain of fire.

Enflamed arrows.

Heading straight towards not them, but *us*.

"SHIELDS!" I yell as loudly as I possibly can. Others yell it as well. I stop my own horse and raise my unbelievably heavy shield over me, frightened by the fiery night sky.

"The arrows will not reach you, my padishah!" Halil yells over the yelping men. "You are far out of its range!"

Oh...

I put down my shield and find his words to be accurate.

Well, that just made me look like a fool.

Angrily I yell, "Order a counterattack, you pompous bastard!"

Unfazed by my words, Halil does just that. With torches now lit, Halil shouts, "*Akinji*, FILE AHEAD AND ATTACK! ATTACK FOR YOUR OWN SAKES AND FOR THE REALM!"

Immediately, the orders are barked out across the battleground in a thunderous and impressive manner. Once the message gets to the *akinji* at the front lines, they gallop forward, bows and arrows in hand, chanting, "YA ALLAH! YA ALLAH! ALLAHU AKBAR! ALLAHU AKBAR! ALLAHU AKBAR!" releasing the arrows from their bows in a uniform manner.

At that moment, another rain of fire is unleashed on us. This time, knowing that I'm much too far out of range, I simply sit on my horse and observe. The arrows are being fired in four different directions. Like precisely four different directions, as though they expected this.

"SHIELDS!" the men yell as the arrows fall right down over them, striking dozens who collapse to the ground. This is when it hits me.

They *did* expect this. They knew our exact plan.

Their counterattack is far too coordinated. The *akinji*'s first wave of attack is miserably failing. They haven't broken through to the camp. The Karamanids are effectively using the ruins of the old wall of Gordion as a barrier, and they're using it to perfection. They've known about this and have planned against it. They basically have my playbook.

So what's a guy gotta do to get around a solid defence?

Improvise. I can do that.

"HALIL PASHA!" I scream. "SEND THE SIPAHI! DEPLOY THE REST OF THE CAVALRY!"

The man looks at me bizarrely, but does exactly as I say, yelling, "SIPAHI! DRAW FORWARD AND CRUSH THE ENEMY!"

The order rings around the battleground as it is yelled out by all the leaders on the plains, reaching the four separate forces as the *Sipahi* draw forward promptly chanting in unison, "YA ALLAH! HAYYDIR ALLAH! HAQQDIR ALLAH!" as they join in the *akinji's* assault on the Karamanids.

Literal chills. No, like, I'm literally shivering because I'm that scared.

But also, THIS. IS. INSANE.

The *Akinji* and *Sipahi* are fighting passionately, however, they are being counterattacked by the strong line of infantry soldiers defending with spears. I guess that's what's used as a defence for a cavalry attack. Even though they are surrounded, the Karamanids are holding their lines, but all they can do is defend. We've got them trapped, but can we knock them over? The cavalry seem to be hitting a dead end. Too many spears are going through the horses, leading to men falling over each other, preventing them from breaking through the line.

I didn't expect the Karamanids to have this much order. I mean, it was *meant* to be a surprise attack, and there is no way they *should* have this much order and uniformity. Curse that buffoon who exposed our plan.

Do I send in the first wave of infantry soldiers now? No, lemme wait and let things play out. It's an even fight between our cavalry and their infantry. All I can really hear are screams of dying men or chants pleading to Allah for help. Men are falling off horses, horses are trampling men, swords are cutting through limbs, and it's just an all-round disgusting shitshow.

I look around at the restless infantry, who are anticipating the moment I send them ahead. Some look scared; most look determined. I look back at the cavalry and yeah, they aren't having any success. In fact, the Karamanids are starting to dominate.

"UNLEASH THE INFANTRY!" I bellow to Halil Pasha. "ALL THE INFANTRY, EXCLUDING THE JANISSARIES! DEPLOY THEM EXACTLY WHERE THE CAVALRY PRESSURE IS HEAVY!"

Halil Pasha yells out those orders, and all of the infantry (not including the janissaries) march ahead, shouting, "YA ALLAH! HAYYDIR ALLAH! HAQQDIR ALLAH!" as well as "YA ALLAH! YA ALLAH! ALLAHU AKBAR! ALLAHU AKBAR! ALLAHU AKBAR!"

I should've sent these fellas first. No, I can't regret stuff right now. There's a battle out there to be won. *Inshallah*, this will work. Oh Allah, please let this work. I don't know what to do if it doesn't.

The infantry soldiers flow in and the field gets even messier. They push back against the Karamanids, so that they no longer dominate.

"*ALHAMDULILAH*!" I yell, even though I feel silly invoking the praise of God in a bloody battle being fought over a piece of land on His magnificent planet. There are no winners here.

Yet I still need to win. I will win. I just don't know how. For now, I'll just observe.

Minutes pass by; the fighting and bloodshed drag on. No edge is being given. I see different banner holders yelling orders, trying to urge on the men, fighting for every inch on the battleground. Those ruined walls are proving to be a problem. Okay, I keep saying they are a problem without explaining why. The Karamanids have stacked up the ruins to sorta rebuild the walls. A number of soldiers, mainly the archers, are using that as a barrier for their own defence as they use their weapons to attack ours. The food supplies, tents, and horses are all behind those very walls. Those ruins have made it hard for our soldiers to do anything. Even with the addition of the infantry, it's an intense struggle. We're barely pushing them back. At the moment, it looks like a 50/50 chance (at best) even with an optimistic lens.

Okay, I should give them some more time while I try to think of my next move. A battle isn't a short event. It can drag on for hours, days. Even though it feels like only seconds have passed, this present battle has been waging on for well over an hour. The fact that I've deployed 50,000 troops to their 30,000 doesn't bode well. Now, I just need to let this marinate for a bit.

And that is exactly what I do. Over the next hour or so, I witness unspeakable horror. Limbs torn apart. Guts flowing out of men. Heads, hands, arms, legs, feet, cut off by swords. One courageous Ottoman warrior got his horse to jump over the defence wall to fight dozens of Karamanid warriors, many of whom he successfully slayed, only to lose his life from a javelin going through his back.

Brutally painful.

I can feel the colour draining from my face as I witness the horrific atrocities. This is the most brutal thing a man can ever see. Dozens of men are dropping like flies. No inch is being given on the battlefield. I only got one card left to play. The janissaries.

I've read the stories of their might. They are *the* greatest infantry in all of Europe. Every single janissary warrior is elite. But they are my final play. If I send them, I have to join the fight alongside the other military leaders.

No. Oh my gosh. I got one more play to run.

I can use the janissaries to give us time to retreat for the night. I need to get this army out before we suffer too many losses. We can return in the morning because it looks as though it's futile tonight. What we *could* do tonight is gain a minor victory. We *could* put them at the brink of a loss.

We must do that.

I look at Jake and yell, "Can you lead your forces straight for the Karamanid supplies and destroy them? The horses as well?"

"You want to slaughter the horses and destroy the supplies?" he yells back in disbelief.

"Yes!" I shout. "And use that as a distraction to escape for the night!"

Jake looks at the battleground. He looks at the place where all the horses and supplies are being kept. He observes the fight around there, then nods at his men before turning towards me, bellowing, "We will do it! We will blow up the supplies with flames that will light up the night sky!"

Halil notices our conversation and yells, "The second the smoke is visible, we order a retreat! We will get the army back to camp safely, my padishah!"

I nod and look at Jake, who doesn't need my direction. He yells, "MY JANISSARY BRETHREN! FOLLOW MY LEAD, AND DO NOT DOUBT! WE WILL LEAD THE OTTOMAN SULTANATE TO A GLORIOUS VICTORY! A VICTORY THAT WILL BE TALKED ABOUT FOR YEARS TO COME!"

With that, they march off immediately towards the supplies like an arrow shot out of a bow. I hear Jake shout instructions and lead the battle cry, "*YA ALLAH! HAYYDIR ALLAH! HAQQDIR AL-*

LAH! YA ALLAH! HAYYDIR ALLAH! HAQQDIR ALLAH!"
as they reach the battleground slashing through everything in their
way.

It's amazing how powerful these warriors are. They are swift,
organized, strong, and unified. They fight as a collective, and they
dominate. Within minutes, they've broken past the Karamanids.

Holy cow, do I push for victory now? I've got a unit that's broken through them. That's all we needed. Just that one break, just that
one edge over worthy opponents. That little sliver of hope. But before I can say anything, I see smoke coming from where the supplies
are supposed to be.

"ALL FORCES RETREAT!" Halil's voice booms through the
dreadful night air. His order is immediately repeated by the leaders
and banner holders of my army.

Too. Damn. Late.

"FUCK THIS SHIT!" I yell in English as I turn back to follow
Halil.

I truly mean that. I just messed up bigtime. I let my inexperience
and impatience cloud my judgment. I could have won this battle
with the breakthrough provided by the janissaries.

But I didn't. Curse this idiotic head of mine. Why do I have to
always overthink shit? Now, I just may never get the chance for a
comprehensive victory.

42. Jake

"ALLAHU AKBAR! ALLAHU AKBAR!" I chant with my janissary comrades as the Karamanid supplies bursts into flames. Destroying the supplies is only part of the plan. Now, onto the next.

The horses are a hundred or so metres away. There is a line of opposition soldiers fighting the Ottoman soldiers who haven't retreated yet for some reason. The Karamanids now outnumber us, so they approach the janissaries, licking their chops, searching for annihilation.

"FEAR NOT, MY BROTHERS!" I roar. "THIS IS A BEAU-TIFUL NIGHT! TONIGHT WE BECOME LEGENDS! WIN OR LOSE! WE SHALL BE HONOURED AS WARRIORS OF THE HIGHEST CLASS!"

The janissaries thunder in reply, so I continue, "NOW FOL-LOW ME, MY BROTHERS! FOLLOW ME TO A GLORIOUS VICTORY!"

With that, we run towards the oncoming Karamanid soldiers. At this point, I've just become a machine. I can't tell if I'm in control or being controlled by some freak force of nature, but I just go insane.

I sidestep the first Karamanid soldier and slash right at his hip, and he goes down crying in agony. I duck under the blade of another and stab his pelvis as he goes crashing to the ground howling in pain.

I slice the head off another Karamanid lunatic and the arm off one more looking to harm me. I reach the first horse successfully without any harm befalling my body. I raise my sword to strike down the stallion's neck, but I hesitate.

Mehmet is wrong here. Hurting innocent animals is plain evil.

I strike down on the horse's neck. I wanna throw up. I hate myself for doing this, but I trust that Mehmet is doing this as a last resort.

I quickly move and execute seven more horses, while fending off the Karamanids tryna kill me. I look around to see that most of the horses have been slaughtered. Now, it's time for the escape.

"JANISSARIES!" I yell at the top of my lungs. "IT IS TIME TO ROLL OUT! FOLLOW ME, BROTHERS!"

With that, I dash away from the Karamanid camp, running as fast as I can, slaying everything in my way.

I'm a beast. An unrecognizable monster.

The world isn't a black-and-white place. Morality is often grey. I don't think I'm in the wrong, but will my loved ones back home think I am? Will Priya think I am?

Perhaps. But I do all this to get back to them. I've become this person to get back to them. What I've done today brings me one step closer to them.

I walk into camp, soaked in blood alongside my janissary brothers. About forty or so have lost their lives in that assault, but we definitely killed at *least* seven times their number. Not even tryna sound arrogant, but this force that I have the privilege of leading is extraordinarily powerful.

I discharge the warriors to their tents and walk straight towards the strategic tent, passing by Mehmet's where Arslan, Demir, Baver, Rizwan, Altan, Barış, and Çetin stand guard.

Arslan, Demir, and Baver smile uneasily at me. I know they're irritated that they must stand guard over Sally instead of participating in battle. They think I'm hiding something about her. They believe I know why she's so important to the sultan. Of course, their instincts are correct, but I hate seeing them so irritated. I just don't know who else to trust to do this job.

Rizwan mockingly shouts out, "Yakub! We're protecting the precious asset, but I fear she might be bored. Perhaps I ought to entertain her by showing off my precious assets!"

At that, Altan, Barış, and Çetin burst out laughing as Rizwan looks on smugly. I glare at him and mouth, "Watch him," to Arslan, Baver, and Demir.

I hate that pompous prick named Rizwan. If I had a choice, he wouldn't be watching over Sally, but I don't have a choice. I duck into the strategic tent, and it feels as though I've walked into a funeral. That's how grim and morbid the place is.

"What's the final count of men lost for us?" Mehmet asks Zaganos.

"7,000 soldiers, my padishah," he replies morbidly. "Most from the ill-equipped infantry force. We estimate that the Karamanids have lost 10,000."

"Add forty janissaries to that," I reluctantly add as Mehmet's face brightens at the sound of my voice. "I also estimate that my force killed at least seven times that number."

"Forty warriors that are gone far too soon," an old, raspy, and gloomy voice states from behind me. I turn to see the actual agha of the janissaries right behind me. "At least they drew their final breaths serving the realm valiantly."

"Yusef Agha!" I spit out enthusiastically. "You're here!"

Mehmet's tone is far more serious. He rather angrily asks, "When did you get here? What took you so long?"

"I just arrived at camp, my padishah," Yusef Agha replies. "Traversing countless kilometres of land takes a lot of time, my padishah, especially for someone of my advanced age who's been on the battle trail for months now."

Mehmet seems unsatisfied. "Stay standing, Yusef Agha," he snaps, "there is no seat for you at the present moment. Yakub has been leading the janissaries in your absence, so I'd rather hear from him."

"It's okay," I say. "Yusef Agha can take my seat. I am okay with standing."

Yusef Agha smugly smiles, and Mehmet looks on enraged. I don't get why he's being so disrespectful to Yusef Agha. I get that he doesn't like him. I know Yusef Agha can be an arrogant schmuck sometimes, but he could, at the very least, fake politeness. Mehmet doesn't need more enemies. Heck, he isn't even being this disrespectful to Halil, whom we suspect to be the *most* averse to Mehmet.

I don't get it, and I don't think I will anytime soon. Mehmet has revealed very little to me throughout this war so far.

Mehmet clears his throat and asks me in front of the room, "Did you accomplish your mission?"

528

"The Karamanid supplies are no more, and they no longer have the use of their horses."

"Good," he replies with a smile. "They no longer have food, shelter, or water. Our camp surrounds theirs. The Karamanids are trapped.

Zaganos stands up. "They may hold us out one night, one day, one week, but they can't hold us out forever."

"Exactly, Zaganos. Somehow, they knew tonight's strategy," Mehmet says, "but they will not know about my strategy for tomorrow. *Inshallah*, tomorrow we will earn that decisive victory."

"What is the strategy for tomorrow, my padishah?" Halil asks.

"I'll let you know tomorrow," Mehmet says. He gets up to walk out of the tent just as it fills with loud conversation. I turn to follow, but Yusef Agha grabs my shoulder to hold me back.

"What is Mehmet hiding in his tent?" he asks. "Don't bother lying to me because I have a good idea who it is, and I have a way of finding out."

"It's a girl," I reply. "To Mehmet, it seems as though there is nothing more valuable, more precious, more important than her."

"Is it love?"

"I don't think so," I lie. "He states that she is of great significance to this realm."

"Do you believe him?"

"Yes, I truly do believe the sultan," I say. "With all my heart."

Yusef Agha releases my shoulder with a smile. "Very well then, have a great night, Yakub Agha."

"That is not my title sir," I reply quickly. "It rightfully belongs to you."

"I would say that you've earned it, lad," Yusef Agha gracefully counters. "You have earned the respect of every janissary tonight."

"This is all because you challenged me to be great, Yusef Agha," I say.

"All I needed to do was place you in the right direction," the old man replies. "The talent has always been there. Challenging you to march along with Vlad and Radu on a difficult campaign helped you earn the confidence you displayed tonight."

I smile at the old man as I walk away. I know he's difficult, and he doesn't really get along with Mehmet. I know he believes Mehmet to be an awful leader, but he's been a mentor to me.

Perhaps Yusef Agha isn't as evil as Mehmet believes.

I arrive at Mehmet's tent to find him in deep conversation with Sally, probably retelling the night's events for her.

I grunt while walking to the corner I'll sleep at tonight. For security purposes, I've been sleeping in Mehmet's tent with both Mehmet and Sally. I feel like an outsider at times with how these two talk when I'm outta earshot. In fact, it was Sally that came up with the strategy for tonight's attack against the Karamanids. It truly feels like Mehmet confides in her before me. I get it, though. Both clearly have love for the other. Mehmet's not gonna keep secrets from her.

When they do notice me, Sally calls out, "Jacob, come here."

Mehmet adds, "We got something to tell you."

"A rarity these days, Mehmet," I say. He ignores my comment and waits for me to sit next to him. "I do hope it's positive news," I add to lighten the mood.

"Far from that," Sally replies.

"Jake," Mehmet says. "What I say cannot leave the confines of this tent. No one is to hear this. Is this understood?"

"Of course," I say, surprised that he thought he even needed to say this.

He looks towards Sally who nods at him. "We believe there's a traitor in the government."

"Who?" I ask. "How? Why?"

"We don't got answers," he replies. "It's obvious that our plans were leaked to the Karamanids."

"You really believe that?" I ask. "Who would do such a thing?"

"It was meant to be a surprise attack. We were so careful to be undetected," Mehmet replies. "Yet they were so damn organized that they actually attacked first. They knew exactly where to fire their arrows. They knew exactly what units I was going to send, preparing a solid defence for that. Is it not obvious?"

I stay silent because I truly don't know.

"Who do you suspect?"

"We have no idea," Sally says. "We've been running through the different names but the only person we've ruled out is Yusef Agha."

"Why rule him out?" I ask with a sense of astonishment. "He doesn't like you and you don't like him."

"Do you really think the traitor would reveal his true colours?" Mehmet says. "They never do so in front of the guys they're betraying. I can't think of a movie, book, or historical event, where a traitor ever has."

"Besides, he's only just arrived," Sally adds.

"Let's just sleep for now," Mehmet says. "We still gotta win this war tomorrow, and we're gonna do that despite the traitorous bastard's hard work."

"That we will," I say. "That we will."

43. Mehmet

Who the hell could it be?

Halil? That muppet could certainly be a traitor. He gets executed for being a traitor right after the conquest of Constantinople. Although if that's what happened in history, he may not be one yet.

Perhaps it's Zaganos. He's supposedly my biggest supporter, but he's been irritated that he doesn't have the same access to the sultan anymore, considering the sultan is Mehmet Ahmet Osman (me) and not Mehmet Ibn Murat. Perhaps that is what led him to the Karamanids. Maybe he wishes to replace the Ottoman dynasty with the Karamanid dynasty. That would mean that my very presence has literally shifted the course of history.

Nah, that's kinda farfetched. It can't be Zaganos.

Is it possibly Ishak Pasha? He idiotically left Ankara to join Aslan Pasha's forces in a very dumb move that gave the Karamanids a slight advantage.

But...that may have been a serious tactical error.

Ugh, I'm not gonna get anywhere with this tonight. I just gotta sleep and come up with a plan in the morning. I know ima offer them surrender with the injured Karamanids we've captured as trade, but I don't know much else yet.

I stretch my arms, ensuring I don't make any contact with Sally, who's comfortably sleeping next to me. She looks so damn beautiful; I don't want to accidently awaken her.

I close my eyes and clear my thoughts. In my mind, a few seconds pass and then...I hear commotion. An uproar. Just like the night of the attempt on my life.

I open my eyes. This must be a dream. I must be dreaming of that horrible night again. I look to my left to find Jake comfortably sleeping. Sally is sleeping to my right. It can't be a dream. Yet, I hear chaos right outside. I reach under my bed for my dagger and kilij. I use the hilt to shake Jake awake and gesture that "there's something going on outside."

Within seconds of saying that, a man, Demir I think, shouts, "DAMN YOU RIZWAN! YOU LEFT YOUR PO—"

Next thing I hear is a violent groan as Demir's voice fades out.

Silence. It just went silent. What the hell is going on? Suddenly, I hear a violent clash of swords, vehemently striking each other.

I gulp and get out of bed.

Seconds pass slowly, but next thing I know, Baver is running into the tent. "My padishah!" he yells. "They've killed Demir! Arslan is holding off five attackers to help you escape!"

"Don't worry about me!" I yell. "I can fight back! Get Salmana Hatun and flee!"

Just as those pleading words escape my mouth, FIFTEEN soldiers rush in. Five of them pushing Arslan back. I only recognize four, the same four leading the damn insurgence. Rizwan, Altan, Barış, and Çetin. Rizwan looks at me and haughtily smiles.

"GET THE SULTAN!" he yells, but before one of his men moves an inch, Baver, Jacob, and I charge ahead with a thunderous roar, passionately defending our lives.

I combat two enemies, slaying one quickly while sidestepping the other. Out of the corner of my eye, I see Jake fighting Altan and Barış. Both Baver and Arslan fight *five men each*. I duck under the slash of the man I'm duelling only to be hit with a sudden realization.

One enemy warrior is unmarked. Rizwan. He's left completely unchecked. I smash the dude I'm fighting on the head fervently, so I can quickly turn around to look for Rizwan. I locate him slinging Sally's sleepy body over his shoulder and running off. Right outta the tent and into the darkness of the night.

"NO!" I yell. "SALLY! SALLY!"

At that moment, everything goes black. Pitch black, as I fall into an abyss of nothingness.

To be continued...

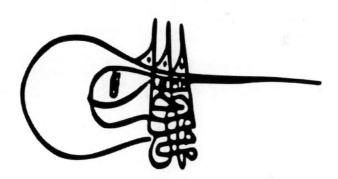

ACKNOWLEDGMENTS

There are so many people I would like to thank, but there aren't close to enough words to do so.

First and foremost, I would like to thank the almighty Allah. Without the help and will of Allah, I would not have been able to write a single word of this novel. Next, I would like to thank my mother and father. They have showered me with love and support my entire life, always helping me pursue my goals. To continue, I would like to thank my nine-year-old brother Isa, who's been my greatest fan since day one. Isa always badgers me with questions about Mehmet, Hamdan, Sally, and Jacob along their journey in the Ottoman world. Next, I would like to thank my sisters, Yamna, Hania, and Lumah, for always reading whatever I put in front of them, even if it was utter trash. Without my sisters and family, I would absolutely not be the man I am today. For that, I am so very grateful.

Furthermore, I would also like to thank my friend Liban, who has stood by me with every step I take. I am so grateful for my friend Hafsah, who is always there for me, hearing me out, and listening to me vent about my novel, no matter the time or circumstance. I would like to thank my friend Hamzah, for being the inspiration behind Hamdan, as well as Nicholas, for being the inspiration behind Jacob. I would like to thank Br. Arssal for helping me navigate writing the first book of this trilogy. His advice was always top tier. I would like to thank my cousins Belal, Ammar, Omar Bhai, and Hiba Baji for their continued advice. I would like to acknowledge my friend Libby, who always is willing to help make sense of my ideas. Lastly, shoutout to my boy Taran, who just is the most chill guy this world has ever seen.

About the Author

Hasan Zia is a twenty-one-year-old Muslim-Pakistani-Canadian currently studying political science at McMaster University in Hamilton, Ontario. From an early age, Hasan took a deep interest in Islamic history and the life of the Prophet Muhammad, peace and blessings of Allah be upon him, which also inspired him to finish his memorization of the Qur'an by the age of thirteen. Hasan's love for writing and storytelling started after reading Rick Riordan's Percy Jackson and the Olympians series, from which he takes great inspiration. When Hasan isn't reading or writing, he loves listening to music, going out with his friends, spending time with his family, trying different types of food, and stressing over his favourite sports teams disappointing him.

You can keep up with Hasan here:

Twitter: novelhasann

Instagram: novelhasann

Tik Tok: novelhasann

Hasan Zia

Printed in Great Britain
by Amazon

16842076R00310